The LIST

The LIST

ROBERT WHITLOW

WestBow
PRESS
A Division of Thomas Nelson Publishers
Since 1798

visit us at www.westbowpress.com

THE LIST

Library of Congress Cataloging-in-Publication Data

Whitlow, Robert, 1954-
   The List/by Robert Whitlow
     p.cm.
   ISBN 0-8499-1640-2 (tp)
   ISBN 0-8499-4518-6 (rpkg)
   I. Title.
PS3573.H49837 L57 2000
813'.54 21—dc21   99-045922
                                            CIP

Printed in the United States of America
05 06 07 08 09 RRD 8 7 6 5 4

To my wife, Kathy.

Without your constant encouragement, prayers, and pratical help, this book would not have been written.

So she became his wife, and he loved her.
Genesis 24:67

ACKNOWLEDGMENTS

As iron sharpens iron, so one man sharpens another.
PROVERBS 27:17, NIV

M any thanks to those who helped in the creation of this book. To my editors and resource providers: Rick Blanchette, Sheri Blevins, Annette Davis (my sister), Traci DePree, Butch Watson, and Scott Wilcher. Special thanks to Ami McConnell, Senior Editor at Word Publishing, who believed in the book from day one, and to my agent, Scott Nelson, who introduced her to it.

And to those who prayed. You know who you are and your reward follows after you.

PROLOGUE

I have set before you life and death, blessing and cursing:
therefore choose life, that both thou and thy seed may live.
DEUTERONOMY 30:19, KJV

Georgetown, South Carolina, November 30, 1863

T he old man pushed open the front door of the inn against the force of the coming storm. Slamming the door behind him, the wind's hand caught his long white beard and whipped it over his shoulder. Leaning forward, he swayed slightly as he crossed the broad porch and slowly descended the weathered wooden steps. He wrapped his cloak tightly around him and pulled his black hat down over his head.

He had feared the group assembled inside would not heed his words. Five years before the first shot was fired on Fort Sumter he began warning all who would listen of the coming conflict:

> "Then the Lord said unto me, Out of the north an evil shall break forth upon all the inhabitants of the land. . . . And I will utter my judgments against them, touching all their wickedness, who have forsaken me, and have burned incense unto other gods, and worshiped the works of their own hands."

Now, the sound of Lee's army retreating from Gettysburg had reached their ears. It didn't require a prophet's vision to see into the future. Judgment was coming. But rather than repenting in the face of wrath, men of power and influence met in Georgetown to save Babylon, not to come out of her.

Because of age and respect he was invited. And he came, not to join them but to warn them. Waiting until their frantic voices stilled, he spoke with all the strength and fervor his spirit could muster. Then, standing in front of a portrait of a stern-faced John C. Calhoun, he delivered a clear, impassioned call: "Lay not up for yourselves treasure upon earth, where moth and rust doth corrupt, and where thieves break through and steal: but lay up for yourselves treasures in heaven, where neither moth nor rust doth corrupt, and where thieves do not break through nor steal: for where your treasure is, there will your heart be also."

Layne and Jacobson had wavered, hesitant to reject completely the words of one they had called sir since first learning to talk. Others sat in silence; a few mocked. He overheard Eicholtz whisper to Johnston that the old man looked more like a scarecrow than a planter. But in the end, LaRochette's smooth speech prevailed. No brands were plucked from the fire—all took the oath; all signed but him.

He had been obedient, but prophetic obedience that fails to accomplish its purpose leaves aching regret for the objects of its mercy. Thus, he felt anger and grief: anger against his enemy, grief for his friends and neighbors. Naturally minded, practical, astute in business, they only saw the need for security and self-preservation. Good churchmen all, yet they were deceived, failing to see the spiritual evil straining for release. "Don't you understand?" Hammond told him. "We must unite and preserve our wealth for the safety and future of our families."

Of course, one knew. He and the old man shared a private moment in the midst of the gathering. LaRochette's eye caught his and flashed the identity and challenge of pure evil. The old man wanted to respond, strip away the pretense of the natural and cross swords in the unseen realm. But there was no call to battle from the Spirit.

"Why don't you let me confront it?" the old man pleaded.

"All things have their appointed time, even the wicked for a day of destruction," came the steady response.

So, upon discharging his trust, he left them to their plans. Holding his hat securely on his head, he stood at the bottom of the steps and looked up at the night sky. The moon and stars flickered on and off as small, dark clouds hurtled across the heavens, clouds without rain but warning of storms to come.

Thinking his task finished, he turned and faced the inn for a final farewell. Light from oil lamps faintly illuminated the windows of the meeting room. Then, as he leaned back against the wind, he felt the seed of another word forming deep within the core of his being, the place where he really lived. Knowing he must wait, he let the word build, push upward, and grow in intensity until its force sent chills through his chest and across his shoulders. Strength to stand against the wind entered his body and brought him to full stature as he stretched out his hands toward the house.

Fueled by a power not found in the oratory of men, he cried out the words of the righteous Judge who spoke with lightning from Sinai:

> "I the Lord thy God am a jealous God, visiting the iniquity of the fathers upon the children unto the third and fourth generation of them that hate me; and showing mercy unto thousands of them that love me, and keep my commandments. . . ."

A solitary bolt of lightning split the heavens high overhead.

> This is what the Lord says; "A son will be born to my house, and he will expose your evil power and execute My righteous judgments against you."

The wind tore the words out of his mouth and swept them up into the swirling darkness. Inside the house, Jacobson shuddered and turned to Weiss, "What was that?"

"Nothing. Only the wind."

The old man remained motionless until the full power of the Word was released. Knowing it would come to pass, he faced the storm, mounted his horse, and rode off into the darkness.

1

Inherit the wind.
<small>PROVERBS 11:29, KJV</small>

The secretary whom Renny shared with two other associates in the banking law section of the firm buzzed the speakerphone on Renny's desk. "Attorney Jefferson McClintock from Charleston calling on line one. Says it's personal."

"I'll take it."

Renny shut the door of the windowless office he had occupied since graduating from law school three months earlier. If he continued working sixty hours a week, he had a fifty-fifty chance of a comfortable six-figure salary and an office with a view of the city in approximately twelve years. But for now he was at the bottom of the legal food chain. Of the 104 lawyers employed by Jackson, Robinson, and Temples in Charlotte, Raleigh, Winston-Salem, and Washington, D.C., his name, Josiah Fletchall Jacobson, was next to last on the firm's letterhead.

Renny picked up the phone. "Hello, Mr. McClintock."

"How are you, Renny?"

"I'm OK. Busy learning the ins and outs of Truth in Lending and Regulation Z."

"Bank work, eh?"

"Yes sir. I have to review all the forms used by the lending institutions we represent to make sure they contain the exact wording required by the regulations and print everything in the appropriate size type."

"Sounds picky."

"It is, but if I make a mistake, the banks can get hit with class-action lawsuits involving thousands of consumers who have a cause of action, even if they didn't suffer any financial harm."

"Our government regulators at work." The Charleston lawyer coughed and cleared his throat. "Well, move the law books to the side for a minute, and let's talk about your father's estate. With the help of two associates, I've almost completed the documents needed to probate your father's will, but there are several matters that need your attention."

Two associates. Renny knew how the system worked. Multi-lawyer involvement was McClintock's way to triple his money: charge for each junior lawyer's time and throw in another fee at time and a half for the senior partner to proofread a stack of papers.

"Any problems?" Renny asked.

"We need to meet and discuss some things," McClintock answered vaguely. "When can you come to Charleston? Tomorrow is Friday. Why not leave early and see me around two?"

Renny had worked until ten o'clock two nights earlier in the week and had billed enough hours for the week to sneak away by late morning on Friday. Besides, he wasn't going to let anything delay moving forward on the estate. "Could we make it three?"

"Let me see." McClintock paused. "Yes. I can move my three o'clock appointment up an hour."

"Do I need to bring anything?"

"No," replied McClintock, "we'll have the paperwork ready. See you then."

"With your bill on top," Renny remarked as he heard the click of the other lawyer hanging up the phone.

Renny let his mind wander as he looked around his office. Even though it wasn't much larger than a walk-in closet, Renny didn't complain. Landing a job at a big law firm in a major city was the ultimate prize for the masses of eager students passing through the law school meat grinder. Each one entered the legal education process hoping they would come out with *Law Review* on their résumés and filet mignon status in the difficult job market. Most ended up as hamburger, relieved to find any job at all.

Renny had an advantage. Although not on *Law Review* or in the top 10 percent of his class, he had something even better: connections. For once, really the first time he could remember, his father had come to his aid. Dwight Temples, one of the senior partners in the firm, had attended college with Renny's father at The Citadel in Charleston. Over the years they maintained a casual friendship centered around an annual deep-sea fishing expedition off the coast of North Carolina. When Renny mentioned an interest in working for the firm's Charlotte office, H. L. Jacobson called Dwight Temples, and the interview with the hiring partner at Jackson, Robinson, and Temples became a formality. Renny was offered a position on the spot.

Today was not the first call Renny had received from Jefferson McClintock, his family's lawyer in Charleston. Six weeks before, McClintock telephoned Renny with the news of H. L.'s sudden death on a golf course in Charleston. No warning. No cholesterol problem. No hypertension. No previous chest pains. The elder Jacobson was playing a round of golf with two longtime friends, Chaz Bentley, his stockbroker, and Alex Souther, a College of Charleston alumnus and restaurant owner.

At the funeral home, Bentley, a jovial fellow and everyday golfer who probably received more stock market advice from Renny's father than he gave to him, had pumped Renny's hand and shook his head in disbelief. "I don't understand it. He was fine. No complaints of pain or dizziness. We were having a great round at the old Isle of Palms course. You should have seen the shot he hit from the championship tee on the seventh hole. You remember, it's the hole with the double water hazards. His tee shot must have gone 225 yards, straight down the fairway. He birdied the hole. Can you believe it? Birdied the last hole he ever played!" The stockbroker made it sound like nirvana to make a birdie then die on the golf course. "We were teeing off on number eight. Alex had taken a mul-ligan on his first shot and hooked his second try into a fairway bunker. I hit a solid drive just a little left of center." Renny could tell Bentley was enjoying Souther's duff and his own good shot all over again. "Then your father leaned over to tee up his ball and, he, uh…never got his ball on the tee," he finished lamely.

Because of the circumstances of his death, the coroner had required an autopsy. The pathologist's report concluded death by coronary fail-ure. H. L.'s family doctor, James Watson, had explained to Renny, "Your father's heart exploded. He never knew what happened. Death was instantaneous. The pathologist called me from the hospital after he examined the body and reviewed his findings with me. Given your father's good health, we were both puzzled at the severe damage to the heart muscle. We know how he died, but not why it happened as it did."

Renny grieved, but he and his father had not had a close relationship. H. L. was a harsh, critical parent whose favor eluded his son like the prover-bial carrot on a stick. Renny tried to please, but the elder Jacobson often changed the rules, and Renny discovered a new way to fail instead. After his mother's death, Renny only visited his father a couple of times a year.

Since there was no one else with whom to share the considerable assets his father had inherited and then increased through savvy invest-ments, Renny looked forward to the trip to Charleston. Once the estate was settled, he would become what some people called "independently wealthy." It had a nice ring to it, and Renny indulged in fantasies of future expenditures.

H. L. was not a generous parent; he paid for Renny's education but never provided the extras he could have easily afforded. After landing the job at Jackson, Robinson, and Temples, Renny sold his old car for three thousand dollars and bought a new charcoal gray Porsche Boxster convertible. The payment and insurance on the new car devoured almost half of Renny's monthly paycheck, but the sporty vehicle was a sign to himself and, subconsciously, to his father, that he had started up the ladder of success. Now he would be able to pay off the car, buy a house, perhaps even quit work and duplicate his father's exploits in the commercial real estate market. His stay at the bottom of the law firm letterhead might be very short indeed.

———

At 2:55 the next afternoon Renny was standing on the hot, humid Charleston sidewalk in front of the semicircular double stairway beckoning him with open arms to the law firm of McClintock and Carney, Esquires. *Some antebellum grande dame must be spinning in her grave,* he thought. *Her house, her home, the common thread of the domestic and social fabric of her life, taken over by legal scriveners and secretaries with word processors and fax machines.* It was not an uncommon fate for a growing number of the homes and mansions lining Fourth Street. An antique dealer rented Renny's ancestral home, near the Battery.

At least Jefferson McClintock had Charleston roots. He wasn't a New York lawyer who came south for the Spoleto festival, unpacked his carpetbag, and hung out a legal shingle. In fact, few current Charlestonians went further back to the city's origins. McClintock's great-great-grandfather, a Scottish blacksmith's servant, could have been the farrier who made sure the grande dame's horses had proper footwear. Now the servant's descendant had his desk in the parlor and law books in the living room.

When McClintock and his law partner, John Carney, purchased the house, they spent the money necessary to maintain the historic and architectural integrity of the 150-year-old structure. They had cleaned the white marble double stairway leading up from the street to the main entrance and made sure the hand railings were kept in good condition by a yearly staining to erase the corrosive effect of Charleston's proximity to the ocean. The exterior stucco had been painted a fresh light peach—only in Charleston could pastel houses reflect good taste. From a low-flying plane, the old residential district looked like a summer fruit compote.

Opening the large front door, he stepped into the law firm's waiting area. As with many large nineteenth-century homes, the foyer was as wide and spacious as the dining room in a modern house plan. McClintock and Carney had turned the greeting area into a gracious reception room, furnishing it with antiques and quality reproductions.

"Good afternoon, Mr. Jacobson," a cheerful receptionist spoke before Renny could give his name. "Mr. McClintock will be with you in a minute."

Noticing a graduation photo of The Citadel's class of 1958 on the opposite wall, Renny walked over for a better look at the black-and-white picture.

"That's our class, a good one," McClintock remarked as he walked out of his office and shook Renny's hand. "There's your father, third from the left in the back, and me, second from the right in the first row."

It was easy to see why McClintock was in the first row. At five feet six, he was barely tall enough to gain admittance to a military academy. But to his credit, McClintock didn't weigh ten pounds more now than he had almost fifty years before. He still sported a Citadel haircut and held himself erect, ready to snap to full attention. Renny knew his father's classmate ran five miles every morning and jumped into the Atlantic Ocean every New Year's Day in a Southern version of the famous Polar Bear Club's annual dip in Lake Michigan.

Renny leaned closer to see his father. Henry Lawrence Jacobson, H. L. to everyone who knew him, was tall and slim. The influence of early military discipline kept his back straight and shoulders square to the end of his days. Even in the grainy picture, H. L. exuded a sense of confidence and control. Not particularly handsome, but without any distracting negative features, it was not his physical appearance but an intangible presence that set him apart from his peers. Whether on the schoolyard or in the boardroom, it did not take long for the elder Jacobson's internally generated power to pervade the atmosphere around him. If austere Southern aristocracy existed in the twentieth century,

H. L. Jacobson qualified as Exhibit A. From the graduation photo, H. L.'s dark eyes seemed to probe the depths of Renny's soul just as they did when he interrogated Renny after he was caught wandering away from school during recess in the second grade.

Renny, with his dark hair, brown eyes, and wry, almost shy, smile, looked more like his soft-spoken mother than his father. Short and solid, Renny had played outside linebacker for three years at Hammond Academy, a private high school in Charleston. In his senior season, he received the Best Hit of the Year award for a play in which he tackled the opposing team's punter. It was fourth down late in a game and the other team was behind ten points. Renny suspected a fake punt was in the works and ran as hard as he could toward the punter. Slipping between two players who were supposed to block him, he hit the punter so hard the punter was knocked several feet through the air. It looked great on the highlight film of the game, and Renny won the award. Neither of his parents attended the game. His mother was in the early stages of the Lou Gehrig's disease that killed her three years later, and his father was out of town at a business meeting.

McClintock ushered Renny into his office. "Come into the parlor. Some of the antiques here, including my desk, were purchased from the Stillwell Gallery," he said, referring to the antique dealer located in the former Jacobson family home.

McClintock sat down behind an eighteenth-century partners desk, a beautiful mahogany piece designed for two clerks to work opposite each other. Of course, McClintock had the desk to himself.

The older lawyer picked up a heavy folder, set it down, and tapped a fountain pen against his desk blotter. "Well, let's get down to business." He hesitated, opening the folder on his desk then closing it again without taking anything out. "I'm not sure where to begin."

"I've reviewed my copy of the will," Renny said. "Everything appears straightforward. Could we look over the documents you intend to file with the probate court?"

"The documents I've prepared for the court?" McClintock said.

"Sure, you said they would be ready."

"Oh, they are. I have them in here." The lawyer patted the still-closed folder.

Renny reached out his hand. "Yes. I'm sure everything is fine. I'd just like to skim through them."

The older lawyer didn't budge. "Renny, did you study holographic wills in law school?" he asked, staring past Renny at a spot on the wall behind him.

Renny stopped. "Of course. It's a will in the testator's own handwriting, usually without all the legal boilerplate language and the formality of witnesses."

"That's correct." McClintock paused. "I don't know how to say this except to ask you point-blank. Did your father ever tell you he had prepared a holographic will?"

A cold chill ran down Renny's spine. "No. He gave me a copy of the will you prepared for him a few months after my mother died."

"I see," McClintock said. "He never gave you an updated will prepared by another lawyer?"

"No. You were the only lawyer he used. Tell me, Mr. McClintock, what's going on."

McClintock sighed. "After your father's death I had my secretary pull his file to prepare the documents for the probate court." He opened the folder on his desk. "Inside was this." He held up a plain white envelope. "As you know, in the will I prepared you were the residual beneficiary of almost all your father's estate. Apparently, a month later he brought this envelope by the office and asked my secretary to put it in his file. I don't know what he told her—she doesn't remember and probably thought it was a list of assets or the location of important records." He handed the envelope to Renny. "Read it."

Renny took out three sheets of paper. No question, it was his father's handwriting, a familiar pattern of printing and cursive. It was dated one month after the lengthy will prepared by McClintock. There were only four paragraphs:

I, Henry Lawrence Jacobson, being of sound and disposing mind, do hereby revoke all prior Wills made by me and make this my Last Will and Testament.

ITEM ONE

I hereby will, devise and bequeath to my son, Josiah Fletchall Jacobson, all my personal belongings and the gold coin collection contained in my safe deposit box at Planters & Merchants Bank. I further will, give and devise to my son all my right, title and interest to any and all assets, tangible and intangible, in the Covenant List of South Carolina, Ltd. This bequest is subject to the usual and customary conditions precedent.

ITEM TWO

I hereby, will, devise and bequeath all the rest, remainder, and residue of my estate, including all real estate, stocks, bonds, certificates of deposit, cash, or other property of any type, tangible and intangible, in equal shares to the Medical College of South Carolina, The Citadel, the Charleston Historical Society, and the Episcopal Parish of St. Alban's.

ITEM THREE

I hereby appoint Jefferson McClintock as executor of my estate.

Henry Lawrence Jacobson

The other sheet was a report from a local psychiatrist, Dr. Lewis Abbott, dated the same day as the will.

To Whom It May Concern:
I have this day examined Henry Lawrence Jacobson and can state that

he is mentally competent to handle his legal affairs. He understands the natural objects of his affection and has informed me of his intention to prepare a Last Will and Testament in which the majority of his assets are bequeathed to charitable institutions. He has indicated that he will make a bequest to his son, Josiah Fletchall Jacobson, consistent with his desire and intentions for him.

Lewis Abbott, M.D.
Diplomate, American Board of Psychiatry

Renny let the papers fall into his lap and stared for several seconds at the floor in front of McClintock's desk. Every ounce of hope for the future drained out of him in the two minutes it took to read the papers. In shock, he didn't even have the strength to ask why.

The lawyer cleared his throat and broke the awkward silence. "We know the law doesn't favor a holographic will or one that disinherits family members. There was little doubt that your father wrote the will, but to be sure, I obtained a handwriting analysis. The results came back just before I called you yesterday."

"And?" Renny managed weakly.

"It's as close to a 100 percent match as possible. I also had an extensive interview with Dr. Abbott. Do you know him?"

"No."

"He is a former president of the South Carolina Psychiatric Association with impeccable credentials. He had detailed records of an interview with your father and stands completely by the report issued at the time of the will."

"Does he have connections with the Medical College?" Renny ventured.

"I thought of that, too. No, he doesn't, and there is no way to claim any self-interest on his part that would raise a question about his medical opinion of your father's capacity."

"I don't care what the psychiatrist says. This is crazy. Why would my father do this to me?" Renny asked, desperation and hurt creeping into his voice.

"I don't know. I'm a father, Renny, and I don't understand."

"But item one is nonsense. I didn't know he had a gold coin collection, and I've never heard of the Covenant List of South Carolina, Limited. What is it? What are the conditions precedent?"

"I was hoping you might shed some light on it. We've gone over every inventory of assets three times and found no record of this company. Since your father was involved in so much commercial development, it could be a real estate limited partnership."

"But you don't know."

"That's right. I'm guessing."

Renny put the papers on the edge of McClintock's desk. "We can't tear this up and probate the other will can we?"

"I'm sorry, but you know the answer to that. Since I'm the executor, I can exercise as much leeway as possible in interpreting 'personal belongings.' There are several valuable antiques at the Isle of Palms house. I'm going to consider those items personal belongings so that you can have them. Also, I would advise you to consider getting another legal opinion about the legitimacy of the will."

"I understand, but the handwriting is on the wall, or actually on these sheets of paper," Renny said bitterly. "Being on the receiving end of a lawyer telling his client what the client doesn't want to hear is painful."

"I can't blame you for anything you feel," McClintock responded. "I didn't want to have to give you this news." He handed Renny a key. "This is the key to safe deposit box 413 at the Planters and Merchants Bank downtown. You are a signatory, aren't you?"

"Yes."

"There's one other puzzling thing."

"What else?" Renny asked, bracing for more bad news.

"Nothing substantive. Included with some routine postmortem instructions was a letter." McClintock read aloud:

Dear Jeff,

    The enclosed information will assist you in probating my estate. As soon as possible, please send a copy of my obituary notice to the people on the attached list.

H. L.

Handing the second sheet to Renny, McClintock asked, "Do you know any of these individuals?"

Renny quickly scanned the names. No one was immediately familiar. As he read over it more slowly, he counted nine names with post office box addresses—no street names, no phone numbers. All men, no women.

"I don't know any of these men," Renny responded slowly. "I recognize several family names, families with a long history in the Low Country."

"It was the same with me."

"As far as I know, none of them are relatives. I don't see the names of any of my father's business associates either."

"Exactly my conclusion as well," the lawyer responded.

"But, this is just like the unknown company mentioned in the will. All we know is that we don't know anything."

Renny and McClintock stared at each other across the desk, each letting his mental wheels grind, both coming up empty.

McClintock spoke first. "Pursuant to your father's instructions, I sent a copy of his obituary to each person. I enclosed a short cover letter notifying them that I was following your father's last wishes."

"Did anybody respond?" Renny asked.

"Not yet," said McClintock, shaking his head. "I'll let you know if they do."

"Should I ask if there's anything else?"

"Fortunately not, I guess. My secretary has duplicates of everything for you."

Still numb, Renny nodded.

"Of course, I will delay sale of your parents' house as long as you need me to."

"It's hard to believe the house will be sold. That everything will be sold and given away," Renny said dully.

McClintock came around the desk and put his hand on Renny's shoulder. "Call me if you need me. I'll contact you as soon as I know anything else."

"Thanks." Renny got up to leave. When he reached the door, he stopped. "I forgot to ask. What is the value of the estate?"

McClintock paused. "Depending on the value of securities at time of probate, approximately $8 million."

2

He being dead yet speaketh.
HEBREWS 11:4, KJV

Going down the steps in front of McClintock and Carney, Renny walked a block to his car, which was parked next to a palmetto tree. His shirt was damp by the time he opened the door. Throwing the folder of information about the estate on the passenger seat, he turned the air conditioner on full blast and drove toward the Battery. Turning down King Street, he slowed in front of St. Alban's Episcopal Church and found a shady parking space under an oak tree beside the entrance to the church cemetery.

The church was one of the oldest in Charleston, and its mottled gray stone walls and muted stained-glass windows often graced the pages of guidebooks and pictorial tours of the city. For families like the Jacobsons, who had lived in Charleston for over two hundred years, St. Alban's was a family gathering place on Christmas Eve, Easter morning, and the site for marrying and burying. The rest of the time it was primarily a brief stop for busloads of hot tourists seeking a cool place on a steamy summer day.

There had not been any new plots available in the original cemetery since World War I. To handle the ongoing tide of death, the church purchased land outside the downtown Charleston area and sold burial plots in what Renny called the "cemetery annex." With the burial of Renny's father, the Jacobson plot at the main cemetery was at maximum occupancy, and Renny guessed he would have to reserve a space for himself at the annex.

The parish had no debt or financial needs—what the vestry would do with a $2 million gift from his father's estate was beyond Renny's comprehension. Buy more cemetery space? Hire an additional worker to keep the hedges trimmed and the few tufts of grass cut? Renny shook his head in shock and disbelief as he gingerly made his way around the ancient markers and tombstones, some so faded it was hard to decipher the names and ages of those who rested under the sandy soil. Maybe he could get a free burial plot. It would be the least the parish could do.

Surrounded by an ornate wrought-iron railing, the Jacobson plot was easily identified by a ten-foot-tall monument with the family name chiseled into all four sides at its base. His father and mother were side by side, his father's grave still a mound of light brown dirt. A few dead flowers from the funeral were strewn on the ground.

Renny stared at his father's name on the headstone and asked the question that had reverberated in his mind since he read the hand-written will at McClintock's office. "Why?" he whispered. "Why?" he said a little louder. "Why?" He wanted to scream at the top of his lungs.

Nothing. A breeze stirred the leaves in the old trees, but it didn't cool Renny's rising anger or assuage his inner pain. Eight million dollars. He had known it would be a lot of money, but the actual amount surprised him. His father had done better financially than he had realized. But for his only child—nothing. It was one thing for H. L. to deny Renny the things he needed while alive; it was almost more painful to experience rejection from beyond the grave. Rage and resentment boiled inside his soul. "Why?" he cried. "Why did you do this to me?" Nothing. Picking up a dead flower stem, he threw it at the headstone. There were no answers here.

Next to his father's fresh mound of dirt, the level grave of Katharine Candler Jacobson was covered with green grass. Turning toward her gravestone, Renny continued his questioning. Wherever she was, did she know what her husband had done to their only child? "Why?" he asked her resting place. Nothing. Shouldn't she share some of the blame? "Why didn't you outlive him?" Nothing. She died first, and the scant protection she offered Renny died with her. She would have done differently, or at least tried to, but she was gone.

He resented her abandonment. But his mother couldn't answer his questions and didn't deserve his blame. She had endured much herself. Although skewed by a child's naturally positive perceptions of his parents and their flaws, Renny knew his mother's relationship with his father was trying. But in the midst of a difficult marriage, Katharine gave her only surviving child memories worth preserving. She sat with him and listened when he told her about his day at school. She was there when he needed wise counsel as a teenager. She kept the lines of communication open until the ravages of disease robbed her of her voice. Even then her eyes had continued to speak of a mother's love . . . until their light went out, too. Now nothing responded to Renny's gaze but marble and memories.

Because of her and her alone he would come back to this place. Retracing his steps to the car, Renny's anger gave way to dejection. How many steps were there down to the depths of hell in Dante's *Inferno*? How much more would he have to endure?

———

Shortly after Renny drove away, another car parked in the space Renny vacated. An older man with a younger man's vigor and energy opened the door and walked briskly to the spot where Renny had stood beside his father's grave. Looking at the tombstone, he smiled. To him, H. L. Jacobson's grave was not a place of rejection, anger, and frustration; it was a place of triumph. Sure of the irrefutable evidence of his victory, he lingered for a moment, savoring his conquest, then left.

It was not yet five o'clock, so Renny decided he might as well stop at the bank and examine the gold coin collection before driving out to the

Isle of Palms. In earlier times, Planters and Merchants Bank, an ancient, square, dark stone, three-story building, contained a waterfront counting house. It was the financial center where traders, planters, and factors—the men who lent money secured by future rice, indigo, and cotton harvests—transacted their business affairs and "counted" their money. Most people viewed banks with a mixture of fear, awe, and distrust, but to Renny, the old bank was familiar territory, and Planters and Merchants Bank, locally known as P&M, was like an honored old grandfather, black and hoary on the outside, but noble and sedate on the inside.

Slipping the safe deposit box key into his pocket, Renny entered P&M through the solid wooden front doors and passed through the marble-floored lobby to the desk of the custodian of the vault, a stoop-shouldered old gentleman resting with his head in his hands.

"I'm J. F. Jacobson. I need access to my box, please, number 413."

Looking up sleepily, the clerk opened a drawer in his desk and pulled out a signature comparison card and a record of access card. "May I see some picture identification? And please sign here, sir."

Renny handed him his driver's license. The clerk pushed the record of access card across the desk, grunting. "Just got back from there."

Renny picked up the card. "Who is this?" Renny asked, trying to decipher the signature. "It looks like Gusto something."

Returning to his drawer, the clerk pulled out three signature cards and put on his reading glasses. "There are two persons besides yourself with access to this box," he replied, somewhat more awake. "Henry Lawrence Jacobson and Augustus Eicholtz."

"Henry Lawrence Jacobson was my father. Who is Augustus Eicholtz?" Renny asked sharply.

"Sir, how should I know? It's your box."

"How long has this Augustus Eicholtz had access to the box?"

"Since June 4, 1981," the clerk replied. Handing Renny the original signature card for Mr. Eicholtz, he added, "See, the signatures match exactly."

Renny examined the signature card. This was déjà vu from McClintock's office—more questions without answers.

"Do you still want to open the box?" the clerk asked as he compared Renny's signature to the signature card in his file.

"I guess," Renny replied. As the clerk led him through the twisting labyrinth of the security area, Renny asked, "Did Mr. Einstein take something from the box?"

"Mr. Eicholtz, sir. I'm sorry, I didn't notice."

Renny had little doubt there was nothing in the box. Mr. Eicholtz or whatever his name was would have taken care of that.

Safe deposit box 413 was a large drawer inset into the metal casing of the vault. The clerk pulled out a master key, turned his side of the lock, and waited as Renny inserted the key's mate next to it. With a click, the lock released, and the clerk pulled the drawer open an inch.

"Let me know when you're finished," he mumbled as he shuffled out of the vault.

Renny slid the drawer out all the way. It was empty except for two white envelopes lying faceup in the bottom. Handwritten on the front of both envelopes was his full name, Josiah Fletchall Jacobson, one in his father's handwriting, the other in an unfamiliar scrawl. No return address.

The envelope from his father contained a heavy coin. Glancing over his shoulder, Renny gently pried open the seal. Inside was an 1864 half eagle five-dollar gold coin in excellent condition. Although possibly worth several thousand dollars, one coin hardly qualified as a collection. Renny let the heavy coin rest in his hand for a moment before slipping it into his pocket and opening the other envelope. Inside he found a plain white cassette tape labeled "Covenant List." The mystery company. Nothing else was in the envelope. No letter, no note.

Renny closed the safe deposit box and navigated out of the vault past the custodian's desk. "Thanks for your help," he said as he passed the sleepy-eyed clerk.

Seated in his car, Renny took a deep breath. Glancing in the rearview mirror, he wondered if he was being followed. He didn't know Augustus Eicholtz, but this man probably knew him. Was he watching him now, planning to attack at a vulnerable, unsuspecting moment?

Picking up the car phone, he called McClintock's office.

"Mr. McClintock, please."

"I'm sorry, Mr. McClintock has left for the day," the receptionist chirped.

"This is Renny Jacobson. I was just in to see him. Do you know if he went home?"

"I'm sorry Mr. Jacobson, he was leaving to pick up his wife and fly to Key Biscayne. He will not be back in the office until Wednesday. Should I leave him a message?"

"No. That's OK. I'll call back another time."

Renny couldn't listen to the tape in the car; he only had a CD player. But his father had a stereo system at the Isle of Palms house. So Renny pulled into the afternoon traffic, heading across the city. As he crossed the short bridge to the Isle of Palms where a few fishermen were casting their lines into the receding tidal river, he wondered what in the world was on the tape. Why did his father ask a man named Augustus Eicholtz to put the cassette tape in the safe deposit box? What else could H. L. do to hurt him?

Then Renny remembered something he saw in McClintock's office. He turned sharply into a convenience store and jammed on the brakes, the car's tires scattering broken seashells across the parking lot. Flipping hurriedly through the paperwork, he found the sheet listing the names of the persons who received copies of his father's obituary notice. There he was, number four on the list, Augustus Eicholtz, P.O. Box 376, Savannah, Georgia. Renny leaned back against the seat and read the names again. Still no one familiar. At least it was a start. He put the car in gear and eased back onto the roadway.

Renny turned away from the Atlantic. His father didn't want to live too close to the ocean, a preference that stood him in good stead when Hurricane Hugo roared through Charleston in September 1989. A massive sea surge and winds exceeding 100 miles per hour had demolished most of the homes and buildings on the Isle of Palms. Mr. Jacobson's home, a federal-style old brick dwelling, was sufficiently sheltered by the highest dunes on the island to survive without serious damage. Renny had brought a key to the house with him from Charlotte. Vacant since H. L.'s death, the house had a musty smell as he entered the kitchen.

The stereo was in the den, a dark-paneled room with a view of the marshes. Pulling a green leather ottoman up to the stereo, Renny inserted the cassette and pressed the play button. Then, like in the old *Mission Impossible* series on TV, he waited for the message of the moment, "Good morning, Mr. Phelps, your mission, should you choose to accept it..." He flinched slightly when his father's familiar voice filled the room.

"Renny, I am recording this message shortly after your mother's death, on the same day I prepared my handwritten will. I assume you are listening to this cassette after meeting with Jefferson McClintock or one of his associates and obtaining this tape and a gold coin from the safe deposit box at P&M. If you are with anyone else, please honor my wishes and ask them to leave now. What I have to tell you is for your ears only."

After a brief pause, the voice continued, "I asked a friend, Augustus Eicholtz, to deliver the tape to the safe deposit box as soon as he received news of my death. I mentioned the gold coin collection in my will to ensure that you went to the box. The half eagle coin has been passed down from father to son in our family for 140 years, and I would ask you not to sell it; keep it to give to your firstborn son. As gold, it is a symbol of the true source of enduring wealth for our family.

"I am aware that the provisions of my will have come as a shock to you; however, if you listen to this tape, you will understand what I have done. In my will I made a specific bequest to you of my interest in the Covenant List of South Carolina, Ltd. Neither Jeff McClintock nor anyone in his office knows what it passes to you. I can now tell you that it is far more valuable than the combined assets of my known estate. The charitable bequests in my will are a fraction of the value of your interest in the List, as we call it."

Renny sat stunned.

"As you know, our family line goes back to the early days of European settlement of the Low Country. Toward the end of the Civil War, most planters and landowners faced financial ruin. Our family, together with ten other families from the local aristocracy, entered into an agreement of cooperation for the common good. The List is merely a way of identifying this group of families. Pooling a significant percentage of its remaining resources, this group smuggled gold and hard assets out of the Confederacy to safe havens in Europe. The eleven male heads of the families also entered into an agreement obligating their firstborn sons to honor a mutual commitment to contribute to and to receive the benefits of the funds sent overseas. Since that time, your forebears have remained true to their word. You are the fifth generation of Jacobsons privileged to take his place on the List.

"The nine men who received my obituary notice are the current members of the List. One of the original families no longer has any direct bloodline descendants. When a member dies, it is necessary to hold a meeting of the survivors to install the next man in line for the family involved. I have a box at the main post office in Charleston. The key is in my desk at the house on the Isle of Palms. You will receive notice of the meeting by letter at the post office box. In the old storage building behind the house on St. Michael's Alley is a trunk containing paperwork you must take to the meeting. Stillwell has let me use the building for many years. The key for the storage shed is also in the desk at Isle of Palms. In the meantime, do not discuss this with anyone. One of the linchpins of our mutual success has been secrecy, an obvious necessity in this day of high taxes."

Renny smiled ruefully. So, his father was probably a felony tax evader.

"There are other, more intangible but nevertheless important benefits associated with membership to the List. You will learn more about all the benefits at the appropriate time. Carpe diem."

"Seize the day," Renny echoed softly. He listened for a full minute to the scratching of the tape as it continued to turn in the machine. That was it.

Children occasionally fantasize that their parents had a different, secret life—a father who worked for the CIA, a mother who was the heiress to a European fortune. Such a thought was no longer fantasy for Renny.

Hitting the rewind switch, he backed the tape to the beginning and listened again. Nothing changed.

Renny pulled open the middle drawer of his father's desk. The two keys mentioned on the tape sat in a tray. One was a standard government-issue post office box key with a string tied to a small round disk, labeled "Box 399"; the other, an old-style skeleton key, was marked "St. Michael's Storage Building." Slipping the keys into his pocket, Renny went into the kitchen. There wasn't anything to eat in the pantry; his father's housekeeper had no doubt cleaned it out already. Dusk was creeping over the marsh when he looked out the window in the breakfast nook adjacent to the kitchen.

Still somewhat dazed by the information he'd received, Renny sat at a small round table for several minutes. His stomach rumbled. Dreams of future wealth could not take the place of a good supper.

Hopping back in his car, he retraced his route to the edge of the city and stopped at a shrimp boil shack. Within forty-five minutes he had peeled and eaten three-quarters of a pound of the pink delicacy and drained two large frosted mugs of draft beer.

Fortified, he did not want to return immediately to the empty Isle of Palms house. Jingling the post office box and storage building keys in his pocket, he decided to drive downtown. The post office was open till 11:00 P.M., and he had plenty of time to check for mail before stopping by the storage building on St. Michael's Alley.

The heat of the afternoon had diminished, and Renny put the top down on the car before navigating the familiar streets. Box 399 was one of the smallest boxes available, not the place for someone expecting a lot of correspondence. Opening it, he took out a sales flyer from Wal-Mart, a sheet of pizza coupons addressed to *Patron*, and a letter addressed to Josiah Fletchall Jacobson, c/o H. L. Jacobson. Renny realized he was following a well-marked path through the woods. The return address was simple, P.O. Box 1493, Georgetown, SC. He remembered two names on the list with Georgetown addresses. It had to be from one of them.

Taking the letter to a table against the wall of the post office, Renny carefully broke the seal and pulled out two sheets of ivory-colored paper. The top one was dated the previous week.

Dear Mr. Jacobson,

Please accept my condolences on the death of your father. As custodian of the List, he provided admirable leadership over the years. He will be missed by all who knew him.

Due to the deaths of your father and Mr. Taylor Johnston, there will be a meeting of the members of the List on August 25, at Rice Planter's Inn, Georgetown, South Carolina. You, as your father's heir and designee, and Mr. Joe Taylor Johnston, Mr. Johnston's heir and designee, will be installed at that time.

In addition, I am sure your father took care to furnish you with the location of the documents he held in trust as custodian. It is imperative that you bring these items with you to Georgetown so that we can conduct our business.

Please do not discuss these matters with anyone.

Respectfully,
Desmond R. LaRochette

The letter was copied to the names furnished by H. L. to Jefferson McClintock. The second sheet was a letter similar to Renny's sent to the other man whose father had recently died, Mr. Joe Taylor Johnston.

Leaning against the table, Renny folded the two letters and put them back in the envelope. Whatever it was, whatever it meant for his future, the List was real. His father did not prepare the taped message as a cruel joke with April Fools as the punch line. H. L. had held some sort of official position within the group; there were real people from several states involved; they held meetings; they communicated through specially designated post office boxes. In a few days he would see them face to face and find out...what? The amount of money involved would be a good start. He was going to have to trade in his fantasies about the wealth from his father's known estate for new ones funded by a different cache of money, which his father considered "far greater than my known estate."

Walking outside, Renny was tired. Like a child who'd stayed too long at the amusement park, he was overloaded from the intense stimuli of the day. However, he still had one stop to make before returning to the Isle of Palms.

Following the quiet downtown streets to St. Michael's Alley, he pulled up to a dark, deserted Stillwell Gallery. Renny's family had built the cream-colored house in 1836. Partially held together by huge earthquake bolts, the structure had survived everything from the Civil War to Hurricane Hugo. It was a typical antebellum home. The original house, a separate cook's house, and an adjacent livery stable were now incorporated into the main dwelling. The building's only distinctive architectural feature was a third-story bay window extending five or six feet out over the street. Legend had it that an early Mrs. Jacobson, an invalid with keen eyesight, ordered the window built to provide an unobstructed view up and down the street so she could keep a close eye on her husband as he drove his buggy to his shipping office near the docks.

No colorful past put the Jacobson house on the cover of guide books or caused busloads of gaping tourists to stop and see a place where the shot was fired, the blood spilled, or the famous slept. Tourists came to shop for antiques, not to gather pieces of historical information.

Renny's family had not lived in the house since World War II. The Charleston waterfront area had deteriorated for many years, so H. L.'s parents sold the house and moved to the Isle of Palms in the late 1940s. When the older areas of Charleston made a comeback, the Jacobson house was renovated by a group of businessmen who bought it as an investment. Glenn Stillwell, owner of Stillwell Gallery, paid five thousand dollars a month for the privilege of displaying a good selection of Low Country antiques. Renny wished his family had never sold the house.

Parking under the bay window, he took a small flashlight out of his glove compartment and wondered if Mr. Stillwell had a security system designed to sense physical presence near the building after hours. Renny doubted it, but he nevertheless moved gingerly around the side of the shop to a small wooden gate leading to the backyard. Lifting an ancient iron latch, he pushed open the gate and stepped onto a slate stone patio that stretched half the length of the house before yielding to a small patch of grass ringed with narrow flower beds. A high brick wall enclosed the yard. The storage building, snugly set against the wall and covered with ivy, sat in the far corner of the grassy area.

Renny's flashlight generated a feeble beam that barely cut through the darkness. He couldn't remember if the storage building was wired with electricity or not. Moving slowly across the grass, he fished the skeleton key from his pocket as he quietly approached the door. Although not a naturally timid person, he had to banish sinister images from old Sherlock Holmes movies that crept into his mind as he approached the shed. Turning the knob, the door creaked open. Relieved, Renny cautiously stepped forward, then recoiled in horror as something suspended from the ceiling struck him in the face. It was a metal chain for an overhead light. Telling his heart to stop pounding, Renny pulled the chain, and a bare bulb illuminated the little room.

To one side was a rotary push mower, on the other side sat several cans of paint, a few garden tools, and against the back wall, a small wooden trunk, obviously old, probably an antique.

Renny picked up the trunk by ornately carved handles on its sides and positioned it under the light. A modern combination lock secured a metal latch plate on the chest's front. Renny pulled on it, but it didn't yield to his tug. Hoisting the trunk onto his left shoulder, he retraced his steps across the yard, alternately shining the flashlight ahead, behind, and to both sides. His booty secured, he drove northeast toward the Isle of Palms.

3

And they covenanted with him for thirty pieces of silver.
MATTHEW 26:15, KJV

When he awoke in the morning, it took Renny a couple of seconds to orient his thoughts in light of the previous day's events. Once assured of his bearings, he dressed and, placing the wooden trunk on the table in the breakfast nook, examined his new possession in the morning light.

Not large enough for a transatlantic voyage or rough enough for storage in a barn, the old trunk was probably intended for use in a business. It was well constructed; the joints fit closely together, and each corner was reinforced with brass. From the dense texture of the wood, he guessed it was made of teak, consistent with an eighteenth-century craftsman's disdain for lesser woods such as oak or maple. The top was rounded and ribbed with a dark red mahogany, and each rib was decorated with the four stages of the moon. The brass lock plate stretched across one-third of the front. The trunk was most likely used as a strongbox that would have been filled with gold and silver coins after sale of the cotton and rice crops.

The original lock had been supplemented with a heavy-duty combination lock. Definitely twentieth century, stainless steel, Masterlock brand, probably from the local Ace Hardware.

Renny went into the den to look for the combination for the lock. Rummaging through the middle drawer of the desk, he found a Mont

Blanc fountain pen, a few paper clips, a yellow notepad, and a slip of paper on which his father had written, "Combination to trunk: 42, 33, 51."

"Hike," he said.

Carrying the sheet back to the kitchen, he sat down in front of the trunk and tried a right, left, right sequence. The lock clicked and popped open. Sliding the lock out of the brass plate, Renny opened the lid and looked inside.

He wasn't expecting a cache of gold, silver, or diamonds. The trunk was too light for gold bullion or pirate treasure. In fact, it was almost empty. On top were a few envelopes with his father's name written on them, and underneath was an old, dark brown ledger. Renny's attention was immediately drawn to the book. Oversized by modern standards, it was about fourteen inches wide by eighteen inches long. "Ledger" had been stamped in faded gilt on a dark leather strip embedded in the brown cover. The inside was decorated in a zigzag pattern of different colors, a pattern common to nineteenth-century bookbinders.

Renny rubbed the front with his hand, enjoying the feel of the old book. Turning to the first page, he saw that all the writing, from beginning to end, was in black ink, some dimmed by age, the more recent, clear and distinct.

On the first two pages Renny read in bold, flowing script:

Georgetown, South Carolina, November 30, 1863

> *Whereas, the current state of civil and military affairs for the State of South Carolina and the Confederate States of America is deleterious to the preservation of domestic safety and security; and*

> *Whereas, the undersigned recognize the need for common action and unified response to the current crises; and*

> *Whereas, the undersigned desire to commit their lives and honor to the common goal of preserving their families during these difficult days; and*

Whereas, the undersigned agree that a mutual covenant and commitment to accumulate resources for transfer to other countries is the best way to insure security for present and future generations:

Now, therefore, in consideration of the mutual promises recited herein, the undersigned hereby agree, covenant, and bind themselves and their male heirs as determined by the right of primogeniture as follows:

i. We each agree to transfer within thirty (30) days to a common fund held in trust at LaRochette & Co. the sum of $10,000.00 each in gold or silver, said sum to be transported to England for deposit in the Bank of England under the name of the Covenant List of South Carolina, Limited, hereinafter the List;

ii. We authorize Messrs. Smithfield and Weiss to arrange transport of said sum to England by sailing vessel as soon as practicable considering the current Northern blockade;

iii. We agree that neither Messrs. Smithfield nor Weiss shall be liable for any loss incurred should said ship be captured by Northern forces or lost at sea;

iv. We agree that distribution of income and/or principal shall be made no more often than every five years from the monies put on deposit or at such other intervals as decided by majority vote of the subscribers hereto;

v. We agree that investment and distribution of all funds shall rest exclusively with the subscribers to the List free from outside influence or control. The subscribers hereto bind themselves and all successors to strict secrecy and confidence, revealing the existence and function of the List to none.

vi. We agree that the purpose of this fund is to perpetuate the financial stability and security of each subscriber family irrespective of the laws of civil governments.

vii. *We recognize and acknowledge our dependence upon, and the authority of the Supreme Being who governs our lives and this world to bless us in the accomplishment of the munificent purposes herein.*

viii. *To the above preamble and recitation of covenant we swear, binding ourselves and descendants as described herein to all the rights and appurtenances hereinbefore recited.*

This 30th day of November, 1863.

Signed by:

Henri LaRochette
George P. Smithfield
Alexander Weiss
Fredrik Eicholtz
J. F. Jacobson
Astor M. Flournoy
Thomas Layne
Pierre Roget
Alexander Hammond
Marcus K. Johnston
Lawrence Maxwell

Renny half expected to see a Rockefeller, Rothschild, or Du Pont as one of the signers.

He knew the cumulative power of compound interest over a long period. A penny invested at 4 percent compound interest at the time of Jesus' birth would today exceed the gross national product of the United States. Depending on withdrawals, the original $110,000, a large sum in 1863, had been churning and percolating for almost 140 years. He again remembered his father's words on the tape, "Far more valuable than my known estate."

Questions blinked in his mind like Christmas tree lights. Was the money still in England? How much and how frequently were distributions made? Who knew the details of the amounts of money and its location? Had there been diversification of investment? Had World War I, the Depression of the 1930s, or World War II affected the funds? Was it time for a distribution? What would be his share?

He examined his great-great-grandfather's signature, a strong first letter trailing off to illegibility at the end. J. F. Jacobson, the same initials as Renny. What did his initials stand for? What was he like? Renny knew some about the branches of his family tree and a little bit about the twigs, but as he stared at the old signature, he felt as if he were looking at the roots of an old oak.

The original Covenant document filled the first three pages of the ledger. Turning the pages, Renny read multiple entries in a common form for successors from each family.

> *The undersigned, eldest legal heir of* _____, *hereby enters into covenant under the terms and conditions of the Covenant List of South Carolina, Limited.*

> _____

> *Sufficient and confident proof of legal succession having been presented and upon administration of an oath of Covenant allegiance,* _____ *is hereby accepted to full rights and privileges pursuant to the Covenant List of South Carolina, Limited.*
> *This* _____ *day of* _____, _____.

In addition to the original signatories, there were at least sixty or seventy subsequent subscribers. Beside each signature was a small brown smudge. Renny located three other Jacobsons: his father, H. L., signed in 1957, his grandfather Philip S. in 1921 and his great-grandfather Hiram T. in 1874. Renny wished each name could come to life, step from the page, and spend an evening telling his tale. He regretted the vow of secrecy and felt a pang of regret that it had prevented his father from sharing this with him. Could it have made their relationship different? A sense of family pride swelled in Renny's chest; he felt privileged, connected with the past, linked to his roots.

Although he had no brothers or sisters, Renny grew up as part of a larger family of Low Country relatives, and the modern twentieth-century notion of the nuclear family, isolated and distant from blood kin, was not his experience. To Renny, the concept of family also included links with other similar families from the same social strata in their geographic area. Among aristocratic Charleston families there was an unspoken understanding that, if possible, suitable unions of young men and women from the pool of established families should be pursued. That way the offspring would, like thoroughbred horses, bring out the best in the line of sire and dam. Renny himself was the progeny of such a union. His mother, although not as well off financially as his father, had roots wrapped around the bedrock of the pre–Revolutionary War settlement of South Carolina.

Renny reread the original agreement. Given his upbringing, he was comfortable with the purpose of the List and its references to honor and family security. It reminded him of a compact between European noblemen in the face of a common enemy.

The most recent entry in the ledger was a man named Bartholomew Maxwell. Checking back in time, Renny found that Maxwell's father, Stephen Franklin Maxwell, entered into membership in 1942. The List was like a necklace, each family a strand of beads connected at the beginning. Shutting the book, he took a sip of water and decided he wanted to learn more about his family before the meeting in Georgetown.

There was a Charleston phone book on top of the desk in the den. Turning to the Cs, he found the entry for Gerald C. Caswell, his deceased uncle. Uncle Gerald had been dead for ten years, but Renny's Aunt Margaret continued to list her husband's name in the phone book. To her thinking, anyone she wanted to talk to would know that she was Mrs. Gerald C. Caswell. She answered on the third ring.

"Aunt Margaret, it's Renny. I'm here in Charleston for the weekend."

"Good morning, Renny," Aunt Margaret said in her high-pitched but congenial drawl. "Do you have time to come by and see me?"

"That's why I called. I had a meeting yesterday with Jefferson McClintock about my father's estate and decided to stay the weekend."

"Good. Come at noon, and I'll fix you a bite to eat."

"Thanks. See you then," Renny responded with satisfaction. His aunt's "bite to eat" would be enough of the four major food groups to last him until the next day. Confident he would not starve to death in the foreseeable future, Renny carefully put the List back in the trunk and snapped the lock shut.

Aunt Margaret, his father's older sister by twelve years, had helped raise H. L. and always viewed him more as a son than a brother. When Renny was born, she transferred some of her maternal affection from H. L. to him. She had three children, all much older than Renny, and a number of grandchildren, two of whom, boys named James and Andrew, were contemporaries of Renny and his frequent playmates while growing up.

Aunt Margaret's home was close to Charleston's air force base, or more accurately, the air force base was close to her home. Long before jet engines, the Caswell family sold the U.S. government a sizable portion of the land needed for construction of the base. Although her house was not in the direct flight paths of incoming and outgoing aircraft, it was noisy on a busy day. Aunt Margaret had adapted to the airport sounds like people who lived beside the railroad tracks in a small town: After a while, the noise of a passing train became so common that it was nestled in a familiar slot of their consciousness without disturbing them.

Renny pulled onto a long driveway and drove several hundred yards through rows of live oaks to the house. Not quite *Gone with the Wind*'s Tara but still impressive, the white-columned house was built around 1900 and originally served as the main house on a large farm. Turning into the circular driveway, Renny parked directly in front of the house and opened the car door to a boisterous greeting from his aunt's two golden retrievers, Johnny and Jay. His aunt had watched *The Tonight Show* with Johnny

Carson every night for years, and when Jay Leno took over for Carson, she transferred her loyalties to the new toastmaster. As a gift upon Renny's graduation from college, Aunt Margaret presented him with one of Johnny's offspring, a beautiful female named Brandy.

True to their namesakes, Johnny was older than Jay, and both loved to chase tennis balls. Jay dropped a slobbery yellow mass at Renny's feet and crouched low, ready to spring into action. Estimating he could make it to the door by the time the dogs returned, Renny threw the ball as far to the left of the house as he could and dashed up the porch steps as the dogs sped off.

Stoop-shouldered by her eighty years of life but still full of energy for her daily tasks, Aunt Margaret waited for him. "I wish I could throw the ball for them like that," she said. "Do you want to wash your hands? Those tennis balls are soaking wet, although I'm sure you know a dog's mouth is cleaner than a human's."

Not having scientific proof available to substantiate his aunt's hypothesis, Renny said, "I'll wash up."

All the years watching *The Tonight Show* had not made Aunt Margaret cosmopolitan. The house was decorated much as it was when Uncle Gerald was a boy. The foyer opened to a large dining room on the right and a smaller living room to the left, with heart pine flooring throughout. A huge kitchen occupied most of the back of the house. In the 1930s, Gerald's father employed fifteen to twenty day men as field hands. The men were paid, in part, by an all-they-could-eat noonday dinner of fried chicken, mashed potatoes, green beans, creamed corn, beets, tomatoes, biscuits, fruit cobbler, and sweet tea. It took two women most of a morning to fry the chicken, fix the vegetables, and prepare the baked goods. For many of the men during the Depression, it was the only meal of the day.

Renny washed his hands in a large bathroom with two freestanding sinks. In earlier times, water to the house had been supplied by a private water tower constructed on the property. The Caswells had used two windmills to pump water from a well to the holding tank, and his aunt still used it to irrigate her flowers and a portion of the lawn close to the house. Renny remembered it as a frigid contrast to the summer heat. He and his cousins would use a hand pump to fill an old horse trough and lie in it on hot days.

His aunt had a bedroom downstairs and kept the upstairs closed except for frequent visits from children and grandchildren. Much of the furniture in the house was wood. She even had a long wood settee as a substitute for a sofa in the living room. It was a handsome piece, with a dip in the seat that made it surprisingly comfortable. Renny smelled dinner as he walked through the living room. This was not going to be a frozen meal for two popped out of the microwave. Aunt Margaret was a good cook who continued to prepare fancy holiday dinners for her children and grandchildren.

The long kitchen had a bank of windows facing the broad expanse of the backyard, a row of huge pin oaks, and the edge of the air base.

"Come out to the kitchen, Renny, we'll eat here."

The combination of smells made Renny's mouth water. He hadn't eaten since the previous evening and he gratefully watched as his aunt prepared a plate with a medium to large portion of everything.

"Go ahead and get started, Renny," she said as she set the food in front of him. "You look hungry."

Renny didn't protest and began feasting like a field hand. "If Jay Leno knew about your cooking, he'd fly in for dinner," he said after he had made a sizable dent in the food piled on his plate.

"Thank you," she said. "How have you been doing?"

"OK, I guess."

Aunt Margaret spread some butter on a homemade yeast roll. "It's hard to believe your father is gone. I miss him."

"Me, too," Renny said, trying to sound sincere.

"Yes, he used to come out every couple of weeks or so and eat with me."

"Really? I didn't know that. How long had that been going on?"

"At least two years. We had some good talks."

"Just the two of you?"

"Yes." She nodded. "You know, he was getting softer as the years went by."

"Um," Renny grunted noncommittally.

"Oh, I know he was hard on you. It was just his way of wanting you to grow up strong."

"I guess so."

"Just a few months ago he told me he had been too demanding with you."

"He did?" Renny put down his fork.

"He never told you?"

"No."

"I'm not surprised. I told him to talk with you, but he was a proud man. He rarely opened the window into his soul." Getting up, Aunt Margaret took some fresh rolls out of the oven. "Let one of these rolls float onto your plate," she said more cheerfully.

Renny filled his stomach with Southern cooking at its best and wondered what his aunt would think about all he had learned about his father in the past twenty-four hours. She was a gracious, hospitable, Southern matron, focused on family activities, serving others, and preserving her little corner of the world. The idea of confederate gold and secret overseas bank accounts was not included in her framework. Perhaps that was why the founders of the List decided that succession pass to subsequent generations by the law of primogeniture, the exclusive right of the eldest son to inherit the estate of his father. Secrecy prevented the jealousy of those who received nothing, although Renny doubted Aunt Margaret would have cared.

Slowing down in order to make sure he had enough room for two servings of dessert, Renny swallowed a bite of chicken and broached the reason for his visit. "Aunt Margaret, I'm interested in learning about the Jacobson ancestors. My father once told me that you had documented a fairly detailed family tree. Do you have something you could show me about the male line back to the time of the Civil War?"

Visibly pleased with his request, she pushed away her plate. "My files are upstairs; I'll be back in a moment." He heard the floor overhead creak under her footsteps. She returned a couple of minutes later with a manila folder.

"This contains what you want to know," she said briskly, not stopping to ask him the reason for his sudden interest in genealogy. Moving her plate farther out of the way, she unfolded a large sheet of paper on the table at an angle so Renny could see it. "This is an overview of the family tree. The records used to compile this outline are upstairs. I prepared this sheet as a summary using what I learned and information collected by your great-aunt Aimee.

"At the top is the first known Jacobson to settle in South Carolina, John Worthington Jacobson, born approximately 1630 in Pelham, England, and died in 1679 in Charleston. He immigrated as an indentured servant in 1650. Freed after seven years, he worked for a shipping company, eventually becoming part owner. In 1659, he married Eliza Rea. They had three children."

Renny was fascinated. The few bites of food on his plate grew cold as he listened to his aunt skillfully navigate the waters of the past.

Tracing his finger back and forth across the page in a miniature game of hopscotch, Renny found Jeremiah F. Jacobson, born 1835, died 1874. "Tell me about him."

Aunt Margaret pursed her lips. "Well, J. F. Jacobson had a good start. As you see, he was born before the Civil War. He was a rice planter and worked with his father as a factor for other planters."

"I wonder if he worked at the old P&M building downtown," Renny interjected.

"Could have. He married at age twenty-two, and his first child, a son, Hiram T., was born on April 12, 1861, the day Confederate forces began the bombardment of Fort Sumter. It's my understanding that J. F. raised his own regiment and fought at Manassas and Fair Oaks. His term of enlistment ended before the war was over, and instead of continuing in uniform he returned to Charleston in early 1863. He was disillusioned with the Confederate cause and became convinced the South could not win the war long before more strident voices were willing to admit the possibility of defeat. The Jacobson family suffered financially during Reconstruction, but did better than most of their contemporaries. The Heywoods, descendants of a signer of the Declaration of Independence, worked as hands in a rice mill. The Jacobsons never had to sell their holdings or work for others."

"My boss in Charlotte is named Heywood, but I don't know anything about his family."

"If he wanted to find out, it shouldn't be too hard."

"You said J. F. had a good start," Renny commented. "It sounds like he did better than most toward the end as well."

"Not really." Aunt Margaret lowered her voice. "He died a hopeless alcoholic, killed in a fight over a high-stakes poker game."

"Are you sure about that?" Renny could not imagine one of his relatives in such a scenario.

"I have a letter written by his widow to a cousin in Beaufort. It's all there."

Renny pointed to Hiram Jacobson, the next name down the tree. "So, he was about thirteen when his father died?"

"That's right. Hiram was your great-grandfather. He was forced by his father's untimely death to assume responsibility for the family at an early age. Fortunately, he had help from an uncle and a man named LaRochette."

The mention of LaRochette startled Renny.

"What is it, Renny?"

"Nothing, nothing. Go ahead."

"Well, by the time he was thirty-five or forty, Hiram was buying interest in banks and some of the textile mills springing up in the South. He and his wife did not have any children who survived infancy until Hiram was thirty-seven. Your grandfather, my father, Philip S. Jacobson, was born in 1897."

"How many children died before Philip survived?" Renny asked, thinking about his mother's multiple miscarriages before his own birth.

"I don't know, but my father was so overprotected as a child he could not leave the house if it started to rain even a few drops."

"How did your grandfather die?"

"He died in 1919. In his later years he became very fearful and suspicious. My father told me he put bars on his doors, convinced someone was planning to break into the house on St. Michael's Alley. One night a neighbor who was locked out of his house came over to ask for help. He knocked on the door and heard a yell and crash. Breaking out a window, he crawled into the front parlor and found Hiram dead. I assume he heard the noise outside, became frightened, and had a heart attack. The cause of death on the death certificate is apoplexy."

"Not a lot of joy in Mudville. Why was he so fearful?"

"He was wealthy, but afraid someone was plotting to take everything from him. As far as I know, his fears were unfounded. After his father's death, my father, Philip Jacobson, lived in Savannah for fifteen years. That's where your father and I were born and where I went to elementary school. Not content to stay in port and run a shipping company, he spent about half the year on board ship traveling all over the world."

Renny had seen some of the curious objects his grandfather acquired during his travels. Aunt Margaret displayed her father's knife collection in a glass case in the living room. It contained knives from Africa, South America, the Far East, India, and Europe.

"I was born when my father was twenty-three and my mother twenty-four. They wanted to have another child, hoping for a son. Over the next ten years my mother had two miscarriages and one stillborn son before your father finally arrived in 1927. My father was so excited I thought he might give me a cigar."

Renny knew this part of the story well. "So, did you get a cigar?"

"I said 'might.' We moved back to Charleston and lived on St. Michael's Alley until World War II. You know the rest, but I brought down the newspaper article reporting your grandfather's death in 1957."

He had not seen the article in years. The small headline read, "Local Resident Lost at Sea."

Local businessman Philip S. Jacobson failed to return from a day sailing excursion this past Saturday. Coast Guard authorities were notified and initiated search activities in coastal waters. No signs of Jacobson or his craft, *The Aramore*, were located and, after three days' unsuccessful search, the Coast Guard listed him presumed lost at sea. Weather conditions have been favorable up and down the coast over the past week, and the Coast Guard offered no explanation for Jacobson's disappearance. An avid sailor, Mr. Jacobson was involved in shipping and real estate development throughout the area.

Renny handed the article back to Aunt Margaret.

"For months we held out hope he would return. The uncertainty was much worse than facing a known cause of death like heart attack or cancer. All we could guess was that his boat sank and he drowned.

"Your father planned on going sailing with your grandfather the Saturday of the last trip, but he canceled at the last minute. They ate breakfast together at the dock that morning, and H. L. was the last family member to see your grandfather alive. Your father changed after your grandfather's disappearance. It was not so much grief as a profound melancholy. He rarely smiled, becoming serious and morbid. If he had not met your mother, I don't know what would have happened. She was the morning star of his life."

Renny's father was forty-five and his mother forty-one when Renny was born. After three miscarriages, they had given up hope for a family. When Renny arrived, his father gladly endured the Strom Thurmond jokes about having children in his old age.

"Are you interested in dessert?" she asked.

No matter how much he ate, Renny always reserved an inner compartment for something sweet. "Sure, I'll help you clear the table."

They didn't talk as they put the dishes in the sink, their thoughts on the past, not the present.

Aunt Margaret gave him a generous slice of apple pie capped with vanilla ice cream. "It's not all happy days, is it, Renny? We just have to make the best of our time here."

Renny took another bite of pie. "I guess so," he responded, not sure of her meaning. "Thanks for the dinner and the history lesson. I'll call Jay Leno and remind him to eat with you next time he's in Charleston."

"Johnny and Jay eat with me every day. They like Purina."

On his way out, Renny saw a fresh tennis ball in the umbrella stand by the front door. Knowing it had only one purpose, he picked it up and, standing on the end of the porch, let it fly.

"Good throw. I sure wish I could give them a better workout."

"Thanks again."

As he headed down the long driveway, Renny glanced in his rearview mirror and saw Johnny and Jay bounding up to Aunt Margaret.

4

Renny decided not to spend another night on the Isle of Palms. A couple of hours after leaving Aunt Margaret's house, he was packed and on his way back to Charlotte. He didn't call Charlotte home. Three months in a place couldn't supplant Charleston in his heart. Charlestonians viewed Charleston much as the Chinese did China; it was the Middle Kingdom, the center of the earth, the focal point of civilization. Situated on a peninsula, the city was bounded by the Ashley and Cooper Rivers. According to local lore, the convergence of the two rivers formed the Atlantic Ocean.

Traveling away from the coast, the landscape changed. Charleston was steeped in elegance and charm, but a few miles inland the hot countryside was untouched by beauty. Driving fast on two-lane roads, Renny passed house trailers and concrete-block houses baking in the heat. Few people stirred. The residents tended their scraggly gardens shortly after the sun came up and in the heat of the day clustered inside, sitting on couches under the breeze of an electric fan. At sunset they came out to the front porch and watched the cars go by. Much of this area never received the news that the Depression was over.

South Carolina was not a homogeneous state. The steamy Low Country was as different from the hilly Piedmont as gumbo from grits. Northward, Renny entered textile country. New England textile manufacturers migrated southward and opened plants that created thousands of new jobs in the South within fifty years of the end of the Civil War at Appomattox. By the 1920s, the transition was virtually complete. The reduction of the South's agricultural base created a pool of unemployed farm workers willing to work for low wages and live in "mill villages," cookie-cutter frame houses clustered around a central factory. Agriculture and shipping decreased in importance. The economic base of South Carolina shifted from the coast to the uplands. During the 1970s and 1980s, highly sophisticated industry arrived on the scene. Renny's convertible was made in Germany, but the new BMW Z3 Roadsters were manufactured at a sleek new facility in Spartanburg, a small city in the northwest corner of the state. At Columbia, Renny merged onto I-77 and set the car on cruise control.

He found it disconcerting that his father had harbored such a significant secret from Renny's mother. Would he be able to do the same someday? What about the IRS? Renny worried that he might go on a spending spree, attract an IRS audit, and go to jail for failing to report his income from the List. How had his father handled these questions? Could he ask the men on the List about these issues without sounding like a naive kid? In the isolated honesty of the car, Renny didn't feel comfortable with tax evasion. Maybe a little fudging on business expenses, but not large-scale tax fraud. He looked forward to the opportunity to talk with the other men and receive some advice.

After a couple of hours, he reached the outskirts of Charlotte, the boom town of the Carolinas. Named after a member of the German royal family who was related to England's King George, Charlotte had grown big and tall since its founding by Scotch-Irish Presbyterians in the 1700s.

Renny rented the second floor of a seventy-year-old home in the Myers Park area of the city. He pulled the Porsche into his half of the detached garage. His landlady, Mrs. Daisy Stokes, drove a massive Lincoln that barely fit in the old garage and dwarfed Renny's sports car.

He took his luggage out of the car, deciding to leave the old trunk until after he let Mrs. Stokes know he was back. Renny had private access to his part of the house via an exterior stairway, but he often greeted Mrs. Stokes when he returned from a weekend trip.

True to form, she was in the kitchen. Renny knocked at the back door, which opened into an eating area overlooking the yard. Seeing the elderly woman at the table, he pushed the door open. "Hey, Mrs. Stokes, it's me. I'm back from Charleston. How's Brandy?"

Johnny's offspring skidded around the corner and rushed toward Renny, shaking and wagging all over from head to tail.

Renny dropped his bag and grabbed the dog's head in both hands. "How's my girl?"

"We did just fine, although she almost jerked my shoulder out of its socket, wanting to chase a squirrel when I took her for a walk." Mrs. Stokes smiled and rubbed her right arm.

Renny never boarded Brandy at a kennel. He had tried it once, and she howled and refused to eat the entire weekend. When he mentioned this to Mrs. Stokes, she surprised him by offering to care for the dog the next time he was out of town.

Mrs. Stokes, a widow for more than thirty years, was barely five feet tall and weighed a shade over ninety pounds. A retired Presbyterian missionary, she and her husband had served as teachers on a mission compound in Taiwan. Her husband died after ten years overseas, but Mrs. Stokes stayed almost forty years. Her brother, a dentist, left her the Charlotte house and the Lincoln automobile in his will, and she was living out her retirement in pleasant surroundings, supplementing her pension with Renny's rent checks. At first, her diminutive size and quiet voice led Renny to assume she was scared of her own shadow. But over the past three months, he had learned that she was not afraid of anything and was even willing to allow something new, like Brandy, to invade her routine.

"How was your trip?" she asked.

"It was fine. I met with my father's lawyer. There are still some things to clear up." Renny scratched Brandy's favorite spot behind her right ear.

"Estates can be complicated. The more property you have, the more you have to worry with it."

Renny looked up at the small face framed by white hair pulled back in a bun. "That's the kind of worry I'd be happy to take on."

"I've seen money cause more problems than it solves. That's all."

"Not me. Anyway, I'm going back to the coast, to Georgetown, next weekend."

"I'll be happy to dog-sit again. Brandy and I had some good talks as we walked over at Queens," she replied, referring to nearby Queens College, Renny's favorite place to jog and Brandy's preferred spot for squirrel chasing.

Renny could picture Mrs. Stokes happily talking to Brandy as passersby glanced in her direction.

"Thanks, we both appreciate it. Come on, girl, let's go upstairs." Renny held the door open for the dog and followed with his suitcase.

"Good night, Renny. Good night, Brandy," Mrs. Stokes's blessing followed them out.

Renny climbed the stairs to the second floor, unlocked the door, and let Brandy bound in before him. Dropping his suitcase, he went back to the car and quietly carried the old trunk up to his living room.

"Here it is, girl, the famous old trunk." Brandy sniffed it and growled.

"Hold on, there's nothing in it but some old papers. This will keep us both in dog food for a long time." Brandy, eyeing the trunk with suspicion, circled around to the far side of the room and curled up on her bed.

"Well, tomorrow I'm going to start finding out how much we've got. I tell you what—we'll split it fifty-fifty, if you can keep it secret." Brandy didn't move.

"I guess you liked Mrs. Stokes's conversation better," Renny said grumpily. Brandy yawned and closed her eyes.

Renny's area of the house was almost too big to be considered an apartment. The living room was connected to a large kitchen, with windows overlooking the backyard. He had an office for his computer, a master bedroom, and a guest bedroom. He had furnished the house with secondhand furniture, so some of the antiques from the Isle of Palms house would be welcome additions. The kitchen area was his favorite spot on Sunday mornings; he fixed a huge breakfast of waffles, eggs, bacon, sausage, and hash brown potatoes, drank large mugs of coffee, and read the *Charlotte Observer*.

Renny turned on the TV. He had been so consumed with his own news he hadn't thought about the rest of the world. Watching the images flash across the screen, he decided a story about the List would make a great human interest/history piece. It would begin with scenes from Charleston and a commentary on the lost lifestyle of the antebellum South. Then the reporter would tell how a group of plantation owners banded together to save their families by smuggling gold and silver out of the dying Confederacy. Now, 140 years later, the money set aside by the original participants has multiplied to an unknown but possibly astronomical sum. At that point Renny's face filled the screen, and he answered questions about his family's history, expressing his gratitude for their foresight. "No, I'm not at liberty to reveal the value of my share of the List," he would tell the interviewer. "As J. D. Rockefeller once said, 'If you know what you're worth, you're not rich.'" Renny chuckled. Better stay on this side of the screen. He turned off the TV and went to bed.

Renny was up by 6:15 because Brandy was up at 6:14. She gently woke him with a nuzzle to the arm. He let her out, and by the time she scratched at the door five minutes later, Renny had the coffeepot percolating and the shower running. After a cup of coffee, he opened the trunk and carefully examined the loose papers. An envelope addressed to his father from a Swiss bank caught his eye. Opening it, he unfolded a single sheet of paper with the name Banc Suisse engraved in small letters at the top and Office de Geneva typed in the upper right corner. In the center it read, "This letter authorizes the holder thereof to funds deposited in account number 23-98730-2, Access Code 8760945-2. Signed, F. Grossman, Clerk." The bank seal was affixed under the bank official's signature.

———

"Listen, I have a letter from your bank giving me ownership of this account. I want you to straighten this out, and if you can't do it, get someone who can!"

"I'll let you speak to Mr. Diegal." The clerk put Renny on hold before he could fire another salvo.

Renny fumed. He was getting the runaround from the Swiss bank—no one would tell him what the balance of his account was. This was what they did to the Jews. Now it was his turn to be robbed of his inheritance. He would find the Swiss equivalent of F. Lee Bailey and make the bank officials quake in their feathered hats.

"This is Mr. Diegal, I have pulled up the information on the account."

"I want some answers," Renny demanded.

"Mr. Broffman told me you have the bank account letter and that your father is deceased."

"That's correct. I'm the beneficiary of this account under his will," Renny added.

"The individual who set up this account specified that it be subject to dual-number access, much like a joint account in an American bank for Mr. A *and* Mr. B."

"Of course." Renny knew about joint accounts. "But with joint accounts either party has unrestricted access to the monies deposited."

"Unfortunately, that is not the case with this type of account. However, though we cannot waive the joint access requirement, there is a procedure that will allow us to give you the name of the other individual or entity designated on the account. You could then contact them."

Knowing something would be better than nothing, Renny responded, "What would be necessary to do that?"

"I will fax you the forms. We need to verify the genuineness of your bank letter. Once this is established, our confidentiality guidelines allow us to reveal the name of the joint account holder to you. What is your fax number?"

"I'm in the U.S.A., Charlotte, North Carolina." Renny gave him the fax number for his office.

"Just a minute—" The line was silent for a few seconds. "Fortunately, we have a representative who can assist you at a Bank of America office in Charlotte." Renny grabbed a pen and wrote down the name and address. The main Bank of America building was only a block south of his office in uptown Charlotte. "I will fax you the information you need before the end of the day."

"Thank you. I want this straightened out as soon as possible."

"Certainly."

Renny tried to immerse himself in his work. After a couple of hours, his supervising partner, Barnette Heywood, called him into his office for a midmorning meeting. Mr. Heywood had achieved partner status the last year of his eligibility primarily because another associate in his class at the firm was killed in an automobile accident. Heywood's responsibilities never increased beyond overseeing a couple of young associates, and his professional frustration made him a difficult taskmaster.

"Renny," the short, balding lawyer barked as soon as Renny sat down, "I need you to give me a memo on current congressional initiatives that may affect our bank clients. We may need to mobilize some lobbying pressure."

Renny saw a vast haystack of federal government records looming before him, and he had no idea where the needle might be hidden. "Anything particular you want me to focus on?"

"That's your job—to give me focus. I have to prepare a quarterly newsletter for our retainer clients, and I want to give them up-to-date information."

"Yes sir."

"I need the memo by five o'clock Thursday."

Renny had logged on to the legal research network and was trying to unravel the labyrinth of House and Senate subcommittees that might be talking about banking when his secretary interrupted him. "Morris Hogan on line two."

Renny leaned back in his chair and picked up the phone. "Hey, Morris, how are you?"

"Fine for Monday. How is the life of the rich and famous?"

"Since I'm neither, I can't comment."

"Can you meet me at Yogi's?"

Renny looked at his watch. "Sure, I'll be there in fifteen minutes."

Morris Hogan, a big, blond-haired Duke graduate, worked as an investment adviser in the trust department of First Union, one of the larger banks in Charlotte. He and Renny became friends before Renny went to law school, and they maintained contact during the next three years. When Renny landed the job in Charlotte, Morris was the first person he called with the news. The two young men spent a lot of time together, eating, playing tennis, and arguing the respective merits of the Duke and U.N.C. Chapel Hill basketball teams.

It seemed to Renny and Morris that every fourth person in Charlotte worked for a bank, and they often wondered who within a twenty-five-mile radius of Charlotte engaged in productive labor. Morris's theory was that most of the money in the United States was counterfeit, printed at shopping center print shops and laundered through grocery stores. His proof was the redesigned hundred. He once held a crisp new bill up to Renny's nose and presented his case: "Now tell me, does this look like legal tender for all debts, public and private, or mediocre play money? Would Ben Franklin consent to such a ludicrous likeness? Why, he would rather be struck by lightning!"

Renny pulled into the restaurant parking lot and found an open space next to Morris's Ford Explorer. Yogi's served a major-league meal for lunch. No quiche of the day or asparagus salad feminized the menu. Hungry businessmen and construction workers could order a half-pound burger with enough fries and onion rings to lay down a serious oil slick in the largest stomach.

Morris was waiting in one of the "cells," a restaurant booth designed to look like a jail cell. Peanut shells littered the floor, a practice encouraged by the management to give credence to its antiestablishment mystique.

"I just ordered you a spinach salad with avocado dressing," Morris quipped. "How was the trip to Charleston?"

"It was OK, but there's more hassle to my father's estate than I expected." Renny decided not to mention the terms of the will.

Morris inspected his friend's face. "Yeah, you do look like you've been negotiating with a group of terrorists. What's up?"

"Nothing much. Heywood assigned me an impossible project, but that's to be expected." Renny paused then asked tentatively, "Do you know much about Swiss bank accounts?"

"Some. Secret havens for money made by selling drugs, weapons, and contraband. You're not planning on selling arms to Iraq, are you?" Morris said, raising his eyebrows in mock suspense.

"Not even a firecracker."

Morris scratched his chin. "I get it. Did your father have an overseas account?"

"Good deduction. He did, and I can't find out what is in it."

"What's the problem?"

"It was a joint account, and I have to get permission from the other party to do anything."

"Who is it?"

"I don't know."

"You do have a problem. What are you going to do?"

"The bank is going to send me some paperwork that may let me find out who else is on the account."

"I wouldn't know anything else to do."

"Actually, I was hoping you could do a little research for me—find out how Swiss bank accounts work . . . ?"

Morris grinned. "What are friends for? Sure, I'll look into it. But you owe me."

The waiter brought their order, and they ate in silence for a few minutes. Morris spoke first, "Have you decided what you are going to do once your father's estate is finalized?"

Renny swallowed a big bite of burger and answered, "I really don't know. My father's death was so unexpected; I'm not sure what to do."

"Will you keep working at the firm?"

Renny shrugged. "At least till I do this project for Heywood."

"It's not such an awful dilemma. Most people would happily trade problems with you."

"My landlady says money sometimes causes problems."

Morris rolled his eyes. "Name one."

Renny thought. "High taxes?"

"Right. Give me the money, and I'll be happy to pay the taxes on it."

"OK, OK." Renny wiped up a spot of ketchup with his last onion ring.

"In case you ever have too much money, my phone number is in the yellow pages under 'Friends Who Need Money.' Since you're feeling so depressed about your money today, I'll buy your lunch."

Renny grinned. "Thanks. Why don't you use one of those fake hundreds?"

———

Renny took the Banc Suisse forms home and filled them out that evening at his kitchen table. A copy of the original letter needed to be certified before a Banc Suisse representative. The next day he set up an appointment and met with with a Bank of America employee, a middle-aged gentleman who asked no questions and accurately reflected the detached approach of his Swiss counterparts. After checking the forms, he inspected the Banc Suisse letter, ran his thumb over the gold seal, and certified the copy as true and correct. He suggested that Renny send the information to the bank via overnight courier so that it would arrive in

Geneva before the close of business Thursday evening. Renny was going to work until noon Friday, and he hoped this would enable him to hear a response before leaving for Georgetown.

At 11:30 A.M. Friday, Renny got a call. "Mr. Jacobson, this is Hermann Diegal at Banc Suisse. We received the paperwork and certified letter on the account. Everything appears to be in order."

"Good. Who else is on it?"

"The joint party on the account is the Covenant List of South Carolina, Limited, Desmond LaRochette, director."

Renny whistled softly under his breath. "I should've known."

"I trust this is helpful to you."

"Yes, I'm sure it will be."

"If I can be of further assistance, please contact me."

"Sure, thank you very much."

"Good day."

Renny set the receiver gently in its cradle. This List was tighter than he thought. Not only did it control the corpus, but it also had its finger on distribution. His father didn't have unrestricted ownership of the Swiss bank account. Why not? It was not typical for his father to relinquish control voluntarily. Therefore, the restrictions must have preceded his father's time. But why? How could this money be of help to anyone if the List held the trump card? He replayed his father's words, "Far more valuable than the combined value of the rest of my estate." But how? If these men were nice old guys, perhaps they would let Renny withdraw a million or two or ten.

Barely acknowledging a greeting from two fellow workers as he headed for the front door, Renny left the office in a preoccupied haze. This knot was not going to be unraveled until he had the end of the string in his hand. That end was in Georgetown.

5

Yes, to smell pork.
THE MERCHANT OF VENICE, ACT 1, SCENE 3

U sually Renny traveled light, and he rarely dressed up unless he had to. For this trip, however, he took his best suit. For all he knew, the members of the List wore tuxedos and sat around in leather chairs, smoking cigars and sipping brandy after dinner.

Georgetown was north along the coast from Charleston. Renny retraced his route of the previous weekend but, based on his renewed interest in his ancestry, decided to take a brief detour through Moncks Corner, South Carolina, his mother's hometown. Located an hour inland from the ocean, Moncks Corner was one of the first places settled when the early pioneers left the coast and began to move westward. Now it was a sleepy town in an out-of-the-way corner of the state.

Renny's maternal grandmother had died years before his birth, but his mother's father, Nathaniel Candler, a pharmacist in Moncks Corner, was in good health up to the day he suffered a fatal stroke when Renny was seven years old.

Renny knew that his mother loved her hometown and felt more at rest there than anywhere else. The community was peaceful, sleepy, or dead—Renny wasn't sure where to draw the line.

Just inside the city limits he pulled into a convenience store for gas. While filling up the tank, he heard a loud flapping sound. Turning, he saw a big red Dodge pickup with a flat tire limping into the parking area beside the store. The left front tire was shredded, and only a few pieces of battered rubber and steel remained on the rim. The truck rolled to a stop, and the sole occupant, a dark-haired young woman, went into the store.

The truck had Michigan license plates, and when Renny went inside to pay for his gas, its driver was handing a phone book back to the clerk.

"Thanks. Do you have a phone so I can call the tire store?" she asked.

The clerk shook her head. "I'm sorry, it's not working."

Feeling chivalrous, Renny broke into the conversation. "You could use my car phone, if you like. I'm parked out at the pumps."

The woman faced Renny, sized him up with her clear blue eyes for a second, and said, "Thanks, that would help me a lot. Let me write the number down on a piece of paper."

Renny held the door open for her. "Is that your husband's truck?"

"No, it was my father's. It's exactly like the truck that went up into the tornado at the end of the movie *Twister*," she said, smiling.

"Yeah, it was a shame about that truck," Renny answered. "Just a second, and I'll be back with the phone."

Renny kicked himself as he walked to the car. *What a stupid thing to say!* It was a toy truck in the movie; special effects could do almost anything. He might as well have said, "What happened to Peter Rabbit in Mr. MacGregor's garden sure was sad, wasn't it?"

As he started his car and pulled forward, Renny had a clear view of the damsel in distress. She was medium height with an oval face framed by fairly short dark hair in loose, casual curls. He guessed she was mid to late twenties, not a Barbie type, but with a figure that looked nice in her white shorts and loose-fitting blue shirt. She was only slightly tanned, consistent with Renny's perception that people in Michigan lived most of the year in snowbound isolation, coming out occasionally to shovel snow or ride snowmobiles across frozen lakes. Parking next to the truck, he unplugged his car phone and was met by a bright smile, blue eyes, and an outstretched hand.

"I'm Jo Johnston," she said. "I really appreciate you taking time to help me."

"Renny Jacobson. It's no problem at all. Let me call the store for you. Do you have a full-size spare?"

"Yes," she answered. "But it's flat, too. I didn't check it before leaving on this trip"

Renny knelt beside the truck, wrote down the size of the tire, and called the store. Holding the phone, he asked, "Do you have any road hazard insurance? You shouldn't drive another block on the wheel rim. It would be better to tow the truck from here to the store."

"Yes, I have a policy with Road Rescue," she answered.

"Do you tow for Road Rescue?" Renny turned his attention back to the phone. "Great, we'll wait for you here." Renny gave the location of the convenience store.

"Thanks for your help," she said when Renny hung up.

"I'll wait here with you until the tow truck comes," he offered.

"I don't want to hold you up any longer."

"I'm not in any hurry. My mother grew up in Moncks Corner, and I was going to drive around town for a while before heading down to the coast."

"What's your name again?" she asked.

"Renny. And you're Jo, right?"

"Yes. J-o," she said, spelling out the two-letter name.

In a few minutes the tow truck came into view and stopped with a belch of black smoke. The driver, a middle-aged man with a well-developed beer belly that threatened to pop the bottom three buttons of his shirt, slid out and walked over to Renny. A large brown dog hung his head out the passenger-side window of the truck.

"Did you call for a wrecker?" he asked, taking a half-chewed cigar out of his mouth and spitting a few pieces of stray tobacco onto the ground.

"Yes. It's my truck," Jo answered.

The driver looked at Jo and looked at the truck. "I'll hook it up. Do you want to ride with me and Hercules?"

Renny spoke up before Jo could answer. "We'll just follow you in my car."

"Suit yourself."

Renny and Jo stepped back. "Are you sure I'm not holding you up?" she asked as the wrecker driver crawled under her truck.

Renny grinned. "I don't mind, unless of course you wanted to hold Hercules in your lap."

As they followed the tow truck through the town's central square to the tire store, Renny pointed out the location of his grandfather's pharmacy, now a ladies' clothing store.

"He died when I was in second grade. My mother said the drugstore was an institution in the town. My grandfather sold everything from thermometers to red wagons."

"What was he like?"

"He lived here before nationwide drugstore chains drove most locally owned pharmacies out of business. In those days the small-town pharmacist had a respected place in the community. He let most folks get the medicine they needed for their children even when they were behind in paying their bills."

"Sounds like a pretty neat gentleman."

"I guess he was. He was a very religious person, a little extreme, you know. I remember watching him pray out loud, asking God to heal a woman who came in for a prescription." Renny shook his head. "It seems to me that divine healing would have cut into business." Renny turned the air conditioner up a notch. "I guess it's never this hot and humid in Michigan."

"Not like this. It makes me wish I was back in my igloo."

"I knew it!" Renny laughed. "I always suspected people up North lived in igloos. I bet you have a huge, shaggy coat trimmed with fur."

"Of course, but it's only cold in winter. During summer the weather is wonderful. Did you grow up near here?" Jo asked.

"No, my folks moved to Charleston years ago. I live in Charlotte now and work for a law firm. How about you?"

"I've spent all my life in East Lansing. I went to Michigan State and work as an operating room nurse in the cardiac wing of a local hospital."

"That must be quite a job," Renny said.

"It is. I always wanted to be a nurse and went into a cardiac OR specialty so I could train with a couple of outstanding doctors at the hospital where I work."

Renny glanced at Jo's left hand resting in her lap. Nice fingers with pretty red nail polish. No engagement or wedding ring. She wasn't Mrs. Heart Doctor yet.

Jo made arrangements with the worker at the tire store. It was a small operation, but Jo's truck wouldn't be ready for an hour. It was a little past noon, and Renny's stomach tank was flashing orange for empty.

"Would you like to get something to eat?" he asked.

"Sure. I don't have to get to the coast until this evening either."

Renny asked the man at the service desk for a phone book. Turning to the restaurant section, he ran his finger down the modest selection. "Yeah, here it is—Moncks Corner Carolina Barbecue. Would that be OK with you?"

"Sure, I'd like to try some ethnic food."

Renny gave her a puzzled look. "I never thought of barbecue as ethnic food, it's just . . . well, it's just food."

"I understand," she said, chuckling, "but to someone from Michigan, it's as ethnic as German sausage would be to you."

Renny asked the serviceman for directions to the restaurant. He wasn't sure barbecue was an ethnic dish, and it seemed almost blasphemous to compare it to German sausage.

The restaurant was less than five blocks from the tire store. The low-slung red building looked as if it had grown out of the red clay. Renny pulled into the gravel parking lot and pointed to a couple of red smokers the size of fifty-five-gallon drums mounted horizontally on legs and connected to smaller black boxes.

"Those are the smokers. The cooks put eight- to twelve-pound pork shoulders inside, build a fire in the adjacent firebox, and smoke the meat for six or seven hours. They slice off the fat, cut up the meat, and cook it inside the building for another thirty minutes. Then it's ready for the touch of genius, the sauce."

"All great chefs are distinguished by their sauces."

"Yeah," Renny agreed. "However, most guys who run barbecue joints would rather be caught riding in a Mary Kay Cadillac than answer to 'chef.'"

The Moncks Corner Carolina Barbecue Restaurant was the genuine article. The outside walls were decorated with old automobile license plates. A large, pink, plywood pig stood beside the banged-up front door and announced the hours of operation in green letters across his chest.

Renny and Jo found seats at a bare wooden table under a picture calendar of the local high school football team. The menu, a single laminated sheet, was simple: barbecue pork sandwich, barbecue pork plate, barbecue pork ribs, or hamburger steak. Brunswick stew, like coastal oysters, was occasionally available: "Ask your waitress." Side dishes included baked beans, French fries, onion rings, and slaw. Peach cobbler was the only option to finish off the meal.

"I thought they made barbecue from beef, too," Jo said.

"Maybe in Texas. Here, some folks refer to barbecue as barbecue pork pig—redundant, but it emphasizes that the only true barbecue is made with pork."

An overweight waitress, her Moncks Corner Carolina Barbecue T-shirt permanently stained by dark red sauce in multiple locations, sauntered up to take their order.

"May I order for you?" Renny asked. "I want to make sure you get a comprehensive ethnic experience."

"Sure."

"Two pork plates with beans, slaw, and sweet tea, please. Do you have stew?"

The waitress turned her head and yelled toward the back of the room, "Fred, is there any stew on?"

A black-haired man with a three-day growth of beard and a completely stained T-shirt leaned out a door and yelled, "Yeah."

"Let me have a bowl of stew, too. Thanks," Renny said.

Renny grinned as the waitress headed to the kitchen. "Pretty classy place, isn't it?"

"Low overhead, I'm sure. I wonder if they have a license plate from every state." The license plate motif continued on the inside walls of the restaurant. "There's one from Guam and a military plate from Saudi Arabia."

"Michigan is over the cash register," Renny said, admiring Jo's profile as she turned her head. "Speaking of Michigan, do you mind if I ask what brought you from Michigan to South Carolina? Most folks from the North come in spring to escape the cold, not in summer to roast in the heat."

Jo hesitated a moment. "This is not a vacation. I'm in South Carolina on personal business."

The waitress brought their food on large plastic plates divided into three sections. Jo leaned forward and said, "I'd like to pray before we eat."

Surprised, Renny simply nodded. Jo closed her eyes and said, "Father, thank you for sending Renny to help me today. Bless his life and your purposes for him. Help me to see my way clearly this weekend. Thank you for this food. In Jesus' name, amen."

Renny kept his eyes open while Jo prayed, first glancing to see if anyone noticed what was happening, then watching Jo's face. It was more like talking than the type of praying Renny was familiar with. After she said amen, her eyes popped open and met his.

"Thanks," he said. "I never thought anyone would say that God used me. It's a novel thought."

They both dove into their food. To Renny's relief, it was a good sample of ethnic Southern fare. The meat was lean, and the sauce was sweet with enough spice to tickle the tongue. "Here, taste the stew before I start," he offered, dipping Jo's spoon into his bowl and feeding her the bite.

"That's good. I like it."

"What kind of business do you have on the coast?"

Jo wiped her mouth and took a sip of tea before answering. "Actually, it's a personal matter related to my father's estate. He died a few months ago."

"My father died a few months ago, too."

Jo looked up and met Renny's eyes. Their mouths dropped open simultaneously. "Are you . . . ?" She started a question, then stopped.

Renny picked up, " . . . going to Georgetown?"

Jo nodded her head. Renny remembered LaRochette's letter to Mr. Joe Taylor Johnston, leaned back in his chair, and laughed.

He put his fork down beside his plate. "So you're *Mr.* Jo Taylor Johnston," he chuckled, emphasizing the mister. "This is unbelievable."

Jo stared past Renny's shoulder at the far wall of the restaurant and muttered, "Incredible."

Reaching across the table, Renny said, "Let me formally introduce myself. I am Josiah Fletchall Jacobson."

Jo took Renny's hand, smiled wanly, and continued muttering, "But why?"

"You said it in your prayer. You thanked God for sending me to you."

"That was about the tire, of course. This is just incredible."

Renny glanced around the restaurant. No one was seated near them, and the waitress was cleaning a table by the rest rooms. "Well, I guess we can talk openly. No vow of secrecy applies to members of the List." Saying "the List" cast a sort of curtain around them.

"But we're not members yet."

"A mere formality."

"Maybe for you. But I'm a woman, and they think I'm a man. Plus, I want to know more about the whole arrangement. What do you know?"

Renny gave her a summary of the past week, leaving out that the only significant bequest to him in his father's will was the List. "You know," he concluded, "the papers I read mentioned transfer of interest from one generation to the next based on primogeniture, the right of the firstborn son to receive all the father's estate. But that was about 150 years ago. Surely things are different now."

"Think about it, Renny. If I don't participate, there is more for the rest of the members, including you."

"Surely it's not that mercenary a group. I don't know any amounts involved, but the taped message my father left me clearly implied there is a lot of money. Plenty for everyone, I would guess."

"The richest man in the Bible said, 'Whoever loves money never has money enough.'"

"Maybe, maybe not." Renny took a last bite of barbecue and asked, "You don't have any brothers?"

"No, I'm my father's only child. He wanted a boy, and when I showed up with a pink bow in my hair, he gave me a unisex name. Now I can guess one reason why."

They ate in silence for a minute, each in thought.

Jo spoke first, "Well, I agree with you."

"Agree with what?" Renny asked.

"That this is a divine encounter. God is in our meeting. I just don't know how." Jo looked at Renny questioningly.

Renny was not used to this God talk. To him, God was the great cosmic clockmaker, a skilled craftsman who constructed the universe, wound the key, and went off to do his own thing. The thought that God was personally involved in an individual's life enough to set up a meeting between two people in Moncks Corner, South Carolina, was new. Normally, he would have politely avoided someone who talked like Jo, but he had an immediate attraction to her that overruled his natural response.

The waitress came to clear the plates from the table. "We have peach cobbler," she mentioned nonchalantly.

"Any ice cream to go with it?" Renny asked.

Turning again toward the kitchen, she yelled, "Fred, any ice cream in the cooler?"

Fred's unshaven face made an appearance for a repeat performance. "Yeah."

"I'd like some of that, please. Jo?"

"No thanks."

"Since we are not two ships passing in the night, tell me about you and your family." Renny settled back in his seat. "There is obviously some connection between our families in the past."

"OK, but I'd better give you the *Reader's Digest* condensed version. My mother's family immigrated to America from Norway in the 1880s and settled in the lower peninsula of Michigan. With a Scandinavian background, you would think I'd have blonde hair, but my mother and I are both brunettes. My parents divorced when I was two years old, and my mother remarried a couple of years later. My stepfather, whom I consider my real dad, was a physics professor at Michigan State. He died of cancer when I was twelve, and my mom has never remarried. She is an amateur naturalist and bird-watcher, traveling all over the world to sit for hours in hopes of spotting a rare species of bird. I went with her to Africa once."

"What about your father?" Renny asked as the waitress set his cobbler on the table.

"He was a consulting engineer, specializing in bridge building. He was raised in Roanoke, Virginia, and went to Virginia Tech. He came to Michigan on a job, met my mother, and asked her to marry him. I was born within a year. He traveled all over the country in his work and while on a job in California wrote my mother a letter telling her he had met someone else and wanted a divorce. Of course, I don't remember anything about that time. He filed for divorce, and I didn't see him for fifteen years. I think he was divorced and remarried five times. Crazy, but it's true."

"Did he have other children?"

"Not as far as I know. He came to my high school graduation, gave me a check for sixty thousand dollars to pay for my college education, and left immediately after the ceremony. I wrote him several times while I was in college, but he never wrote back. About two years ago he called me at my mother's house on Christmas Day. I think he had been drinking. We talked a few minutes, and he told me I would know how much he loved me after he died. I asked if I could see him, and he hung up. The next news I received was a call from a lawyer in Chicago. He told me my father was dead and that I was the sole beneficiary in his will."

"How did he die?"

"He suffered a massive heart attack while driving the red truck you saw at the convenience store. He had it at a stoplight; the truck slowly rolled forward and swerved into a small ditch. He was in Chicago and apparently had been to the grocery store because there were several bags of groceries behind the front seat. He was dead when the ambulance arrived. He was only fifty-three and had no record of heart trouble. The lawyer had a copy of an autopsy. I called the doctor who performed the autopsy—"

"And he said your father's heart exploded."

"That's right, but . . . ?"

Renny shrugged. "It's like I'm hearing about my own father. Go ahead."

"I would have suspected suicide if not for the autopsy report. He had already been buried when I got the call. No funeral, just a simple marker in a Chicago cemetery. My journey here began when I went to the lawyer's office."

"I can imagine. How did it all come up?"

"My father was not married at the time of his death. It had been several years since his last marriage ended in divorce. All the failed marriages, divorces, and unknown tragedies had depleted his financial resources, and at the time of his death he didn't have a whole lot except a modest bank account and the truck. The lawyer who contacted me did not prepare the will. A lawyer in Valparaiso, Indiana, drafted it, but he had retired and moved to Florida. The executor was a man who worked at the Chicago bank where my father kept his money. He delivered the will to the lawyer after my father's death."

"Did the will mention the List?"

"Yes. I met with the lawyer, a nice old gentleman who told me everything was straightforward about the estate except a reference to an organization called the Covenant List of South Carolina, Limited. He wanted to know if I knew what it was. I told him no. He also told me that a copy of my father's obituary was sent to nine men listed in a separate item in the will. I looked at the list and didn't know any of the men, but thought that because they all lived in the South they might be cousins or other relatives. The lawyer also gave me an envelope addressed to me from my father."

Renny went for the daily double. "Inside was a cassette and a key to a post office box."

"Half right. It was a letter and a post office box key. Would you like to read the letter?"

"Sure." Renny scooped up the last bite of cobbler and ice cream while Jo picked up her purse. Reaching inside, she took out a plain white envelope and handed it to Renny. Jo's full name was scrawled in a spindly script across the front. Taking out three sheets of lined notebook paper, Renny read silently, slowly at first, then faster as he adapted to the writing.

Dear Jo,

I just hung up the phone after talking with you. I wanted to say yes when you asked to see me, but I believe it is best that you have no personal contact with me. My life has been marked by nothing but tragedy for myself and those around me. I have failed as a husband and father, and my words here are crippled messengers of what should have been said and done.

Please forgive me for not truly being a father to you. I can do nothing about it now except ask you to forgive me. I am convinced part of my problems come from some deception I perpetrated. I know this sounds strange to you, but it has to do with the Covenant List of South Carolina, usually referred to by its members as the List. Formed in Georgetown, South Carolina, during the Civil War, the List was a cooperative venture of eleven families to preserve financial security in the face of certain ruin near the end of the war. Working together, they were able to transfer gold and silver out of the South before seizure by the North.

This group has continued to the present time, with membership passing to the eldest male of each generation. The current assets of the List are enormous. I took membership upon the death of my father, but every dollar I have withdrawn has been lost through bad investments and business deals. I now believe I made a very serious mistake by deceiving the members of the List about you. I know it sounds archaic in this day, but I was concerned we would lose our stake in the money if they knew you were a girl.

There has not been a major distribution of funds from the List for years. I hoped I would live to see my share transferred into my name so I could give it to you. Then, even if you couldn't succeed me as a member of the List you would still get something from it. Since you are reading this letter, my plan failed, just like everything else.

I will let you choose what you want to do. I have left instructions for the members of the List to receive notification of my death. They will schedule a meeting in Georgetown to install you on the List because they will think you are my son. Enclosed is a post office box key for a branch office in Chicago on Ashland Avenue. We communicate only via post office boxes. A notice will be sent to you there.

The existence of the List is secret. *No one knows about it but the members.* Upon joining, we all take a series of vows, including ones of secrecy and truthfulness. My mother never knew about the List; your mother never knew either. I don't know what you should do. All I know is that everyone has always honored the vow of secrecy. I broke the vow of truthfulness. I lied and have paid the consequences. I don't know if it's better for you to run from it or face it. Do what seems right to you.

Good-bye,

Dad

Renny folded the letter and put it down on the table, shaking his head. "Crippled messengers. I'm sorry."

"I cried off and on for a week. His life slipped through his hands like sand, never taking form, never having substance. The letter explained some things but raised more questions than I had before reading it."

"Did you talk with your mother?"

"Selectively. She knew I went to Chicago and met with the lawyer. She is aware of the known estate, but I didn't tell her about the letter or the List. I wasn't sure reopening her pain was the responsible thing to do. I wanted to sort it out myself. That's what this trip is about."

Renny looked into Jo's eyes again. He saw a steel there he hadn't noticed before. "It took a lot of courage for you to get in his truck and come down here."

"I thought it over from every angle. In the end I decided I had to see what this thing is all about for myself."

Renny pulled his chair closer to the table. "I have a proposal. Do you want to hear it?"

Jo raised her eyebrows. "What?"

"First, let me buy your lunch. Agreed?"

"Agreed."

"Second, you follow me to Georgetown. Who knows, you may have another flat. Agreed?"

She smiled slightly. "Agreed."

"Third, you have supper with me tonight at the nicest seafood restaurant we can find in Georgetown. Agreed?"

"Agreed, if we go Dutch treat."

"We'll negotiate that last stipulation later." Then, mustering every ounce of earnestness he possessed, he said, "Fourth, I want to help you through this situation. Agreed?"

Jo considered Renny's offer for a moment. "I'm not sure. We don't know what's involved, and we just met an hour ago."

"Well, we're together so far, and you said I was divinely sent to you."

"Are you serious?"

"Very serious."

"Agreed," she said, the hint of a smile returning.

"Let's shake on it." Renny extended his right hand across the table.

Jo placed her left hand in his and squeezed lightly. Renny was unprepared for what he felt—a brief, intense tingle, almost as strong as a low-voltage shock, swept up his arm, down his back, and vanished. Startled, he looked at Jo. Her eyes met his, but her face revealed nothing.

"Good," he said, not at all sure what he meant or what had happened.

They walked to the cash register where five bottles of Moncks Corner Barbecue Sauce stood at attention. Fred came out of the kitchen. Renny handed him a twenty. "The food was good, especially the stew. My compliments to the chef."

"Yeah." Fred's eyes narrowed as he handed Renny his change.

6

The eye is the window of the soul.
ANONYMOUS

Jo's truck was ready when they returned from lunch. After she paid for the tire, Renny walked her to the truck.

"I'll take you through the Francis Marion National Forest," he said. "It's the more scenic route to Georgetown from here."

"Who was Francis Marion?"

"A Revolutionary War hero known as the Swamp Fox."

"Fine. Just keep me away from any alligators."

Traveling seldom-used two-lane roads, Renny set a leisurely pace. It was a little less than an hour's drive from Moncks Corner to Georgetown, and Renny spent most of the time replaying his lunch with Jo, occasionally casting covert glances toward her in the rearview mirror. Between his thoughts and glances, it seemed only a few minutes until they passed the city limits sign.

Georgetown was almost as old as Charleston, but much smaller, nestled beside the Winyah Bay near the confluence of the Black and Pee Dee Rivers. Because innumerable rivers, streams, and inlets intersected the rainy Low Country coast, some of the earliest settlers found the area suitable for growing rice. Within a generation, thousands and thousands of slaves toiled in rice paddies dispersed along the low-lying coastal area. Georgetown became the point of arrival for the slave ships and the point of shipment for the bags of rice produced by the slaves' backbreaking labor.

Only a handful of antebellum homes and other pre–Civil War structures dotted the modern Georgetown waterfront. The largest of these relics, the Rice Planter's Inn, faced Front Street, one block from the bay. A large rectangular structure, the three-story inn was the oldest continuously operating hotel in South Carolina. Built by a sea captain from slave trading profits, the dark green structure had survived storm, war, and the pressures of twentieth-century economics.

They parked in back of the inn. "Welcome to Georgetown," Renny said when they got out of their vehicles.

"Whew, it's muggy."

"That's why things slow down the closer you get to the coast. People can't get in a big hurry—it just makes them and their cars overheat faster."

They climbed the steps to the front porch, a wide expanse that circled the building. Several ceiling fans vainly stirred the soupy air. No one sat in the row of white rattan chairs lined up behind the porch rail.

Inside, they entered a dark, cool foyer. "The air conditioning works," Renny said. "That's a good sign."

To the left of the entrance was the front desk, and a clerk who looked nearly as ancient as the inn gave them a raspy greeting, "Welcome to the Rice Planter's Inn. May I help you?"

"Hello, I'm J. F. Jacobson. I should have a room reserved for the weekend."

The man squinted at a large date book a moment, then, as if he had made a surprising discovery, said, "Yes, here it is, Josiah Fletchall Jacobson. You have room 6. It is located at the east end of the second floor. May I help you and Mrs. Jacobson with your luggage?"

It was Renny's turn to look surprised. "This is not Mrs. Jacobson."

"I see." The clerk's squint narrowed further.

"This is Jo Taylor Johnston. She should have a reservation of her own."

"It may be under Mr. Jo Taylor Johnston," Jo added.

The clerk examined Jo and, satisfied that she was female, ran his finger down the right side of his reservation book. "Here it is. You are correct. It is in the name of Mr. Johnston. Is Mr. Johnston coming?"

Renny interjected, "She is Mr. Johnston. I mean the reservation is for her because her name is Jo Taylor Johnston."

The clerk put both hands on the ledge that separated him from Renny and Jo, paused, thought for several seconds, and as if reaching a momentous decision, handed Jo a key and said, "You can have room 12 at the west end of the third floor. If Mr. Johnston should arrive, I will notify you and you will have to find another place to stay."

Jo chuckled as they climbed the stairs to the second floor. "I felt like I was on *To Tell the Truth*. Will the real Jo Taylor Johnston please stand up?"

The second floor had six rooms, three overlooking the street in front of the house, three facing the bay. Renny opened the door to a modest-sized room, simply furnished with a large four-poster bed, a beautiful armoire that took the place of a closet, and a couple of chairs. The wall on the left opened to a small bath.

Jo's room upstairs was the same size, but had a smaller bed, a tiny closet, and a finely crafted vanity sink. "I can wash my face like my great-great-grandmother did on the plantation. By tonight I'll be a Southern belle."

"Your Michigan accent will need some work before you take your Southern belle test," Renny responded.

"I could take lessons."

"You wait here. I'll get your luggage," Renny said. "Southern belles don't carry anything heavier than a parasol."

"Right, but as you said, I've not passed my test yet."

They carried the luggage without the desk clerk's help. Renny was concerned the old man wouldn't survive a trip up to the third floor. Besides, Renny wanted to handle the old trunk himself. As he lifted it out of the back of the Porsche, Jo asked, "What's that?"

"We'll talk about it at supper," Renny said quickly. "Is seven-thirty OK? You'll have time for a nap, if you like."

"Yes, that will be great."

Once in his room, Renny lay down on the bed, stared at the ceiling, and replayed the afternoon's events. He lingered at the moment he held Jo's hand in the restaurant. A strange but pleasant experience, he had never felt anything quite like the sensation that came over him from such a simple touch. An attractive woman, Jo exuded life, and Renny wanted to get to know her better. Also, they had an involuntary link because of the List. She was the only woman on earth with whom he could discuss it. A shared secret, a joint adventure, a common challenge inexorably draws people together.

Closing his eyes, he began to unwind. Tomorrow would be soon enough to meet a room full of old men. Tonight, he wanted to eat some seafood, have a good time with Jo, and maybe do a little more than touch her hand. He dozed off with pleasant thoughts.

———

Jo poured some cool water into the metal basin nestled in the washstand, splashed her face, and dried it with a soft green hand towel. Because her room faced the rear of the house, she pulled up a chair to the window so she could look out over the bay. Directly in front of her, two shrimp boats gently swayed at anchor, their nets draped over their sides like old-fashioned petticoats drying on a clothesline. Farther out, a small sloop, hoping to find a breeze in the bay, motored slowly away from shore. She watched the peaceful scene for several minutes. She, too, wondered about the effect of Renny's touch at the restaurant.

Staring out the window, she remembered an incident at the hospital in April. She was working in the OR during a five-level bypass procedure for a forty-five-year-old man. Dr. Leonard Starks, the cardiologist, had harvested veins from the patient's leg and had completed the last of the five bypasses. When he ordered the patient brought off the heart-lung machine, the patient's vital signs began to drop. Jo had her hand in the man's chest holding a clamp and silently began praying for her patient. At the moment the man's heart should have resumed beating, nothing happened, and the operating room erupted in activity. Jo intensified her silent petition. An inner voice whispered, *Touch him*, and as soon as she briefly laid her free hand on his arm, a warm tingle flowed from her. The man's heart fluttered slightly, then started beating. "It's beating!" one of the OR techs yelled in her ear. Dr. Starks completed the final portion of the surgery, and the man had a full recovery without any residual damage to the heart muscle. Jo was ecstatic.

The sensation in the restaurant had been the same.

———

Dressed in light khaki slacks and a white shirt with the sleeves partly rolled up, Renny knocked on Jo's door at 7:25.

"Come in. I'm almost ready." She was wearing a yellow-and-white sundress. Barefoot, she sat in the small chair near the window and strapped on some white sandals. For an instant, Renny wished he was a shoe salesman and could help her put them on. Looking up, she smiled. "That's it. Let's go."

Neither spoke as they descended the stairs. Holding the front door open, Renny followed Jo onto the porch.

"Let's walk" Renny said. "The desk clerk told me about a restaurant two blocks down the street."

The restaurant, a rectangular building not much bigger than a train car, nestled beside the bay and a small grassy area next to the wharf. Renny and Jo sat at a table for two beside a window overlooking a restored frigate resting at anchor.

"Tea with lime please," Renny told a young waiter. Jo ordered the same. They sat in silence for a few moments.

Jo spoke first. "Let's relax."

"That's easy to do over a plate of barbecue," Renny said.

"Then, let's consider today's lunch as our first date," Jo suggested.

"Sounds good to me."

The waiter took their order. Jo selected the blackened salmon; Renny opted for broiled scallops. After the waiter left, Jo said, "Tell me about the trunk. It looked pretty old."

"It was my father's, or at least he had possession of it for a number of years. He held an official position with the List, something called Custodian."

"What kind of custodian?"

"He kept possession of the original List agreement, an old ledger book that contains the covenant signed during the Civil War and a record of all the members down through the years. Our ancestors all signed it. A cassette tape from my father and a letter from Desmond LaRochette ordered me to bring it to the meeting tomorrow."

"Cassette tape?"

"I'd better start at the beginning. You had a letter from your father; I had a cassette message from mine." Renny told Jo about the safe deposit box and the cassette tape from his father.

"Did he say anything personal to you?"

"Not unless 'carpe diem' counts as personal. It was very businesslike, typical of my father. It didn't surprise me that he didn't say anything personal, and I didn't really think about it. I was so stunned by the existence of the List."

"Don't you think it strange that he didn't say he loved you or would miss you?"

"Not really. I can't ever remember him saying he loved me."

"He sounds cold-hearted."

Renny bristled. Jo was right, and it stung. "I guess he thought he showed it in other ways. He would, uh—" Renny stumbled, unable to think of an example.

Jo softened. "I know there are different ways of demonstrating love, but it's still important to say the words. You read my father's letter to me. He never showed his love, and although I don't mean to be disrespectful to your father, it sounds like he never let you know how he felt either."

"I don't disagree with you," Renny admitted. "Except for my aunt, my father came from a reserved family, and 'I love you' was not part of their family vocabulary."

73

"Then someone needs to break the cycle."

Hearing Jo talk gave Renny a tightness in his chest, a sense that there was something inside that could not get out.

Jo continued, "Several years ago, a major magazine did a survey of the three phrases people most want to hear. Number one was 'I love you.' Guess number two."

Feeling the constriction in his chest loosen, Renny ventured, "The check is in the mail."

Jo smiled. "Good answer for a lawyer. Actually, number two was 'I forgive you.' Unforgiveness and broken relationships go hand in hand."

"Grudges can be a problem," Renny said, remembering one he carried like a sharp nail in his pocket involving a former girlfriend who had lied to him.

"Number three is appropriate for us tonight."

Renny erased the picture of his old girlfriend from his mind. "Let's see—" He glanced out the window at the water. "How about 'Surf's up'?"

Jo laughed. "We're at the beach, but too narrow." The waiter set their food on the table. "Good timing," Jo said. "The third thing people most want to hear is 'Dinner's ready.'"

The food was good, but Jo's presence made the meal superlative. Renny had never met anyone quite like her. With most people the eyes are the windows of the soul, and Jo was no exception. Her eyes could shift quickly from challenging to quizzical to compassionate. She was open, her openness flowing out of honesty and an "I've got nothing to hide" attitude that was like unclouded sunshine. There was something indefinable about her. She was attractive, but there was something more. She had a delightful personality, but there was something more. She was intelligent, but there was something more. He could not put his finger on it, but whatever it was, he liked it.

When Renny described some of his experiences growing up, she leaned forward as if she were listening with her whole body, not just her ears. She was undeniably, completely, alive.

Renny ordered dessert to fill his spot for sweets and prolong their time at the table. "Key lime pie with two forks, please."

While they waited, Jo said, "I'd like to see the trunk sometime."

"You will. Since I may not have it after tomorrow, you can have a look when we go back to the inn."

They finished the pie, Renny paid without protest from Jo, and they stepped out into the fading light of the August evening. Walking slowly over to the restored frigate as a steady ocean breeze cooled their faces, they stood silently while three fishing boats chugged out of the harbor to begin their night's work.

Renny wanted to reach out and take Jo's hand in his, but something restrained him. In usual circumstances holding a date's hand in a peaceful moment would have been a natural, casual response to a pleasant evening, but this was different. He cast a furtive glance in Jo's direction. She was facing the bay, watching the fishing boats, her silhouette etched against a pinkish-red sunset. Renny felt the tightness in his chest return, but he felt no pain. Taking a deep breath, he slowly exhaled.

At the sound, Jo turned her head toward him. "It's beautiful, isn't it?"

"Yes, it is." Renny took another deep breath. "Let's walk back along the wharf."

They strolled toward the inn, taking a short detour onto the weathered black boards of the dock to inspect a sleek overnighter rocking to sleep in its slip.

The desk clerk was on the phone when they came through the door.

"Come up to my room, mademoiselle," Renny said with an exaggerated French accent as they started up the stairs. "I would like to show you my rare stamp collection."

"Is that a Charleston French accent?"

"*Mais oui,* and that exhausts my repertoire of the French language."

Renny unlocked the door and switched on the light. Jo sat in a small wooden chair as Renny put the old chest on the bed. "There's no pirate gold in here." He quickly dialed the combination, opened the trunk, and took out the List. Renny handed her the old book. "Here's the ledger with the original agreement. There is some other stuff you may want to look at after you read the book."

Jo rubbed her hand across the cover, opened it, and began reading. At one point she stopped, closed her eyes for a moment, then continued. Renny watched her face as her eyes went back and forth over the lines, but he did not interrupt her. She flipped through the pages, looking for her ancestors, pausing at each one. Closing the book, she looked up at Renny. "It's real, isn't it?"

"Yes, I know what you mean."

"What was your reaction the first time you read it?"

Renny thought back to the morning on the Isle of Palms. "I thought about the effect of compound interest—$110,000 expanding and multiplying since 1863. How much money is involved today? Then I wondered about practical matters: the subsequent history of the agreement, the decisions made about investments, the frequency and amount of distribution, you know, what a banker or accountant would like to know. Later, I started wondering more about the people—my ancestors, what they were like, how they lived, how they died. I even called my father's older sister and went to see her so I could learn more about the men who signed that book."

"What did you find out?"

"Stories of prosperity mixed with personal tragedy. The cycle of life, I guess."

"Life without God," Jo murmured.

"What do you mean? My ancestors were Christians. You'll find their graves in the cemeteries of some of the oldest churches in South Carolina."

"Where someone is buried is not proof of their Christianity."

"I don't know what you mean," Renny said. "You read what it said about God or the Supreme Being in the original agreement. These men established the List for the good of their families. Isn't that a Christian thing to do?"

"Maybe. Don't take me wrong, Renny, but words and substance are not always synonymous. It is not where they're buried or the sincerity of their motivation that counts. I'm just wondering about the results, or as the Bible says, the fruit of their lives after entering into this agreement. Remember what my father said in his letter."

"I don't think you can evaluate this based on the Bible or your father's vague fears. He was obviously something of a misfit." As soon as he said "misfit," Renny wished he could take it back.

Jo bit her lip and nodded. "You're probably right about him. I guess he looks like a bum to a Charleston blue blood." She handed him the ledger and stood to leave.

"Wait, I'm sorry. Please don't go."

"I understand. It's OK. I just need some time alone. Thanks for dinner."

Hearing her steps as she hurried down the hall, Renny shut the door and threw the book on the bed. The initial dinner meeting with the members of the List was not until seven o'clock the next evening, and he had hoped to spend the next day with Jo, taking her for a ride up the coast, maybe going for a walk on the beach. Now, he would be looking for seashells alone. He repacked the trunk, berating himself for not watching his words.

———

Jo wiped away the final tears that had coursed down her cheeks as she hurried down the hall and climbed the stairs to her room. Renny's callous comment breached the dam of pent-up emotion that still flowed from grief over her father's tragic life and death. After splashing her face in the vanity's sink, she put on her nightgown and sat in bed, leaning back against the headboard. As her breathing stilled, she prayed a simple prayer and waited for the familiar inner calm, the peace that passed understanding.

After a few minutes she reached for her Bible, read a psalm, turned off the light, and went to sleep. During the night she dreamed she was on board a frigate like the one anchored near the restaurant. She was a passenger, the only woman on board. A storm was brewing, and the ship began to toss to and fro. A young junior officer on the ship came to her and asked if she had seen the ship's maps because the captain had misplaced them. She said she would look for them. When she got to her cabin, she found a map rolled up under a chair, but when she tried to take it to the young officer, she could not find him. The ferocity of the storm increased, and searching with increasing anxiety, she lurched onto the deck, stopped, and cried out for help.

———

Renny tossed and turned for almost an hour. Finally, he switched on the light and found a piece of stationery with the inn's name across the top. The sheet had a palmetto tree in one corner and a rice plant in the other. He quickly sketched in black ink a seashell and a simple picture of two people walking on the beach. Under the picture he wrote:

Once again, I apologize. I would like to take you for a ride up the coast. I will be on the back porch at 9 this morning for your RSVP.

Sincerely,
Renny

He looked at the word *sincerely* as if he had never seen it before. It had so much meaning in that moment; he was sincere—sincere about the apology, sincere about wanting to spend the day with Jo. Honesty equaled vulnerability, but if he was going to be vulnerable, Jo seemed the least likely person he had met in a long while to take advantage of someone's openness. Folding the note, he put it in an envelope, slipped on a pair of pants, and went quietly up the stairs to Jo's room. Sliding the note under the door, he started to offer a quick prayer but decided it was not a situation that warranted disturbing the Almighty. Besides, *he* was probably mad at Renny, too.

7

*I shall endeavor to enliven morality with wit,
and to temper wit with morality.*
JOSEPH ADDISON

The air was stirring outside when Renny woke up at seven the next morning. Looking out the window, he saw the trees beside the inn swaying in the breeze and white caps on the waves in the bay. A storm was brewing in the Atlantic, and he needed to check the forecast. Many years of life on the coast made him cautious.

Putting on shorts and running shoes, he grabbed fifty cents to buy a paper, raced down the steps and out the front door. Heading northeast along the shore of the bay, he ran against the wind for two miles. The stiff breeze had banished the humid heat of the previous day, and Renny, knowing the wind would be a friend not a foe on the way back, enjoyed the invisible wrestling match of the unseen force against his body. The path ended at a marina, and he retraced his route into town, stopping to buy a paper at a rack near the inn. Sure enough, a tropical storm was churning two hundred miles out at sea; however, it was not expected to make landfall in the Georgetown area and, at most, could bring some rain during the night. In the meantime, it would be cooler and breezy— a perfect day for an excursion with Jo. All he lacked was her acceptance.

It was close to nine when Renny finished his shower. To reach the back porch, he walked down a hall that opened to a large dining room on the right and a smaller dining room on the left. A handful of people in the larger dining room were eating breakfast.

He looked through a windowpane in the upper half of the door. Jo was sitting in a wicker rocker, her knees under her chin, her toes wiggling in the breeze. A stiff breeze swept her hair back from her face as she gazed at the bay.

She turned at the sound of the door and smiled. "Good morning! Isn't it glorious! I love the breeze."

"Yes, it's going to be a beautiful day."

"I got your note. I wrote my answer on the bottom." She held the note toward Renny, who walked over to her chair.

Renny saw his crude sketch, and underneath was a much more detailed picture of two figures, a male and a female, riding down the road in Renny's Porsche with the top down. She had simply written, "Oui."

Renny grinned. "Great! Are you ready to go?"

"I'd like to get some fruit for breakfast. What do I need to take with me to the beach?"

"They probably serve fruit here in the dining room, and we can have lunch somewhere along the coast. You might want a hat, some sunscreen, and a towel to sit on. I wasn't planning on swimming in the ocean. Is that OK?"

"Sure. Except for the hat—I'll need to buy one—I'm set. I'll be ready in a few minutes. You get what you need while I check on the fruit."

"See you here in a few minutes."

Renny hurried down the hall and through the lobby. He cheerily greeted an elderly couple creaking down the stairs as he bounded past them. In his room he stopped in front of the mirror to conduct a quick inventory. He was as excited as an adolescent on his first date.

———

Renny put down the car's top, and they drove north on the highway. After crossing the Pee Dee and Black Rivers, they hugged the coast for a short distance, then turned a few miles inland and passed a succession of vacation, retirement, and residential developments. It was a perfect day to enjoy a convertible, and Renny and Jo were like bugs on the back of an elephant, able to see the entire panorama of the landscape for miles around.

"My grandfather owned several miles of beach north of Charleston," Renny said. "He sold it in the 1920s, long before the major boom along the Grand Strand."

"Grand Strand?" Jo asked.

"The local term for the beach area from the North Carolina border to Charleston. I can't guess what the property would be worth today."

They passed a sign for Debordeau Beach. Pointing to it, Renny asked, "How do you think they pronounce the name of that beach around here?"

"No telling. I could probably say it the French way. What do they call it?"

"I'll let a native tell you, and here's a likely place to find your hat." Renny turned into the parking lot of a small store advertising beach wares.

The store catered to the forgotten or misplaced needs of tourists and vacationers who were looking for everything from aloe lotion to inflatable rafts. Jo tried on several hats, finally narrowing the decision to a large, round straw, and a floppy, brightly colored cloth hat. Renny knew better than to express a preference. "They both look great," he said.

She opted for straw. "It's more appropriate for beachcombing."

As Jo was paying for the hat, Renny asked the owner if he grew up in the area.

"Lived here all my life. Born in Georgetown."

"What's the name of the beach just south of here?" Renny asked.

"You mean Debby-do?" the man replied. "Now that's a real nice place. They have more deer than you can count and a few alligators lying up in the marsh along the golf course."

"That's the place. Thanks."

Walking out to the car, Jo remarked, "Debby-do is a lot easier to say than Debordeau."

"Especially if you're not French. That's the way down here: Follow the path of least resistance."

Jo put the hat behind the front seat, and they continued north for a few miles before turning east toward the ocean and Pawley's Island.

Slowing down, Renny said, "Pawley's was first settled by local vacationers in the 1930s. It's commonly described as 'shabbily elegant.' The beach is open to the public, so I thought it would be a good place for us to hang out."

They crossed an earthen causeway flanked by marshes. The island was home to a mix of 1950s-era bungalows. It had a homey, comfortable aura, and they leisurely drove the length of the island, looking at the different homes and cottages. There was one with a pair of faded pink flamingos precariously perched along the narrow, sandy roadway.

"There's some of the local fauna," Renny said.

"We don't have many of those in Michigan. Maybe my mother could add a plastic flamingo to her bird list." Jo grinned.

Finding a public parking area behind a high row of sand dunes, they unpacked the trunk of the car. As they were walking toward a narrow wooden boardwalk, Jo stopped. "Wait, I forgot my hat."

Retrieving the hat, she put it on her dark curls and faced the wind. The stiff breeze blowing off the ocean flipped up the brim of flexible straw, and she put one hand on her head to keep it from flying off as Renny reached out his hand to help her step up onto the boardwalk. Her hand felt cool in his as they walked between two large clumps of dune grass.

The beach was crowded near the parking area, so they continued on several hundred yards along the edge of the water. Children were playing in the ocean; the smaller ones would run furiously toward a breaking wave, hop over the crest, and dart back onto the dry sand to make sure their parents saw their brave exploit.

Spreading out their towels on the soft sand, they sat down and watched the people passing by. Jo searched in her bag for the sunscreen and coated her legs, arms, neck, and face while Renny watched out of the corner of his eye.

"We rarely went to the ocean when I was growing up," she said, leaning back on her arms when she had put the lotion away. "My parents rented a house on Kelly's Island in Lake Erie for a month in the summer while my stepdad was between semesters at the university. It took about an hour to reach the island by ferry. We played in the water some, but my best memories are of times curled up reading a book on the back porch. Any book seemed better when read on a beautiful summer day on an island. It was incredibly peaceful."

"Have you ever thought about writing a book?" he asked. "You express things vividly."

"I keep a personal journal, but after I decided to become a nurse, most of my courses in college were in the sciences. I made a B- in freshman English, but I got an A on a chemistry paper one time."

Renny smiled. "It would be hard to make chemical equations vivid."

"Do you do much writing in your legal work?"

"Memos, mostly. A few legal briefs that are anything but brief and an occasional document with a healthy quota of 'heretofores' and 'whereinafters.'"

"Do you write anything on your own?"

Renny stared out over the water. "I'd like to."

"I thought so," Jo said. "When you asked about me writing, it seemed more for yourself than for me."

"Good insight, Nurse, but I'm a lawyer. Heretofores and whereinafters are not the building blocks of best-selling novels."

"You are avoiding the question, Counselor. What have you written?"

Renny faced her. "Nothing yet. I've had no time between school and learning a new job, but I have an idea for a book."

"Would you tell me about it?"

"You won't laugh?"

"Of course not."

"You know I love barbecue," Renny said seriously. "So I thought I could write a book about the twenty-five best barbecue restaurants in the South. I'd have to eat at hundreds of places to cull the list to the top twenty-five. It could take years, but think of the contribution to hamanity, I mean humanity."

Jo laughed. "And when you were finished, you would smell as smoky as one of the pork shoulders you told me about. Tell me the truth."

Renny looked crestfallen. "You promised not to laugh."

"I believe there's more between your ears than a chopped pork sandwich."

"OK." Renny held up his hands in surrender. "I yield to your probing cross-examination. I'd like to write a novel set in the South during the Civil War era. *Gone with the Wind* has already been written, and I don't know one-tenth as many descriptive words as Faulkner, but I have an idea."

"A concept?"

"Right. Nothing more at this point. The book would be based on an historical event. Most people don't know that in 1867 ten thousand Southerners emigrated from the former Confederacy to Brazil and settled about five thousand miles below the Mason-Dixon Line in the jungles near São Paulo. Called the *Confederados*, they started raising sugarcane and named their community Americana."

"Did they have slaves?"

"No, they were pioneers who worked their own land. Their descendants still live in the area and have reunions where they wear antebellum costumes and celebrate their heritage."

"What's your idea?"

"A historical novel that follows the struggles, failures, and triumphs of a Georgia family. I'd begin with their life before the war but quickly move to the war years, incorporating Sherman's March to the Sea and the early days of Reconstruction. The father, mother, and five children reach the momentous decision to move to Brazil where they face the challenges of a new culture and the dangers of establishing a new life in South America. Oh yes, my hero, one of the sons, gets the girl."

"Is she a Brazilian?"

"I'm not telling."

"I'm hooked already."

Renny grinned. "I made an A in freshman English, and the professor encouraged me to take some creative writing courses. When I told him I was going to major in business to please my father, he shook his head and asked me to reconsider, saying, 'Your time in college is your best chance to develop what is in you. Don't waste this opportunity.' I didn't heed his advice and spent the next four years slightly bored and generally regretting my decision."

"Renny, I think you should do it. With your dry wit, I bet it would be funny, too."

"Yeah, I would want it to be a little humorous. But what if I spend a lot of time working on it and then it doesn't get published?"

"So what? You spent four years in college not following your heart. Why keep making the same mistake?"

"I've thought that the money from the List would give me the option of quitting work so I could spend time writing."

Jo looked out over the water a few moments, then said, "Even if the List doesn't work out, you should do it. I heard John Grisham used to write on a legal pad while he was waiting in court."

"I don't know."

Jo reached in her bag and pulled out a tangerine. "Let's go for a walk down the beach."

"Better have a sip of water before we start." Renny opened a bottle of spring water and handed it to her.

As they walked along the edge of the surf, four or five sandpipers accompanied them, scurrying in front and to the side, stopping to poke their beaks in the sand for tiny mussels, then running off as Renny and Jo drew closer to them. Jo peeled the tangerine, dropping the skin in the shallow water where the pieces floated like tiny orange boats until capsized by the next wave. She offered the first piece of the fruit to Renny, who opened his mouth to receive it directly from her hand.

"Best tangerine I ever tasted," he said.

It was not oppressively hot, and the ocean breeze cooled their faces. Jo had a small plastic bag for collecting shells, and they walked slowly, hoping to spot unbroken shells or sand dollars in the shallow water. It was slim pickings, but to Jo each find was an individual treasure.

The farther they went, the more deserted the beach. The northern spit of the island was so narrow residential development was not possible.

"Let's walk to the very tip," Jo suggested.

As they drew closer to the end of the island, they passed pieces of driftwood that had washed up on the sand. Jo found a tiny piece shaped like a stylized bird and put it in her bag. The beach wrapped around the shore a short distance before giving way to the marsh on the landward side of the island, and finding a large, dry log to lean against, they sat down.

Jo dug her toes in the sand while Renny put his head back and watched the clouds move slowly overhead. After a few minutes of silence, Jo asked that most personal of questions: "What are you thinking?"

Renny answered without moving, "I was watching the clouds and thinking they are so random and free, just going where the wind blows them. I feel so tied to the earth, if that makes any sense."

"Sure it does." She gestured toward the limitless expanse of the ocean. "The panorama of the sky and water is a much better sermon about freedom and the nature of God than you would hear in many churches."

"Is that like the guy who says he doesn't need to go to church because he can meet God in his bass boat?" Renny said, continuing to look up at the sky.

Jo laughed. "There is some truth to that old excuse. 'The heavens declare the glory of God; the skies proclaim the work of his hands.' However, you have to be looking for God to see him."

Bringing his gaze back to earth, Renny muttered, "When I look at the clouds, my mind tells me I'm looking at suspended water vapor responding to shifting air currents. I admire their beauty and freedom to go with the wind, but I don't see God."

Jo popped her toes up out of the sand. "How badly do you want to see?"

"Um, I'm not sure," Renny muttered.

"I mean, are you really looking, Renny? You have to be looking. You will look when God calls you."

Renny shook his head. "Come on. Do I need to give God my car phone number or e-mail address so he can send me a message?"

"He has already given the message; it's in the Bible."

Remembering his blunder the previous evening, Renny chose his words carefully, "I've read some of the Bible, and it was more confusing than instructive. I know Jesus said some good things, but the Bible is filled with contradictions and scientifically impossible events. If the daily newspaper has mistakes, how much more something written hundreds and thousands of years ago."

"The Bible is not God's newspaper; it's the revelation of God's love and purpose for us. I don't know about any serious contradictions. And Bible accounts of 'scientifically impossible events,' or miracles, simply reveal that there is a spiritual world that can affect the physical one."

"Don't tell me you believe it hook, line, and sinker," Renny said mockingly. "You don't believe Jesus walked on water, do you?"

"I sure do."

Renny shrugged. "I think it's more likely he knew where some rocks were located just under the water."

"It was in the middle of a lake."

"Do you believe he fed thousands of people with a few pieces of bread and a couple of fish?" Renny said, gathering a little steam.

"Yes."

"Don't you think it's more likely the generosity of the fellow who contributed the bread and fish caused other people to be generous with what they brought so that everyone was fed?"

"Then it wouldn't be a miracle."

"Exactly my point. Swallowing the miraculous gives me problems with the Bible. Speaking of swallowing, how about Jonah?" Renny gestured toward the ocean. "You don't really think he was swallowed by a whale, do you? Even the largest whale would choke on something the size of a grapefruit."

"Actually, the Bible says it was a great fish, not necessarily a whale. I guess I can ask Jonah how it happened when I get to heaven."

Seeing his chance, Renny sprang, "Jonah lived in the Old Testament. What if he's not in heaven?"

Jo picked up some sand and let it run through her fingers. "If he's not in heaven, Renny, then I guess you'll have to ask him."

Renny sputtered, then burst out laughing. "Touché. Perry Mason couldn't have said it better."

Jo stretched out her legs on the warm sand. "Perry Mason was a pretend lawyer, and I'm no theologian, but I do know God is real. It's not as much a matter of logic as encounter. Once you meet somebody, it would be foolish to say they did not exist. Remember, you thought I was a man before we met. Now you know the truth. It's the same with God. We have to meet him to know him, and we meet him at his invitation. That's why I asked if he's ever called you."

Laying down the sword of argument, Renny asked, "How would I know if he has?"

"Think back. Have you ever been in church, had a conversation, read a book, or been in some situation in which you felt a tug inside to respond to God? If you did, that was probably God calling you."

Renny's contact with church was more of a desert than an oasis. Given his upper-class roots, he sporadically attended St. Alban's as a child, but he viewed churches and denominations as a reflection of the social and economic strata, not places to meet God. On the bottom of the ladder were the blue-collar Baptists, next the middle-management Methodists, followed by the professional-level Presbyterians, with the aristocratic Episcopalians perched on top of the heap. The Catholics were shrouded in mist and incense, and he tried not to look at a Pentecostal church in fear something might leap out the door and jump on his back.

Renny was baptized as an infant in a beautiful white gown, but the pictures of the occasion were more embarrassing than inspiring. He couldn't figure out why the church wanted every baby to look like a little girl. It seemed more fitting to baptize a baby boy in a tiny baseball uniform; the priest could take off the baseball cap, sprinkle the water, and tell the little fellow he was ready to play ball in the game of life because God was on his team. By his teenage years, Renny occasionally trolled for dates in the church youth group, but generally considered the hour from eleven till noon on Sunday the most boring of the week.

Renny's college experience was a mixture of studying and hedonistic haze that left no room to consider the divine. He remembered a couple of occasions when he prayed to get out of trouble and sent up a desperate prayer or two during the bar exam, but he never came close to what might be called a conversion. No, he couldn't think of a time God called his number, unless . . .

"Jo, I need to tell you about a conversation I had with my mother before she died. It was during my senior year in college. She was very, very sick, and I had gone home to see her."

Jo turned and faced him. "What happened?"

"She had Lou Gehrig's disease; it affects the central nervous system. Well, you're a nurse; you probably know more about it than I do. She had reached the stage where her speech was incomprehensible. A lady who had worked for us since before I was born was staying almost full time at the house taking care of my mother. I came in on a Friday afternoon and told Mama A, that's what I called the lady who helped us, she could go home because I would stay with my mother. My father was out of town, so it was just the two of us in the house.

"My mother was in a hospital bed and motioned for me to raise the head of the bed. I gave her a sip of water through a straw. After that . . . she began to speak in a weak but clearly understandable tone of voice. I guess you could call it a miracle," he added sheepishly.

"What did she say?"

"It was strange. She told me her father, you know, the pharmacist in Moncks Corner, had written down some things God told him about his children and grandchildren. I asked her, 'Why are you able to talk so clearly?' but she ignored my question and said that someday I would need to know what he had written about me. She said he'd named me before I was born, something I'd never known before, and told me when the time came to ask Mama A about it, but not now, because Mama A didn't know yet. I could understand her words, but not their meaning.

"Her voice started fading, and she asked me to come closer. When I did, she kissed my cheek and said, 'God loves you, Renny. I love you.' Then she closed her eyes and slept. She died a month later."

Jo said nothing for several moments. A single tear ran down her cheek. "Renny, that was to prepare you for the time when God would call you."

"You may be right," Renny said, "but the whole conversation was so confusing I thought the disease had affected her mind. My father came home the next day, and I asked him if she had been talking to him. He said that she had not been able to communicate except by gestures for weeks."

"Did you say anything to Mama A?"

"I started to talk to her but decided not to mention what happened because I didn't know what to say. Besides, my mother said Mama A wouldn't know anything, and it seemed pointless to bring it up."

"What about your mother's faith? What did she believe?"

"I'm not sure. She was more of a churchgoer when she and my father were first married, but then didn't attend as often until she became sick. After that she would occasionally go to church with Mama A. It was a racially mixed congregation, quite radical for Charleston. My father thought it was crazy, so she only went when he was out of town. I went with her two times, and it was definitely more lively than the old parish, but too wild and emotional to be considered church."

"So you don't know what your grandfather wrote about you?"

"I haven't a clue and never thought about it since her death until now."

"Is Mama A still alive?"

"Yes, she came to my father's funeral."

"Are you going to contact her?"

"I might."

"It sounds like she's part of the answer to your search."

"What search?"

"Your search for God; his search for you. The Bible says no one can come to Jesus unless Father God draws them and that God rewards those who earnestly seek him. It's a process on our part and God's part."

"You're assuming what I want to do."

Brushing the sand from her shorts, Jo stood up. "You do; you will. I can tell."

Jo picked up the shell bag, and they started back down the beach.

When they were almost back to their beginning point, Jo found a large, unbroken sand dollar skimming through the surf. It was as big as Renny's palm, and a real beauty by Pawley's Island standards.

"There are folks who comb this beach for years and never find one like that one," Renny said.

"What's it worth?" Jo asked.

Renny stopped and gave her a puzzled look. "Nothing. You can buy one at a beach shop for two dollars. Finding it on your own is what makes it valuable."

"Good answer. Think about it." Jo laughed, kicking some sand and water back toward Renny.

They gathered their belongings and returned to the car. It was early afternoon, and even with sunblock, Jo needed to avoid further expsure to the sun's rays.

Noting the effects of the sun on Jo's forehead and nose, Renny suggested they drive with the top up. Once in the car, he remembered his stomach. "Would you like to get something to eat?" he asked.

"I have another tangerine," Jo responded, "but that's probably not what you had in mind."

"Like I said, those are the best tangerine pieces I've ever tasted, but I think a foot-long sub would do more to sustain my high-octane metabolism."

A shopping area on the mainland had a sub shop. They took their food to a small table, and Jo said, "I want to pray again."

"Sure."

"Father, thank you for the ways in which you are calling Renny. Help him to hear your voice. Also, please don't let him choke on his sandwich, just as the great fish didn't choke on Jonah. Amen."

"Hey, I already admitted you won that round. Don't rub it in. And you'd better be careful joking with God," Renny said, taking a bite out of his sandwich. "And are you sure he understands what you say without the thees and thous?"

"He understands, and it seems to me the joke is on you, not God."

"Whatever. It's tough being a straight man for either you or God."

"I'll try to go easy on you," she said lightly, "but you'll have to talk to him about what he does."

Renny shook his head. "Are you sure you're not a lawyer?"

Jo grinned and shook her head. "Eat."

On the highway back to Georgetown, Jo identified several types of birds perched in trees near the road or flying overhead. Renny knew some of them, but Jo was a walking Audubon Society. They grew quieter as they neared Georgetown. Jo yawned a couple of times as they drove over the bridge into town.

"I want to rest for a while. What are you going to do?" she asked.

"I may read or go down to the docks. I'll probably make a few notes about questions I want to ask tonight. Can we get together before the meeting? I meant to talk to you today, but I never got around to it."

"OK, let's meet in your room at six-thirty. We can go down together at seven."

"And don't worry about the meeting," Renny said. "You're better than Perry Mason. You'll handle every objection with class. Little did I know when I offered my help how little you probably need it."

"No, don't say that. I don't feel very confident or comfortable."

"Everything will be OK. You'll see."

They pulled into the parking lot. There were several expensive cars in the area, most with South Carolina license plates. Renny counted. "It looks like the boys are here."

———

Envelopes waited for Renny and Jo at the front desk. Jo's was addressed to Mr. Joe Taylor Johnston, and the elderly clerk did his usual double take, squinting at the lettering on the envelope, squinting at Jo, then squinting once again at the envelope before shrugging his shoulders and handing it to her. They stepped off to the side of the small lobby to open them. Inside were identical messages, except for a P.S. on Renny's.

Dear Mr. Jacobson,

Welcome to Georgetown. We will meet this evening in the private dining room at 7:00 for cocktails, followed by supper and a meeting of the members. We look forward to seeing you then.

Sincerely,
Desmond LaRochette

P.S. I trust you brought the List and other documents entrusted to your father as custodian.

"Here we go," Renny said. "I feel like a kid who has never ridden a roller coaster about to go to the county fair for the first time."

Jo folded her letter and put it back in the envelope.

"Are you sure you will be able to rest?" Renny asked. "I'm getting too psyched up to sit still."

"Probably not, but I need some time in my room before the meeting." Jo touched Renny's arm. "Thanks for today. It was great."

Renny spent a second basking in the glow of her upturned face, which continued to radiate some of the sun they had gathered on the beach. "We'll have to do it again sometime soon. I liked it, even when you cross-examined me."

"Next time, I'll let you be the lawyer."

———

Renny cooled off by taking a shower. He reread the covenant and organized the contents of the old trunk. Taking a yellow legal pad, he outlined some notes and questions for the meeting.

- Where are the List assets invested?
- What was my father's role as custodian?
- How often are meetings held?

He would be humble and non-confrontational, asking general questions before getting more specific. The items on the sheet of paper grew.

- What is the amount of current List assets?
- Who keeps the records?
- What safeguards are there against embezzlement?
- When and how are monies distributed?
- What about the IRS?
- Why couldn't he directly withdraw funds from his father's Swiss account?

Pausing, he said softly, "What else?" He knew there was something else. Then he remembered. Of course, how could he forget?

- What about Jo, primogeniture no longer viable?

He tore out the sheet, folded it, and put it on the edge of the bed.

It was after six. Putting everything back in the trunk, Renny dressed in a dark blue suit, white shirt, and silk tie—dressed for success. Butterflies flitted around inside his stomach as he worked to get his tie straight. A soft knock at the door pulled him away from the mirror.

It was Jo, but not the Jo of the convenience store or his companion who dug her toes in the soft sand of Pawley's Island.

He opened his mouth, closed it, and opened it again before saying, "Wow!"

She wore a white-and-blue tinged gown that rushed up to her shoulders, opened expansively in the back, brushed snugly past her hips, and swept gracefully to the floor. A large sapphire pendant on a white gold necklace hugged her neck. Her dark hair had not totally submitted to her efforts to pull it back, but the few rebellious strands made her look softer than if every lock of black was successfully held captive.

"Thanks. Nice compliment." Jo's eyes sparkled more than the blue stone.

"Come in," Renny said, grabbing the room's only chair for her to sit in as he closed the door behind her. "I was trying to straighten my tie."

"Here, let me do it."

Renny stood at attention as she reached up. While she worked to flatten the knot, her fingers reached inside his collar and touched his neck. Renny's knees almost buckled.

"Are you OK?" she asked, stepping back.

Renny knew it was the moment of truth. He could lie and say "Sure," or he could tell her, "You are the most incredibly beautiful woman I have ever met. Your slightest touch has an overwhelming effect on me that I can't begin to explain or understand." He decided to lie. "Sure, I'm fine. Thanks for fixing my tie."

Sitting in the chair, Jo asked, "What do you think about tonight?"

Renny handed his yellow sheet to her. "Here are some comments and questions I wrote down."

Jo unfolded the paper and read it. "Renny, these questions presume you want to join the List. I thought you wanted to check it out first."

"Yeah, I did say that, didn't I?" Renny admitted. "But I'm optimistic that my questions will be answered and I can participate, like my father, grandfather, great-grandfather, back to the original Jacobson who signed in 1863."

"I understand," Jo said. "And we know this could involve an astronomical sum of money."

"It is a factor. I mean it wouldn't make sense not to consider how much money is involved in reaching a decision." Shifting the subject, he asked, "What about you? What do you want me to do or say on your behalf? You saw I had a question about primogeniture on my sheet."

"Yes. I appreciate it." Jo hesitated. "Here's what I want you to do."

"OK, shoot."

"I want to walk into the room downstairs a few minutes after seven. Hopefully, all the men will be there when we come in."

"Yes."

"I want to walk in on your arm."

"Of course, my pleasure."

"I would like you to introduce me to the group. Like our friend at the front desk, they will probably think I am your wife."

"What do you want me to say? 'Guess who's coming to dinner?'"

"Something simple, 'Gentlemen, this is Miss Jo Taylor Johnston.'"

"I can handle it. What then?"

"I believe I will know what to say after I see their response."

"That's it?"

"Yes, that will be enough."

"Do you want my odds on their response?"

"What do you mean?"

"Well, the Georgetown/Las Vegas line has you a 3-1 favorite to be a hit."

"In case I'm not, I will probably retire gracefully from the field. If I do, don't feel like you have to leave the room. I mean that," she said with emphasis. "Agreed?"

Part of Renny wanted to say, "No, we are in this together," but he knew it wouldn't be true. Jo's statement at the barbecue restaurant came back to him: *You need to do what you need to do.*

"Agreed."

"Thanks. I'm going back to my room for a few minutes." Jo held out her hand toward Renny, who took it in his. No shock treatment this time. She gave him a firm, appreciative squeeze. "I'll meet you downstairs near the front desk."

"I'll be there."

8

To be or not to be: that is the question.
HAMLET, ACT 3, SCENE 1

The old desk clerk glanced up when Renny came downstairs and sat in an armchair in the tiny lobby. "Your group is meeting in the private dining room on the left down the hall. It's across from the main dining room."

"Thanks, but I'm waiting for someone."

"Of course," the clerk said.

"Yes, here *he* comes now." Renny smiled as Jo, the white-and-blue apparition, descended the stairway.

The clerk squinted harder than ever at Jo before continuing to rapidly shuffle a stack of papers on the counter before him.

"Are you ready?" Renny asked as he took Jo's arm and started down the hall.

"Yes," she replied in a quiet, confident voice.

Renny wished his mother could see him with Jo on his arm at that moment. He knew she would approve.

The door to the private dining room was closed. A solitary waiter stood guard outside. Renny and Jo stopped before him.

"May I help you?" he asked, opening a small black booklet hidden in his left hand.

"Yes, I'm Josiah Fletchall Jacobson, and this is Jo Taylor Johnston. We have invitations to join the group inside."

"Yes, sir, I have your names here." The waiter put a check beside their names on a page in his book.

"Has everyone else arrived?" Renny asked.

"Yes sir."

The waiter opened the door to a magnificently decorated dining room illuminated by a large crystal chandelier. Walls paneled in solid cherry surrounded a long table covered with white linen, gold-rimmed plates, and cut-crystal goblets.

Renny and Jo stepped into the room. Eight men, clustered in three groups, stopped all conversation, turned as one, and stared in stunned silence. Someone blurted out with a gravelly voiced Southern accent, "A woman!"

Jo smiled. "Thank you."

A short, slender man with a thin mustache and neatly groomed gray hair stepped forward from one of the groups.

"I'm Desmond LaRochette. This is a private party, and the doorman must have made a mistake."

"No," Renny responded as he shook LaRochette's hand. "I'm Josiah Fletchall Jacobson"—and nodding toward Jo—"this is Jo Taylor Johnston. There is no mistake."

The same voice echoed, "A woman!"

LaRochette took a step back and glanced toward the speaker. "We can see that, Gus." LaRochette turned to Jo, bowed, and took her hand. "My pleasure, Ms. Johnston."

Jo smiled again and said, "Thank you, Mr. LaRochette." Then addressing the room, she continued, "Gentlemen, I am Taylor Johnston's daughter and only child. I'm here in response to a bequest in my father's will and by invitation received from Mr. LaRochette."

The room responded in silence, all eyes turned toward LaRochette.

A voice piped up, "What's the precedent on this, Harry?"

"I'm not sure," another answered.

LaRochette stepped in. "Enough. We can talk business later. Come, Mr. Jacobson and Ms. Johnston, I want you to meet everyone."

LaRochette took Jo's hand in his and led her to an open space at the end of a long dining table. They stood in front of a painting of John C. Calhoun, the fiery pre–Civil War senator from South Carolina.

One by one they filed by, dutifully shaking Renny's hand and calling him Josiah until he corrected them, then lingering longer with Jo who, after her initial speech, graciously deflected all questions with a simple, "I've told you what I know. It's a pleasure to meet you."

The deep-voiced Southerner proved to be Augustus Eicholtz. Renny thanked him for serving as deliveryman for the tape from his father.

"Your father was a great man. One of the best in the history of the List. I hope the apple hasn't fallen far from the tree," Eicholtz said cryptically.

One hundred and forty years had disrupted any uniformity of generations. Renny estimated LaRochette, Eicholtz, and Harold "Harry" Smithfield as the oldest members, contemporaries of Renny's father, all at or near seventy years of age. Next was a group of three who looked to be in their fifties, Michael Flournoy, Thomas Layne V, and Robert Roget. Then came Jerrod Weiss, a forty-year-old from Virginia, followed by Bartholomew "Bart" Maxwell, a lanky young man in his early thirties. Renny and Jo, the only representatives of Generation X, rounded out the group.

After all the anticipation, the men seemed boringly ordinary, no different from a corporate board gathered for its annual getaway or a planning retreat scheduled by the directors of a charitable foundation. Renny felt little different than he had when with his father and his business associates. In a few minutes, the initial hubbub about Jo died down. Everyone poured another round of drinks from a self-service bar in the corner and drifted back into small groups. Renny saw LaRochette and Smithfield huddled in a corner. Jo was momentarily alone, and Renny seized the opportunity to go over to her.

"Well, what do you think?" he asked.

"Too soon to tell."

"They seem like bankers or lawyers, not mobsters," he said, answering his own question.

"Is there any difference?" Jo said mischievously.

At that moment Bart Maxwell joined them. At least six foot four, he was the tallest man in the room. Stoop-shouldered and pale, he looked like a subterranean creature who rarely saw the light of day. "You made a big splash in our little p-p-puddle," he said to Jo with a pronounced stutter. "I-I-I would say Mr. LaRochette and Mr. Smithfield are h-h-huddling in the corner trying to decide what to do about you."

"What do you think?" Renny interjected.

Bart peered at Renny through glasses as thick as the bottom of the proverbial Coke bottle.

"I-I'm a real estate lawyer. Do you know about the rule of p-p-primogeniture?" he said, almost exploding out the last three syllables.

"Yes I do," Renny interjected, "and I explained it to Jo."

"Of course, the r-r-rule no longer exists, and someone is free to leave his estate in trust for his d-d-dog; n-n-no offense," he added, giving Jo an embarrassed look and stooping even more. "I-I don't think there should be any g-g-good reason not to let you participate. I'm about to get married, and if I d-d-don't have a son, I would want my daughter to take my interest in the List."

"Thank you. I appreciate your willingness to tell me what you think is right," Jo said, turning the sunshine of her countenance on his barren features. "That's very kind of you."

"Well, there is no *stare decisus,* or r-r-rule of law over the List. We m-m-make our own law. It's like having your own c-c-country. B-b-but you have my support," he finished a little breathlessly.

"Thanks again."

Bart turned and loped across the room.

"What an odd guy," Renny remarked. "He must be the product of a seriously watered-down gene pool. Lucky he found someone to marry him."

Jo cut her eyes toward Renny. "Don't be cruel, Renny. He's the only one thus far bold enough to say something supportive to me. There's probably more to him than you think."

"OK, OK. Let me get you a drink."

"Straight tonic water on the rocks with a lime twist; no liquor, please."

"A woman who knows what she wants," Renny responded. He crossed the room to the bar, poured Jo's tonic water, and fixed himself a Chevas Regal on the rocks. He wasn't ready to climb on the wagon quite yet, especially not tonight.

When he returned to Jo, Gus Eicholtz, having recovered from his shock at her gender, was telling Jo about her father. A barrel-chested old man with the build of a prizefighter, Eicholtz had the skill of a true Southern storyteller.

"Your father was a brilliant engineer. He could have designed the Golden Gate Bridge, but he never got the chance to show the extent of his talents."

"Did you see him often?" Jo asked.

"Not really. He always kept to himself, but one time about twenty-five years ago, right after you were born, I guess, I persuaded him to meet me in Savannah and drive down to Key West. He saved my life on that trip. We decided to do some fishing in the Gulf and rented a boat for a couple of days. Your father navigated the boat like an old sea captain. It was a good thing, too, because we spent the night on the water and had to weather a severe storm. The boat was rocking and rolling all over the place. I came up from below deck, and while I was trying to walk along the edge of the deck, a big wave hit the side of the boat and pitched me right over the side into the water. Fortunately for me, your father was at the wheel holding the boat into the wind and saw me wash over the side. He grabbed a life preserver, tied the rope to the railing of the boat, and jumped over. I was flailing around in the water and didn't know which end was up. The next thing I knew he had me under my arms and pulled me in like a big tuna. I thanked him, of course, but never got the chance to tell anyone else in his family what he had done. I tried to spend time with him off and on for years afterward, but he always put me off."

Wanting to know more, Jo asked, "Why do you think he was so withdrawn from other people?"

The big man rubbed his chin. "I wondered the same thing myself. He had so much going for him, yet I know he was never happy. Why, look at you! What father wouldn't want to see you every chance he could? Of course, we all thought you were a boy."

Jo mimicked Eicholtz's "A woman!"

Eicholtz grinned. "Your accent needs some refining."

"Renny mentioned the same thing. But how do I start?" she asked.

Eicholtz thought a moment. "Lesson number one. When speaking, slowly move your jaw while keeping your tongue as relaxed as an old dog lying under the porch on a hot summer day. That way the words roll out on top of one another. You remember *My Fair Lady*?"

"Sure. The rain in Spain falls mainly in the plain," Jo said, trying to stretch out the vowels.

"Excellent."

"That's it?"

"No, no. Just the beginning, but with a willing pupil like yourself I could do a reversal of Professor Henry Higgins's work with Eliza Doolittle. Before you knew it, *y'all* would be as comfortable to your lips as a pair of old moccasins on your feet."

Turning toward Renny, she asked, "What do you say, Renny, should I try to learn a new language?"

"Absolutely. You know, the Southern dialect is close in enunciation to Elizabethan English. Shakespeare would feel more at home in Charleston than he would New York. My only disagreement with Mr. Eicholtz would be who should be your teacher."

Before the debate could continue, LaRochette, standing at the head of the table, tapped an empty wine goblet with a silver spoon, and conversation ceased.

"If everyone would move to their seat, it is time for dinner. Ms. Johnston and Mr. Jacobson, it is our custom to sit in the same order our forefathers did when they first met in this room almost 140 years ago."

Everyone but Renny and Jo quickly took position, standing behind a chair. LaRochette was at the head of the table, with Smithfield, Eicholtz, Layne, an empty chair, and Roget on his right. To his left was an empty chair, and he motioned for Jo to take the seat of the Johnston family. Jo stepped quickly to the table. Next to Jo was Flournoy, followed by an empty chair, then Weiss, Bart Maxwell, and another empty chair. LaRochette indicated Renny's spot next to Weiss.

"The perpetually empty chair is for the family of Alexander Hammond, an original signer of the List, whose wife died in 1868 while giving birth to a son who also died. Hammond never remarried and died childless in 1884. Please be seated."

Dinner came in courses, a "soup to nuts" affair orchestrated with precision at the long table by a trio of waiters. The entrée was a succulent cut of prime rib.

Michael Flournoy separated Renny from Jo, and the table conversation broke up into groups of three or four. Renny's group included Jerrod Weiss and Thomas Layne. LaRochette and Michael Flournoy focused on Jo. Every so often Gus Eicholtz's booming laugh echoed around the room.

Weiss, a stocky, dark-haired man with a thick neck and bushy eyebrows, ate hunched over his soup. The comptroller of a Virginia corporation that imported electrical equipment from Europe and Asia, he contributed little to the conversation beyond a few grunts.

On the other hand, Thomas Layne V, handsome and tall with a full head of carefully coifed gray hair, was the most aristocratic, suave, and overtly arrogant person at the table. If born in the seventeenth century, he would have made a perfect courtier during the reign of Louis XIV, but in today's world he had to settle for a life of self-indulgence on Hilton Head Island south of Charleston. He entertained himself during dinner by perversely teasing Weiss, whom he described to Renny as a "bean counter."

Weiss finally rose to the bait. "I'm a money counter, Layne. Maybe you should count more and spend less yourself."

"I'm sure you're right, Jerrod, but money is a means to an end, the means to acquire *la joie de vivre*, the joy of living, not the end in itself."

Weiss shrugged and went back into his shell.

Layne turned toward Renny. "I'm sorry about your father. He was a very impressive man, respected greatly by everyone in this room."

"Thank you."

"I'm glad he has such an obviously well-prepared and successful son to follow after him."

Renny nodded, wondering at Layne's sincerity and motivation.

"Desmond tells me you live in Charlotte?" Layne said.

"Yes."

"My sister and her husband, a CPA, live there."

"Is he with a big firm?"

"No, he has a small group, Berit and something. His name is Jack Berit."

"I've met him," Renny said, remembering a short, gray-haired man who had provided an audit for an acquisition Heywood handled at the firm.

"You don't say," Layne said. "It is a small world."

"Jack's a bean counter like you, Jerrod. You'd get along great."

Weiss didn't look up from his plate.

"Aren't you glad Renny has been able to join us?" Layne continued.

Weiss muttered, "Sure, sure, welcome aboard."

Layne leaned across the table and asked in a low tone, "What about the young lady? Do you think she should be on the ship?"

Weiss grunted with greater emphasis. "I know what I think."

"What do you think?" Layne acted surprised that Weiss had a thought.

"I'll keep it to myself," Weiss growled, vigorously cutting his prime rib.

Giving up on Weiss, Layne returned to Renny. "Tell me, did you meet Ms. Johnston before this evening?"

"Yes, we arrived at the same time yesterday," Renny answered, not wanting to tell about the chance encounter in Moncks Corner.

"Her presence makes this meeting different from the previous ones I've attended," Layne said. "Very interesting indeed."

Dinner was superb. Renny counted four bottles of Tignabello, a Tuscany port, that made the rounds and were emptied of their rich, red contents. Jo's glass remained full, but by meal's end the rest of the group, with the exception of Weiss, who obviously could hold his liquor very well, were becoming more and more mellow and fraternal. Bart Maxwell was visibly intoxicated, and his stutter, now combined with a slur, was twice as bad as before the meal. The dessert cart rolled back into the kitchen, and LaRochette tapped his glass again.

"Gentlemen," he began, then smoothly added, "and lady. I would like to call to order the 247th meeting of the Covenant List of South Carolina, Limited."

The room settled into silence. Renny took a sip of water and peeked around Flournoy at Jo. Catching his look out of the corner of her eye, she gave him a quick smile and turned back toward LaRochette.

LaRochette continued, "As you recall, we were all here together at our regular meeting last November. Now, due to the deaths of H. L. Jacobson and Taylor Johnston, we are required by the rules of the List to call a meeting of the members to install successors. On behalf of us all, I have expressed our condolences to Mr. Jacobson and Ms. Johnston on the deaths of their fathers. Let us have a moment of silence to honor their passing."

Everyone bowed their heads. Renny closed his eyes and imagined his father sitting in the room the previous year. It was eerie sitting in the same spot at the table as his father, grandfather, and back through time.

LaRochette broke the silence. "As is our custom when uninitiated members are present, I would ask the historian of the List to give a summary of our background and purpose."

Renny felt like a freshman pledge during fraternity rush week.

At his cue, Harry Smithfield rose and opened an old leather-bound book thicker than the one Renny had found in the old trunk. Reading in a monotone, he said, "The Covenant List of South Carolina, Limited, was established on November 30, 1863, by our forefathers to provide financial stability for our families as the adverse outcome of the War Between the States became apparent. . . ."

Smithfield, a short, rotund man, recited the original language of the Covenant in a friendly voice, making it sound more like the Four Laws of Rotary International than the foundation principles of a 140-year-old secret society with untold financial fortune. "Since the time of the original signers, all successor generations of the member families have subscribed to the Covenant without break except for Alexander Hammond." He then read the names of the current members, giving the dates each signed the List, then sat down.

LaRochette took over. "The presence of Ms. Johnston raises a question regarding current applicability of the rule of primogeniture, the exclusive right of inheritance for the eldest male heir, established in the original List agreement. I have talked to Harry, and we believe the issue needs to be brought before the group for discussion. During dinner, I mentioned this to Ms. Johnston, and she is agreeable to proceeding in this manner. She has requested the opportunity to speak first."

Jo began, "Thank you for your hospitality to me this evening. I know it was a shock when I walked through the door." She smiled toward Gus Eicholtz. "It seems obvious that when my father named me Jo, he did so with participation in this group in mind. However, I realize there is a question as to whether my gender disqualifies me from participation, and I want to make it clear that I am not here to try to pressure or coerce you into accepting me. Primarily, I am seeking answers to some troubling aspects of my father's life, and my purpose is more personal than related to anything in my father's will."

Roget, a short, pudgy man with a receding hairline and dark eyes, cleared his throat and looked questioningly across the table at Renny.

Taking the letter from her father out of her purse, Jo unfolded it and continued, "I suppose, like all of you, I learned about the List after my father's death. Before you discuss my status in this group, I would like to read the letter he left for me."

The room listened in silence. When she finished, Jo took a deep breath and asked, "What can you tell me about my father's concerns?"

Michael Flournoy, a small man with gold-rimmed glasses, spoke first in a soft, Southern voice. "Ms. Johnston, I'm not sure the answers to your questions are in this room. Once the immediate threat to our families from the war and Reconstruction subsided, the List became nothing more than a business relationship we maintain from one generation to another. We are simply a group that has found the key to the accumulation of wealth: longevity of investment. I'm sure no one in this room had ill will toward your father, and while his failure to inform us of your gender violated our mutual trust, I think it is more superstition than fact to conclude that his personal problems have a relationship to his conduct vis-à-vis this group. I don't say this to denigrate his memory or hurt your feelings, but I believe you are seeking an honest answer, and I must give you my sincere opinion."

Eicholtz followed on Flournoy's heels. "Your father seems to have been burdened with guilt, a rare commodity in our day, but as Michael said, a guilt that had no foundation in fact. He mentioned God punishing him in the letter. I frankly don't know if the Almighty cares, but if he does, I doubt he would be concerned with such a trivial offense. There are a lot more serious criminals on the loose. As I told you before dinner, Taylor Johnston saved my life. I'm sorry he allowed this issue to prevent him from being a part of my life, and I'm sorry it kept us from spending time together."

Layne piped in, "I would ditto what Michael and Gus said. I think it is a question of misplaced emphasis. We are responsible for our future and our fate. Life is simply a matter of choices. The List is designed to help us financially and has no other significance."

"So there is no record of unusual problems in your family backgrounds?" Jo asked.

Smithfield spoke up, "I may know more about the families of everyone in this room than anyone else. I've read the records of our family histories. There is a lot of tragedy in the past, but I don't think you can give a comprehensive reason or explanation. My father died before he was forty, and I was the only one of five children to reach age twenty-one."

Renny remembered his conversation with Aunt Margaret and the tragedies that had plagued his ancestors.

"I would say it's just a part of Southern melancholy and malaise," Michael Flournoy interjected dryly. "Every Southern family with roots and history has a lot of insanity in the back sitting room and illegitimate children in the woodshed."

"What a happy thought, Michael," Eicholtz grunted.

"There's no way you could prove or disprove any idea or theory," Weiss growled. "Each man is entitled to his own opinion, and everyone's got a different one. I don't think we are going to be able to answer Ms. Johnston's questions. I think we are wasting our time."

"I don't want to waste your time, Mr. Weiss," Jo said quickly. "I was troubled by my father's letter, and this seemed the place to come for information."

Weiss responded in a gentler tone, "I didn't mean your questions are not important. I mean that we"—gesturing to the men around the table—"do not have the answers."

"I must say Jerrod is right," LaRochette said. "The answers to your questions do not lie in this room. We are ordinary people with ordinary problems. With all due respect to your father, I do not think his failure to tell us about you had any connection with his personal problems. As to the supernatural, we do not bring our personal religious beliefs into this meeting. We are tolerant, not coercive. All we require is that we enter into covenant with one another under the terms and guidelines set out long ago. This protects and benefits everyone. It always has and always will."

Jo opened her mouth, closed it, then said, "Thank you for your comments. I guess I will need to look elsewhere for insight."

LaRochette took the floor. "This brings us back to the question of primogeniture and Ms. Johnston. She is willing to leave the room while we discuss this matter. Is that agreeable with everyone?"

Renny wanted to say no, but remembering his previous conversation with Jo, he kept quiet. A general nod of heads supported LaRochette's suggestion.

Eicholtz motioned toward Renny. "I suggest young Jacobson stay since his succession to the List will be in the usual way."

"Any problems with Gus's recommendation?" LaRochette asked.

No one spoke.

"Fine. Mr. Jacobson, please take Ms. Johnston to the parlor adjacent to the main dining room. It would also be an appropriate time for you to bring in the original documents in your father's possession as custodian."

Everyone stood as Renny pulled back Jo's chair and escorted her to the door. The parlor, down the hall from the main dining room, was furnished with a love seat and two comfortable chairs. A pair of windows overlooked the back porch, the parking area, and the bay beyond. The wind was picking up, and it was obvious the storm offshore was going to dump some rain on land before the night was over.

"This is perfect," Jo said. "I can sit in here with my friends."

"What friends?" Renny asked.

"The angels. They hang around with me," she said, laughing as Renny rolled his eyes.

"I think you might be an angel," Renny responded. "However, we don't have time to debate about angels. What do you want to happen in there?"

"That's not the question, Renny. The question is, what do you want to do?"

"But you're the reason for the discussion. What do you want me to say on your behalf?"

"Nothing. I've said what I wanted to say. I know what I am supposed to do."

"What is that?"

"I'm not saying, but listen to what they say about me with your own situation in mind."

"Why should I do that?"

"So you can get a clearer picture of what is really going on here."

"It seems simple enough."

"Really?"

"Don't be so obscure," Renny said with a hint of frustration. "I understand what is going on in the meeting better than I do this conversation."

"There are some powerful forces in that room, and I don't know where they are coming from."

Jo was not making any sense, and he didn't want to keep the other men waiting any longer. "Well, I've got to go. I need to get the trunk from my room."

"I'll say this much," Jo said slowly and deliberately. "If you don't know what to do, I would say don't do anything."

"OK. I've got to get the trunk. I'll see you later."

"I'll be here," Jo said as Renny turned to go.

Renny bounded up the stairs in an effort to release the tension he felt. Angels, family tragedies, riches, powerful forces. What was going on? Why was an intelligent, twenty-six-year-old woman acting this way? Who could know if there was a "right" thing to do? Reaching his room, he entered and grabbed the trunk. The old clerk glanced up as he passed by the desk with the old box in his arms. Opening the door, he reentered the dining room.

Layne had lit a pipe. Eicholtz was puffing a huge cigar, and LaRochette snuffed out a cigarette as Renny came into the room. Every man had pushed his chair back from the table.

LaRochette motioned for Renny to bring the trunk to the head of the table. Renny deposited it at LaRochette's feet.

"Let's have a quick look inside," the old man said eagerly.

Before Renny could offer to help, LaRochette leaned over, quickly twirled the lock, and popped it open.

"You know the combination?" Renny blurted out.

LaRochette didn't answer. He took out the old book, and, oblivious to Renny, he held it reverently, opening it to glance at the first few pages before quickly turning the signature pages. "Good, good," he said. "Thank you for delivering this treasure."

Addressing the group, he said, "Gentlemen, everything seems to be in order. Let's proceed."

Turning to Renny, who had returned to his seat, he continued, "While you were out of the room, we decided it best to proceed with your acceptance onto the List as the first order of business. That way you can participate in our other discussions as a full member."

Renny met LaRochette's gaze and felt slightly lightheaded. Forgetting about the sheet of questions in his pocket or his comment to Jo that he would wait until her status was decided to make his own decision, he said, "All right."

Smithfield took over. "Since your father was custodian, I'm sure you've had opportunity to look over the documents in the trunk. Particularly, have you read the original Covenant List agreement?"

Shaking his head in an attempt to dispel the fuzziness and sense of detachment he felt, Renny heard himself answer, "Yes sir." Too much dinner wine.

"Good," Smithfield said. "All you need to do is verbally acknowledge and submit to the terms of the List agreement and agree to covenants of secrecy, truthfulness, and mutual security."

Renny nodded. He felt a little queasy and desperately thought this would be a very inappropriate time to throw up.

LaRochette's voice penetrated the haze and nausea. "If everyone would stand, please. Josiah Fletchall Jacobson, come forward."

LaRochette's command was nonnegotiable. As he walked to the head of the table, Renny took a couple of deep breaths, hoping the extra oxygen would quiet the turbulence in his stomach and clear his head. Flournoy and Roget moved to the front as well.

LaRochette opened the List to the faded ink agreement. "Please put your right hand here and repeat after me."

Renny had never had an out-of-body experience. He'd never fallen on his head as a child, choked on a chicken bone, or been knocked unconscious in a car wreck—the type of events commonly known to trigger the reported sensation of "watching" yourself from outside your body. Not until now. On the way to the head of the table, he became detached from himself and saw his body standing before LaRochette. The air seemed heavy, almost thick, and Renny's physical activities went on autopilot. He numbly watched himself repeat the words intoned by LaRochette while his hand rested on the faded black ink.

"I, Josiah Fletchall Jacobson, the eldest legal heir of Henry Lawrence Jacobson, hereby enter into covenant under the terms and conditions of the Covenant List of South Carolina, Limited. I bind myself and my heirs by the terms of the Covenant List of South Carolina, Limited, and receive on behalf of my family all the rights and benefits arising out of said Covenant. So help me God."

As he spoke, the nausea left. "I further agree and covenant with the current and future members of the Covenant List of South Carolina, Limited, to keep existence of the said Covenant confidential and inviolate from all persons. I further agree and covenant to conduct myself with complete truthfulness and for the purpose of mutual security and benefit as outlined and contemplated in the Covenant List. So help me God."

"Sign here," LaRochette said as Roget put a quill pen in Renny's hand.

Someone had written in fresh ink an entry notation in the old ledger book.

The undersigned, eldest legal heir of Henry Lawrence Jacobson, hereby enters into covenant under the terms and conditions of the Covenant List of South Carolina, Limited.

_____

Renny watched himself sign his name on the blank line.

LaRochette looked to Flournoy, who produced a small knife with an intricately carved ivory handle and handed it to LaRochette.

"For millennia, binding covenants have been sealed with blood. Blood represents life, and your life, as was that of your father, grandfather, and others of the Jacobson line, is joined with our lives and our families in an irrevocable bond of support and cooperation. Let me have your left hand, please."

Renny watched himself hesitate, and then he was back in his body, looking into LaRochette's eyes. He did not try to resist LaRochette's compelling gaze and slowly extended his left hand, palm up. LaRochette took his hand, mumbled something in a language Renny took to be French, and pricked Renny's ring finger with the point of the dagger.

Renny flinched but felt no pain. LaRochette pressed the bleeding flesh to the page next to Renny's signature. It left a bright red spot below all the dark brown and black ones that preceded it.

"Here, here," Renny heard Layne's voice.

The air cleared, and Renny was again fully himself. He commanded his left index finger to wiggle, and it obeyed instantly. LaRochette shook Renny's hand warmly. Beginning with Flournoy, Roget, and Smithfield, the other men filed by, dutifully welcoming him to the fraternity of the List.

Renny felt a euphoria that erased the confusion and nausea experienced just moments before. It must have been the pent-up tension. Now that the ceremony was over, he could shift back into normal gear. He returned to his seat, a member of the elite group.

LaRochette said, "Let's move to our next item of business. I have asked Harry to give some brief background on Ms. Johnston's status. Then we will open the floor for discussion."

Smithfield remained seated while he spoke. "I have looked over the historical records and find, as we suspected, no instance where a woman served, even briefly, as a member of the List. Taylor Johnston had no male heirs, and he expressed his desire in his will for his daughter to take his family's place on the List. As we all know, the rule established in the original Covenant mandates succession only to the eldest son. If we change the rule, it will require a change in the Covenant."

"We c-c-can do what we w-w-want," Bart Maxwell stuttered. "We m-m-make the rules."

"I think we need to respect what our forefathers decided," Roget interrupted before Bart could generate a head of stuttering steam. "If we change the rules, we lose stability. Next, someone will want younger sons or relatives outside the direct family line to inherit. A sure rule has served us well, and I don't want to change it. You heard what Ms. Johnston said. She didn't seem overly interested in subscribing to the Covenant."

"She doesn't know how much money is involved," Michael Flournoy said. "Money has a way of persuading."

"How much money is involved?" Renny blurted out.

LaRochette raised his eyebrows and looked to Roget. "Robert is our treasurer. Would you address that issue?"

Roget looked condescendingly at Renny as he spoke, "We are doing very well, very well indeed. We will have a financial report later, but for now, we need to focus on Ms. Johnston."

Renny wanted to punch Roget in the nose. He didn't like the man and felt he was being treated like a kindergartner. But he kept his mouth shut and relieved the tension by clenching and unclenching his hand under the table.

"I think we ought to let her join," Gus Eicholtz said bluntly. "I'm sorry for all her father must have gone through worrying about this issue. If he had brought it up while he was alive, I think we would have told him not to worry, that his daughter would be welcome. I think it is the only sensible thing to do. There is plenty of money for everyone, and the purpose of preserving family involvement seems more important to me than whether a male or female serves as family representative. I mean, look at Margaret Thatcher. She was the best leader Europe's produced in the past twenty-five years."

"That raises another concern I have," said Roget. "What if we ended up with a majority of women? Would we want women to control the List? Can we count on women to maintain secrecy? It's just not in them to keep a confidence. As it is, we have always been able to run this group without female intervention, interference, or intuition."

"Whoa, Robert," Layne interjected. "I think you need to see my psychiatrist about your anger toward the weaker sex. I don't think we should punish this young lady for the sins of every woman since Eve. She seems bright and capable to me. My concern is more a matter of, how shall I say . . . conscience."

"Spare us," Roget said, bristling. "You checked your conscience at the door of your first-grade classroom."

"No, no, you're mistaken. I'm not concerned about my conscience." Layne grinned. "I have it well sedated. It's her conscience that raises a question in my mind."

"Explain yourself," Eicholtz said.

Layne waited until sure he had everyone's attention. "While the rest of you were gnawing on the prime rib, I was watching young Ms. Johnston. She bowed her head and prayed before we ate, and she failed to sample the excellent Tignabello. She's a 'true believer' and a teetotaler."

"So w-w-what. W-w-we're not alcoholics," Maxwell said with effort to sound more sober than he was.

"I agree. Appreciating a fine wine is not a prerequisite for membership to the List, and religion is the harmless opiate of the people. But I think Ms. Johnston believes some of the nonsense in the letter from poor old Taylor about God, curses, tragedy, and the vague culpability of this group in it all. That troubles me. We don't need someone conducting a witch hunt that upsets our apple cart, to mix my metaphors. My sense is that this young lady is a religious fanatic. It's trouble with a capital *T,* and we don't need that. Ask Mr. Jacobson. He has been around her some for a day or so. I dare say he will confirm what I'm saying."

LaRochette nodded toward Renny. "Do you have an opinion about Thomas's categorization of Ms. Johnston?"

All eyes now turned to Renny.

Renny was impressed with Layne's insight. Although skewed by personal prejudice, he'd read Jo like a book. He instantly replayed some of his own "religious" moments with Jo and debated his options. He could say, "I don't know her well enough to give an opinion," "I think you are mistaken," or "You are right. She is very religious." He decided to answer as Jo might.

Addressing Layne, he said, "You're right. She is very religious. I haven't been around her before this weekend, but I think she has the type of conscience you described. She believes in a God who is involved in her life in a way I would call somewhat mystical. How she would relate to this group is something I don't know. She marches to the beat of her own drum." As soon as he said it, Renny knew Jo's fate was sealed. The members of the List didn't want individualism. Everyone had to beat his drum to the same cadence. There was one sheet of music, and there would be no drum for Jo.

Layne nodded with satisfaction. "I call for a vote."

"I second," Roget responded.

Renny, Eicholtz, and Maxwell voted to accept Jo for membership; LaRochette, Flournoy, Smithfield, Layne, Roget, and Weiss voted against it. Renny knew Eicholtz's vote was sentimental. It was his way of honoring Jo's father. Maxwell's tenaciousness surprised Renny. Jo had been right—there was more to him than Renny had thought. Renny voted yes, but knew in his heart she would never have joined.

"Renny, please ask Ms. Johnston to come back in for a moment," LaRochette said. "I'll explain our decision to her."

Renny left the room and leaned against the wall in the hallway. What had he done? He went into the agreement blind. He hadn't asked any of his questions. He hadn't waited until they voted on Jo. He knew nothing more than he did before the meeting started. Why did he feel so rotten, then so wonderful?

Looking at his left ring finger, he could barely see any sign of the cut. No redness, nothing. He pressed the finger at the site of the cut to see if it was sore. Nothing. Well, he couldn't stand there and give himself a physical. He needed to retrieve Jo.

She was sitting in the parlor with her eyes closed. Renny cleared his throat as he walked through the door. It seemed like hours since he had left her there.

"Not asleep, were you?" he asked.

"At rest, yes. Asleep, no," she said, opening her eyes and blinking a couple of times. "What's the verdict?"

Renny held his thumb down.

Jo shrugged. "I'm not surprised."

"Come back in for a minute. LaRochette wants to give you the news."

Renny didn't mention his own decision, and they walked down the hall in silence. He held the door for her as she reentered the dining room.

LaRochette turned on the charm. "Ms. Johnston, please have a seat."

Renny held her chair for her. Several of the men occupied themselves with another glass of wine.

"Deciding your status has been a difficult issue. We respected your father greatly and have considered his request designating you as his successor on the List. However, the terms of the relationship established by our forefathers do not make provision for your membership to the List, and we have voted accordingly. However, while Mr. Jacobson was getting you, someone suggested we demonstrate in a small way our sentiments to you and your family. For this reason we would like to transfer one million dollars to you as a gift. All we ask is that you honor your family's commitment to keep the List confidential."

Jo arched her eyebrows and said, "I understand the reason for your decision and appreciate your offer. But I did not come here seeking money. Frankly, it would be better if I didn't take any money or make any promises."

"Are you sure?" Layne asked.

"Yes, very sure. Good night, gentlemen." She got up quickly and swept out of the room.

As the door shut behind her, Eicholtz said to no one in particular, "I've never seen anyone like her."

Neither have I, Renny thought dolefully. He felt alone. Alone, although he was surrounded by men seated at the same table. Maybe *empty* was a better word. Empty, alone. The words themselves sounded hollow.

9

And let all mankind agree.
JOHN DRYDEN

"I would have thought she could have taken the money and given it to her favorite church or charity," Layne said dryly as the room collectively digested Jo's refusal of the million dollars.

"Maybe Taylor had a secret stash and she doesn't need any money," Weiss grunted.

Renny started to answer, then changed his mind.

"I am more than a little concerned about Ms. Johnston breaching the confidentiality of this group," Roget said quietly.

"We all are," LaRochette agreed, clearing his throat. "Perhaps you could help us, Renny."

Renny, already missing Jo's presence, shrugged. "How? I just met her yesterday, and I assume she'll be leaving town to return to Michigan in the morning. I doubt I'll ever see her again."

"You could have a say in that, couldn't you?" LaRochette responded. "We saw how the two of you exchanged glances all evening. It doesn't take a savant to see there is a mutual interest."

Renny flushed. "If there was, it was probably dealt a deathblow by the rejection of this group."

Eicholtz interrupted, "Hogwash, boy. She looked at you like you were the finest crabmeat soufflé in Charleston." Turning to LaRochette, he continued, "What do you have in mind, Desmond? Get to the point."

LaRochette clasped his hands together behind his back. "All I have in mind is for Renny to embark on a goodwill, fact-finding mission. Whether he admits it or not, he wants to spend time with Ms. Johnston. I merely suggest that he give her a positive perspective on the List and find out if she intends to violate our rule of confidentiality."

"What are we g-g-going to do if she d-d-does? B-b-break her legs?" Maxwell asked.

"Don't be silly, Bart. If we have information, we can give Renny advice on how to respond. Also, I am not convinced she will continue to refuse a financial incentive."

Everyone turned toward Renny, who found himself nodding in agreement and saying, "I can't promise anything, but I will see what I can find out."

"Excellent," LaRochette said with a satisfied smile. "One of us will stay in touch with you. Next we need a financial report. Robert?"

"Just a minute, Desmond," Flournoy interjected. "Before we get into the figures, I would like to propose a toast honoring the upcoming wedding of Bartholomew Maxwell. It appears he will avoid the unfortunate fate of Alexander Hammond."

"Rightly so," added Layne with a nod toward Bart, who rose unsteadily from his seat and stammered, "Th-th-thank you."

Eicholtz retrieved a bottle of Dom Perignon from a side table and pulled the cork with a pop. "Here, Harry, please help me with the glasses."

Smithfield took a round silver tray with the delicate goblets around the table, and Eicholtz followed, pouring the pale champagne.

Once all were served, Eicholtz held his glass aloft and said, "To Bartholomew Maxwell. May you prove Euripides wrong and your marriage have more joy than pain."

A few of the members echoed, "Hear, hear," as they drained their goblets.

"I-I-It is an honor t-t-to be here," Bart stuttered and drained his glass in a single swallow.

Everyone sat down except Bart, who stared ahead with a startled look on his face, turned toward LaRochette, and crashed forward face-first onto the table.

Eicholtz said, "He's passed out."

Remembering Jo's training as a cardiac care nurse, Renny ran out the door and up the stairs. Pounding on her door, he yelled, "Jo, it's Renny! Come quick!"

Jo opened the door, barefoot, but still dressed in her evening gown. "What's happened?"

"It's Bart Maxwell. He's passed out. Come back downstairs."

As they quickly went down the steps, Renny said, "We had a toast honoring his upcoming wedding and he fell face-first on the table."

As they passed the front desk, Layne was on the phone. "It looks serious! I'm calling an ambulance!" he shouted as they went by him.

They entered the dining room and saw Maxwell lying face-up on the floor. Someone had placed a damp dinner napkin on his forehead.

Jo quickly knelt beside him. "Let me see." Taking his wrist, she held it in her hand. "He doesn't have a pulse!"

Layne thrust his head inside the door. "An ambulance is on the way. It should be here any minute."

Jo put her ear to Bart's chest. "Did he appear to choke on anything?"

"No, no," Harry Smithfield answered. "He just drank his champagne, got a strange look in his eyes, and fell on the table."

Renny glanced up and saw Robert Roget standing with his arms crossed, calmly watching.

Jo was administering CPR when the ambulance siren wailed in the distance. A few seconds later, the emergency medical personnel burst through the dining room's door.

Jo immediately yielded to the EMT. "I'm a nurse. I can't pick up a pulse."

The EMT continued with CPR as they lifted Bart onto a stretcher and hurriedly rolled him out to the waiting vehicle.

"Where are you taking him?" Jo asked as she followed them down the hall.

"Georgetown Memorial," the EMT replied. "It's one block south of Highway 53 on Seventh Street."

"Renny, can you take me?" Jo asked.

"Sure, sure. Put on some shoes and we'll go."

Jo looked at her bare feet. "I'll be right back."

Renny stood by the front desk. The meeting was obviously over. LaRochette, Smithfield, and Roget passed by on their way to the hospital.

Renny rubbed his eyes and shook his head. This was not a good picture. Before he could further sort his thoughts, Jo appeared, still dressed in her formal gown but without the sapphire necklace. She said nothing as they walked quickly down the back steps of the inn to the parking area. Renny started the car as Jo slammed her door shut.

"What do you think is wrong with him?" Renny asked.

"I don't know, but unless they get his heart beating, he's gone."

"Did he have a heart attack?"

"Possibly, or a seizure of some kind. He didn't appear to be choking, did he?"

"No. It was like Smithfield said. He drank his champagne and crashed onto the table."

"Strange," Jo said.

Renny wove in and out of traffic. He went through two stoplights just as they turned red, pulled up to the hospital, and parked next to LaRochette's Mercedes. A few big drops of rain hit the roof of the convertible.

LaRochette, Roget, and Smithfield met them as Jo and Renny walked into the ER.

"He's gone," Smithfield said, shaking his head. "They tried electric shock, but they were unable to revive him."

"The hospital is trying to reach his sister in Savannah," Roget added.

"Are you coming back to the inn now?" LaRochette asked.

Jo addressed Renny, "I'd like to see if I can talk to someone inside."

LaRochette touched Renny's arm as Jo passed through the doors. "We'll see you back at the inn as soon as you finish here."

Renny nodded and followed Jo inside the hospital.

There was a small waiting area to the left of the entrance where two registration clerks were taking information from patients. Jo walked up to the nearest clerk. "A man named Bartholomew Maxwell was brought in by ambulance a few minutes ago. I would like to talk to the attending doctor."

"Are you a relative?" the clerk asked.

"No, I'm a nurse who gave him CPR at the Rice Planter's Inn when he collapsed after dinner."

"I'll check with the doctor," the clerk said, disappearing into the area behind the registration desk.

She reappeared in a few seconds with the doctor. He held out his hand to Renny. "I'm Dr. Davidson."

Jo stepped forward. "Dr. Davidson, I'm Jo Johnston, the nurse who gave Mr. Bartholomew CPR after he collapsed. Could I have done anything differently to help him?"

The doctor shook his head. "I don't think so. He was dead on arrival here at the hospital. We tried to revive him by electric stimulation without success. It appears he died immediately after his collapse."

"What was the cause of death?" Renny asked.

"We're going to conduct an autopsy as soon as we contact the next of kin. At this time, I would have to say unknown causes. I'm sorry."

"Thanks anyway." Jo turned away, and they headed outside.

It was raining, and Renny ran to the car and drove up to the ER entrance to pick up Jo.

"I've never seen someone die," he said. "One minute he was talking in his stuttering voice; the next he's unconscious on the floor. I'm sure you've seen death at the hospital. How do you get used to it?"

"You don't. If you did you would be better off working at a mortuary instead of a hospital."

Renny had a hard time seeing in the heavy rain, and he drove slowly, the windshield wipers flicking back and forth as quickly as possible.

"It's just hard to imagine he was here one second and gone the next," Renny said. They stopped for a red light. "So, where is Bart Maxwell now? In heaven?"

The light turned green. A passing truck plowed through a puddle and splashed the car.

"It goes back to our talk this morning," Jo said. "It depends on whether Bart ever responded to God's call and was born again."

"Born again? Like Jimmy Carter or Billy Graham?"

"They made the term well known to a lot of people, but it was first used by Jesus himself when he talked to a religious leader named Nicodemus."

Renny slowed to a stop as a second light turned red. "What does it mean?"

"Jesus told Nicodemus, 'The wind blows wherever it pleases. You hear its sound, but you cannot tell where it comes from or where it is going. So it is with everyone born of the Spirit.' It's a supernatural, spiritual experience."

"You've lost me," Renny said.

"It's a spiritual birth, the point of beginning for spiritual life. That's why it's compared to a newborn infant passing from the womb to the world."

"So serving a couple of times as an altar boy when I was a kid won't get me into heaven?"

"No. That's why I asked you whether God had ever called you when we were on the beach today."

The beach seemed like a long time ago in a galaxy far, far away.

As they turned into the inn's parking lot, Renny remembered he had not told Jo about the List. "In all the confusion about Bart, I didn't get a chance to tell you that I was accepted on the List."

"Oh, weren't they going to wait until after they discussed my situation?" Jo asked, puzzled.

"No, when I came back into the room with the trunk, LaRochette said they wanted me to participate as a voting member. To do so it would be necessary for me to take the Covenant. It took me by surprise, and I was off balance, but his comment made sense since there was no reason I couldn't join. It was over in a few minutes. A very strange experience—almost like I wasn't there at all. I don't know how to describe it except that I watched myself walk to the front, agree to the Covenant, and sign the book."

"What about the marks in the book beside each name?" Jo asked.

"They prick your finger and put the blood beside your name, just like a couple of kids might do. They used a little dagger. Look"—he turned on the car's interior lights and held his finger out for her to see—"there's no mark where I was cut."

Jo leaned over and inspected Renny's finger. There was no visible sign of a cut.

"I don't know, Renny. How do you feel about it now?"

"The way it happened. So easy, it seemed inevitable. It's my destiny, I guess."

They got out of the car and walked to the inn.

Jo turned to go upstairs. "I'm going up to my room, but I won't go to bed until I see you after the meeting."

"OK."

Renny walked down the hall to the private dining room. His stomach was acting up again. It was almost midnight; Eicholtz and Weiss, each with a large tumbler in his hand, were the only people in the room.

"Renny, join us," Eicholtz beckoned when he saw Renny standing in the doorway. "Everyone decided to call it a night. We're going to get together at ten o'clock in the morning."

Gus Eicholtz was the most genuine person on the List, and Renny wished he could talk with him in private and ask him some questions. But with Jerrod Weiss morosely nursing a double scotch, now was not the time.

"I'm going to have a Coke and go to bed," Renny said.

While Renny fixed his drink, Eicholtz and Weiss sat in silence.

Weiss said, "We've had some significant attrition on the List the past twenty-four hours. First, the Johnston family goes aground on the rocks of primogeniture; next, Bart Maxwell follows the way of Alexander Hammond and dies childless."

Renny didn't detect a hint of regret in Weiss's voice.

The Coke was not helping Renny's creeping nausea, and he wasn't sure he could stomach much more of Weiss's meanspiritedness.

"I wonder who's next?" Weiss added.

"Who knows?" Eicholtz responded. "This has been a sad night."

"I think I'll go up to my room," Renny said. "I'm beat."

He took a couple of steps and felt the hair on the back of his neck stand up. Turning his head, his eyes met Weiss's gaze, a malevolent stare that almost pushed Renny out of the room. Eicholtz, his back to Renny, was pouring another drink and didn't see the exchange. Renny stumbled slightly as he walked out of the room.

———

"Come in." Jo opened the door at Renny's knock. "Sit down."

Renny slumped into a small chair.

"That was quick. Are you all right?" she asked a little anxiously.

"Yes, I feel like I did after a hard-fought football game in high school. A little shaky in the legs, but I guess I'm OK." He took a deep breath.

"I'd say you have been fighting, but not with flesh and blood," Jo responded. "Here, let me get you a glass of water."

The water tasted better than anything Renny had drunk the entire evening. His stomach relaxed, and he was able to think without being distracted by nausea.

"Thanks. My stomach has been acting up since dinner, but I think it's settled down now."

"Good. Why did you come up so soon?"

"They canceled any further meeting tonight; we'll get together in the morning. The only men in the dining room were Eicholtz and Weiss. Eicholtz seemed sorry about Bart, but Weiss . . ."

"What?"

"I don't know. He is a cold fish. He said, 'I wonder who's next?' It was creepy."

"Um, maybe he's glad less people have an interest in the money."

"Could be." Renny closed his eyes tightly. "I've aged a couple of years in a single evening."

"We both need some rest," Jo answered. "I have to be at work by Monday afternoon, and it will be a long drive home to Michigan. I need to get an early start."

"Let's have breakfast together?" Renny asked.

"What time?"

"About seven-thirty?"

"OK."

———

Renny was asleep within seconds after his head landed on the pillow. At two o'clock he woke up with a splitting headache. The rain was beating against the window, and the wind howled. Turning on the light, he stumbled into the bathroom and ran hot water over a washcloth. It provided little relief, so he searched through his travel kit for some pain pills. Taking two, he tried to go back to sleep. Twenty minutes later, he took two more. At four o'clock he dozed off to fitful, disjointed dreams. When he awoke at six-thirty, he heard the storm fading outside. His head was still producing a muffled pounding, so he swallowed two more pain pills and lay back down.

Then he remembered his father's headaches. Although in excellent health until his death, H. L. suffered occasional, severe headaches that the doctor diagnosed as migraines. Not frequently—maybe six or seven times a year—he would be knocked out for a day, usually spending the time in bed in a darkened room. Now Renny knew how his father felt. Renny moaned a prayer, "God, I don't want to have headaches like my father," and fell back asleep.

An hour later, he woke up with some residual pain and pressure behind his left temple. The worst had passed, and the storm was almost spent as well. It was overcast and cloudy, but no longer raining. Renny took a long shower and dressed in casual clothes.

Opening the door to go downstairs and meet Jo for breakfast, he saw an envelope with his name on the outside. He opened it and read,

Dear Mr. Jacobson,

Due to the tragic events of last night, we have decided to postpone our meeting to discuss a possible distribution from the List. We will notify you concerning the date and time.

Sincerely,

Desmond LaRochette

Renny wondered who the "we" referred to. The List was not a democracy. Like the law firm, Renny was a peon, not an equal partner who participated in the decision-making process. A peon with a sore head.

It hurt to look outside, and Renny sat with his back to a window in the main dining room, positioning himself so he would see Jo come through the door. He distanced himself from Layne and Roget, who were drinking coffee and reading the Charleston newspaper on the other side of the room.

Jo appeared in a short white dress that made her dark hair appear darker and the sunburn from yesterday seem a little redder.

"You look bright and Jamaican this morning," Renny said as he stood to greet her.

"You look like you were hanging on to a palm tree in the middle of the storm last night. What's wrong?" Jo asked.

"Is it that obvious? A horrible headache kept me up off and on all night. I feel lousy."

"Do you want some coffee?"

"No. I think I would do better with juice."

Breakfast was a buffet, and Jo went to the table and poured Renny a large glass of orange juice.

Renny took a couple of swallows and leaned back in his chair. "I could have used Nurse Johnston last night. I have never had a headache so bad in my life. It kept me awake until after four this morning. My father had occasional headaches that knocked him out for a day or two, but I've never had any problem with them until now. I hope I'm not following in his footsteps."

"It may be the result of tension from last night."

"It sure wasn't the booze. I was sober when I went to bed, but I had some crazy dreams."

Before Jo could comment, a waiter came up to the table. "Would you like the buffet?"

Renny looked at Jo. "All I want is another glass or two of this juice."

"I'll do the same. Here, Renny, let me get you another glass."

Jo poured a glass for Renny and herself. Renny glanced over to the table where Layne and Roget were sitting. Layne caught his eye and raised his coffee cup with a smile.

Renny didn't know what he thought about Layne. He couldn't figure out how much of his arrogance was show and how much was genuine conceit.

Jo took a sip of juice. "Can I pray for you this morning?"

"Sure. Believe it or not, I prayed for myself last night. I don't have total faith in aspirin."

Jo closed her eyes. Renny looked at her face for a second, then closed his eyes as well.

"Father, I ask you to touch Renny and remove the cause and effects of this headache. In Jesus' name, amen."

Renny started to say, "Is that all?" when he felt a warm tingle flow down the side of his head to his cheeks. The last remaining pressure on his left temple lifted.

"It's gone! I felt a tingle on my head, like warm water, and the pressure and pain left. It worked!"

"Great!" Jo exclaimed.

"Can you do that whenever you want?" Renny asked excitedly. "I can't believe it!"

"I can ask, but I don't always see instant results. When I was getting the juice, I asked God to touch you this morning. I think it's just a token of God's love. He knows your address."

"Removal of pain I can understand." Renny drained his juice glass. "Speaking of addresses, can I have yours?"

"Of course. I'd like yours, too."

Renny wrote his home phone number on the back of one of his business cards. "I've added my landlady's number, too."

"Let me put my phone number on one of your cards." Jo took a card, wrote her number, and handed it back to him.

"I'd like to talk as soon as you get back to Michigan."

"OK. Will you promise me one thing?" Jo asked.

"Up to half my kingdom."

"It's not that demanding, but I think it's important. After the meeting today, contact the lady who helped your family. Now is the time to follow through on what your mother told you before she died."

"I forgot to tell you. There isn't going to be a meeting. I had a brief note from LaRochette this morning telling me the meeting would be rescheduled because of Bart's death. He mentioned the next item of business was the distribution of money."

"Since there's no meeting will you have enough time to go to Charleston?"

"Before you prayed, all I wanted to do was limp back to Charlotte and go to bed. But I feel great, and I agree with you. I need to see Mama A."

10

Whose wealth arithmetic cannot number.
PHILIP MASSINGER

The old desk clerk seemed relieved when Jo returned her room key and paid her bill. Having avoided the embarrassment of the "real" Mr. Joe Taylor Johnston learning that his room had been rented to an impostor, the clerk placed the key back on its numbered hook with satisfaction.

Renny carried Jo's luggage down the stairs to her truck. The sun shot rays through the clouds, and Renny marveled at how quickly a storm could roll in from the ocean then dissipate, leaving the air clear and fresh. He began to look forward to driving south to Charleston.

Climbing the stairs back to Jo's room, he met Gus Eicholtz carrying his bag down the steps.

"Good morning, good morning," he greeted Renny heartily. "I want to see you for a minute before you leave if I can."

"Sure, when and where?"

"I need to put my bags in the car and check out. I'll be in the meeting room in about ten minutes."

"OK. I'll see you then."

Jo had her back to him, partly opening the curtains over the bayside window when he came through her door. A ray of liberated sunlight pierced the gap and shone on her. Renny paused to imprint the scene on his mind. He couldn't believe the change in his feeling and mood between the night before and this glorious morning.

Renny cleared his throat to announce his presence, then asked, "Is that all your luggage?"

"Everything except a tote bag and my beach hat." Jo reached over and took the large straw hat from the bed and positioned it on her head. "I'll take care of it. It will not get a lot of use in the cold, cold North."

Jo grabbed her bag, and Renny closed the door and followed her down the hall.

"I passed Gus Eicholtz on the steps. He said he wanted to talk a minute before he leaves town, so I'm going to meet him in the private dining room as soon as you're on your way."

"I liked him and Bart Maxwell the best. Are you going to ask him some of your questions?"

"I might, but I'll listen to him first. One thing I've learned since all this started is that you can't plan what will happen when the List is involved," Renny said.

"I'm going to contact Dr. Davidson at the hospital in a day or so and try to find out the results of the autopsy."

"I would like to know that myself."

"I'll call you one way or the other."

Renny opened the truck door for Jo, and she climbed into the cab of the big vehicle.

"When you decide to sell your father's truck, I can get you top dollar for it in western North Carolina. There are men who would sell their wife, children, and maybe their favorite hunting dog for a truck like this one."

"I may take you up on that."

Renny didn't want to let go of the door. He stood with his head down, rearranging the crushed seashells of the parking lot with the toe of his shoe.

"Well, bye," he said.

"Thanks for all your help. We'll see each other soon."

Renny shut the door and watched as Jo backed out of the parking space and drove slowly toward the highway. She waved as she rounded the corner of the inn and passed from sight.

———

The door of the dining room was ajar, and Renny pushed it open. Eicholtz was examining an old oil painting on the opposite wall. It was a picture of the inn.

Eicholtz shook Renny's hand. "This is probably what this place looked like when our forefathers first met here. It hasn't changed much."

Renny joined the big man in front of the picture. Sure enough, except for the electric service wires, a fresher coat of paint, and removal of the hitching posts for horses and buggies, the inn was much the same as it had been in 1863.

"The inn hasn't changed much, and neither has the List," Eicholtz said. "But something makes me think change is coming." The big man sat down in a dining room chair and motioned to Renny to take a seat.

"What do you mean?" Renny asked.

"Bart dying in the meeting, the appearance of Ms. Johnston; I feel like we need to check the bolts on the wheels of this wagon."

Renny waited.

Eicholtz shifted in his chair and leaned forward, placing his hands on his knees. "Renny, the List has been run almost like the private property of the LaRochette family. We discuss issues as if we're equals, but the LaRochettes have always controlled everything."

"Mr. LaRochette didn't dominate the discussion," Renny said slowly, not wanting to commit to an opinion until he saw more clearly the direction Eicholtz was steering the conversation.

"We may talk, but almost everyone looks to Desmond when it's time to make a decision. You were a neophyte, so your vote in favor of admitting Ms. Johnston will probably be overlooked. I can't say the same for myself or Bart Maxwell. Of course, now Bart's dead." Eicholtz stopped, and Renny had the distinct impression the older man was internally debating what else to say.

Eicholtz took a deep breath and continued, "Did you try to access some of your family's money once you learned about the List?"

Renny nodded.

"It was frozen, wasn't it? You couldn't even find out an account balance without List approval, correct?"

"Yes. And I intended to raise that in the meeting last night but never had the chance." Renny's palms started to sweat a little.

"That's not unusual. If you had brought it up, you would have been told joint control is standard operating procedure. It ensures that nothing will be lost from the List corpus, the common fund of money from which distributions to each family are made. To get the right to access the money in your account, you have to sign a durable power of attorney that allows the List to reclaim the money from your family's account in case you died childless or became mentally incompetent. Otherwise, because no one knows about the List before his father's death, the money would grow moss in those old Swiss banks. People have questioned the practice in the past, but it was always refuted by the example of Alexander Hammond. Because he died childless, his family's portion of a distribution from the List corpus could have been lost when there was no one to claim it. It was not a large amount when he died in the 1870s, but through use of the durable power of attorney the monies were recovered and placed back in the corpus."

"That means the Johnston and Maxwell money—"

"Will revert back to the List. And unlike the 1870s, we are not talking about a paltry sum. Both Taylor Johnston and Bart Maxwell signed the papers necessary for the List to recoup their funds if they died childless, or as it turns out in Taylor's case, without a son."

"But a power of attorney is ineffective once the person who signed it is dead."

Eicholtz shrugged. "Who tells the foreign bank the person has died?"

"But, but, that's fraud."

"Self-preservation, my boy, self-preservation. It's the bedrock motivation of the List."

Renny tried a different tack. "What would prevent someone from withdrawing all their money before their death and transferring it to another account?"

"Remember, all withdrawals have to be the result of joint activity by the individual and the List. Everybody plays by the rules because he either doesn't care or is afraid to rock the boat."

"If someone tried to jump ship, the List might refuse to authorize a distribution or withdrawal?"

"Potentially, although as far as I know it has never happened. There have not been as many withdrawals as you might think. All of the families weathered Reconstruction with modest help from the List. After that, I think the ruling LaRochette decided to see how large the money tree could grow. With the advent of the income tax in the U.S. after World War I, everyone saw the List as a way to accumulate tax-free wealth, safe from the federal government's greedy clutches.

"I talked about the control issue with your father before he died. He and I were getting old and cranky enough to think about attempting to change the process. I also mentioned it to Bart after last year's meeting, and he was interested in reforming the procedures."

"What about Jo's father?"

"I never contacted him, but your father and I discussed talking to him."

Renny decided to pop the question burning in his mind since listening to the tape from his father. "How much money is in the corpus of the List?"

With a sigh, Eicholtz said, "Of course you want to know. Normally that is not discussed until the new member signs the durable power of attorney. That will be the next step for you in the overall process. It's like the proverbial carrot on the stick; they keep something out there to lead you down the designated path. However, as my first act of independence and rebellion…"

Eicholtz picked up a cocktail napkin and pulled out his pen. He put a dollar sign on the napkin followed by a twenty-five and eight zeros.

"Two and half billion dollars!" Renny was staggered. "How?"

"Compound interest. We've profited on wars, revolutions, and depressions for almost 150 years. That's another one of LaRochette's strong cards, an uncanny ability to hit an occasional home run in the investment market. Roget is treasurer in name only. He does what Desmond tells him to do."

"Is there an investment committee?"

"Yes, but I've never been on it, another fact that concerns me."

"Only LaRochette knows everything that's going on?"

"And whomever he brings into his circle."

"Which is?"

"I don't know for sure. For years I didn't care so long as I received a distribution."

"Understandable." Renny hesitated. "So what would be a typical distribution amount?"

"That has varied. Remember that the List was set up to accumulate money to survive hard times, and there is a kind of paranoia that keeps the vast majority of the funds in the corpus account. Did you notice no one responded in a positive way to my comment last night that we ought to accept the charming Ms. Johnston because there was enough money for everyone?"

Renny remembered Jo's comment on the beach, "He who loves money never has money enough."

Eicholtz continued, "To answer your question, last year we discussed a substantial distribution, but Desmond tabled any motions until this year. I would hope for a distribution of at least twenty-five million each, with a right to withdraw as much as we wanted from our individual accounts."

"I could use an extra twenty-five million," Renny said, shaking his head in disbelief.

"I would ask you to think about the other parts of our conversation as well."

After hearing the amounts of money involved, Renny was already having trouble remembering what Eicholtz had said before writing the astronomical figure on the napkin.

"What do you want me to think about?" he said, a little distantly.

"I've lost you, boy, haven't I?" Eicholtz said with resignation. "Maybe I shouldn't have told you about the pot of gold. Oh, well, we'll reconvene this meeting after you have time to come down to earth. Remember, the pot of gold at the end of the rainbow is an elusive prize. As far as I know, no one has actually found it. Do you want to continue this conversation later?"

"Sure. I need to learn all I can." Renny brought his focus back to the room. "I don't have a post office box in Charlotte yet. Here's my card."

The big man heaved himself out of the chair and patted Renny on the shoulder. "I like you, Renny. I also like Ms. Johnston. She was like a fresh breeze that hasn't blown through this room in many moons. Let me give you some fatherly advice. A girl like her is worth pursuing. Contrary to popular opinion, all women are not alike."

Renny rose to his feet. "You're right. I've never met anyone quite like her."

As Renny followed Eicholtz out into the hall, the door to the kitchen closed slowly with a creak.

11

Who knows what prayers offered in faith
by those who have gone before us are yet unanswered.

Iain Murray

Within fifteen minutes, Renny was on the road to Charleston. Driving south along the coastal highway, he occasionally caught a glimpse of the ocean, but even when it was out of sight, he knew the water was just past the trees or on the other side of a line of sand dunes. In the air was the faint but pungent smell of salt water. Renny loved the Low Country.

It took an hour to reach the outskirts of Charleston. Renny put his mind in neutral, not thinking about anything but the sights of the roadway. For the first thirty minutes he read each billboard as it flashed by the windshield.

When he crossed into Charleston County, he pulled into the parking lot of a fishing tackle and bait store where there was a pay phone with a tattered Charleston phone book hanging by a steel cable. Thumbing through the white pages, he found the listings for Flowers. Mama A's husband, Clarence, had died over ten years before and she used her initials, A. D., for Agnes Darlene, in her phone book listing. He wrote the number on a slip of paper and called from his car phone.

A familiar voice crackled on the other end of the line. "Hello."

"Mama A, this is Renny."

"Why hello, Renny. Where are you?"

"I'm on Highway 17 coming into Charleston. I wondered if I could come by and see you."

"Of course. I decided not to go to church today, so I guess I was just here a-waitin' for you to call."

Renny had forgotten it was Sunday morning. Normally, Mama A would leave the house at nine and not return until midafternoon. Meetings at her church were not run on a tight schedule, and she often ate lunch with someone after the church service was over.

Renny glanced at his watch. "I should be there in about twenty-five minutes."

"Good. I look forward to seeing you, son."

"Bye."

Mama A lived in a small white house built in the 1940s. Renny's father had financed the house for Clarence and Mama A when they purchased it shortly after Mama A began working for Renny's family. Clarence worked on the docks at the Port of Charleston, and they paid off the debt to Renny's father two years ahead of schedule. H. L. respected Clarence Flowers—but from a distance. For their generation, the racial gulf was still unbridged except along narrowly defined points of contact.

Clarence and Mama A had two sons and one daughter, all of whom were several years older than Renny. Renny liked their youngest daughter, Julia, the best. In fact, it was Julia who gave him his name. When he was just three years old, Julia, who was thirteen, came with her mother to the Jacobson house in the summertime to help with looking after the little boy. Mama A would make wonderful home-cooked meals for them each night, but finicky little Josiah would just pick at his food. "Eat, little bird," Julia would tease. "You just like a little Carolina wren, boy, peckin' that way at your food. Come on, little wren, eat some o' these peas." Eventually Julia's teasing turned into a full-fledged nickname and everyone came to call Josiah Jacobson "Renny."

Many nights, after playing outside all day, Julia would make the two of them real lemonade. No one could make lemonade like Julia. She squeezed the lemons by hand and knew exactly how much sugar to add without making it too sweet. After they enjoyed a cool refreshment out on the veranda, she would read to him. Julia read with expression and feeling, changing her voice for different characters in the story. It was as good as an old-time radio drama.

When Renny was twelve, Clarence died after suffering a massive stroke. His funeral was one of Renny's most vivid childhood memories. At the time, the Flowers family belonged to an A.M.E. church, which Renny later learned stood for African Methodist Episcopal. The A.M.E. was nothing like St. Alban's Episcopal in downtown Charleston. The two groups were as similar as ham hocks and filet mignon. Each church had its liturgy and protocol, but to an uninitiated observer it would be hard to place the two approaches to Christian worship on the same planet. During the funeral, three matronly ladies dressed in white did nothing but fan Mama A and Clarence's three sisters. The first man who spoke eulogized Clarence for half an hour. Amazed at the power of the man's oratory, Renny thought he was the preacher, but he turned out to be one of Clarence's coworkers from the docks. Clarence's younger brother followed the dock worker and spoke for forty-five minutes. It was a muggy, overcast day, but toward the end of the brother's remarks about the reality of Clarence's faith, a shaft of sunlight pierced the clouds and shot a beam of light onto the wooden casket. Several people shouted "Glory" and "Hallelujah." Renny had to admit it was high drama with visual effects from another realm. The preacher spoke for an hour. By the time he finished it was so hot Renny would have given a week's allowance for one of the fans used by the ladies in white.

Because her children were all out of the house by the time Clarence died, Mama A worked an extra day each week for Renny's family and, in a way, became his mother's best friend during the years prior to her death. For them, the racial gulf was not a canyon; it was a narrow ditch they could easily step across at any point.

Mama A lived in a predominantly black residential neighborhood not far from downtown Charleston. People were sitting on their front porches or front steps as Renny entered the area. Several groups of younger children playing in the street scattered at the sound of Renny's approach, then stared wide-eyed when he drove by in the fancy sports car.

Renny had spoken to Mama A for a few minutes at his father's funeral. Before that, he had last seen her when he graduated from college. She and Julia, who was married with two children, came by the Isle of Palms house with a graduation present before he left to start law school. Mama A had made Renny his favorite dessert, a graham cracker cake topped with a brown sugar icing that was a quarter-inch thick. As a child, Renny remembered savoring every bite, rolling it around in his mouth until it dissolved. To reciprocate, Renny found a couple of his old children's books as gifts for Julia's children.

Renny pulled into Mama A's driveway and parked behind her aging white Oldsmobile. As he walked past the old car Renny saw a cushion strategically positioned in the driver's seat so the five-foot-one Mama A could see over the dashboard. He knocked loudly on the white wooden door.

"Come in, come in," Mama A said as she opened the door. In her late sixties, a little overweight with graying hair, a happily wrinkled face, and sparkling dark eyes, Mama A wore a loose-fitting, faded blue seersucker housedress.

Leaning over, Renny gave her a quick hug and followed her through the small foyer to a combination dining room and den to the left of the front door.

"Sit down where it's cool and comfortable," Mama A said.

A window-unit air conditioner hummed in the background. Pictures of children and grandchildren covered an entire wall.

"Do you have any new grandchildren?" Renny asked as he scanned the gallery.

"As a matter of fact, I have one so new she doesn't have a picture on the wall yet. Joe and his wife have a brand-new daughter named Amber Nicole. She's two weeks old today."

It would be joyful chaos when Mama A's brood crowded into the small house. Renny settled back in the chair and stretched his legs.

"Did you get together on the Fourth of July?" he asked.

"Of course we did. This past Fourth we had twenty-four people here. I wish you could have tasted the ribs my brother Garner cooked on the grill."

"Don't torture me," Renny begged.

Though it was almost exclusively a Flowers family affair, Renny twice participated in the Fourth of July event. Besides the food, the highlight for Renny was a softball game at a schoolyard a couple of blocks away. Everyone from age six up played. Mama A served as all-time catcher, encouraging players on both teams as they came up to bat.

"Would you like some lemonade?" Mama A asked. "And I have some leftover ham for a sandwich and some sweet potato casserole from supper last night."

Renny hadn't realized it was lunchtime until she mentioned the food.

"Do you have plenty for yourself?"

"Plenty for both of us. And I made a fresh graham cracker cake this mornin'. We can have some for dessert."

"You're kidding!" Renny exclaimed. "Are you sure I didn't call you yesterday instead of half an hour ago?"

Mama A didn't answer as she got up and went to the kitchen. "You stay there. I know how you like your sandwich. I'll be back in a minute."

Renny slid down farther in the chair and looked up at the ceiling. It was creased with tiny cracks in the plaster that looked like a map of the interstate highway system. He had identified I-40, I-85, and I-75 by the time Mama A came back into the room carrying his plate and drink.

"There's a TV tray behind your chair. You can put your food on it while I get my plate from the kitchen."

"Thanks, this looks great."

Mama A settled into her chair and arranged her food. "Let's bless the food, Renny," she said.

Renny bowed his head, but kept his eyes open to watch the elderly lady as she prayed.

"Thank you, Lord. You are always good and always wise. Bless Renny and this food. In Jesus' name. Amen and amen."

Watching Mama A, Renny concluded she looked a lot like Jo when she prayed. Same friendly way of talking to the Almighty.

He took a bite of sandwich. "This is perfect." The sweet potato casserole, topped with pecans and brown sugar, was equally good. "I bet this casserole is better warmed up than it was last night."

They ate in silence. As the minutes passed, Renny began to unwind from the stress of the weekend.

Mama A broke the stillness when she finished her sandwich. "What brings you to Charleston?" she asked.

"I was in Georgetown for some business related to my father's estate. I met with Jefferson McClintock, the lawyer, a week or so ago, but needed to come back to take care of some additional matters in Georgetown."

"Is everything OK?"

"Yes, but while walking on the beach at Pawley's Island yesterday, I remembered a conversation I had with my mother shortly before she died. She told me I needed to come see you after she was gone."

"What about?"

"It was after she lost normal use of her voice. She was able to communicate in an amazing way with me one day and told me to ask you about my grandfather. I had forgotten about it until the other day."

Mama A slid her tray back and slowly pushed herself up from the chair. "Wait here. I'll be back in a minute."

Renny could hear her opening doors and drawers in her bedroom. He finished his sandwich and was rolling the first bite of graham cracker cake around his mouth with his tongue when she returned.

"Here they are. I think this is all," she said, putting two old manila envelopes and a small, tattered, leather Bible down beside his chair. The metal clasps on the envelopes had rusted and streaked the faded yellow paper.

Renny opened the Bible and saw his mother's name neatly printed on the dedication page and his grandfather's name underneath it with the date of the gift. His grandfather had given it to her when she was about twelve years old.

"A gift Bible from my grandfather to my mother. Do you know what is in the envelopes?" Renny asked.

"I never opened them. You can see they are sealed, probably by your mother. Just like you, I was alone with her one mornin' near the end, and she was able to talk with me in a way I can only explain as the hand of God. She told me your grandfather had a vision or dream about you before you was born, gave me these envelopes, and asked me to save them for you until you asked about him."

Renny was mystified. "Why didn't she just give the information to me directly? It seems there was a risk involved if I hadn't decided to come by and see you."

"The Lord works things out accordin' to the pattern of his will and that don't always make sense to our common sense. It seems to me the important thing is that you're here now, right?"

"Yes."

"Then, I'd guess it had to do with timin'. You may need this information now in a way that you didn't before."

"OK," he said. "Let's have a look."

Mama A got up to leave.

"No, please stay. You have a part in this, and I may need to ask you a question."

"That's fine," she said, taking a bite of cake.

Renny picked up the envelopes. Turning them over, he recognized his mother's handwriting. The thinner of the two was addressed "To Josiah." On the thicker one, his mother had written "Daddy's Papers."

Renny pulled open the seal of the envelope addressed to him. The glue was so old and dry that the flap easily gave way to his tug. Reaching inside, he pulled out two sheets of unlined paper. It was a letter dated five years before his mother's death, about the time she first learned she might have Lou Gehrig's disease. Her handwriting was not as small and precise as it was before she became ill, but it was still easy to read.

Dear Renny,

I have said prayers for you that I believe will be answered after my death. Your reading this letter is one of them.

It is a difficult thing to entrust this message to the future. It has been a great step of faith, but I know you will read this when you are ready for it and not before. I wanted more than you know to talk to you about these things while I was alive, but everything has to be done in the fullness of time as God defines it.

Your life has a purpose ordained by God. The fact that you have come to Agnes is proof that you are looking for the right path. This letter and the papers from my father may help you.

Before you were born, your grandfather told your father and me that you would be a boy and asked us to name you Josiah. Knowing he had at least a fifty-fifty chance of guessing right, your father and I didn't think much about his prediction, and because Josiah is a Jacobson family name your father agreed to it. You were born after a difficult delivery.

I've never fully understood the reason behind your grandfather's request regarding your name, but you can read about your namesake, King Josiah, in the Old Testament. According to your grandfather, he believed the life of King Josiah would be a source of God's direction for you.

I know this probably sounds unusual and strange to you, but there is more to life than we can see with our natural eyes or know with our finite minds. Please ask God to lead you.

My prayers for you live on after I'm gone.

I love you,
Mother

Renny handed the letter to Mama A. "Read this." It was Renny's turn to wait. He could picture his mother sitting at her cherry writing table with its straight thin legs in the bedroom of their home, writing a letter she prayed he would read someday. It was hard to fathom. But here he was, just as she'd hoped and prayed. He waited until Mama A handed the pages back to him. "Why did she write this?" he asked.

"I don't know, except that she wanted you to know about your birth and name."

"But couldn't she have told me?"

"I suppose, but that gets back to the question of timin'. I suspect you're more able to appreciate this information now than when you were a teenager."

"I guess so. Still, I don't…" Renny folded the letter and put it back in the envelope.

Mama A continued, "You'll need to read the story of King Josiah yourself, but he was a boy king who rediscovered the Book of the Law and brought the nation of Israel back to the Lord. He also fulfilled a prophecy by destroyin' a pagan altar at a place called Bethel."

"Well, things get more complicated every time you hope they are going to get simpler," Renny said.

Mama A nodded. "But if we walk with the Lord, most things get worked out in the end."

"I hope so."

Mama A picked up her plate. "Do you want another piece of cake?"

"No thanks."

"I'll wrap up a piece for you to have later."

While Mama A was in the kitchen, Renny picked up the other envelope and started to break the seal, but stopped, deciding to wait until he was alone.

Mama A handed him the cake.

"I'll read the papers from my grandfather later. Thanks for . . . for everything," Renny didn't know where to start thanking her. "I need to get on the road to Charlotte. I'll call you soon."

"You call or come anytime, day or night."

Renny picked up the Bible and the two envelopes.

"Bye, Mama A."

"The Lord bless you. Thanks for comin' by."

Agnes chuckled to herself as the screen door slammed behind Renny. She watched through the front window as he backed his car into the street and drove away. The chuckle blossomed into a laugh as she threw back her head and let the joy flow through her. It was the joy of the Spirit bubbling up from within, a joy known only by those who have the opportunity to participate with heaven in the unfolding of the divine plan for a precious life. No, God wasn't up there anxiously wringing his hands, hoping everything was going to be all right. He was a confident Father who enjoyed watching the adventure of life. "Yes," she said aloud, "he knows the end from the beginning, the Alpha from the Omega."

Agnes wasn't surprised by Renny's visit. She had seen him in the night; whether in a dream or vision, it didn't really matter to her. He appeared to her, walking into a woodland clearing in the moonless darkness before sunrise. But he was not alone. Clarence was with him. The two men stopped, talked a moment, and Clarence pointed toward a path on the other side of the opening. Renny hesitated. There were other paths out of the clearing, and the young man was not sure which one he wanted to take. She left him there, not knowing his choice. Half-awake, she looked at her clock. It was 3:21 A.M., but to her blurred vision it looked like 30:21. Shaking herself fully awake, a familiar verse dropped into her consciousness, "This is the way, walk ye in it." Flicking on the table lamp she found it. It was Isaiah 30:21. Then she knew; Renny was searching for direction and needed to hear from God.

Whenever Clarence appeared to her, Agnes knew the call to prayer was serious. Shortly after Clarence died, a five-year-old girl from the neighborhood was abducted from a local playground. Agnes learned about the kidnapping through a phone call from a lady in her church. Filled with concern, Mama A went to her back porch to rock and seek the Lord's mercy for the child. Her head bowed as she prayed, she heard a noise and looked up. It was Clarence standing on the back step. He looked steadily into her eyes and said, "Pray Matthew 16:19, Agnes," and was gone. Grabbing her Bible, she read, "And I will give unto thee the keys of the kingdom of heaven: and whatsoever thou shalt bind on earth shall be bound in heaven: and whatsoever thou shalt loose on earth shall be loosed in heaven."

Holding up her Bible, she shouted, "Thank you, Lord!" Then she prayed aloud, binding the evil and releasing the good. On the evening news that night, a TV reporter described how the little girl escaped when the kidnapper's car stalled at a traffic light in front of a convenience store. The child hopped out of the car and ran into the store. Driving away at a high speed, her abductor hit a telephone pole and was captured.

Mama A kept the back porch encounter to herself, and, after studying the Scriptures, decided she probably saw an angel appearing in a form familiar and friendly to her. On two subsequent occasions, one involving a friend with throat cancer and another involving a marriage with potential for serious domestic violence, Clarence appeared in dreams and gave her instructions for intercessory prayer on behalf of others. She prayed: the woman was healed, the marriage restored.

Mama A knew the battle for Renny had been long—it took time to bring forth a statue from a block of marble. Thinking back, she calculated the years since Renny's birth. His grandfather had a vision. Katharine had a hope. Now it was Mama A's turn to help bring the promise to fulfillment. Picking up her Bible, she decided to go out on the back porch and rock awhile.

12

If Renny retraced his route through Moncks Corner, he could still be back in Charlotte by supper. A quiet spot in Moncks Corner would be an appropriate place to open the envelope containing his grandfather's papers. It seemed right to read the words in the town where they were written.

Little was stirring in downtown Moncks Corner on a hot Sunday afternoon. Renny drove through the town square and turned onto a side street that passed in front of his grandfather's former home. Two stories tall with a broad wraparound porch and a trio of enormous oak trees shading the front yard, the white frame house peacefully surveyed the street. There were no cars in the driveway, and Renny parked in the shade alongside the curb.

Breaking the seal on the envelope, he slid out several sheets of crinkled onionskin paper covered with neat blue handwriting.

There were three poems, a sheet with Bible verses on it, a genealogy of the Candler family, and a page entitled "The Promise—Josiah," dated January in the year of his birth:

I have been praying for ten years that Katharine would be able to conceive and deliver a child. There has been tremendous resistance. She called this morning with the news that she is once again pregnant.

After spending some time waiting on the Lord, I was impressed to turn to 1 Kings 13—the promise of Josiah. I believe she will have a successful pregnancy and deliver a boy with a Josiah call on his life. I claim this promise in advance for this tiny life today. Lord, bless my grandson. It will be so. Amen!

Tears welled in Renny's eyes, forcing their way through blinking eyelids. A soft, tender spot deep inside, a place he didn't know existed, was touched by the thought of a man rejoicing over his life, calling him "my grandson," and blessing his future before Renny drew his first breath. Wiping his eyes with the back of his hand, he looked up at the house and felt a link with his grandfather in the stillness of the quiet afternoon; a connection with the past that in some way held importance for the days and years to come.

Carefully placing the papers back in the envelope, he started the car and drove slowly down the street. At the corner, he saw a small sign pointing the way toward the Methodist church where the Candler family worshiped and the cemetery where several of his relatives, including his grandfather, were buried.

Located one block from the town square, Moncks Corner Free Methodist Church was established in 1756. The original sanctuary, made from red-clay bricks molded by slaves on nearby plantations, had a slender spirelike steeple and steeply pitched slate roof. Narrow stained-glass windows with pointed tops lined each side of the building like sentinels. Today, a large, modern sanctuary obscured from view the older structure, which was used primarily for weddings and more intimate church functions.

It was midafternoon, so the Sunday-morning crowd had gone home to dinner and a nap. The main church parking lot was empty as Renny pulled up to the entrance of the older building. *It's probably locked, but worth a try,* he thought.

To his surprise, the dark wooden door opened smoothly when he pulled the brass handle. The interior of the church was cool and dark, and he paused to let his eyes adjust. It had the smell of old wood, well oiled and polished. The stained-glass windows, six on each side, were magnificent, each depicting one of the twelve apostles with his name across the bottom. St. Paul took the place of the fallen Judas Iscariot. Renny walked slowly down the center aisle, admiring the wide variety of light and color that only expertly crafted stained glass could produce. Remembering how dull the windows looked from the outside, Renny marveled at the beauty and detailed artistry revealed within the sanctuary. Hearing a creaking board, he turned and saw an old man with a cane come in from a side door to the left of the first pew.

"Hello, sir," Renny said, hoping the elderly gentleman wouldn't be startled by his presence.

The man squinted through rimless glasses and smiled. "Good afternoon. I hope I didn't disturb you."

"I was admiring the windows."

"They're beautiful, aren't they? They were made in Charleston and patterned after larger versions in a cathedral in France. Pretty fancy for small-town Methodists."

"They're magnificent." Renny covered the distance between them in a few strides and extended his hand. "I'm Renny Jacobson."

"Michael Harriston," he responded with a firm handshake.

"Are you the church historian?"

"Some might say so. I've been in this church for many years, and you pick up a lot by osmosis if you stay around a place long enough."

"Then you would probably remember my mother and her father, Katharine and Nathaniel Candler."

"Sure do. Is your mother still in Charleston?"

"No, she died several years ago. I'm on my way back to Charlotte and decided to visit my grandfather's grave."

"Have you been to the graveyard?"

"Not yet."

"Do you know where he's buried?"

"Not really. He died when I was a little boy, and I haven't been here in years. All I know is that he attended this church and his grave is in the cemetery."

"Come with me. I can take you right to it."

Without waiting for an answer, Mr. Harriston walked across the front of the sanctuary. A narrow door opened into a small hallway which led to a tiny study containing a single wooden chair and a small writing table.

He stopped. "In the old days, this was where the ministers always prayed before going in to begin the service. It was a way to remind them of their continuous need to rely on God."

Renny peered into the plainly furnished little room before following the old man again.

"What can you tell me about my grandfather?" he asked as they stepped into the blinding sunlight.

Mr. Harriston put on a white cloth garden hat as they walked toward the cemetery. "He was a generous man. Easy to meet and friendly. Much like you, I would suppose."

No one had ever compared Renny to his grandfather.

Mr. Harriston continued, "It's obvious you have some of his physical gestures; the way you walk and move reminds me of him."

The cemetery was open without a surrounding fence or definite boundary line. Within a few steps of the first marker, tombstones of various sizes and designs surrounded them. The older graves were close to the church, the ancient markers thin and streaked in black. Mr. Harriston zigzagged his way along paths obviously familiar to him.

Then he stopped, removed his hat, and wiped his forehead with a red bandanna he had pulled from his pocket. "Here is the Candler plot."

There were several simple markers, the oldest a small, black-streaked slab. Renny leaned over to read the inscription:

Amos Candler
June 5, 1800–April 12, 1875
Though dead, he speaks.

"I left the Candler genealogy in the car. Is he a direct ancestor?"

"Let's see." Mr. Harriston counted on his fingers. "Amos Candler was your great-great-grandfather, the first Candler to settle in this area."

Nearby was a more modern marker: Nathaniel Candler, January 20, 1905–August 26, 1982. Next to him was his wife: Marie Candler, October 15, 1904–April 24, 1971. A sprig of fresh-cut flowers in a small glass vase balanced on top of the marker. This was the resting place of Renny's grandparents.

"Did the church put the flowers on the grave?" Renny asked.

"I did," Harriston said with a small smile. "Today is August 26, the anniversary of Nathaniel Candler's death."

Renny's mouth dropped open. "Thank you. I didn't know that. I've been living more day-to-day than paying attention to the date."

"Nothing wrong with that."

"So, were you good friends?"

"We were close for a number of years." Mr. Harriston stepped next to Renny and shaded his pale blue eyes from the sun's glare with his left hand. "I do a little something every year. Your grandfather is where he belongs. He was as fit for heaven as anyone who ever set foot in Moncks Corner. He lived life to the fullest by giving of himself to the fullest."

"That's what I've been told before."

They stood in silence, Renny wishing for memories, Mr. Harriston enjoying some.

"I'm going back to the church for a minute," Mr. Harriston said, mopping his brow again. "You take your time."

"No, I'm done. I'll walk back with you." Renny felt closer to his grandfather with Mr. Harriston than he did without him.

The cool interior was a true sanctuary from the heat. "Have a seat," the old man offered. They sat down on the front pew.

"Your grandfather always sat on the end of the pew behind where we are today. He's probably looking over our shoulders right now."

"How's that?" Renny asked, not sure if the old gentleman was joking or serious.

Gazing upward toward the narrow arch of the ceiling, he said, "He's part of the great cloud of witnesses mentioned in Hebrews 12:1, the crowd in the grandstand of heaven."

Renny followed his gaze, but saw nothing. "That's an unsettling thought," he said, not at all sure he liked this notion. He did a quick inventory of a few things he'd done and places he'd gone that he hoped no one knew about, much less a great cloud of witnesses.

"Only if you have something to hide, which, of course, all people do," the old man said with a wrinkled smile. "But I like to think of the positive side. There is a vast throng cheering you on to victory. Like a home crowd at a football game."

"I can imagine that, I guess," Renny said, accepting the metaphor. Turning in the pew, he asked, "If my grandfather were here, what would he be yelling from the grandstand?"

"Given our surroundings and your short pilgrimage, as you described it, I think he would be shouting, 'Pray, Renny, Pray!'"

Before leaving Charlotte to come to Georgetown, Renny would not have seriously considered Mr. Harriston's suggestion. But Jo and Mama A had softened up the beachhead of his resistance to spiritual activities like prayer.

"That's something I honestly don't know much about."

Mr. Harriston pointed toward an altar rail supported by dark wooden spindles that spanned the front of the church. A narrow purple kneeling cushion was slightly raised above the level of the wooden floor of the church.

"Your grandfather would often leave his pew and go to the altar for prayer," he said, pointing to a place to the right of the Communion table. "I suggest we go there, too."

Offering no resistance, Renny followed Mr. Harriston to the designated spot and knelt beside him. All his senses heightened a notch, and instead of being distracted by the unusual setting, he became focused. "Would you pray?" he asked.

"Certainly, but I suggest you make my prayer your prayer." Mr. Harriston began in a soft voice, which increased in authority and volume as his prayer continued. "Lord, you are the God of Abraham, Isaac, Jacob, and Nathaniel Candler. All are alive to you. I pray now for Josiah Jacobson and ask you to meet him in his pilgrimage. Bring into his life the full blessings and promises of his grandfather and others in his family line, and break every curse or influence that would hinder him from knowing you and walking in his God-ordained purpose. Answer every prayer uttered on his behalf before he was born and cause every good thing you desire for him to come to pass. In Jesus' name. Amen."

The prayer filled the small sanctuary, and Renny felt his own soul fill with something he could not identify or label. It was similar to what happened outside his grandfather's house but without the tears. As he heard phrases in the prayer similar to words in his mother's letter and grandfather's papers, he bowed his head lower. When Mr. Harriston said, "Amen," Renny didn't stir or lift his head, not wanting to come back too quickly from the place where the prayer took him. After several moments he raised his head to thank Mr. Harriston and ask him how he knew his name was Josiah.

Mr. Harriston was gone.

Renny, still on his knees, glanced quickly around the church. The sanctuary was empty. Getting up from his grandfather's place at the altar rail, he went to the side door where Mr. Harriston had first entered, the floor creaking with each step Renny took. The door opened into a short hall with a room on either side. One room was filled with choir robes, music folders, and costumes for the church Nativity play; the other room had boxes of Sunday school material and a couple of chalkboards. No Mr. Harriston.

Back in the sanctuary, Renny shook his head. The old fellow was either very light on his feet or he flew out of there. Walking up the aisle past the apostles, Renny looked up and down each pew to see where Mr. Harriston was hiding. Seeing no one, he made his way to the back of the church, pushed open the heavy door, and stepped into the sunlight.

13

But when he was yet a great way off, his father saw him.

LUKE 15:20, KJV

Renny cracked open the kitchen door and stepped inside. "Mrs. Stokes, it's me."

Brandy came skidding around the corner to greet him.

"I'm leaving you too much, aren't I, girl?" Renny held his dog's head and scratched behind her ears.

"Did you have a good trip?" Mrs. Stokes followed Brandy at a more sedate pace from the den.

"Good? Honestly, I couldn't summarize it in one word, but it's good to be back with you and Brandy."

Brandy barked, and Renny corrected himself, "I mean Brandy and you."

"Have you had supper? I thought you might want some home cooking after eating out all weekend, so I saved you a plate."

Renny hadn't stopped to eat on the drive back. He used the time alone in the car to mull over bits and pieces of all that had occurred since leaving Charlotte for Georgetown. "Anything would be great."

"You wash up, and I'll get it ready."

Three minutes later Mrs. Stokes placed a plate of meat loaf, carrots, and green beans on the table in front of Renny.

"Oh yes, you had a phone call about an hour ago from a young woman named Jo Johnston. She asked me to tell you that she was in southern Ohio and hoped to be home by late tonight."

"Someone I met this weekend in Georgetown," Renny said between a mouthful of meat loaf and carrots. "You'd like her. She's a nurse at a hospital in Michigan, but probably ought to follow in your steps as a missionary."

"Really? I liked her over the phone."

"Did Brandy behave?" Renny asked, rubbing the dog's neck with his foot as she lay at his feet beside his chair. He didn't want to answer too many questions about his weekend.

"More civilized on our walks. We had a long talk, and she agreed not to jerk my arm so hard if I would take an extra lap around the campus."

Renny ate while Mrs. Stokes gave a detailed account of her time with the dog. "She tried to chase down some wild geese that landed on the lawn in front of the administration building at the college. I told her it's not good manners to retrieve live birds."

"Good advice, Brandy. You could get your head pecked."

Fortunately, the Georgetown trip wasn't mentioned again. Renny didn't want to sort out what he could and could not say.

"Thanks, Mrs. Stokes. I'm going upstairs."

"Here's your mail."

Renny took the handful of envelopes and magazines up the steps to the apartment.

After letting Brandy inside, he brought up his luggage. He thought about the handsome old trunk. Where was it tonight? Probably locked up in the bowels of LaRochette's castle.

———

Tuesday evening he called Jo. An unfamiliar female voice answered the phone. "Hello."

"Yes. This is Renny Jacobson. May I please speak to Jo?"

"She's on her shift at the hospital until eleven, but I'll tell her you called. This is her mother."

"Hello, Mrs. John—" Renny stumbled. He didn't know her last name.

"Carol Edwards. Jo said you might call."

"Thanks, Mrs. Edwards. I'll be up when Jo gets home, or she can call me tomorrow at work."

"I'll tell her."

The phone rang as Letterman finished his monologue. Renny didn't dare tell Aunt Margaret he divided his late-night viewing between Leno and Letterman. She would have considered it talk-show infidelity.

"Hey, Renny, it's me."

"Hello, me." Renny aimed the remote at the TV and vaporized Letterman. "Thanks for calling. Are you tired?"

"No more than usual. I finally recovered from my Georgetown trip lag this morning."

"Good."

"Did you visit your mother's friend?"

"Yes."

"And?"

"It was, uh, interesting."

"Is that all?"

"No, I also went back to Moncks Corner and visited my grand-father's church and spent a few minutes in front of his house."

"How was that?"

"It was unusual."

Jo laughed. "I feel like we're communicating in a chat room on the Internet and you can only type in eight words at a time. At this point I would type LOL and ask you to go into a private room for some mean-ingful communication."

"Good idea," Renny said quickly. "I have a plan to improve our com-munication. I want to buy you a plane ticket to Charlotte as soon as you have some days off work. You can stay with Mrs. Stokes downstairs. She's a retired missionary, and you two are like bookends. Once you're here, we can play twenty questions to our hearts' content."

"LOL. I think that would be better than prying you open one sardine at a time. I have three days off beginning next Thursday, but I'll take care of the plane ticket."

"Great. I mean great that you can come, not that you'll buy your own ticket." Renny kicked the sofa and wished he didn't sound like such an airhead. "Let me at least pay half of the ticket. I can get a good deal through the travel agency used by the law firm."

"OK, that's fine."

"I may have to work some, but I'll try to get in some extra hours before you come, and I'll talk to Mrs. Stokes tomorrow."

"You haven't asked her yet?"

"No, but she'll say yes."

"Let me know if there's a problem."

"I'll call about the ticket tomorrow."

"I'll work late the night before, so don't make it too early."

"OK. By the way, what does LOL mean?" Renny asked.

"Laughing out loud."

"Oh. I'll call you tomorrow or leave word with your mom about the flight."

"Or you could send me an e-mail. Here's my address."

"Got it." Renny wrote her Internet address on a notepad he kept by the phone.

"I've never been to Charlotte. How's the barbecue?"

"Available by the ton."

"I may be craving it by next week."

"No problem. A craving is completely natural. Once you've eaten good Southern barbecue, the body requires a regular refill. You're hooked for life."

"Well, I need to get some sleep."

"Bye."

Renny was slightly disappointed as he hung up the phone. He had hoped LOL stood for lots of love.

———

The next day, Renny was in his office reviewing loan documents for a shopping center renovation when he received a call.

"Line three. Says it's important and won't give me a straight answer about who he is."

Renny picked up the receiver and said, "Hello, Morris."

"Hey, hey, hey, you are still smarter than the average bear."

"Drop the Yogi Bear imitation. You do a better Fred Flintstone."

"I disagree, but you can't hurt my feelings. Do you want to steal a pic-a-nik basket in about forty-five minutes?"

"Sure."

"I've been researching the Swiss banking system night and day since last week. My consultation fee is going to be in the thousands, or I'll settle for a double order of onion rings at my namesake."

"You're on."

Renny arrived at the restaurant first. He cracked open a handful of peanuts and threw the shells in Morris's seat while waiting for his friend to arrive. Morris slid into the booth with a crunch.

"If we shared a real cell, I'd make you clean it twice a day," Morris said as he knocked the shells onto the floor.

"If we shared a cell, I'd take the top bunk and hang my feet in front of your nose at least four hours a day. What can you tell me about the Swiss?"

"All business, I see. Well, as you know from the newspapers, Congress and some Jewish groups here and overseas are holding a mirror in front of Swiss financiers, and the reflection is not rosy cheeks and fair hair."

"That's limited to the Holocaust issue, isn't it?"

"Mostly, but I would think they would be more willing to disclose information to family members following a death than ever before. They want to prove they are aboveboard when, in fact, they probably have a lot of loot stashed under the boards."

"What do you suggest?"

"Here's where I earn my onion rings. We have a financial contact in

Bern who advises us from time to time. I mentioned your situation to Mr. Thompson without telling him your name and asked him to help. He made a call and cleared the way for me to speak with Herr Born, an independent Swiss banking consultant. The Swiss man's English is perfect, and he said, 'Perhaps I could be of assistance to your associate.' Here's his number." Morris handed Renny a slip of paper. "It's worth a try."

"Thanks. Tell Mr. Thompson thanks, too."

———

He took a break from paperwork about four and called a travel agent for Jo's ticket. Logging on to his computer, he sent Jo an e-mail phrased like an old-time telegram.

> Jo. Stop. Have ticket. Stop. Leave Lansing 11:00 A.M. Arrive Charlotte via Detroit at 2:40 P.M. Electronic ticket at USAirways counter. Stop. Renny. Stop. I mean, go. I mean, come.

Renny went in to work at 4:00 A.M. Saturday morning and didn't leave until 5:00 P.M. Mentally exhausted, he decided to go for a long run. With Brandy on a leash, he ran through the tree-lined neighborhoods of south Charlotte. As his feet hit the concrete sidewalk, inner tension oozed out like the sweat that soon soaked his shirt. It was an hour before he slowed and walked the final block home. He and Brandy panted in unison as they climbed the stairs to his apartment.

There was a message on his answering machine from Jo. After toweling off, he sat down with a quart of Gatorade and dialed her number.

Jo answered, "Hello."

"I got your message. I was out for a run with my dog. What's up? Are you still coming?"

"Yes, it's not about that. I talked earlier today to Dr. Davidson about Bart Maxwell."

"What did he say?"

"They did an autopsy. Bart died from a massive heart attack."

"At his age?"

"Yes. Dr. Davidson and the pathologist who did the autopsy obtained copies of Bart's prior medical records. Other than occasional alcohol use, he had no significant risk factors for heart problems."

"So what does that mean?"

"I don't know, but it's not typical. I may ask a doctor at the hospital some questions."

"OK. We can talk about it when you get here."

"By the way, I liked the e-mail. Creative and to the point for a lawyer."

"I told you that I'm not wordy."

Renny heard an unidentifiable sound on the other end of the line. "What was that?"

"A long-distance yawn. I've been up all night and all day and need to get to sleep."

"Good night, then. See you Thursday."

Renny spent the rest of the evening cleaning his apartment: putting things in order, discarding unneeded papers, mopping, vacuuming, dusting, organizing. It felt good. Brandy, never certain if the vacuum cleaner was friend or foe, barked anytime the noisy creature threatened to invade her space. By the time Renny finished, everything was neat and clean. Stepping back, he admired the shine on the white kitchen floor. He was ready in case *Southern Living* or Martha Stewart knocked on his door.

He awoke Sunday morning earlier than usual and brought the paper up from the driveway. There was the tiniest hint of autumn in the morning air, and he took a deep breath, enjoying the first sign of release from the oppressive summer heat. Prepared to settle in for a leisurely couple of hours, he poured a cup of coffee. Usually, Renny read the sports section first, but this morning he picked up the living section and for the first time noticed ads for churches. There were scores of them of every stripe and color—denominations and affiliations as unfamiliar to him as a list of European soccer teams.

He'd enjoyed the feel of his grandfather's church in Moncks Corner.

Could he find someplace similar in Charlotte? How did one shop for a church? One ad caught his eye: St. Catherine's Episcopal, a ten-minute drive from the house. The church offered an "open worship" service at 10:00 A.M. Why not? Closing the paper he decided to check it out. They were open; he was open. Finishing his coffee, he shaved and showered.

Renny didn't know if the church would be "open" to a visitor in casual clothes, so he put on a blue sports coat, gray slacks, and a blue-and-red striped tie, an adult version of the outfit he wore to church as a child.

St. Catherine's was on a major thoroughfare, and Renny passed a shopping center, three apartment developments, a golf course community, and an upscale collection of shops and boutiques before almost missing the small sign for the church. Set back from the roadway in a grove of newly planted Bradford pears and red maple trees, the modern white church was square with a sharp, slender steeple. No stained-glass windows, just long, clear casements extended from one end of the building to the other. He parked between a pair of shiny new minivans. From the looks of the other cars in the asphalt lot, it was an upper middle-class crowd. But what else was he expecting? It was, after all, an Episcopal church.

He joined a stream of people walking to the church entrance. Several families with freshly scrubbed children and a smattering of solos like himself squeezed through a narrow door into the foyer of the church at the same time. Almost every adult was carrying a Bible. Half the men wore ties; the rest were more casually dressed. A golf shirt wouldn't have caused a ripple.

Two men in clerical collars and robes greeted people as they came inside. This was different. Renny was used to the rector dutifully shaking hands with those in attendance on the way out, not welcoming people with a smile and friendly enthusiasm on the way in. Both men appeared to be in their thirties, and the taller of the two shook Renny's hand.

"Good morning. Welcome to St. Catherine's. I'm the rector, Paul Bushnell."

"Renny Jacobson."

"Have you been here before?"

"No, this is my first time."

The priest waved over a short, medium-built, gray-haired man in his fifties.

"Jack, this is Renny Jacobson. Renny, meet Jack Berit."

"We've met before," Renny said, shaking Jack Berit's hand.

Berit gave him a puzzled look.

"I work for Barnette Heywood at Jackson, Robinson, and Temples. We met at the Foursquare Securities closing."

"Of course." Berit smiled. "Sorry, I didn't remember."

"No problem."

Berit gave Renny a program of the service. "Come into the sanctuary."

Renny followed his host into a square room. There weren't any pews; about three hundred dark blue chairs arranged in a semicircle filled the airy room. The clear windows he'd seen from the parking area let in natural light, supplemented by four skylights set near the top of the four ceiling sections. Renny's eyes were drawn upward to the clear view of the sky above.

"Neat building," he said.

"It is, isn't it? Everything is designed to communicate an open heaven."

"A little different from my parents' church in Charleston."

"Are you from Charleston?" Berit asked.

"Yes. All my life until I went to college."

"My wife's family is from Charleston. Been there for generations. Here she is now."

Mrs. Berit, a tall, attractive, middle-aged woman, tanned and gray like her husband, extended her hand. "Good morning, I'm Lois Berit."

Renny took her hand. "Renny Jacobson." Yes, Lois Berit and Thomas Layne had a definite family resemblance.

Renny started to sit toward the back of the sanctuary.

"Would you sit with us this morning?" Lois asked.

"Sure. I don't know anyone here."

She led him halfway to the front and slipped into a row of chairs.

As soon as they sat down, Paul Bushnell came through a side door followed by a group of seven or eight men and women with musical instruments. The rector prayed, "We welcome you, Father, Son, and Holy Spirit, in this place and in our hearts this day. Let us meet with you as you meet with us."

Two women and a man in the group picked up microphones. Another man tuned an electric guitar while a third took his place behind a keyboard. A teenage boy positioned himself in back of a full set of drums and cymbals. Hearing a jingle, Renny looked to his left and saw Lois Berit retrieve a tambourine from beneath her seat. This was definitely going to be different.

One of the women at the microphones picked up a trumpet and blew a solitary note that grew in intensity until Renny felt the hair on the back of his neck stand up. Reaching a crescendo, she held the note to the last possible second, then released it into the stillness of the room. It sounded like a call to war. The band then began to play and sing, the congregation joining to words projected on a screen to the side of the chancel area. All the songs were new to Renny, as unfamiliar as a Latin Mass to a Southern Baptist, but for most of the congregation it was familiar territory, and they joined in with exuberance. They didn't just sing one song. Several fast songs followed without a break, and Lois Berit handled her tambourine with the skill of a gypsy dancer.

Then the pace slowed, and people throughout the room, their eyes closed, lifted their hands in the air or slipped from their seats and knelt in front of their chairs. During an instrumental interlude between congregational songs, one of the male singers started singing, and after a few lines, Renny realized it was a spontaneous song in which the man described a mountain he called the mountain of God. The characteristics of this place—its majestic beauty, panoramic vistas, the fellowship of those who climbed it—began to capture Renny's imagination and sparked an inward longing to go to the mountain, to see it, to feel it, to be with those who wanted to go higher. Glancing at Lois, he saw that her face was lined with two wet paths down her cheeks. When the final note faded, Renny looked at his watch. It was almost eleven o'clock.

Father Bushnell stood and faced the congregation. Without additional comment, he led them through traditional sections of the *Book of Common Prayer.*

The familiar words had an extraordinary effect on Renny. He was amazed. Instead of mumbling phrases in a meaningless rote, the beauty and power of the words pierced his consciousness in a way he'd never experienced. The rector finished by praying:

> "O God, who declarest thy almighty power chiefly in showing mercy and pity; Mercifully grant unto us such a measure of thy grace, that we, running to obtain thy promises, may be made partakers of thy heavenly treasure; through Jesus Christ our Lord, who liveth and reigneth with thee and the Holy Spirit, one God, for ever and ever. Amen."

A deacon read the New Testament lesson for the day, the story of the Prodigal Son from the book of Luke, and the rector delivered the sermon with quiet but relentless intensity. Two things impressed Renny as the priest talked about the story. First, he was chagrined by the misguided eagerness of the son to receive his inheritance before he was mature enough to handle it. But more powerfully, he was touched by the father who, keeping a constant vigil while the son was away from home, looked with unwavering longing for the son's return. The love of the father even after the son had blown it staggered Renny. The rector's points hit around Renny like bolts of lightning. Love based on relationship, not performance. Love without the expectation of control. Love for love's sake, not expecting anything in return. Unconditional love. The type of love Renny had never received from his earthly father. God's love. Renny heard the words and felt the power of the story; yet even so, something inside kept him from believing that it applied to himself. In a world of five billion people, how could God have a specific, personal interest in him?

The priest called the people to Communion as an invitation to meet with a Father God who loved them.

"None of us are as close to the Lord as we could be. None of us can see him as he sees us. All of us can draw closer to him. All of us are in the center of his vision. Come, come, come."

For Renny, Communion had always been a ritual without reality. But as with the readings from the prayer book, he had an almost tangible awareness of God as he moved deliberately to the Communion rail, knelt, and tried to picture himself as a son before the Father, receiving a feast prepared for him upon his return from a far country. But the image remained fuzzy.

The service closed with a blessing. Lois Berit touched his arm lightly. "Do you have any plans for lunch?"

"Not really."

"Would you like to join Jack and me? We're going to go to La Jolla."

"That's nice of you, but I don't want to intrude."

"Don't be silly. We invite visitors to lunch all the time."

"OK, thanks."

Most of the people were not in a rush to leave the sanctuary, and Renny shook several hands on his way to the door. The other priest was standing at the exit.

"I'm Chuck Southgate. Thanks for coming." Reaching inside his robe, he pulled out a card and handed it to Renny. "Here, call me if I can ever be of help to you."

Jack Berit walked up. "We'll meet you at the restaurant. Lois is praying with someone."

Renny glanced back in the sanctuary and saw Lois Berit and another lady seated, their heads bowed. "Sure, I'll put in a reservation."

La Jolla, named for an exclusive suburb of San Diego, was a

California-style bistro with a spacious seating layout and a sense of out-door dining. The restaurant's windows allowed the sunlight to form shifting patterns on the Spanish tile flooring. The only thing missing was the roar of the Pacific.

The hostess wrote Renny's name on the list, and he sat on a wooden bench to wait. The after-church crowd was streaming into the restaurant, and in a few minutes Jack and Lois Berit walked up the sidewalk.

They sat at a table in an area laid out like a greenhouse, with hanging plants and white orchids in pots on the floor.

"We're glad you came this morning," Jack said when they settled in their seats.

"Me, too. It's certainly different from my parents' church in Charleston. A good difference."

"That's right, Lois. I forgot to tell you—Renny is originally from Charleston."

"How long have you been in Charlotte?"

"About four months. I went to undergraduate and law school at Chapel Hill. My parents are deceased, but my father's family has been in the Charleston area forever."

"I lived in Charleston until I went to college at Converse in Spartanburg," Lois said. "Jack was at Wofford and we met while in school. My brother still lives in Charleston."

"Really?" Renny said casually.

"Yes, my maiden name was Layne, L-a-y-n-e. I was teased a lot, Lois L-a-n-e, you know," she said, laughing.

Renny took a sip of water and played dumb about his knowledge of Lois's family. "What's your brother's name?"

"Thomas Layne V. Sounds like old-time Charleston, doesn't it? Have you ever run across him?"

"The name sounds somewhat familiar, but I can't say I've seen him in Charleston." A lousy liar, Renny felt his deception must have been obvious to everyone in the restaurant.

Lois continued, "He's quite a bit older than you and doesn't work a regular job. He's been very smart in some investments."

"Has he ever visited the church?" Renny asked, seeking a way to change the subject.

"No, but he is coming to visit in a couple of weeks, and we hope to take him. Frankly, he doesn't see a need for God."

Renny thought about Marx's statement quoted by Layne at the meeting in Georgetown: "Religion is the opiate of the masses." Wrong. "Money is the opiate of the wealthy" was closer to the truth.

Jack Berit spoke up. "How did you find out about St. Catherine's?"

"Reading the ads in the Sunday paper. I haven't been to a church since I moved to Charlotte and hadn't planned on going anywhere today."

"We're glad you came."

"I am, too. I think I heard God calling me today."

The waiter came to take their order.

———

Two hundred miles away in Charleston, Mama A had not been able to stop humming all morning. Something good was happening somewhere. "What's up, Lord?" she asked out loud as she prepared for church. "Are you messin' with somebody I've been praying for? Who is it?"

She ran down a list of people she carried like babies in the cradle of her heart. Pausing at Renny's name, she felt the confirmation of the Spirit. "So, is that boy thinking about meetin' with you today? Well, do it, Lord, do it!"

14

Pray to thy Father which is in secret.
MATTHEW 6:6, KJV

Renny arrived an hour early at Charlotte's Douglas Airport. It was one of the hottest days of the year. Finding a parking space near the crosswalk to the main terminal, he let the car idle for a minute, the air conditioner on high in a life-and-death struggle against the oppressive heat. In an hour, Jo would be sitting in the car with him. And he was glad.

There were several telephone company vans parked along the edge of the roadway between the parking lot and the airport entrance. Workmen were climbing in and out of two manholes on opposite sides of the road like ants on a mission. Communication was vital to the life of the airport. Communication. Before he met Jo, Renny had considered it a buzzword used to sell women's magazines at the grocery store. Now, it was beginning to have a new, richer meaning. Was he turning into one of those sensitive male types, just a shade this side of effeminate? Remembering Jo's legs stretched in bas-relief against the Pawley's Island sand, he smiled. Not likely.

Beyond the sliding glass doors of the terminal, he checked an overhead monitor for arriving flights. Four out of five flights listed were USAirways, the dominant air carrier in Charlotte and one of the city's biggest employers. Jo was on a connecting flight from Detroit, flight 409, gate C-14, arriving at 2:20 P.M.

Unlike Hartsfield, O'Hare, or LaGuardia, Charlotte's airport did not overwhelm a traveler with a vastness that made the trip to the proper concourse more intimidating than an overseas flight. Rocking chairs lined the walls in the main lobby and gave it a homey look.

Renny stopped at a novelty shop to admire a popular University of North Carolina T-shirt that proclaimed, "If God Isn't a Tar Heel, Why Did He Make the Sky Carolina Blue?" Tar Heel religion had its adherents, and he considered buying one of the shirts for Jo, but it wasn't her. Maybe after she visited the campus.

While waiting at the gate for the plane to land, Renny leaned against the wall and read the newspaper headlines over the shoulder of a short, bald man. Outside the plate-glass windows, three USAirways jets, their tires smoking as they made contact with the tarmac, landed in quick succession and streaked past like silver fish with red-and-blue streaks down their sides. One of the planes taxied ponderously toward the gate. Renny waited impatiently as the first-class passengers came through the skywalk.

Jo was behind a huge man with an XXXL T-shirt and the largest Nike swoosh Renny had ever seen.

"Welcome to Charlotte," Renny said when she popped into view. He gave her a quick hug. "Flight OK?"

"A lot faster than driving my truck. Sometimes it's nice seeing America from the air at 600 miles per hour."

"Baggage claim is this way." Renny led the way into the concourse and turned left.

They walked rapidly past a couple of gates until Jo grabbed Renny's arm. "Where's the race?"

"Sorry." Renny slowed. "My natural gait is a little fast, isn't it?"

"No kidding."

"I run for exercise; it's my great stress reliever. I love to take my dog for a no-time-limit run through the neighborhoods where I live."

"Well, I like to jog, too, but let's save it for later."

"Did you bring your running gear?" Renny knew Jo would be cute even when she was sweating up a hill.

"Yes, maybe I can join you and your dog—Brandy, isn't it?"

"I'll ask Brandy. If she says no, I'll leave her in the backyard."

They rode down an escalator to baggage claim and found the zone assigned to Jo's flight. The luggage was still on its way from the plane.

"Guess where I went Sunday?" Renny asked as Jo's blue suitcase rolled into view.

"Well, it's too early for football, and we're not close to the ocean." Jo paused. "You went to church, didn't you?"

"Bingo."

"You played bingo?" Jo replied, smiling. "I thought they did that on Friday night."

"No bingo, but it was different from the high church services I went to as a child. Something happened."

"How? What?"

"The rector spoke on the love of the father in the story of the Prodigal Son." Renny lifted her blue suitcase and set it between them.

"And?"

"It was powerful the way he talked about the love of God." Renny slid the cardboard box protecting Jo's garment bag from the beltway and set it next to the suitcase. "That's not all."

"Yes?"

"I met someone at the church with a strong Charleston-Georgetown connection."

"Who?" Jo picked up the garment box and Renny grabbed the suitcase.

"Do you want to guess?"

"Let me think." Jo followed Renny through a labyrinth of taxis and airport shuttles. As they crossed under the shade of the parking deck, Jo said, "I don't know anyone in Charlotte except you, so it must have been someone from the meeting. I'll go with Gus Eicholtz."

"Not bad," Renny said as they walked up behind his car. "It was Thomas Layne's sister, a lady named Lois Berit. She and her husband attend the church, and I sat with her during the service. Afterward we ate lunch together." Renny put the luggage in the tiny trunk, and they drove out of the garage, the air conditioner blowing full blast in their faces.

"Did you tell her you knew her brother?"

"No, I didn't."

"Why not?"

"The secrecy thing, I guess. It caught me off guard."

"Group paranoia."

"Whatever. Layne is coming to Charlotte for a visit in a couple of weeks. His sister wants me to meet him."

"That should be interesting."

Renny turned onto Billy Graham Parkway, and the Charlotte skyline rose into view to the east.

"Are you going back to the church?" Jo asked as Renny shifted into a higher gear.

"Probably."

"Maybe we could go together sometime."

"If I can convince you to stay until Sunday, we could go this weekend. When do you have to be back at work?"

"I am off duty until Saturday night, but that could probably be changed to Sunday night. I told another nurse about the trip, and she offered to help if I needed her."

"I can call the travel agent tomorrow and change your return ticket."

"I just got here. We'll see."

Along both sides of Queens Road, the main access road into the Myers Park neighborhood, huge oaks mingled leaves forty feet overhead and created a green canopy that blocked most of the sun's rays from the street below.

"It's beautiful," Jo said as the car entered a long stretch of green tunnel. "Somebody eighty years ago planted these trees for people to enjoy today."

"It was before electricity, that's for sure. The utility company agreed to build its lines behind the houses so that the trees could be spared."

"Is this close to your house?"

"Yes. I often run through this area on Saturday mornings. Sometimes there are more joggers and walkers than cars."

Renny turned into Mrs. Stokes's driveway and turned off the engine. "This is it."

Jo got out and walked over to the backyard fence, an old chain-link completely covered by English ivy. Brandy was on the other side, barking and turning in circles.

"Brandy, meet Jo, that's J-o not J-o-e," said Renny, carefully spelling the two names.

"So she's a good speller." Jo reached over the fence and let Brandy sniff her hand. After a few seconds, the dog gave her knuckles an approving lick.

"Mr. Ed has nothing on Brandy. You'll see."

Renny opened the trunk and carried Jo's luggage to the side entrance. "Mrs. Stokes is nice, but don't expect her to run in circles and give your hand a lick."

Daisy Stokes opened the door. "Come in where it's cool," she said as she ushered them into the kitchen.

"Mrs. Stokes, this is Jo Johnston."

"It's a pleasure to meet you, Mrs. Stokes. Thanks for letting me stay with you."

"A little hospitality is my pleasure." Renny noticed the always neat kitchen was more sparkling than usual, and Mrs. Stokes had an arrangement of fresh flowers on the table in the breakfast nook. "Have a seat for a minute. Would you like something to drink?"

"Do you have some iced tea?" Renny asked.

"Yes."

"Mrs. Stokes makes the best iced tea."

"I'd love some," Jo replied, choosing a seat that provided a view of the backyard. "You have a beautiful yard. Do you have many hummingbirds? I see at least three feeders."

"Yes, there are two pairs zipping around from spring to fall. Sometimes I wonder how they ever finish a meal. Every time one comes to the feeder, another one dives down to run him off. It's been a little better since I put in the third feeder, but I don't think anything will convince them to tolerate one another."

"My mother is a bird-watcher. Do you have a lot of different birds visit?"

"Quite a few. I feed the local varieties all year, and they're loyal to me. I can recognize my long-term guests, and they add color, sound, and personality to my corner of creation." Mrs. Stokes set down two glasses of tea.

Jo took a long drink. "This is good. I didn't realize how thirsty I was. What did you put in it besides tea?"

"A little grape juice. I stir it in after brewing the tea and pouring it over ice and sugar in the pitcher."

Renny just sat at the table smiling. Everything in his world was right.

"Renny tells me you're a nurse."

"Yes, in the cardiac section of the main hospital in our area."

"I roomed with a missionary nurse for five years in Taiwan in the early 1950s. She was from Michigan, too."

As Jo and Mrs. Stokes talked, Renny let his mind wander, daydreaming about things he and Jo could do over the next few days.

"Renny, what do you think?" Mrs. Stokes said.

"About what?" Renny came out of his fog without knowing where the conversation had gone.

"I was suggesting we eat around six-thirty. That will give Jo time to rest a little bit."

"Sure, sure. I'll take your luggage into your room." Renny led Jo down a hall lined with black-and-white photographs of people and places from Mrs. Stokes's many years as a missionary. "The bath for the room where you're staying is on the left, and here's the blue room," he said.

"She's a sweetie, Renny," Jo said as he put her suitcase on the white chenille bedspread. "This room is perfect. I'm going to enjoy it here."

"I knew you would hit it off. I'll see you later."

Jo took her clothes from the garment bag and opened the closet door to hang up her things. The closet was not the small cubbyhole typical in older homes built before massive walk-in closets became common. It was more like a long, narrow room extending at least ten feet to the back wall. There was even a tiny window two-thirds of the way up the wall toward the ceiling. A beveled-glass Star of David the size of a man's hand was suspended on a string in front of the window. The little room was totally empty except for a clothes bar, a narrow chair facing the window, and a deep blue cushion on the floor in front of the chair. There wasn't a speck of dust or hint of a musty smell in the little enclosure. Jo hung up her clothes and stared curiously at the chair and cushion for a few seconds. Then it dawned on her—*It's Mrs. Stokes's prayer closet.*

She could imagine the elderly woman, isolated and insulated from outside distractions, sitting in the chair with her Bible open on her lap as the early morning sun sent its first rays tumbling through the beveled glass of the star, which diffused cascading colors against the wall and floor. Then a passage of Scripture would speak to the old woman's heart, and she would carefully slide to her knees on the cushion and bow down with her face to the floor. Motionless, her lips moving in silent petition or intercession for others, she would wait before her God. Jo guessed the tiny window faced east—toward Jerusalem. It had to. She stepped back, whispering, "This is a holy place; there must be angels in this room."

After unpacking her suitcase, Jo showered and changed. The house was quiet, and she took a few moments to study several of the old photos as she walked back to her room. One in particular caught her attention. Two Western ladies, one of whom appeared to be a much younger Mrs. Stokes, stood with a Chinese woman in front of a primitive-looking wheelbarrow. Jo made a mental note to ask about the story behind the picture.

It was an hour and a half until supper, and Jo wasn't sleepy enough to take a nap. She opened the closet door again, and the feeling of awe and reverence she had felt earlier returned. She wanted to sit in the chair and kneel on the cushion, but she hesitated, wondering if she should ask permission. No, the right to enter the closet was part of staying in the room.

A King James Bible sat on the nightstand. Jo picked it up, slipped into the closet, and closed the door. Sitting carefully in the chair, she opened to Matthew 6:6 and read: "But thou, when thou prayest, enter into thy closet, and when thou hast shut thy door, pray to thy Father which is in secret; and thy Father which seeth in secret shall reward thee openly."

An unexpected tear rolled down Jo's left cheek. Wiping it away with the back of her hand, she couldn't think of a reason to be sad.

Then, suddenly, the undeniable inner Voice came into the tiny room and exploded in her spirit: *"Jo, I am thy Father."* And a dam broke. Through the blur of tears now cascading without number, she saw the verse again, but this time the only words she could bring into focus were, "thy Father." *Thy Father, thy Father, thy Father* echoed inside her. She wept until the corner of her robe was soaked.

"Father, what is this?" she asked, rubbing her eyes with the palms of her hands as the tears slowed.

The answer came in a thought whose origin was not in her conscious mind. *"I'm healing your heart."*

Jo breathed in and out slowly several times, then asked, "From what?"

"The absence of a father's love."

A new wave of weeping swept over her as the enormity of her need opened before her understanding. She'd thought her stepfather's acceptance filled the void of abandonment created when her natural father left her life. Now she knew it had not. In fact, she had a need for fathering beyond the capacity even the best earthly father could provide, a fathering that could only come from "thy Father," the One who would never leave her nor forsake her, who was forever faithful in everlasting love.

The second wave of tears subsided. She continued to sit, immersed in the divine love that saturated the tiny room. Then, unbidden, another wave, less intense than the previous ones, demanded a release of emotion. Another wave, another pause, another wave, another pause; however, the tears began to have a different meaning. Beyond healing, she felt a profound gratitude; a deep appreciation for what the Lord had done filled her heart and overflowed through her eyes.

"Thank you," she murmured, slipping from the chair to the cushion on the floor. "Thank you, thank you."

It was not a moment to be hurried or rushed. Finally, Jo's eyes lost the capacity for tears. Their work was done. Sitting on the floor and leaning against the wall, she let the Presence fill her with peace.

Opening the closet door, Jo looked at the clock. It was six. Through the open bedroom door she could faintly hear Mrs. Stokes clattering pans in the kitchen. Walking down the hall to the bathroom to fix her hair, Jo looked in the mirror. Two swollen eyes and puffy cheeks returned her gaze. Her appearance couldn't be helped, but she had no regrets. She splashed water on her face and spent the next few minutes getting ready for supper.

———

Renny was sitting on a stool with Brandy lying at his feet on the kitchen floor when Jo came into the room. "Did you rest any?" he asked, then blurted, "You look like you were hit by a truck."

"Thanks, Renny. Do you recognize the tread marks?"

"No, I mean, what happened? Are you OK?"

"I'm better than OK," Jo said, smiling.

Mrs. Stokes glanced up from the sink where she was draining some vegetables and studied Jo's face. "You look fine to me. I'd even say you have a little glow about you."

"I don't want to talk about it right now. Let's wait until after supper."

"OK." Renny knew he didn't understand women, but it was always unsettling to have his ignorance revealed.

They ate informally in the kitchen. Renny told stories about his growing-up years in Charleston. Both Mrs. Stokes and Jo were especially interested in Mama A and her friendship with Renny's mother.

"Your mother and Agnes Flowers had a remarkable relationship," Jo said. "You know, how they were friends both inside the home and outside in the community."

"It was not common, then or now," Renny admitted.

"It's the same with the Chinese," Mrs. Stokes said. "We think they are all one people, but they have as many walls between themselves as if they were from different ethnic groups."

"Were you able to do anything about prejudice in the places you served?" Jo asked.

"Only after people had walked with the Lord for a period of time. As part of learning that God's ways are higher than man's ways, we let them see the need to act against the dictates of their culture. We respected their way of life in every way we could without compromising the essential truths of the gospel, but prejudice has no place in the kingdom of God."

"That reminds me," Jo said, "I wanted to ask you about one of the pictures in the hallway. You and another Westerner are standing with a Chinese woman in front of an old wheelbarrow."

"I'll go get the picture and tell you about it." Mrs. Stokes put down her fork and disappeared down the hall. She returned, wiping the glass frame with her sleeve. "This is the one." She set the photo in the middle of the table so they could all see it. "It was taken about thirty-five years ago. The other white woman is Juliana Tobler, a Swiss missionary who worked as a translator. The Chinese woman is standing in front of a homemade wheelbarrow. Both of the woman's legs were severely injured during a Japanese bombing of her home city during World War II, and she hadn't walked since. Some family members who had become Christians brought her in this wheelbarrow to one of our meetings. After the service, her brother asked us to pray for his crippled sister. Juliana and I prayed, and the woman held up her hands to her brother, who helped her to her feet. Her first steps were tentative, but within a minute she could walk normally. It is hard to describe the effect this had on the congregation in the room. People were shouting, jumping, crying. Supernatural events like that woman's healing were more common in Taiwan than they are here."

"Did you see a lot of miracles?" Jo asked.

"Not as many as we wanted. Desperately ill people came all the time for prayer. Some were healed, some were not."

"Why was that?" Renny asked.

Mrs. Stokes shook her head with a wry smile. "That's a question I can't completely answer. People occasionally ask me why we saw so many miracles among the Chinese and so few here in the U.S."

"What do you say?"

"The only answer I know: simple faith."

———

As they were finishing up the last bites of deep-dish apple pie with ice cream, Jo leaned forward. "Mrs. Stokes, thank you for letting me stay here."

"You're very welcome."

"No, I really want to thank you," Jo's voice trembled. "I spent some time praying in your prayer closet."

Mrs. Stokes smiled. "I'm glad you recognized it for what it is."

"It's incredible."

"Yes, it is."

Jo and Mrs. Stokes exchanged a long look, and the older woman said, "Thank you, Father."

Jo's eyes brimmed with tears. "That was part of it."

"That was part of what?" Renny asked, bewildered.

Jo shook her head. It was clear she could not speak and keep her composure. Mrs. Stokes came to her rescue. "Renny, there is a closet, actually more like a narrow room, that opens into the blue bedroom. I cleaned it out soon after I moved into the house, and I use it as a place to pray and meet with the Lord. The term *prayer closet* comes from a verse in Matthew that says we are to go into our prayer closet and pray to our Father in heaven in secret. Jesus taught that the secret life we have with God is one of the true tests of the genuineness of our relationship with him."

Jo took a deep breath. "It surprised me. I sat in the little chair you have in the room and read Matthew 6:6, the verse you just referred to. I began to weep without any apparent reason."

"Did you figure it out?" Renny asked.

"Oh yes. The Lord spoke to my heart that he is my Father, or as the verse says, 'thy Father.' Thy Father, my Father—not just the Father of us all, but my very, very own."

"Like what I told you about the love of God?" Renny asked.

"In a way, yes."

"What a blessing," Mrs. Stokes said softly.

"Renny knows things about my past. My earthly father abandoned my mother and me when I was very young. My stepfather was great, but he died when I was twelve. There was something missing inside me that I didn't even know I was lacking until I met with the Lord today. I wept with joy and gratitude until there wasn't a tear left to shed. My eyes were completely cried out. That's why I looked like I'd been hit by a truck," Jo said, smiling weakly at Renny.

"I'm sorry—" he started.

"No, don't worry about it. But I don't want to analyze it too much because my heart is so tender right now. I'm afraid if I talk about it too much, I'll somehow lessen the power of the experience."

"Of course, of course," Mrs. Stokes said. "You must carry treasures like these in the deepest places of your heart. But thank you for telling us what happened. It blesses me to know he met with you so wonderfully and so deeply."

Mrs. Stokes began to clear the table. "Let me help," Jo said.

Renny pushed his chair back. "I'll take Brandy out for a walk. Be back in a few minutes."

Hearing her name and the word *walk,* Brandy came to attention, her tail wagging so fast and furiously it threatened to clear the table before Jo could get to it. Renny fastened the dog's leash to her collar and opened the kitchen door. Still dusky light outside, the edge of the day's heat was gone. Walking down the driveway, he turned left and set a slower than normal pace down the sidewalk. Brandy pulled hard on the restraint until she realized this was not going to be a run, then she settled back in sync with his steps.

Renny thought about what Jo had said—he wasn't sure about miracles. Maybe if he saw one himself, he'd believe. And as far as hearing God's voice, did God sound like Charlton Heston?

But Renny could not deny the intensity he felt when Jo described her afternoon experience in the prayer room. He remembered his own sensations while sitting in front of his grandfather's house in Moncks Corner and his reaction when Paul Bushnell described God's love at St. Catherine's. It must have been something like that. But he had never considered that God's touch could produce such a powerful emotional reaction. He had always linked the words *religion* and *emotionalism* in a totally negative way: rolling on the floor, swinging from the rafters, weeping at an altar. Nothing but hype and nonsense.

He knew he was not on the same page of life's coloring book as Jo and Mrs. Stokes. They were coloring a picture of Jesus walking on water. He was coloring, what? A sports car parked in front of a beach house? A Van Gogh–like self-portrait?

He walked five blocks, then did a loop around a small park. Turning in the direction of the house, he came to a crosswalk, stopped, and waited for the light to turn green. That was what he needed to do, he realized: stop, not overanalyze. He knew he was on a path, but like the sidewalk at his feet, he couldn't see very far ahead. What was the Chinese proverb? "A journey of a thousand miles begins with the first step."

"Come on, Brandy. One step at a time."

15

Come, let us go up to the mountain of the Lord.
ISAIAH 2:3, NIV

Mrs. Stokes and Jo were sipping a cup of coffee in the living room when Renny returned.

"Do you want some coffee? It's decaf," Mrs. Stokes asked.

"No, thanks, it's a little too warm outside for coffee."

"I was telling Jo about a bed-and-breakfast I love to visit in the foothills of the Blue Ridge. It's one of my favorite places on earth."

"I'd like to go," Jo said. "Do you think we could go up for the day while I'm here?"

"Fine with me," Renny answered. "How far away from Charlotte is it?"

"Maybe a hundred miles."

"Who owns it?" he asked.

"George and Helen Manor, a couple who lived in Charlotte for years before moving to the mountains. My friend Paula Phillips took me up for a visit three years ago, and we spent a couple of days. I've been back several times since."

"Could you call them for us?" Jo asked.

"Of course. I'll call Helen in the morning and see if it's a convenient time."

Mrs. Stokes rose from her chair. "I'm going to my bedroom and give you some privacy." She patted Jo's shoulder as she passed by her. "Have a good night."

"Good night," they echoed.

"Well, are you having a good time?" Renny asked when Mrs. Stokes left the room.

"Better than good. Mrs. Stokes is a special woman."

"I knew you would like each other. You're kindred spirits."

"Kindred spirits?"

"Yeah. I heard the phrase in a movie. It applies to people who can communicate heart-to-heart."

"Oh, I'm familiar with it from the book *Anne of Green Gables*," Jo said. "Anne Shirley is one of my inspirations."

"That's it. I've not read the book, it was, uh—"

"A girl's book."

"Right, but I saw the movie on TV. It was well done. Made me want to visit Prince Edward Island, Canada, but not in the winter. It's probably colder than Michigan."

"That's hard for you to imagine, I'd guess."

"Impossible," Renny said. "You would like the movie. It has a lot of snow in it, but you and Anne are different. You don't have red hair, and your name is Jo without an *e.*"

Jo laughed. "It wasn't her hair color or the way she wanted to be elegant by adding an *e* to her name. It was who she was as a person. That's the attraction."

Renny studied Jo a moment in mock analysis. "I can see it now," he said.

"What?"

"Do you want me to puff you up?"

"How?"

"You remind me of Anne."

"This should be interesting. Tell me how."

"Well, we've eliminated the possibility of red hair or an *e* on your name. But from what I remember, the greatest thing about Anne Shirley was her ability to draw others out of their comfort zones of sterile protection into the excitement of living. Some viewed her as selfish, but actually, she only drew people to herself so they could come alive in their own unique way. She was a life giver. And she was without guile. So are you."

Jo beamed. "Well done, Mr. Movie Critic. And thank you. That's the desire of my heart."

Renny bowed.

"Which brings me to a moment of confession," Jo said, turning serious.

"Yes, my child," Renny responded.

"Please, I'm not joking. I came to Charlotte because I wanted to see you. But there is a part of me that came here to fix you."

"I'm sure I need some fixing."

"Sure, but there was an arrogance in my attitude, a wrong sense of superiority. I need to apologize for that because I need fixing as much as anyone. I realized that this afternoon."

"Apology accepted," he said simply.

They sat quietly.

Renny spoke first. "I have to go by the office for several hours in the morning to review some papers that weren't finished when I left to pick you up at the airport. Maybe Mrs. Stokes can call the folks from the B and B in the mountains while I'm gone."

"OK, I'll ask her."

"And I'll call when I'm finished at the office."

"That's fine. I'm pretty tired from working so many hours; nights and days have run together. I could use some sleep."

Renny walked into the kitchen and poured a glass of ice water from a pitcher Mrs. Stokes kept in the refrigerator. "Do you want some?"

"Sure."

Handing a glass to Jo, Renny raised his own. "A toast. To tomorrow."

"Tomorrow," Jo said. *"L'chaim,* to life."

Later, Renny lay in bed, excited that Jo was just a few feet away in the main house below. At first, he hadn't liked the idea of driving to the mountains, but it was not where he went but whom he was with that mattered. For that reason, tomorrow would be a good day.

———

Mrs. Stokes lay awake long after Renny and Jo went to sleep. Most people considered her retired, but Daisy had simply relocated to a different mission field. According to the evangelization society's guidelines, she had to leave Taiwan when she turned sixty-seven; however, she couldn't find a strong argument in the Bible for retirement from the kingdom of God. Thus, the provision of the house and car in Charlotte from her brother's estate became the ticket to her next port of call. Taiwan or Charlotte, people were people. They all needed a touch from God.

The upstairs apartment had proven to be a fruitful avenue for ministry. During the past ten years, a succession of singles and couples had passed through Mrs. Stokes's life and home. Each one left blessed and closer to the Lord than when they came.

She had not rented the upstairs area to Renny on a whim. The apartment was prime residential space in an area convenient to uptown, but it remained vacant for several months after the previous tenant, a young woman who worked for an international Christian ministry based in Charlotte, moved to Houston. Six people inquired about living in the house, and although Mrs. Stokes needed the extra income a renter provided, she patiently waited until the right person came along.

Within a few minutes of their first meeting, she sensed that Renny wasn't a Christian, but the unmistakable inward nudge of the Spirit said *Yes.* That settled it for her, and she offered him the apartment. The night before he moved in, she walked through the vacant rooms, pausing to pray in each one, gently touching the walls and windows, asking the Father to impart a blessing to Renny during his stay. That was four months ago.

Their relationship had developed gradually. Renny was an ambitious young man on the way up in the legal world, but true to the ingrained influence of his Southern upbringing, he frequently took time to greet her and stop for a few moments of polite conversation. Of course, he benefited from an occasional home-cooked meal and the older woman's willingness to take care of Brandy when he was out of town. Mrs. Stokes didn't push. Early in their relationship she received the word, *"Go easy with this one. I'm doing this on my timetable."* And as far as she was concerned, the young lawyer's spiritual destination was sealed.

However, she had been uneasy following Renny's trips to the coast. Something was not right. There had been an anxiety in his eyes after the trip to Charleston regarding his father's estate. She went to the Lord for directions. Nothing. Then, after his second trip, Renny asked her if Jo could come for a visit. She agreed, but wondered if Jo was the cause of Renny's tension.

She went back to the Lord again. "Does it have anything to do with the girl?"

"No."

"What is it?" she asked.

"Fast."

For three days she ate nothing and drank only water. The evening of the third day, she concluded that Renny was under spiritual attack—a state of affairs for which Renny had no frame of reference or understanding. He was as vulnerable as a child playing at the entrance to a rattlesnake's den. Mrs. Stokes prayed, "I want to stand in the gap for him."

The answer surprised her. *"Yes. And there are others, too."*

She knew that spiritual conflict, like earthly warfare, often involved several participants, some battles more than others. She'd learned the danger of solitary action on the foreign mission field and appreciated the power of people praying in the unity of spirit. Now, she asked the Lord to direct not only herself but the unknown co-laborers he had called to come to Renny's aid.

When Renny had described Mama A, Mrs. Stokes smiled in satisfaction and anticipation. Surely Mama A was part of Renny's troop of intercessors. The time might come when they would need to talk. "If one can put a thousand to flight, two can put ten thousand to flight." Perhaps the two women could pray together for their young charge.

She hoped Renny's time to encounter the Lord for himself was at hand. He needed the divine connection for himself and the battle he was facing. "Hasten the day, Lord," she asked. "Bring him to the time of his visitation."

———

Jo awoke at dawn and thought for a second about rolling over to continue her slumber. Then she remembered the prayer closet, and sleep dropped off her list of options. Bible in hand, she quietly opened the door. There was not yet enough sunlight to read, so she sat in the chair and silently thanked her Father for the day before. Eyes closed, she leaned her head back and relaxed as a stillness flowed over her, a stillness that could be felt. Unlike the previous day, she did not experience intense emotion, only peace. But what a peace it was. As she lingered, the sense of well-being became more pervasive. "Shalom," she said. *Shalom*, the Hebrew word for peace, a word that encompassed more than quietness or the absence of conflict. Shalom, a state of being in the center of Jehovah's blessing and favor. Her Bible remained unopened in her lap as uncounted minutes passed until she heard a knock on the door of the bedroom.

Opening her eyes, the room was flooded with light and, just as she'd imagined, the prismlike edges of the Star of David, scattered red, yellow, orange, blue, and purple across the room.

"Come in, Mrs. Stokes. I'm in here."

Mrs. Stokes's white-haired head and bright eyes appeared around the doorframe. "Good morning. How do you like my sanctuary this morning?"

"I doubt there are many cathedrals more beautiful," Jo replied, turning sideways in the chair.

"His mercies are new every morning."

"Yes, they are."

"Do you want to come out for some coffee?"

"Sounds good. I'll just come in my nightgown and robe. Renny has to go the office this morning."

"I heard him leave hours ago. I'd say he wants to get his work done and come back as soon as possible."

Mrs. Stokes had a cup of coffee and a plate of tiny pastries iced with frosting and topped with chopped pecans waiting in the kitchen. "Will this be enough?" she asked as Jo sat down in the chair that had the best view of the backyard.

"Perfect," she replied, putting a couple of pastries on a small plate. "I'm not a big breakfast eater. Oh, I almost forgot something." Jo went back to the bedroom. "Here." She handed Mrs. Stokes a small decorative jar of raspberry jam topped with a little silk bow. "A Michigan specialty. It's homemade on a farm up north, near Lake Michigan."

"Thank you," Mrs. Stokes said. "I have some homemade bread that will be perfect for this jam."

Jo nibbled a pastry and enjoyed the scene in the backyard. The more she looked, the more beautiful and serene it was. The inexpressible peace she'd felt earlier in the prayer closet flowed over the whole property.

Mrs. Stokes placed a piece of warm, buttered toast in front of her. "If you go to the mountains today, you'll have a big supper at the lodge and, knowing Renny, a barbecue sandwich on the way up."

"He promised me some barbecue. He was shocked that I considered it ethnic food."

Mrs. Stokes chuckled. "Renny is a Southern boy when it comes to his stomach."

A hummingbird swooped down and hovered at one of the feeding stations. Its bill siphoned the sweet juice in three sips before it zipped back up in the air. Jo took a less frantic sip of coffee as Mrs. Stokes joined her at the table.

"May I ask you something, Mrs. Stokes?"

"Yes."

"I am really attracted to Renny."

"And he to you, from what I've seen."

"There's something special about the times we've had together. When I'm with Renny, I sense the Lord's involvement and favor."

"But you're concerned about the possibility of being unequally yoked, as the Scriptures describe it."

"Right. I don't want my heart drawn further into what I feel is happening between us and then wake up in a situation that does not have Jesus at the core of the relationship. I've heard too many tales of women who married in the hope their husbands-to-be would come to the Lord, only to experience years of frustration and shallowness. Or worse."

"That's true. It's wise to avoid that type of situation."

"So what do you think I should do? How do I guard my heart and yet respond to what I believe the Lord is doing in bringing us together?"

"He hasn't kissed you yet, has he?"

Surprised, Jo said, "No, he hasn't even tried."

"I didn't think so. In the midst of all that's happening, I believe there is a divine protection surrounding you. Oh, you could violate this safeguard if you choose to do so. But you have stayed in the shelter of the Most High up to this point."

"Yes. That's probably true."

"Stay in that place while the Lord works on Renny's heart."

"But what if it takes a long time?" Jo said with a sigh.

Mrs. Stokes smiled. "I'd guess sooner rather than later. People have been praying for Renny a long time. You heard about his mother and Mama A. He is an egg that is about to hatch, and I think I can see a little beak poking through the shell."

The phone rang, and Mrs. Stokes got up to answer it.

"Hello. . . . That sounds good. . . . Bye."

"Renny?" Jo asked.

"The little chick himself. He is finished at the office and walking out the door to come home. He should be here in fifteen to twenty minutes."

"Is it too early to call the couple in the mountains?"

"Oh no. I'll do it right now."

"I'd better get ready." Jo hopped up from the table and started toward the hallway, then stopped and quickly walked over to Mrs. Stokes and gave her a hug. "Thanks."

"You're welcome. Very welcome."

———

Jo was in the bedroom when Renny knocked on the kitchen door. Mrs. Stokes let him in.

"Good morning," he said. "Where's Sleeping Beauty?"

"She's getting ready. I called Helen Manor, and you are welcome to come up for the day and stay for supper. Do you want some coffee and a pastry?"

Renny popped a couple of pastries into his mouth. "I don't want to ruin my appetite. I promised Jo some barbecue and thought we might stop at a place I know about in Newton for lunch."

"Here are directions to the Manors' place. It's near Starkeville," Daisy said, laying a sheet on the table.

Renny studied the paper.

"Is it a little cooler today?" Mrs. Stokes asked.

"Yes, and since it's not going to be scorching hot, I thought we might ride with the top down." Jo walked in as Renny finished his sentence.

"Take down the top? That would be fun."

"According to these directions, most of the roads are two-laners through rural areas."

"Do you have a scarf I can wear on my head?" Jo asked Mrs. Stokes.

"No, I don't think I do."

"I've got a brand-new Duke cap," Renny offered. "A friend named Morris gave it to me, knowing I would never wear it."

"OK."

"The cap is upstairs. I'll get it."

———

Renny put on a well-worn UNC cap and turned the car around in the driveway. Jo adjusted the size of the Duke cap and tucked most of her dark hair under it.

"This way no one from either Chapel Hill or Duke will throw a rotten tomato at us," he said. "They'll just wonder what the nice-looking girl from Duke is doing with the scruffy guy from UNC."

As they wound through the tree-lined streets with the top down, they enjoyed the full effect of the ever-changing jigsaw puzzle created by the contrasting sun and shade.

"We'll go through Uptown so you can see the skyscraper that houses my cubicle."

"You've got more than a cubicle, don't you?"

"Just barely. You've not seen me in my work environment. I'm a lot like Dilbert."

"Collection of curved ties and all?"

"You bet."

Turning on Trade Street, Renny slowed before the four huge statues to Industry, Commerce, Transportation, and the Future that flanked the roadway like sculptured meteors dropped from the sky.

"There it is. I'm on the twenty-second floor. Now you can visualize my habitat from Monday to whenever."

"I suppose you don't have a window, do you?" Jo leaned her head back in the seat so she could look straight up as they passed the sleek black structure.

Renny laughed. "That's at least twelve years in the future."

They left the city, traveling northwest through a succession of small North Carolina towns. It wouldn't be accurate to describe them as pearls on a string. They were mill towns—lined up like a row of hubcaps nailed to the side of an old toolshed, shiny in spots but with quite a few dents and scrapes picked up along time's highway. There would be a few nice houses surrounding the main square, but most of the inhabitants lived at a subsistence level and were more interested in a new pickup truck than developing a picturesque community. It was close to noon when they entered Newton.

"You know who lives in Newton, don't you?" Renny asked as they reached the city limits and the wind noise in the open car died down.

"I'm a little rusty on my Newton, North Carolina, trivia," Jo said, taking off her cap and shaking out her hair.

"I guess you don't follow the races much in Michigan, do you?"

"Horse races?"

"No, stock cars, NASCAR."

"Is that supposed to be a hint?"

Renny slowed to a stop at one of the two traffic lights in the sleepy town. "I'll put you out of your misery, or suspense, whichever the case may be. Newton is the home of Dale Earnhardt."

"Never heard of him."

"Don't say that too loud. Remember the top is down." Renny eyed a man in blue jeans and a T-shirt who was crossing the street in front of them. "Do you see that guy's shirt?"

"The one with a black car on it."

"That's it. The one that says 'The Intimidator,' Earnhardt's nickname."

"Why do they call him that?" Jo asked.

"He has a reputation for knocking other drivers off the track at 200 miles per hour, if that's what it takes to win."

Jo thought a moment. "Anne Shirley of Green Gables is one of my inspirations. Are you trying to tell me Mr. Intimidator is one of yours?"

Renny laughed. "Not really. I'm just trying to educate you on points of local interest. Here's the restaurant." He pulled into the freshly paved parking lot. "New asphalt. Business must be good."

Renny and Jo sat at a table for two in front of a window with a view of the parking lot. They ordered Carolina-style pork sandwiches with slaw on the sandwich and pickles and chips on the side. The waitress brought two big clear-plastic glasses of iced tea. Renny munched in satisfaction until only a few potato chips were left on his plate.

"Do you think it's time we talked business?" he asked.

"What business?"

"About the List?"

"I guess so."

"Well, we first discovered our common denominator at the barbecue restaurant in Moncks Corner."

"True. What do we need to discuss?"

"Well, I'm in and you're not," Renny began.

"So have we lost our common denominator?" Jo asked testily.

"No, no. Now, we know each other in our own way. But even though you're not a part of the List, you are the only person I can talk to. And I respect your opinion."

"OK. What have you been thinking?"

"I'm still frustrated in my efforts to gain direct access to my family's money. Gus Eicholtz told me the approximate amount of money that has accumulated."

"I don't want to know that," Jo interjected.

"All right, but there is going to be a sizable distribution to the members in the next few months. I can't give you a figure, but it would be enough that I could quit my job at the law firm and, with conservative investments, never work again."

Renny waited.

Jo completed his thought. "Then you could do what you want to do—write."

"That was my plan. I don't want to wait twelve years for an office with a window. What do you think?" Renny popped the last potato chip into his mouth.

A part of Jo wanted to grab him by the collar and yell, "Renny, can't you see the List is a trap luring you into the same kind of paranoid greed that made your father a mean, stingy man!" But her mouth couldn't form the words, and her heart couldn't release the passion necessary to validate the warning. Instead, she said as calmly as she could, "What I think was made clear in Georgetown. No matter how much money is involved, I'm not interested. I really can't see how I could feel any differently about your involvement than I did for mine."

Renny shrugged and looked out the window. "I guess I knew that was what you would say, but that's not a step I'm ready to take. At the least I want to get the next distribution in my hands."

Jo sighed. "You have some time. Keep an open mind."

"I will. Anyway, it all seems less important when I'm around you."

"I'm glad," Jo said seriously. "I'm very, very glad."

From Newton it took forty minutes to drive to the Manors' bed-and-breakfast. Jo wanted to help Renny sort through his questions, and she was frustrated by the invisible gag that at times kept her from expressing what she knew to be true. Then she remembered something she heard a guest speaker say at her church: "The right word in the wrong time is just as useless as the wrong word in the right time." Closing her eyes as the wind rushed by, she prayed, "Don't let me make either mistake."

Renny slowed the car as they passed a fruit stand advertising locally grown apples for sale. "We're getting close. The road we're looking for is past an apple warehouse." As they came around a bend in the road, the red Phillips Apple Barn came into view on the left. "That's it. I remember the name." A hundred yards beyond the apple barn, Renny turned onto a narrow side road and began climbing upward. "It's somewhere toward the top of the ridge."

They passed several houses, some brick, some wood. Renny pointed out three long, low chicken houses nestled against the hillside. "Let's hope we're not downwind from a chicken house," Renny said. "There's nothing like the fragrance of ten thousand chickens on a hot day."

As they climbed higher, small apple orchards began springing up on both sides of the road. An ancient stand of apple trees whose limbs looked like gnarled arthritic hands thrusting up from the earth appeared on a steep hill to the right. Rounding a corner, they came out on top of the ridge and saw a sign on the right that read, "Zion Hill Lodge." A huge mailbox with "George Manor" painted on it sat beside a single-lane driveway.

"This is it," Renny said.

Turning, they passed through a continuation of the ancient orchard. A small apple-shaped sign warned, "Beware of Falling Apples."

"This is nice," Jo said.

"There's the lodge." Renny pointed across the side of a steep slope to the left of the driveway.

Three stories tall with cedar siding and a broad deck overlooking the orchard, the red tin-roofed Zion Hill Lodge commanded the surrounding area. They parked in a gravel lot to the side of the building. Jo took off her cap and brushed her hair.

Renny knocked on the solid wooden front door, and a petite, gray-haired woman with large, observant eyes opened it.

"Hello, I'm Renny Jacobson, and this is Jo Johnston."

"I'm Helen. Come inside and sit down. George is downstairs getting a jar of apple butter for Daisy. We didn't want to forget it, so we'll give it to you first thing."

South of Georgetown, two men walked slowly to the end of the weathered pier that stretched like a long finger through the surf into the deeper waters beyond the breaking waves. They passed a few fishermen, shirtless men baked such a deep bronze by the long South Carolina summer that the tattoos of mermaids and sea creatures on their forearms had almost disappeared.

"What do you think of Jacobson?" the younger asked when they reached the end of the gray planked walkway.

The older man leaned against the wooden rail, took a cigar from a pocket humidor, and stared out to sea. "Unrealized potential."

"Potential for what?"

The first puff of cigar smoke disappeared as the afternoon breeze began to blow gently off the land. "You'll see."

"Come on. Tell me."

"He's a closed house waiting for a skillful hand to unlock the door."

"Closed house? Does he have more potential than me?" the younger asked.

"Don't be jealous. Each one to his assigned place. Trust me. I've not selected a successor—not yet."

16

So it is with everyone born of the Spirit.
JOHN 3:8, NIV

Renny and Jo entered a large great room with a cathedral ceiling and dominated by a massive stone fireplace and a magnificent view of the mountains. Two dark green leather couches and a pair of side chairs provided seating. Renny and Jo sat next to each other on one of the sofas.

They could hear heavy footsteps coming up the wooden stairs from the basement, and in a moment George Manor came into the room and introduced himself. "Let me put these jars in the kitchen. One of them is for Daisy," he said and disappeared through a door on the opposite side of the great room. When he reappeared, he took a seat in one of the chairs by the fireplace.

A noble-looking man who could pass for a medieval baron, George Manor had a large head topped with a mane of brown hair mixed with gray, an oversized nose, full lips, bushy eyebrows, and a room-filling voice.

"You have a beautiful place," Jo said when everyone was seated. "I liked it as soon as we turned onto the property."

"Thanks," George replied.

"Mrs. Stokes said you moved here from Charlotte?" Jo asked.

"Yes, I was a happy dentist. You know, pulling teeth and filling cavities. Then, in the 1960s, the Jesus Movement swept out of California and hit our home in Charlotte."

"What do you mean?"

"It all started as a small Bible study for teenagers in our living room, but quickly grew until all kinds of people—from drugged-out hippies to children of conservative Christian pastors—came to seek Jesus. Many were converted and went on to become leaders in Christian circles in Charlotte and beyond."

Helen picked up the story. "After that, we decided to move to the mountains and provide a place of healing for burned-out Christians and refreshing for anyone else. Right now we have a recently divorced minister staying in a cabin on the other ridge," Helen said. "He'll be here for a while and then will move on, opening up an opportunity for someone else to come."

"Mrs. Stokes told me the area around the lodge was a prayer mountain," Jo said.

"We try not to publicize that too much," George said. "We only want the serious, not the curious. A woman traveling around the world and visiting places where people have experienced supernatural things in prayer came by a few weeks ago. She intends to write a book about her findings, but I asked her not to mention Zion Hill. As you can see, we don't have facilities to handle a big crowd wanting to see a shrine or something."

"What is here that would cause that kind of reaction in people?" Renny asked. "You don't have a piece of the true cross in a glass case or weeping statue of a saint in the foyer, do you?"

George smiled and shook his head. "No, the basis for what happens began with the prayers of Moravian settlers who came to this area over two hundred years ago. They dedicated this land to God, and from what I've seen, he is still answering their prayers. Many people who visit find it easy to meet with God here. That's the attraction."

Although sitting on a soft leather sofa, Renny felt uncomfortable and shifted uneasily in his place. Prayers uttered two hundred years ago by people long since dead still being answered today? Impossible to prove and unlikely to happen. He was irritated and sorry he'd wasted valuable time with Jo coming to this strange place. A suburban dentist turned Christian guru? An improbable vocational change. One geographic location better suited for prayer than another? The product of an overactive imagination.

Most of the supernatural stuff Christians talked about was simply too hard for him to swallow, and he was more acutely aware than ever that he didn't understand God, not the way these people did. But on the other hand, he didn't know if he wanted to. What if he ended up as a religious fanatic out of touch with reality? In his inner confusion and frustration, he blurted out his next thought before he could trap it in his mind. "What is God really like?"

George turned his big head like the turret on a tank, and in his deep voice fired an answer that exploded in Renny's consciousness, "Renny, he is not like your father."

George Manor didn't know whether Renny's father was alive or dead. He didn't know Renny's background and the negativity and harshness that characterized his relationship with H. L. He didn't know a single word that ever passed between them. He didn't know if they went camping together or shared a bag of peanuts at a baseball game. He didn't know the provisions of H. L.'s will. He didn't know the sermon Renny had heard the previous week about the love of the father for the Prodigal Son. And he didn't know Renny's questions and doubts about the supernatural realm. But George's brief statement needed no supporting validation or explanation; he spoke a truth that Renny needed to hear at that precise moment of his journey through life. Renny's focus shifted from criticism of others to frank honesty about himself.

Renny started to say, "You're right," or "Could you explain what you mean?" but the tongue that had betrayed his innermost thoughts seconds before now refused to utter a syllable. Unable to stay seated, he got up, opened a glass door, and went onto the deck that extended across the back of the house.

Resting his hands on the railing, he stared sightlessly across the open expanse to the next ridge. A mountain breeze brushed past his face. He wasn't emotional and didn't feel like crying; he simply needed to let the significance of the few words he'd just heard find their proper place in his soul.

Renny had never thought about the influence of his natural father on his understanding of God. Children with harsh fathers accept much of what is thrown their way as normal because they don't have a frame of reference for anything else, and this twisted template unfortunately becomes the basis for their picture of the heavenly Father. Renny didn't need an expert to tell him his relationship with his father had not been good, but he knew George Manor's words revealed the main obstacle in Renny's journey toward faith. Doubts about miracles and questions about the supernatural were pebbles, not stumbling blocks. Renny didn't believe because he couldn't trust. How could he trust a heavenly Father when the only example of a father he'd ever known had proven so untrustworthy?

George Manor's statement broke the back of Renny's deep-rooted, unconscious misconceptions about God. "Renny, he is not like your father." Though a negative statement, it was actually the first positive brushstroke on a blank canvas entitled "The True Nature and Character of God." The old picture of fatherhood dominated by H. L.'s penetrating dark eyes and critical countenance began to fade. God was not like his father, and in the light of this truth, old perceptions no longer held absolute power over him. No lie can survive when exposed to the light of truth. The light had shone on Renny, and God could begin to paint his own portrait, a portrait only a divine artist could produce.

A hungering curiosity welled up inside Renny. *How can I really know what you are like?*

Before the thought had time to leave his mind, he heard the still, small Voice resound for the first time in his inner man, *"Read my Word."*

———

While Renny was having his epiphany on the deck, Jo and the Manors sat for a few moments in a circle of silence. Six eyes watched Renny walk to the railing of the deck and rest his hands against it.

George spoke first, "That was quick, wasn't it?"

"Very quick," Helen agreed.

Jo looked at George and raised her eyebrows in an unspoken question.

George responded, "Helen and I prayed after Daisy Stokes called this morning. We had the sense God was going to touch one or both of you in a powerful way today."

"Why did you say that about his father?" Jo asked. "Did Mrs. Stokes tell you anything about his background?"

"No. Of course, what I said is true for all of us to some degree."

"But the effect on Renny . . ."

George shrugged. "It was God's key to unlock Renny's heart to the possibility of a heavenly Father who loves him more than he can imagine."

Wondering about the next step in Renny's pilgrimage, Jo asked, "What's going to happen next?"

The gun turret turned toward Jo. "He's going to ask you to marry him."

Jo flushed. "We haven't even known each other for a month."

"I'm not telling you to say yes," George said, smiling. "That's not my place. Just don't be surprised if he asks you sometime soon. That way you can be ready and won't be caught completely off guard."

"It would have done that."

"And it doesn't mean he's going to come in from the deck and pop the question, but it's coming down the road and around the bend."

"What else should I ask you?" Jo asked somewhat apprehensively.

"How about, 'Can we stay for supper?'" George responded with a wave toward the kitchen.

"And the answer to that question is yes," Helen said. "You two might want to drive or walk over to the ridge behind the house. It's only a couple of hundred yards to the top. There's a gazebo where you can sit and talk and a short footpath along the crest."

"The view of the Blue Ridge Mountains is wonderful," George said.

"OK. But I'll be a lot more nervous about sitting and talking with him than I would have been a few minutes ago."

"You'll be fine." Helen gave her a reassuring smile. "You have a listening heart and a gracious spirit. Now, if you'll excuse us, we have a few errands to run in town before starting supper. Make yourself at home."

Jo pretended to relax on the sofa—too much was happening too fast to truly relax, and she didn't have time to assimilate it. Taking a deep breath, she asked for peace and received an immediate return of the shalom she'd felt that morning. Her heart slowed, her mind cleared, and her anxiety lifted. She closed her eyes until she heard the door open and Renny come in.

"The Manors left to run some errands," she said.

Renny sat down beside her. "Whew, that statement George made about God not being like my father blew me away."

"What happened while you were out on the deck?"

"I'm not sure about everything, but I realized that I shouldn't superimpose my father and his ways on top of God."

"Good insight. Anything else?"

Renny leaned forward. "There are people who would think I'm nuts to say this, but fortunately none of them are in this room, so I'll go ahead. I was wondering how I could find out what God is like—it was more of a thought than a prayer. No sooner had I framed the idea than God spoke to me, not out loud, but as clear as I'm talking to you, and he said, 'Read my Word.'"

Jo's eyes widened. "That sounds like God to me. Short and to the point."

"Like what happened to you in Mrs. Stokes's prayer room?"

"Exactly."

"The Word is the Bible, right?"

"Yes."

"I want to read it. It sounds nuts, but I'm excited about reading the Bible."

Jo laughed. "Then as the commercial says, 'Just do it.'"

"In fact, I'd like to spend a little more time alone, if it's OK with you," Renny said.

"Uh, sure. I'm going to walk over to the ridge behind the house. Helen said there is a gazebo and a path along the crest."

"I'll come in a while." Renny picked up a well-worn Bible from the coffee table. "Any advice on where to start?"

Jo didn't hesitate. "John. The Gospel of John."

Renny already had the Bible open by the time Jo reached the door and looked back. What a sight! She imprinted the scene in her mind as a picture never to be forgotten.

Accompanied by Whitney, the Manors' collie, Jo set an easy pace down a short, steep slope and up a steeper path to the gazebo. Pausing a moment to catch her breath, she continued to the top of the ridge along a well-worn trail. It was higher than the lodge and on one side she could see the lodge's red roof. On the other side the rounded tops of the Blue Ridge Mountains formed a semicircle of bluish green. These were old mountains. Worn smooth by weather and time.

The path led to a fire ring surrounded by several short logs, cut and placed upright for crude seating. Jo sat facing the mountains, stretched out her legs, and enjoyed the breeze that strengthened its force as it swept across the elevated spot. The dog sat beside her quietly, head resting on Jo's knee.

"This place is glorious," she spoke to the wind. "Let your wind blow over Renny." A shadow flashed across her, and she looked up to see an eagle gliding overhead on the currents rising from the valley below. As if delivering her prayer, the bird swooped low over the roof of the lodge and sailed back up on an updraft. "Thank you, Father," she prayed.

———

Following Jo's suggestion, Renny opened the Bible and found the book of John. It was a red-letter edition, and he noticed that Chapter 17 was almost entirely in red. Starting at verse 1, he read through verse 3, "Now this is eternal life: that they may know you, the only true God, and Jesus Christ, whom you have sent." He stopped. *Eternal life is knowing God, not just believing some true things about him.*

He continued to the end of the chapter. Jesus concluded by praying, "May they be brought to complete unity to let the world know that you sent me and have loved them even as you have loved me. . . . I have made you known to them, and will continue to make you known in order that the love you have for me may be in them and that I myself may be in them."

George Manor believed Moravian prayers were still being answered. How much more the prayers of Jesus—even if it had been two thousand years ago? What did Jesus pray? The love of the Father for the Son—in him, and Jesus—in him. But how?

Guided by a skillful Hand that had pointed the way for countless pilgrims down through the ages, Renny turned to John 3. "Flesh gives birth to flesh, but the Spirit gives birth to spirit. You should not be surprised at my saying, 'You must be born again.' The wind blows wherever it pleases. You hear its sound, but you cannot tell where it comes from or where it is going. So it is with everyone born of the Spirit."

Renny looked up from the page. Jo was right. The born-again idea did not originate with Billy Graham or Jimmy Carter. *It's in the Bible. It's Jesus' explanation of a new birth by the Spirit. It's something God does inside you.* Renny's thoughts, with precision and order, turned one way then another, like the dial of a massive safe. He remembered Jo's question when they walked on the Pawley's Island beach, "Has he ever called you?" That's the wind blowing where it wills. *Click.* He remembered his mother's letter and Grandfather Candler's prayer. That's the prayers of my family. *Click.* He remembered the sermon at St. Catherine's on the love of the father for the Prodigal Son. That's the heavenly Father waiting for me to come home. *Click.*

Turning to John 1, he read down to verses 12 and 13: "Yet to all who received him, to those who believed in his name, he gave the right to become children of God—children born not of natural descent, nor of human decision or a husband's will, but born of God." The dial turned the last round, the tumblers fell in place, and Renny opened his heart to the Son of God. "I believe. I receive," he spoke the words out loud, and heaven rejoiced.

Sitting in the chair next to the fireplace, he leaned his head back and allowed himself to know, really know for the first time in his life, what it meant to have a personal relationship with God. Now he could understand why Jo's eyes were so swollen when she had come from Mrs. Stokes's prayer closet. Renny didn't cry, but he understood. God loved him.

———

Mama A stood next to her bed folding a load of clothes. Every few seconds she shouted, "Praise the Lord," "Hallelujah," or "Thank you, Jesus." The day hadn't started out on such a positive note. She hadn't been feeling well that morning, canceled a trip to go out with a friend, and decided to stay around the house.

At noon she felt a little better and, after eating a sandwich, lay down for a nap on the sofa in her living room. She dreamed. She saw Clarence, a sheet of paper in his hand, standing in a brightly lit room next to a simple wooden table. Tall windows, stretching from floor to ceiling, let in light from every direction. The room was bare except for the table and a ladder-back chair with a new cane seat. The door opened and Renny, dressed in a suit, came in. Mama A thought Renny looked like a preacher! He walked up to Clarence with a big smile and shook his hand. Clarence returned the smile, pulled back the chair, and motioned for Renny to sit down. Then, Clarence laid the sheet of paper on the table. Renny leaned over and spent several moments reading it carefully. When he finished, he looked up at Clarence and nodded his head. Clarence handed him a pen, and Renny signed the sheet. The two men disappeared as the room dissolved in light.

The old woman woke up with a hallelujah echoing in her spirit. "He's signed on the dotted line, Lord," she exclaimed. "He's crossed the Jordan! Do you know that, Katharine? Did you know your boy is in the kingdom?" she asked the heavens. "Of course you do. Of course you do."

17

Shout unto God with the voice of triumph.
PSALM 47:1, KJV

Renny suddenly remembered his promise to meet Jo on the ridge. Hopping up, he left the house and walked quickly to the top. As he looked around, Renny felt as if he were seeing with a new set of eyes. Everything around him looked different. The trees more distinct, the touch of the breeze more refreshing, the sound of a chipmunk scurrying in the leaves more clear.

Jo wasn't at the gazebo, but as he neared the crest of the hill, he saw her standing with her back to him, hands raised to the sky. Just like Lois Berit. He slowed, not sure if he should disturb her, but she lowered her hands and beckoned him forward. He covered the distance between them in a few bounding steps and faced her.

"How was John?" she asked.

Renny stood close in front of her and looked into her eyes. Jo saw a light that had not been there when they sat on the sofa in Mrs. Stokes's living room the night before. "You did it, didn't you?"

"Yes."

"I can see it in your face."

"I'm glad. I know it's true. I know it's real." Sitting on a brown stump, he told her what happened, concluding with his simple prayer of declaration and faith.

Jo listened intently. When he finished, she quietly said, "Amen."

Renny couldn't sit still. Jumping up, he said, "What next? I feel like running across the tops of these mountains."

"I think you should shout," Jo responded.

"What do you mean?"

"If you were at a football game and your team scored the winning touchdown on a long pass play as time ran out, what would you do?"

"I'd scream my head off."

"The Bible says to shout unto God with a voice of triumph. You've got something to celebrate and shout about. If we were in most churches, I couldn't suggest this because the ushers would escort you outside the building. But we're not in a church; we're here by ourselves on top of a mountain that has been created by God."

"What should I say?"

"Whatever is in your heart." Jo took a step back. "Go for it."

Renny paused, put his fingers in his mouth, and blew a long, shrill whistle. Raising his right fist in the air, he closed his eyes and yelled, "Yeah, yeah, yeah!" He opened his eyes and looked questioningly at Jo. "How was that?"

"Sounded like a field goal in the third quarter. You can do better. Don't hold back."

He stopped and looked down at the lodge to reassure himself that no one but Jo was within earshot. Taking a big breath, he cried out at the top of his lungs, "Thank you, Jesus!" He said it again, just as loud, but pausing between each word for emphasis, "Thank . . . you, . . . Jesus!" Again and again, with increasing freedom he proclaimed his gratefulness to the heavens and the hills. "Thank you, Jesus! Thank you, Jesus! Thank you, Jesus!" Heaving for breath, he asked, "How was that?"

Jo nodded. "We just had church. That felt good, didn't it?"

"Yes it did. Why?"

"Probably for a lot of reasons I don't know, but there is something powerful in thanking God for saving us and setting us free. Things we don't want hanging around our necks fall off when we acknowledge him in a bold way."

"I do feel lighter."

"We believe in our hearts and confess with our mouths that Jesus is Lord. Try this one, 'Jesus is Lord.' I'll join in with you."

So, atop a small mountain in western North Carolina, two young people declared a reality more important than the sum total of mankind's accomplishments since the beginning of recorded history—the ultimate authority of Jesus Christ.

As he and Jo grew quiet, Renny felt something welling up inside. Sitting on the stump, he said, "Jo, I think I am supposed to tell you something."

Remembering George Manor's words, she hesitated before asking, "What is it?"

"A verse from Psalm 23, one of the few chapters I'm familiar with in the Bible, keeps coming to my mind. The part that says, 'Yea, though I walk through the valley of the shadow of death, I will fear no evil: for thou art with me.' That's it. Why would I think about that?"

Relieved that he hadn't proposed, Jo sat down across from him. "I'm not sure."

"Maybe it's my imagination. I'm sorry."

"Oh, don't be. I'll pray about it." Jo wiped her hands on her shorts and stood. "Let's walk back to the lodge."

Renny followed Jo down the path. When they reached the gazebo, he came alongside her and said, "Let's stop here for a minute."

Jo saw the Manors' car approaching the house through the orchard. "Look, George and Helen are back. Let's see if they need any help." Without waiting for a response from Renny, she kept going. She did not want to test the accuracy of George Manor's prophecy.

Jo and Renny grabbed the last two sacks of groceries from the trunk and carried them into the kitchen, a long, narrow room divided by a wooden island that provided plenty of workspace and seating for eight people on high four-legged stools. An adjacent breakfast nook nestled in a bay window had a mountain view on three sides.

"How was the prayer ridge?" Helen asked.

"More of a proclamation ridge for us," Jo said.

"That's good," George said. "I've had a few meetings myself around the fire ring."

"Would you like something to drink?" Helen asked.

"Water would be fine," Jo said.

They each sat on a stool, holding a glass of ice water.

Renny cleared his throat. "Thanks for what you told me earlier."

George nodded.

"It answered my question about God in a way I'd never suspected."

"Good," George said.

Renny continued, "After I came in from the deck, I spent some time alone reading the Bible. A lot of things became clear to me, and I knew God was calling me to come to know him. I prayed, and it happened."

"Congratulations!" George slid off the stool and clapped him on the shoulder.

Helen gave Renny a hug. "Our supper tonight can be your celebration meal. I'll get started right away."

"May I help you?" Jo asked.

"You can keep me company," she answered.

Ambling toward the door, George said, "Come on, Renny, we can go on in the other room."

Going into the great room, George took his accustomed seat to the left of the fireplace. Renny sat on the sofa.

Renny's earlier irritation was gone, and he saw George Manor in a completely different light. Although his simple words had impact and power, the baron of Zion Hall had the nonthreatening approachability of a giant teddy bear.

"I believe God spoke to me on the deck. Not out loud, but in here," Renny said, pointing to his chest.

"What did he say?"

"It was short. *'Read my Word.'*"

George nodded. "Then that's what you need to do. You'll find the Bible is a different book today than it was yesterday. Only a Christian can fully understand the Bible's message because it's a spiritual book. In 1 Corinthians 2, it states that the man without the Spirit considers the truth of God foolishness because it is only through the Holy Spirit that the words can be understood. You now have that capacity."

"OK, I read something similar in John."

George nodded and continued, "In the new relationship you have with the Lord, you must continue to hear and obey his voice. That's the key to repentance and faith. Those things, together with the assurance that God loves you, are the foundations upon which the Lord will build your life. A lot of people worry about the things they don't understand in the Bible. Mark Twain once wrote, 'It's not what I don't understand in the Bible that troubles me; it's what I do that worries me.' My focus has always been listening to what God is saying and walking in obedience."

George picked up the Bible Renny had used earlier and patted the cover. "By understanding, I don't mean knowing the dictionary definition of the words used or memorizing a bunch of principles and rules. The Bible is full of principles and rules that are important, but spiritual understanding produces change the same way a close relationship between a husband and wife can, after the passage of time, cause them to look like one another. God is not as interested in the facts we know about the Bible as how much we look like Jesus in our character and conduct."

With resolve in his voice, Renny said, "I want this."

"The strength of your desire is important because God rewards those who diligently seek him. That's your part, to make the right choices by an exercise of your will. But real, lasting change is ultimately the result of God's activity in us. It's like my apple trees. They must stay in constant contact with the soil, moisture, and light—the things that give them life and cause them to grow and produce fruit. Stay connected to the Lord, and you will grow as a Christian."

George handed Renny the Bible. "Why don't you go upstairs to one of the empty guest rooms and read John 15."

Helen prepared four pan-fried steaks for supper. Heavily seasoned with pepper and spices, the meat was cooked in its own juices and was complemented by a salad with a homemade apple vinaigrette dressing and scalloped potatoes. Instead of praying before the meal, George led everyone in singing the doxology.

"We've done that a time or two in restaurants," he said as they sat down. "It definitely attracts attention. One time, most of the people in the place joined in before we got to the end."

During supper, George entertained them with stories from his past. "Once I spoke to a group of men in a prison-release program. Toward the end of my talk, a big guy in the back raised his hand and said, 'I have a question. It says in the Bible that you have to turn the other cheek if someone hits you. Do you believe that?'

"Everyone looked at me, wondering what I would say. Not seeing any wiggle room, I said, 'Yes.'

"The guy jumped up from his seat and came up in front of me with a belligerent look on his face. 'If I hit you, you won't hit back, right?'

"Trapped by my own words, I said, 'That's right,' and closed my eyes waiting for the blow to fall.

"But nothing happened. In a few seconds, I opened my eyes and he was gone. I looked down, and he was on his knees, asking God to forgive him. Later, he told me that when I closed my eyes, he lost all interest in hurting me. All he could think about was the mess he'd made of his life."

Listening to George, Renny lost his fear of becoming a religious fanatic. It was simple—unusual things happened to Christians because the Christian life was not designed to be boring. George had gone to exotic places, seen miraculous events, and met fascinating people.

After supper, Helen cleared the table and brought a pitcher of grape juice, four tumblers, and four large pieces of Jewish matzo from the kitchen.

"Let's celebrate," George said as he poured a full glass for each of them and gave them each a large square of the unleavened bread.

Eyeing the large glass filled to the brim, Renny asked, "Is this for Communion?"

"Yes. Jesus was not stingy in the way he gave himself for us. He didn't use little plastic cups and tiny bits of crackers at the Last Supper. It was part of a real meal, just like we had this evening."

George said a few words about the Last Supper and invited them to remember the Lord's sacrifice. As Renny drank the juice and munched on the matzo, he didn't have a vision of the cross or see the wounds on Jesus' body. Rather, he had a deep sense of appreciation for what Jesus had done for him, for Renny Jacobson, a man whose struggles with God had, on one level, come to an end. The prodigal was home.

18

Experiment to me is everyone I meet.
EMILY DICKINSON

R enny and Jo drove slowly through the orchard as the sun cast its last rays upward in an arch from behind a hill to the west.

"I'd like to come back when the blossoms are on the trees in early spring," he said.

"If I lived in North Carolina, I'd come every season of the year," Jo replied.

The ride to the bottom of the mountain seemed shorter than the trip up. Renny pulled into the parking lot of the Phillips Apple Barn and put up the car top. "We'll have a starlit ride another time," he said.

Jo settled into her seat as Renny shifted the gears and the car hugged the gentle curves of the road. Neither spoke as their minds traveled separate journeys through the events of the day. In a few minutes, Jo dozed off.

While he drove, Renny admired Jo's face as the lights of passing cars and trucks illuminated her profile. She didn't wake up until the Charlotte skyline came into view.

"Good nap?" he asked as she stretched.

"Yes. That was a quick trip."

"We should be home in about fifteen minutes."

When they arrived at the house, a light was on in the kitchen, but Mrs. Stokes was already in bed.

"What's the plan for tomorrow?" Jo asked as Renny quietly opened the door for her.

"I have to go to the office for a few hours."

Jo yawned. "I'll see you when you get back," she said, turning toward the hallway.

"OK." Renny reached for the kitchen door handle, then stopped. "Jo," he said, and waited until she turned around. "Uh . . . thanks."

———

Jo needed time alone. Now, rested from her long nap, she sat in the dark in Mrs. Stokes's prayer closet. Several minutes passed. Then she asked the waiting silence the question that had been at the head of the line in her thoughts: "What am I supposed to do if he asks me to marry him?"

"Thank me."

"For what?" she asked. "That's not an answer."

"For saving Renny."

Jo's eyes watered. "I'm sorry. Thank you, Lord."

Many would rejoice—Renny's mother, Mama A, Mrs. Stokes, and other unknown voices whose prayers were the coinage of reward in heaven. Then she remembered that one saint who had invested in Renny was close enough to tell the good news in person—she needed to tell Mrs. Stokes.

Leaving her sanctuary and walking quietly down the hall, Jo saw light shining under the closed door to Mrs. Stokes's bedroom. She knocked softly. "Mrs. Stokes, it's Jo. May I come in?"

A sleepy-eyed Daisy Stokes opened the door. "Come in. I fell asleep reading a book. How was your trip?"

"Wonderful. Renny gave his heart to the Lord."

The news brought Mrs. Stokes fully awake. "Praise the Lord! I thought it would be sooner rather than later, but this *is* soon."

"I wanted you to know. I'll let you go back to sleep."

"I want to hear all about it in the morning."

Jo backed out of the room. "Of course. Good night."

"Jo?"

"Yes?"

"I have a verse for you. 'Except the LORD build the house, they labour in vain that build it.' Psalm 127:1. The Lord will build your house, don't you worry about it."

Jo returned to the prayer closet with the verse reverberating in her heart. It was the answer to her question about marrying Renny, and it gave divine perspective to her circumstances. She prayed, "Thank you, Lord. I ask you to build my house, to oversee every aspect of my relationship with Renny." God was in control. After a quiet half-hour, she went to sleep, untroubled by worrisome dreams of unknown tomorrows.

———

It was still dark when Renny woke up the following morning. He lay in bed, replaying the previous day's events. Once fully awake, he got out of bed and brewed a cup of coffee. In a bookshelf in the living room was his Bible, a gift from his mother when he started high school. Opening it, he read a forgotten inscription, "To Renny upon your high school gradua-tion. May this book find its way into your heart and provide light to your path. Psalm 119:105." Sitting at his kitchen table, Renny took a sip of coffee and turned to the verse. It confirmed George Manor's advice, and its words became the second prayer of his young Christian life.

Turning to the New Testament, he began reading about the life of Jesus recorded by Matthew. At first he read rapidly, but when he came to the Sermon on the Mount, his pace slowed. Jesus' words about the nature of righteousness were disturbing. He stopped. *It's not just doing wrong, it's thinking wrong that Jesus labeled sin. Calling someone a fool, looking at a woman with a lustful thought, hating someone who wrongs me, petty jealousies.* He had done all those things—repeatedly. Renny knelt on the kitchen floor, a posture he'd never assumed except on cue in the Episcopal church.

He spoke out loud, "You know what I've done. You know what I've said. You know what I've thought. Forgive me. Change me."

As he stayed on his knees, particular incidents of wrongdoing from his past came to mind. At first he tried to dismiss the thoughts as distractions, but then he realized it was a chance to clean the slate. Each memory surfaced, and he acknowledged his deeds as sin and asked for forgiveness. By the time he stopped, the first rays of sun were coming in the window. He let Brandy out for a romp in the backyard while he shaved and showered. As the warm water rushed over his head, he felt clean, outside and inside.

Jo and Mrs. Stokes were in the kitchen when he knocked on the door.

"Good morning," Mrs. Stokes said. "Is this the new Renny Jacobson?"

"New and improved," he answered, smiling.

"Coffee?" Jo asked.

"Thanks. My first cup cooled before I finished it."

Jo went to the counter and poured him a fresh cup. "I thought you were going to the office?"

"It can wait. I had some other business to take care of this morning."

"Oh?"

"I went to confessional in my kitchen."

"What?"

"In reading the Sermon on the Mount, I realized some of the creative ways I've sinned."

Jo nodded. "That makes sense, but don't say any more. Those times are confidential between you and Jesus, your High Priest." Setting the cup in front of him, she asked, "What's on for today?"

"Since I've done the serious work already, would you like to play tennis this morning?"

"Sure. Are there courts nearby?"

"It's about a mile. We need to go early so we won't have to wait in line."

"Do you have an extra racquet?"

"I'll let you use my good one."

"Don't give me an unfair advantage."

"Let me fix you a good breakfast, Renny," Mrs. Stokes said. "You may need extra energy."

The tennis courts were past their prime. The green paint had faded through in spots, and the concrete was pocked with several small dips where moisture had undermined the surface. Jo had a smooth stroke, but Renny was able to hold his own. The first set was tied at five when Renny broke Jo's service to take a one-game lead. Confident of victory, Renny served for the set, but Jo unleashed a succession of crosscourt backhands that left Renny gasping as the shots eluded him.

"You've been holding out on me," he panted after failing to run down a shot to the back corner. "You can always tell a real tennis player from a hacker like me by the way they hit those ground strokes."

Jo wiped the perspiration from her forehead with a towel. "You're not a hacker. Remember, you gave me the best racquet."

"Where did you learn to play tennis?"

"I played on my high school team. One of the other girls was a nationally ranked junior, and all of us who played with her improved."

Jo broke Renny's serve and won the tiebreaker five to two. Her last shot was a lob over Renny's head as he charged the net. He watched the shot fall a couple of inches inside the baseline, and he sat down in the middle of the court.

"I thought Christians were supposed to be merciful."

"I was merciful. I could have run you around for a few more points."

They stopped at the video store on the way back to the house and rented *Anne of Green Gables.*

"We can watch it this afternoon before I take you to dinner," Renny said. "It's already too hot to do anything else outside."

"I can fix you some popcorn. It's one of my specialties. Mrs. Stokes offered me some the other night."

"I didn't know Mrs. Stokes had any secret sins," Renny said.

"Oh yes, she even melts real butter and pours it on top."

Renny turned into the driveway. "Have you decided if you can stay through tomorrow? I'd really like to take you to St. Catherine's."

Jo hesitated. "Are you sure?"

"Yes, even though you hit that last ball over my head."

Jo laughed. "OK, I'll call the travel agency and my friend who agreed to cover my shift at the hospital."

———

Mrs. Stokes would be gone all afternoon visiting a friend who lived near the UNC-Charlotte campus. After cleaning up, Renny went downstairs and mentally replayed a few points of the tennis game in his mind until Jo, her dark hair wet from the shower, came into the kitchen.

"I called the travel agency and changed my flight to 5:35 tomorrow afternoon," she said.

"Did you talk to your friend about taking your shift at the hospital?"

"Yes, she was glad to do it. She's bought a new car and needs extra money."

"Great."

"And, most important, I found some popcorn in the pantry."

Popcorn in hand, Jo followed Renny upstairs to his apartment. Brandy greeted them at the door.

"She's not used to a lot of company up here. She likes you, but she didn't tolerate my friend Morris until he started bringing her a bone every time he came over to watch a ball game."

Renny gave her a tour of his dwelling. She stopped in front of a collection of pictures from Renny's childhood.

Pointing to a shot of Renny as a small boy sitting beside a sandcastle complete with a tower almost as tall as he was, she asked, "Was this taken at Pawley's Island?"

"No, that was on the Outer Banks of North Carolina. We often vacationed on Okracoke, a barrier island with miles of deserted beaches. My parents liked it, but I wanted to go to Myrtle Beach because it was more fun for kids."

"Did you build the sandcastle all by yourself?"

"I imagine I did. There wasn't much else to do, and my father was not the castle-building type."

"What about this picture, the one with the golf club?" Jo asked. "How old were you?"

"Sixteen. I look like David Duval with the sunglasses, don't I?"

"Uh, maybe a shorter version."

Renny ignored the dig. "That was at my father's country club in Charleston, the same course where he had his heart attack. We played a round of golf, and I shot a hole in one on a par three. My moment of glory. I still carry the ball in my golf bag for good luck."

In the lower left-hand corner of the frame a gap-toothed Renny with short hair and a plaid shirt buttoned up all the way to his chin looked out with childlike innocence. "And this one? It looks like a school picture."

"That's my absolute worst ever picture. First grade."

"I think it's adorable," Jo replied.

"I didn't have an older brother to help me along the way, so it took me a while to learn how to dress for elementary school success. Come on, we'll watch the movie in the living room."

———

Jo loved the film. From the opening scene in which Matthew Cuthbert picked up Anne from the train station and drove her in a horse-drawn buggy to Green Gables through the flower-bedecked avenue, until the *Titanic*-like incident when Anne floated down the river lying in the bottom of a leaky rowboat while quoting Tennyson, Jo was riveted to the screen.

Renny paused the picture. "Popcorn time."

Jo hopped up and went to the kitchen. "Do you have a popcorn popper?"

Renny opened a cabinet door under the cooktop and handed her a stainless steel pan with a lid. "I have some oil in the cupboard next to the sink." In a couple of minutes the kernels were playing a staccato beat around the inside of the pot.

"I memorized *The Highway Man*," Jo said, referring to a poem recited by Anne in the film. "I would have thought it was impossible, but once I got started, the story carried me along."

"I memorized twelve lines of Rudyard Kipling's *Gunga Din* in the fifth grade," Renny said.

"You're a better man that I am, Gunga Din," Jo responded.

"That line was repeated enough to let me catch my breath. If I ever own an elephant, I'll name him Gunga."

Jo laughed. "Good planning. It would be embarrassing to buy an elephant at the pet store and not have a name selected to put on the collar."

Jo melted the butter in a small pan and poured it over the steaming white kernels. Taking a whiff, she said, "That's the way God intended popcorn, the perfect snack."

With the popcorn bowl between them on an end table between the sofa and chair, they resumed their seats.

"Do I remind you of Gilbert Blythe, Anne's suitor?" Renny asked before restarting the tape.

"You mean when he teased her about her red hair and she broke a slate tablet over his head?"

Turning sideways, Renny said, "No, my profile."

"Not as a boy. Maybe as a man," she answered.

"Hmm, is that good?"

"Yes, it's good."

Jo cried quietly when Matthew Cuthbert suffered a heart attack in a field and died in Anne's arms.

"That was different than the book," she said as her sniffles subsided and the film credits scrolled across the screen. "In the book, Matthew died on the steps of the house when he learned they'd lost their life savings in a bank failure."

"What did you think about Matthew's dying words when Anne apologized for not being a boy who could help on the farm?" Renny asked. "You know, the way he said, 'You're all I ever wanted, Anne.'"

"Quit it, Renny, you're trying to make me cry again."

"OK, OK. I thought it was a good scene."

The popcorn bowl was empty except for a few unpopped kernels rolling around in the bottom.

"Good popcorn," Renny said, "but don't eat anything else. I am going to take you to a nice restaurant tonight and don't want you to ruin your appetite."

"I need to go downstairs and get ready," Jo said.

"Our reservations are for seven-thirty."

"I'll see you later, then. I enjoyed the movie."

"Me, too."

Renny opened the door for her and, leaning against the doorframe, watched Jo without an *e* descend the stairs.

———

The two men sat across from each other, a speakerphone between them in the middle of the polished walnut table.

"Do we have any other questions?" the heavily accented voice on the phone asked.

"Yes. Is the rate of return the same on all transactions?" one of the men responded.

"Always 100 percent."

"Payable within sixty days?"

"Yes."

The two men nodded to each other across the table.

"All right. We will make a trial investment."

"How much?"

"We'll start modest. Seventy-five million."

"Excellent. I'll give you the account information."

After the phone connection ended, one of the men asked, "What about security?"

"I've contacted some local people. They have access to information within the organization and can let us know if anything goes amiss."

"I hope this isn't a rat hole."

"Don't worry. I have everything under control."

19

Let him kiss me with the kisses of his mouth.
SONG OF SOLOMON 1:2, KJV

Jo frowned as she zipped up the low back of the peach-colored dress. Although not immodest by most standards, the dress was the most revealing gown in her wardrobe. She liked to wear it with a double strand of pearls that gracefully looped around her neck. Now, she second-guessed her choice.

She stood in front of a full-length mirror in the bathroom. There was nothing artificial or contrived about her appearance. No Hollywood starlet, Jo possessed an intangible beauty, the same beauty Leonardo da Vinci captured when he painted the *Mona Lisa* and revealed to all the world a woman's most important physical characteristic— her countenance. Like her young Italian counterpart, Jo's countenance revealed the same qualities of poise and inner peace, coupled with a hint of mystery.

If Renny asked her to marry him, what would she say? She searched for direction in the eyes that faced her in the mirror. Nothing gave her the answer. However, she saw something else, a depth, a spiritual reservoir within her spirit, a source of strength that she knew would sustain her. But, in answer to her question. Nothing.

"Lord, why do you always seem to talk to me about something different than what is on my mind?" she asked softly.

"My ways are not your ways, and my thoughts are not your thoughts."

She could see that. She would have to accept it. But she still needed to know what to do.

Trying not to become frustrated or anxious, she continued to wait. Then, after several moments, understanding dawned. She already had the answer. The living Presence within her would provide the wellspring of wisdom for responding to Renny. All she need do was draw upon the infinite resources of God's grace. *His grace is sufficient for any situation or circumstance.* Confidence returned to her face. Rearranging the pearls, she straightened her shoulders and walked down the hallway toward her future.

———

The Clairmont was a yuppie bistro known for steak and lobster. Renny had reserved a table for two, and the maître d' led them to the quietest corner of the busy restaurant. When they were seated, a voice behind Renny's left shoulder said loudly, "I recommend the cheese fries and a bowl of chili."

Turning in his chair, Renny said, "Jo, this is my friend Morris Hogan."

Morris bowed and shook Jo's hand. "Some people call me Hulk, you know, after the professional wrestler."

"What do you like to be called?" Jo asked.

"I'd answer to any name you chose. Renny usually calls me Mr. Hogan."

"Right, Hulk," Renny responded. "Be careful or I'll throw you into the turnbuckle."

"What?" Jo asked.

"Wrestling term," Morris said.

"Jo is not a big fan of the professional wrestling circuit, Morris," Renny said. "She's not up to speed on NASCAR either."

"Stay in town a few days, and I'll teach you everything you need to know about the WCW and NASCAR," Morris offered.

"I'm sure you'd be a great teacher," Jo said with a smile.

"And she could teach you a few things about tennis," Renny added.

"She has a backhand that could run Earnhardt into the wall of turn number three at Talledega."

Morris glanced over his shoulder. "I wish I could pull up a chair and join you, but I'm supposed to be entertaining a couple of boring guys from Los Angeles. It's nice meeting you," he said to Jo. "Renny, I'll see you in the ring on Monday."

After Morris left, Jo said, "I can see you two spending an entire lunch hour trading one-liners."

"That's pretty accurate. Morris has a job with one of the megabanks. We get together regularly and compare notes from our respective cubicles. He's the one who gave me the Duke cap you wore yesterday."

"Next time you talk to him, tell him he has too much personality to be a brainy guy from Duke."

"If I tell him that, his head will swell so much he'll have to buy the biggest Duke hat they make."

They both ordered steak. After the waiter brought their salads, Renny said, "Let me pray."

Jo, a little wide-eyed, nodded.

Bowing his head, Renny said, "Thank you," paused, "thank you," paused longer, and said more softly, "thank you. Amen."

"Amen," Jo said.

"Short prayer, huh?" Renny asked. "Did it work?"

"I'm sure there is no more blessed food within a hundred miles."

The meal was perfect; the conversation relaxed and fun. They finished eating and ordered coffee. The conversation waned.

Leaning forward with his eyes shining, Renny said, "Jo, I want to tell you something."

Jo put down her coffee cup.

Without taking his eyes from Jo's face, Renny began, "I think you are the most wonderful, beautiful person, inside and out, I've ever met."

Everything in the restaurant faded, and they became a universe of two.

Speaking gently but confidently, he continued, "I love you and want to spend the rest of my life with you. We're not perfect people, especially me, but I believe we're perfect for each other."

The previous day, Jo resented the internal upheaval caused by George Manor's prediction. Now she appreciated the preparation his warning had given her. She was not caught off guard. Drawing from her well, she found the grace to answer.

"Renny, there is a big part of my heart that wants to say yes, but I know we are not ready to take this step."

As the first flicker of disappointment crossed Renny's face, she reached across the table, and took his hand firmly in hers. Remembering what Daisy Stokes told her, she said, "I want to encourage what is happening between us, but if we are going to join our lives together, we need a solid foundation. We've only known each other for a couple of weeks."

"It's been a great two weeks," Renny countered.

"I know, but we need to go deeper before we build a home together. God's doing things in our lives that take time."

"What sort of things? I promise I would learn to enjoy Michigan cooking," Renny said with a weak grin.

"It's not about barbecue or bagels, and I wish I could be more specific. All I know is that we're not ready to come together as husband and wife."

When she said "husband and wife," chills ran through Renny.

"I like the sound of that."

"Me, too, but not yet." She squeezed his hand and let go.

Hope renewed, Renny signaled the waiter and asked for the check.

———

They pulled into the driveway and got out of the car. "Do you want to come up and look at some more of my baby pictures?" Renny asked as they walked toward the door.

Jo laughed. "Clever maneuver. I enjoyed the ones you showed me this afternoon, but I think I'll go on inside."

"What if I cued up your favorite scene from *Anne of Green Gables*?"

"Equally clever, but not tonight. What time do I need to be ready in the morning?"

"About a quarter till ten. The church isn't far from here."

Jo reached for the door knob, then turned. "I don't want you to regret anything you said tonight, OK?"

"I don't."

Renny moved close. Jo lifted her face to his and looked into his eyes. He gently held her shoulders as their lips met.

It was a full kiss, sensual without being overbearing, intimate without being intrusive. Neither held back, their wills sacrificing every ounce of individuality on the altar of oneness. It was a kiss completely satisfying in itself.

Renny pulled back and opened his eyes. Jo met his gaze. "I love you," he said, then put his finger on her lips before she could respond. "Good night."

"Good night."

Renny smiled as he walked up the stairs to his apartment. Stopping on the landing he looked at the stars slowly marching across the clear night sky. *You stopped for an instant to watch tonight, didn't you?*

Inside the kitchen, Jo sat down and raised her index finger to her lips, touching the same place as Renny. If he'd asked her a second time to marry him, would she have given the same answer?

———

As Renny shaved and dressed the next morning, he thought about Jo and "The Kiss," as he now labeled it in his memory bank. Any hurt or embarrassment over her refusal to say yes to his proposal was swept away before his confidence that they would be united. For now, he was left with the exquisite pleasure of unfulfilled anticipation reserved for lovers.

While waiting for Jo in Mrs. Stokes's kitchen, Renny poured himself a second cup of coffee.

Mrs. Stokes joined him at the table. "How are you this morning?" she asked.

"Great," Renny said. "I've been reading the Bible, and it's incredible. Things are leaping off the page."

"It's personal, isn't it?" she said.

"Yes."

"Jesus said, 'My sheep hear my voice.' Hearing the voice of the Spirit is the birthright of every Christian. To me it's one of the surest proofs of the new birth."

"Put me on your list—" Renny stopped. When he said the word *list,* a brief wave of queasiness passed over him. He was already on one List.

Unaware of Renny's feelings, Mrs. Stokes continued, "One of the most important things you need to do is maintain that open line of communication with God. Being a Christian is a process. There is a beginning, but that is only the first step."

Renny's uneasiness subsided. "Like the Chinese proverb?"

"Yes," she said. "A journey of a thousand miles begins with the first step. We often used that with new believers. It's a true statement for the Christian life."

"What I've experienced in three days has been so intense I can't imagine it going away."

"Unfortunately it can. We are infinitely creative in ways to grieve the Holy Spirit. Walk in sensitivity and obedience if you want unbroken fellowship with the Lord."

"That's what George Manor told me. I think he said to hear and obey because it was the basis for faith and repentance."

"That's right. Truths such as faith, repentance, love, and grace are like huge precious stones with thousands of facets. You can't appreciate every facet and reflection of light in a single glance; it takes a lifetime of walking with him. Every time the Lord opens our eyes, we receive new levels of understanding that bring transformation to our lives. Transformation simply means becoming more like Jesus."

Jo, her hair pulled up with curls softly framing her face, appeared in a black-and-white dress. "Are you having a deep theological conversation?"

"As a matter of fact, we were," Renny said. "We usually do this on Sunday mornings."

"Careful, I think lying is covered in the Ten Commandments," Jo said.

"What does it say about kidding?"

"I'll have to study the Hebrew and get back to you," Jo said.

Renny stood. "We'd better go. We'll eat lunch out, Mrs. Stokes."

When they were seated in the car, Renny said, "Good morning."

"Good morning. Did you have pleasant dreams?"

"I didn't need any. I had something real to think about. "

"I'm glad you liked it."

"Oh, I did. How about you?"

"It was OK."

"Only OK?" Renny stopped the car. "What was that you said in the kitchen about lying?"

St. Catherine's parking lot was almost full, and Renny dropped Jo off at the entrance to the church before parking the car. As he locked the door, he heard a car horn and saw Jack and Lois Berit coming around the adjacent row of vehicles. They parked a few spaces away from Renny. Someone else was in the car. It was Thomas Layne.

Lois waved. "Renny, come meet my brother from Charleston."

Renny, his mouth suddenly dry, nodded a greeting to Lois and walked over to their vehicle. Layne, the familiar smirk on his face, extended his hand. "Hello, I'm Thomas Layne. My sister was just telling me about you as we pulled in the parking lot. It's a pleasure to meet you." He shook Renny's hand.

Renny mumbled, "Pleased to meet you."

Lois chirped, "I know you two will want to compare Charleston notes. Thomas wasn't going to visit for a couple of weeks but had a change in plans and came early. I'm so glad you came back this Sunday, Renny. Maybe the four of us can go to lunch together after the service."

"I've brought someone with me this morning," Renny said.

"Good, your friend would be welcome to join us as well."

Jack and Lois led the way across the parking lot. Layne held back a little and touched Renny's arm. "Your friend isn't a dark-haired young woman from Michigan, is she?" Layne asked.

"You guessed it," Renny said, trying to act casual.

"Brilliant. I'm glad you're following LaRochette's request to keep an eye on her." Layne kept his voice low. "We'll talk later. Tell her not to let on that she has ever met me. Avoid any awkward explanations with my sister, you know."

Renny grunted.

"By the way, you're not becoming a religious fanatic, are you?" Layne chuckled. "You don't strike me as the type."

Renny didn't answer.

———

Jo was inside the foyer talking with a woman who had greeted her. Touching her back, Renny leaned down and whispered, "Thomas Layne is here. Act like you've never met him."

Jo turned and asked, "What?"

At that moment Layne stepped forward and took Jo's hand. "Renny, this must be your friend. I'm Thomas Layne."

Lois came up on the other side and introduced herself. "I'm Lois Berit. My husband, Jack, has already gotten away from me. I want you to meet him, too," she said looking around for him.

"This is Jo Johnston," Renny said to Lois.

Jack motioned to them. "I have five seats on the left side of the sanctuary, but we need to go ahead and sit down."

Renny was sandwiched between Layne on his left and Jo on his right.

It was impossible to talk to Jo. Out of the corner of his eye, Renny could see the firm cut of her features. She was not smiling.

The worship was similar to the week before. Paul Bushnell, the rector, welcomed the Lord to the meeting, and the instrumentalists and singers began to celebrate.

Renny was flat. His anticipation and excitement about the service evaporated like a drop of water on the hot asphalt of the church parking lot. Lois was banging her tambourine, but it might as well have been a trash can lid to Renny. Jo started clapping her hands a little, and when the music turned softer, she closed her eyes. Layne looked straight ahead. Renny wondered if he ever blinked.

As the worship flowed out of the room and it grew quiet, Renny tried to regain the sense of the Lord he had felt earlier in the morning. Nothing. They all sat down as Paul and Chuck Southgate came forward and led the congregation through the morning readings and prayers.

Afterward, Paul Bushnell said, "Chuck Southgate, who works with our youth, is going to lead us this morning."

Southgate stepped to the microphone. "This morning I want to speak about our identifying with Jesus Christ in the world. It's one thing to express our love and devotion for him within the safety of this sanctuary, surrounded by those who support our faith. It's quite another to do so in the places we live day by day. To help me make my point this morning, I've asked two of the teenagers in the church to share their experiences with you. First, Jeremy Davenport."

Jeremy, a lanky young man with close-cropped brown hair and blue eyes, began by describing typical adolescent struggles with peer pressure at school and harassment from others when he refused to go along with the crowd. He expressed appreciation for the influence of his father and mother, then said, "It was not until my father's death from cancer nine months ago that I learned to stand on my own for God. For me, it was a make-it-or-break-it time. I was mad at God for a while, but although I miss my dad, I decided not to let go of the good things he taught me. I've faced the fact that I will die someday, and this has made me bolder in letting others know that I'm a Christian. Last week, two guys who have hassled me about my faith came to me after they had some problems at school, and I was able to tell them the gospel. One of them prayed to receive Jesus into his heart. I can see now that each step I've taken toward God has always been the right step. That's the journey I'm on."

A junior high girl named Kelli spoke next. She told how she had reached out to Sarah, a neighborhood friend. After a few months, Sarah became a Christian. Sarah's parents were considering a divorce, and their daughter asked Kelli and her family to pray about the situation. One evening when Sarah's parents came to pick up their daughter, Kelli's parents invited them inside. The two families became friends. Now, six months later, both families were in the church. When Kelli finished, Chuck Southgate asked everyone involved in the story to stand, and the congregation applauded.

Renny was amazed at the willingness of the people to allow their lives to be exposed to public view.

Southgate said, "Let me read Mark 8:38: 'If anyone is ashamed of me and my words in this adulterous and sinful generation, the Son of Man will be ashamed of him when he comes in his Father's glory with the holy angels.'"

Closing the Bible, he continued, "My purpose is not to burden you with the wrong kind of guilt this morning. If you are not active in sharing your faith, don't try to pull yourself up by your bootstraps and attempt to do better. Rather, come to the Lord in repentance and ask him to overwhelm you with his love. He loves you; you love him; he loves others through you. Then, because you have something real yourself, you will want to share that reality with others."

When it was time for Communion, Southgate held his arms wide in invitation. "The first place to acknowledge the presence of Jesus in your life is safe—before this congregation. I want to invite anyone who has never done so to confess publicly Jesus as Lord. If you have never openly identified with Jesus and want to do so this morning, we want to serve you first."

In classic sawdust-trail fashion, Renny's hands grew clammy, his heart started pounding, and he felt everyone in the room watching and waiting for him to get out of his seat. He hesitated. Chuck Southgate seemed unhurried as the seconds passed. A young boy, accompanied by his mother, went forward and knelt at the altar. An overweight woman in her twenties followed him. Tissue in hand to blow her nose, she was greeted by Paul Bushnell. Renny hesitated. He would have to crawl over Layne to get to the aisle. He saw himself getting up and tripping over Layne's foot. That would never do. He hesitated. Southgate smiled as if everything was great. "Please pray for these two as we serve them."

Renny was relieved, but the relief lasted less than a full second. It was followed by regret, then before regret could gain a hearing, accusation pushed its way to the front of his consciousness. He was an idiot and a fool who had been playing a silly religious game. *Get real,* he told himself. A splitting headache pierced his skull with pain, and when the others on the row got up to go to the Communion rail, he put his head in his hands and shook his head.

"What's wrong," Jo whispered.

"Terrible headache."

Jo sat down beside him and motioned for Lois and Jack to go ahead. Layne was already in line to go to the front.

"Remember when I prayed for your headache in Georgetown?"

Renny nodded without looking up.

Jo continued softly, "Father, I ask you to touch Renny now and heal him."

She waited; Renny kept holding his head in his hands.

"Do you feel any better?"

"No. You go on up. I just need to be still a minute."

Jo hesitated then slipped past him. A place opened at the altar rail, and she knelt to receive the bread and wine. She lingered and Paul

Bushnell came back to her as the crowd at the altar thinned and asked, "Is there something I can pray about with you?"

"If you have time, could you pray for my friend after the service?"

"Sure. Don't leave. I'll come back into the sanctuary as soon as most of the people are gone."

———

After the rector gave the benediction, Lois Berit asked, "Renny, can you and Jo join us for lunch?"

"No thanks, I've got a migraine and don't feel like eating right now," Renny said.

"I'll be in town for a couple of days. Maybe we can get together," Layne spoke up. "Do you have a card with you?"

Renny pulled out his wallet and gave him one.

"Hope you feel better," Lois said. "It was nice meeting you, Jo. Hope you visit again."

Jo motioned for Renny to wait as the Berits and Layne walked toward the door. "I asked the rector if he would pray for you. He said to wait here until he finishes greeting the people."

"Why did you do that?" Renny asked. "I barely know the man."

"That's your headache talking. Let's give it a chance."

Renny sat down grumpily. "I feel like a calf waiting to be branded."

They sat in silence until Bushnell came over to them. He shook Renny's hand. "We met last week, didn't we? Ronny, isn't it?"

"Yes, uh no, it's Renny."

"Sorry. What's the problem?"

"I didn't want to bother you. It's only a headache."

"A bad one though?"

"Yes."

"Let me get some oil."

Renny looked at Jo as Bushnell went to the front of the sanctuary. "Oil?"

"Anointing oil. It's a symbol of the Holy Spirit. The New Testament gives guidelines about praying for sick people and anointing them with oil. It's in the book of James."

"Oh." Renny knew he was going to have to submit to the ritual whether it was motor oil or castor oil.

"Do you know about anointing with oil?" Bushnell asked when he returned with a small vial of golden liquid in his hand.

Relying on his education of the past thirty seconds, Renny said, "Yes."

"Good. Let's pray and ask God to touch you."

Bushnell moistened his finger with the oil and put his hand on Renny's right temple. "Is that where it hurts the worst?"

"Yes, it is."

"OK. Lord, we ask you to touch Renny with your healing power." He waited several seconds, then said, "It's really bad, isn't it?"

"Yes, it still hurts," Renny said.

"I may have suffered the type of pain you're feeling. It's a sharp, knifelike sensation centered in your right temple. Makes you feel a little nauseous?"

"Yes."

"Is this the first severe headache you've experienced?"

"No. They started recently. I've had two or three since my father's death."

"Did he have headaches?"

"Yes. All his life, as far as I know."

"There may be a connection. Let's pray again. Father, we ask you to remove this headache and rebuke its origin in Jesus' name." He waited again. "It's not gone, is it?" It was more of a statement than a question.

"No."

"Why not?" Jo asked.

"When I prayed for you, Renny, I saw a picture in my mind of two swords coming down out of heaven. They clashed in the air then fell to earth, sticking in the ground in a crossed position, blade to blade."

"What would that have to do with a headache?" Renny asked.

"It means the basis for the headache may be more spiritual than physical."

"Well, it hurts in the physical," Renny said.

"Granted. Many headaches have a physical explanation—stress, fluid pressure, poor circulation, blows to the head. Do you have a history of a physical condition that could cause you to have headaches?"

"No."

"Then I would think even more strongly that it is a spiritual issue."

"Whatever." Renny was ready to leave. The rector was getting on his nerves.

"What do the swords represent?" Jo asked, ignoring the tone of Renny's response.

"I would interpret the clash of swords as a battle over your spiritual vision or understanding. It's so fierce you are having effects in your body. Does anything I've said make sense to you?" Bushnell asked.

Renny wanted to say no and shut the rector up, but he answered, "Perhaps. But I still don't know what to do."

"I don't know either, but I'm willing to help. Could the three of us get together later this week and spend a longer time praying about this?"

"I'm going back to Michigan this afternoon," Jo said. "But Renny lives here in Charlotte. You could come by this week, couldn't you?" she asked Renny.

"Maybe Wednesday," Renny said reluctantly.

"I'm here in the morning, but I usually play golf Wednesday afternoon. I can skip it, though, if that's the only time you can meet."

"Thanks," Jo said.

They stood, and Bushnell shook Renny's hand. "Give me a call, please."

Renny dreaded walking out into the sunlight, but the pain lifted as he walked across the parking lot to his car.

"Do you want me to drive?" Jo asked.

"No, I can do it. Maybe it's a delayed reaction to the prayer. Does it work that way sometimes?"

"Yes, it can." Jo sat in the passenger seat. "Do you want to go home? That would be fine with me."

"No, I'm better. Really. Let's get something to eat."

"Are you sure?"

"Yeah. Mexican OK?"

Jo turned in her seat and faced him. "Wait a minute. This is strange. One minute you're so sick you can't go forward for Communion and the next you want to eat Mexican food."

Renny shrugged. "I don't know. Neither did the good rector."

———

The phone rang four times while the old man took a tentative sip of his Bloody Mary. Like Renny, he was recovering from the remaining vestiges of the morning's headache.

"No, I feel terrible," he said in response to the caller's greeting. "Get to the point."

He listened and took a few more swallows of his first cocktail of the day. "Satisfactory. Keep me posted."

He put on dark glasses before walking into the sunny kitchen.

20

Parting is such sweet sorrow.
ROMEO AND JULIET, ACT 2, SCENE 2

Renny turned onto Park Road, an open boulevard flanked by newly developed residential areas that fed a steady stream of minivans and sport utility vehicles onto the busy roadway.

"It shook me up a bit seeing Thomas Layne in the parking lot," he said.

"That was obvious. I could tell you were uptight as soon as you came into the church."

"He's intimidating."

"Did he tell you to pretend you'd never met him?"

"Yes."

"I'm glad it wasn't your idea, but I didn't like it. At best it was phony; at worst it was deceptive."

"I didn't know what to say. It caught me off guard. The parking lot of the church on Sunday morning didn't seem the place to open a discussion with Layne and his sister about a 140-year-old secret society that neither he nor their father ever told her about. She seems happy enough without the information."

"That should tell you something about happiness."

"You mean that ignorance is bliss?"

"Not exactly, but go ahead."

"Well, I had trouble concentrating in the meeting, and I knew you were upset when I asked you to play dumb about Layne. Worst of all, I think I should have gone forward at the end."

"I wondered why you didn't. I thought about giving you a nudge but decided you were able to hear from the Lord yourself."

"Earlier today I would have thought so, too. I know what happened at the mountain and the times I've had with God in the mornings the past couple of days have been real, very real. But at the church everything was thrown into a barrel of doubt and questioning."

Renny turned into the restaurant parking lot. Inside, they sat across from each other in a high-backed booth under a multicolored piñata. Dipping a tortilla chip in the salsa, Renny continued, "When the rector asked people to come forward and openly acknowledge Jesus before the congregation, I knew it was my opportunity to take the next step. I was a little hesitant to walk forward in front of a group of people, but the real reason I stayed in my seat was concern about Layne. What would he think? I doubt he would have approved of an open religious display."

"Probably not. But remember what George Manor said."

"What part?"

"God is not like your father."

"How does that apply to Thomas Layne?"

"Don't let your father, Thomas Layne, or the List determine how you respond to God."

The waiter took their order.

"You're right," Renny said thoughtfully. "I'll try not to miss my opportunity to respond to what God is telling me. And before I eat this whole basket of chips, will you pray a blessing?"

Jo prayed.

"Hearing you pray reminded me of something," Renny said when Jo finished. "Speculation about your religious beliefs was a hot topic in Georgetown. While you were out of the room, they asked me about your Christian faith. I didn't think it was relevant, and I bet most of the men on the List are church members, probably more 'whiskeypalian' than Episcopalian in their theology. But I'd guess they're tolerant of casual religion; it's part of their tradition."

"What did you say?"

"Oh, I told them Christianity was very important to you. I'd already heard you pray and felt your missionary zeal toward me as a potential proselyte when we went to Pawley's Island."

Jo smiled. "You were a difficult prospect. Too much of a know-it-all."

"Hey, I think I've been easy. Anyway, I think some of them were scared by your religious fanaticism. Religion is not a threat unless it affects behavior. And since the List operates on the edges of law, some of the other members were concerned you might create problems. Why else would they offer you a million dollars and ask you to keep everything confidential?"

"I was interested in learning about my father, not upsetting their apple cart."

"You said that, but most people aren't as straightforward as you are. They have hidden agendas."

The waiter brought their food and set it down on the table. "Careful, the plates are hot," he warned.

"We need to work through this," Renny said, suddenly uninterested in the steaming burritos and rice in front of him. "There are people on the List who are scared of you because you are a loose cannon, not committed or controlled. I almost wish you had taken the million dollars and given it away; you were entitled to a lot more than that. From their perspective, you are a potential threat because you don't have any stake in the game, so to speak."

"Do you think I'm in danger?" Jo asked, startled.

"When there is money involved, people will do things. We can't be naive."

"Do you think you're in danger?"

"I doubt it. I'm part of the fraternity."

"I'm not sure that's protection."

"Why not?"

"Would you consider it a good health insurance policy? Ask Bart Maxwell."

"You have a suspicious feeling, but that could be coincidence. We need to think about facts, not theories."

"Excuse me," Jo said testily.

"Sorry. That was too blunt. But one fact you don't know is that LaRochette asked me to keep an eye on you after you walked out of the meeting in Georgetown. I guess he wanted to know if I thought you were going to tattle. This morning in the parking lot, Layne asked me if I was doing my job."

"Why didn't you tell me this before?"

"I forgot about it. I was too busy watching you on my own time to think about it from LaRochette's point of view."

"Forgiven. What did you say to Layne this morning?"

"Nothing really, but maybe I should now."

"Why? What would you say? That I'm not interested in what they do?"

"No. I've a better idea. I can tell them the truth. That I am in love with you and want you to marry me. Then, even though you know about the List, you aren't likely to do anything that would harm your husband-to-be."

"That means you have to stay involved. I'm not comfortable with that approach."

"All I want to do is hang around for the next distribution. It's only a few months off."

"I'm unconvinced. I've already told you—"

"I know, I know," Renny cut her off. "Don't worry. Let's eat. There's nothing worse than cold Mexican rice."

———

Renny drove under the canopy of trees on Queens Road. "It doesn't have the beauty of Anne's Avenue on Prince Edward Island, but it offers a stately welcome, don't you think?" he asked.

"Yes, the old oaks are royal greeters on Queens Road."

Mrs. Stokes was listening to music and humming when they knocked at the kitchen door. "How was church?"

"Ugh," Renny said.

"What?" she asked.

Coming to his aid, Jo said, "Renny was sidetracked, but he'll get it straightened out. How long will it take us to get to the airport?"

"We need to leave a couple hours before your flight. You've plenty of time to pack, then I'd like you to come upstairs for a few minutes before we leave."

"OK."

As the door closed behind Renny, Jo leaned against the counter. "Renny missed a golden opportunity to acknowledge Jesus publicly. Then he felt shut out from the Lord."

"I see."

Tears gently pooled in Jo's eyes. "He's under a lot of pressure from several angles, Mrs. Stokes. I'm worried about him."

The old lady took Jo in her arms and held her with firm strength. A single tear escaped and ran down Jo's cheek onto Mrs. Stokes's shoulder.

"I know he's special," Mrs. Stokes said. "He's special to you, to me, and to the Lord."

Jo sniffled. "I'm going to leave my phone number with you. Call me and let me know how things are going with him."

"I will, I will. Now, go pack your things."

———

Jo reluctantly said good-bye to the blue bedroom with its secret holy place. Putting her suitcase on the bed, she noticed a small white box on the pillow with a loosely tied blue bow on top. A card was lying beside it. Opening the card, she read, "This gift is a symbol of God's promises for you and our connection in him. With love, Daisy Stokes." Inside the box, Jo found a crystal Star of David identical to the one in the prayer closet. Jo held it up to the light and turned it so it cast its display of color across the white bedspread. Mrs. Stokes was one of those unique people grown so used to the path of blessing others that no other walkway was familiar to her feet.

Jo carried her suitcase and garment bag into the kitchen. She could see Mrs. Stokes outside the window filling her hummingbird feeders with sweet red liquid.

Mrs. Stokes came back into the house. "Ready to go?"

"I think so. Thanks for the Star of David. I love it."

"I bought two of them in Jerusalem when I visited Israel three years ago. I knew someone who would appreciate it would cross my path."

"I have the perfect place for it in my bedroom."

"I know you'll enjoy it."

Jo picked up her bag. "Thanks. Thanks for everything. I'm going to leave my suitcase by the door while I go upstairs to get Renny."

"I have a meeting to attend, so let me give you a hug before I go. Come back anytime." Mrs. Stokes blessed Jo with a final smile. They walked outside together.

"Bye."

Jo walked up the steps and knocked once. Renny opened the door, and Brandy gave a welcoming bark.

Jo entered and scratched Brandy behind the ears.

"I wanted you to meet one more person before you leave. She's a special lady, and I know you want to talk to her," Renny said.

"Who is it?"

"I'm going to call Mama A. Unless she is spending the day with her family, she should be at her house by now."

"That would be great."

"Here's the cordless phone. I'll call on the extension in my bedroom."

Renny dialed the number, and Jo listened in as the phone rang in Charleston. On the third ring, Mama A answered, "Hello."

"Mama A. It's Renny. Are you doing OK?"

"Fine, fine. A little tired today, but I took a nap after church. How are you?"

"I'm good. Guess what happened?"

Mama A was silent a moment, then said, "You tell me; I'm too old for guessing games."

"I've become a Christian, a real one."

"Praise the Lord, Renny."

"It happened Friday up in the mountains."

"Your mama is jumpin' for joy," Mama A exclaimed.

Renny hadn't considered his mother's reaction to the past two days' events. On earth, she never owned a pair of sneakers to jump in.

"Maybe she is," Renny conceded. "I've got someone else on the phone, Mama A, a girl I've met who helped me down the path toward God. Her name is Jo Johnston, and I think she is the most beautiful woman in the world."

In the living room, Jo blushed and said, "Hello, it's a pleasure to meet you. Renny's told me some wonderful things about you."

"It's good to meet you, too, though this is a poor substitute to seein' you with my own eyes. Renny, I wish you were here. I'd give you the biggest hug you've ever had."

"I want to see you again soon," Renny said. "Next time I'm down that way I'll call you."

"Jo?" the old lady said.

"Yes."

"You come, too. Renny doesn't throw around compliments like horseshoes. I can tell from your voice that you are something special. Where are you from?"

"Michigan."

"Jo's a nurse," Renny said.

"Well, if I have to pretend to be sick to get you to bring her here to meet me properly, I will."

"I hear you, Mama A. Thanks for all you've done for me, especially the time I had with you the other day."

"I told you, you're like one of my own, Renny. Always have been, always will be."

"I'll talk to you soon."

"OK. Bye, Renny. Bye, Jo."

"Good-bye," they echoed.

"Do you have a picture of her?" Jo asked when Renny came into the living room.

"I'm sure I do. Let me check." Renny did an about-face and disappeared. Jo could hear him opening drawers. "Here's one," he called.

He set a picture album on the coffee table in the living room, and he and Jo sat next to each other on the couch. "These were taken a few years ago on the Fourth of July. Her family had a big cookout, and I was invited. This is Mama A."

Agnes Flowers, a proud smile on her face, was cradling a newborn baby in the catcher's mitt. "This is one of her grandchildren. She is always the catcher in a family softball game, and I came up with the idea of taking a picture with the baby in the baseball glove."

"Is there one of the two of you?"

Renny turned the page. "Here's one. Typical. I've got barbecue sauce all over my face." Renny was standing next to Mama A with his head tilted toward her so she could kiss him on the cheek.

"She loves you, doesn't she?" Jo picked up the album and looked closer.

"Yes. I wish I had kept in closer contact with her the past few years."

"She doesn't seem to hold it against you."

"She's not that way at all."

"Do you think we could see her sometime?"

"Of course. It will give me another reason to buy you a plane ticket."

"Speaking of planes, is it time to leave?"

Renny glanced at the clock. "Unfortunately, yes."

The airport was crowded, and they had to walk quickly to the boarding gate.

As they called her flight, Jo said, "Phone or e-mail after you talk with

Layne, and don't forget to set up something with Paul Bushnell."

"Yes, dear," Renny said teasingly. "Are you going to call me?"

"If I need you to pick up something at the grocery store on the way home."

"I wish."

Jo laid her hand on his shoulder. "Also, remember what I said last night."

"I will."

"And remember everything else, too."

"I will." Renny leaned over for their first good-bye kiss. "See you soon."

"Bye." Jo stepped away, handed her boarding pass to the attendant, and walked down the ramp. She didn't look back, afraid that if she did, she might not have been able to keep walking away.

21

Yond Cassius has a lean and hungry look.
JULIUS CAESAR, ACT 1, SCENE 2

The faces of the people in the airport concourse were as indistinguishable from one another as cornstalks in a field. Renny felt sharply the pain of separation and muttered his first airport prayer as he jostled his way through the throng to the parking deck. "Soon, God. Let me see her soon."

At home, he put Brandy on her leash, and they ran until both were gasping for breath. Upon returning to the apartment, Brandy lay down on her side in front of the air-conditioning vent next to her bed. Renny was finishing a second glass of water when the phone rang. It was Thomas Layne.

"Are you feeling better?" Layne asked. "You looked a little under the weather at the church."

"I'm fine now."

"Glad to hear it."

Renny didn't respond, and Layne cleared his throat. "I want to get together, just the two of us, while I am in town. Is tomorrow a possibility for lunch?"

Renny couldn't remember any scheduled conflict, but stalled, "I'll need to check my calendar when I get to the office in the morning."

"Of course. I hope you're not tied up; it's important that we talk as soon as possible."

"Sure. Do you want me to call you tomorrow morning?"

"No," Layne said quickly. "Since I'm here with Lois and Jack, it would be better if I called you. I have your work number."

"OK."

"I look forward to seeing you tomorrow."

———

At 9:30 the next morning, Renny was at his desk when the phone rang.

"Mr. Layne on line one," the secretary announced.

After Renny picked up, Layne got straight to the point. "Are you free for lunch?"

"Yes."

"Let's meet at Alton's at noon."

"All right."

"I'll see you there."

Renny started to sweat. He decided to call Jo. Her mother answered the phone. "Hello, Mrs. Edwards, this is Renny. Is Jo available?"

"Good morning, Renny. No, she worked from seven last night until seven this morning. She collapsed into bed an hour ago; I'd hate to wake her."

"That's OK. I'll try to catch her this evening."

"She said you two had a good weekend."

"Yes, we did."

"I look forward to meeting you. You need to visit us soon, before we build our igloos."

"Did she tell you about that?" Renny laughed. "I'd like to come. How about today?"

"We'll find a time, and I'll tell her you called."

"Bye."

———

Renny pulled into the Alton's parking lot a couple of minutes before noon. Except for a few uptown clubs, Alton's was the most expensive restaurant in the city. Many businessmen considered it the perfect setting for a power lunch. More deals were settled over Alton's steak roulade than in corporate boardrooms, but Renny would rather have a grilled cheese sandwich with Jo than steak with Layne.

A snooty maître d' greeted Renny in the foyer of the restaurant. "Are you meeting someone, sir?"

"Yes, Mr. Thomas Layne."

"Mr. Layne is in the lounge waiting for you."

Everyone in the restaurant wore a coat and tie, and the air conditioner hummed at maximum capacity. Renny shivered, but not from the cold. Taking a breath, he entered the wood-paneled lounge. Layne saw him and, scotch in hand, stood up to greet him. "Can I buy you a drink?"

"No, I still have an afternoon of paper shuffling to endure at the firm. I'd hate to miss a comma or apostrophe."

"Well, let's have a seat. They have a table waiting for us."

Layne led the way to a table for two. As soon as they sat down, a waiter appeared with another scotch and took Renny's order of water with a twist of lemon.

"How are you doing?" Layne asked in a fatherly tone as he set his glass on the table. "Things going well for you and the beautiful Ms. Johnston?"

"Very well," Renny said. "I hope we're going to get married."

"A whirlwind romance."

"Yes, it has been."

"No date yet?"

"Just serious discussions, but I'm sure it won't be long. "

"I see."

Renny continued, wanting to complete his presentation. "And I also see our marriage solving the questions raised about Jo in Georgetown. I've been keeping an eye on her as Mr. LaRochette asked. And although I'm seeing her for personal reasons, I think it will help us all if she agrees to marry me. Then there would be no reason to be concerned that she would compromise the secrecy of the List. It would be against my interest, and therefore her interest."

"Good. I hope it all works out for you. But I didn't ask you to lunch to talk about Ms. Johnston."

"You didn't? But you asked me about her in the parking lot at church."

"Just a casual remark. Frankly, I'm not a bit worried about her telling anyone about the List. There's nothing she could do to interfere." The waiter arrived, and Layne stopped to order a seafood bisque and crabmeat étouffée.

Renny, intent on delivering his monologue, hadn't looked at the menu. "Uh, the same, please. I'm confused. What did you want to talk about?" he asked.

"Something far more important. But first, I must ask if you are willing to keep our conversation confidential. Confidential from everyone."

"I don't know," Renny said uncertainly.

"There's nothing sinister involved. But to have any chance of success, my proposal must not be discussed with anyone else."

"Including Jo?"

"Yes, although she's not my primary concern. I emphasize everyone to include all the others on the List."

"And it's nothing illegal?" Renny felt like a schoolboy asking if it was OK to take only one piece of bubble gum without permission from the grocery store.

"Don't be silly. It's really just an issue of corporate protocol. Do I have your agreement?"

Renny conducted a three-second internal debate, decided corporate protocol was safe, and said yes.

"Good. First, I know you talked with Gus Eicholtz in Georgetown about his dissatisfaction with Desmond's domination of the List." Layne held up his hand to keep Renny from interrupting. "Don't worry. I've talked with Gus myself, and we have devised a plan to break Desmond's grip on our money. Here's how. There is going to be a meeting of the List this Saturday in Georgetown. You haven't received notification because you don't have a post office box in Charlotte yet. A courier service will probably deliver a notice to you this afternoon or in the morning. The purpose of the meeting is to set the amount of distribution to members. I've talked with Robert Roget, who is a member of the investment committee, and I believe Desmond is going to recommend five to ten million apiece, a ridiculous amount."

Still, an amount, Renny thought.

"Here's the plan. Now that Bart Maxwell is gone without an heir and Ms. Johnston was excluded on primogeniture, there are eight voting members. Before we give rubber-stamp approval to Desmond's distribution plan, I want to call a vote replacing Desmond as president of the corporation."

"On what grounds?"

"None are needed, but if Desmond wants to get ugly, I think there is a good chance he has embezzled funds from the corpus of the List."

"Can you prove it?"

"You're a lawyer. The circumstantial evidence is strong. Think about it. Did you contact the Swiss bank to gain access to the account?"

"Yes."

"Did you receive authorization to withdraw funds?"

"No."

"Whose name was on the account as legal representative of the List?"

"Desmond LaRochette."

"Who has possession of a power of attorney from your father authorizing access to the account?"

"I don't know."

"Do I have to tell you?"

Renny shook his head.

"What would prevent Desmond from accessing the account as representative of the List and as holder of a power of attorney from your father?"

"I don't know."

"Nothing. And I believe the LaRochettes have made a practice of pirating money using different powers of attorney for generations."

"Then do we really know how much remains in the corpus? Mr. Eicholtz said there was at least two billion."

"There is at least that much, but the LaRochette fortune—made with the help of our personal money—is probably much more."

"But can you document all this?"

"I don't really have to. I'm just mentioning it to convince you that we need to act, and act now. The removal of Desmond can be accomplished by a simple corporate resolution based upon a majority vote."

"Who would be the new president?"

"C'est moi," Layne said with a self-satisfied smile. "And my first act would be to make a motion for distribution of a substantially, and I mean substantially, greater amount of money to every member."

"How much greater?"

"One hundred million dollars apiece."

Renny gasped, started to speak, then said, "Whew." Finding his tongue, he said, "One hundred million would go into our individual accounts?"

"That's right. And we would authorize everyone to withdraw the full amount for his personal use as soon as possible."

"Do you have the votes?"

"Gus is in Singapore and will not attend." Layne pulled an envelope from the inside pocket of his jacket. "He has given me proxy to vote on his behalf. Do you want to read it?"

"No, that's all right. Who else is committed?"

"Weiss hates LaRochette. He thinks Desmond is an effeminate wimp and would vote with us just to watch Desmond turn red in the face."

"Who else?"

"I have one more stop to make after I leave Charlotte. I'm going to talk with Michael Flournoy. Desmond's father once insulted Flournoy's father, and they got in a big fight after a meeting in Georgetown. The elder LaRochette pulled a derringer out of his hat and shot Michael's father in the kneecap. He never walked without pain again. I think we can count on Michael's vote."

"I see."

"So you're in."

Renny was convinced. "Yes. One question more. What if LaRochette doesn't agree with the vote and pulls a derringer out of his hat?"

"Desmond doesn't have his father's spunk. But don't worry, I've got that covered. There is, however, one other thing I need you to do."

"What?"

"I want you to make the motion nominating me as president of the corporation. I obviously can't do it myself. You don't need to go into all the embezzlement suspicions—just make a motion. Weiss has already agreed to second it."

"I'm not sure I want to do that."

"If you want to share in the spoils, you must enter into the fray."

Renny shrugged. "OK. Let me know when to make the motion."

"Good. Here comes our overdue bisque."

Layne spent the rest of lunch talking about a stable of racehorses he kept on a farm in Maryland. One had been nominated for the Preakness two years before but came up lame a week before the race. Layne paid for lunch with a hundred-dollar bill, telling the waiter to keep the balance.

"I look forward to a most interesting and profitable weekend. I'll call after I talk with Flournoy to verify that we are set to proceed."

"Thanks for lunch," Renny said.

As he drove back to the office, Renny wondered how he could endure the rest of the afternoon. Shuffling loan documents was not a job for multimillionaires-to-be. He toyed with the idea of walking into Heywood's office and quitting but decided against it. Instead, he spent the afternoon enjoying a fantasy in which he counted crisp hundred-dollar bills until they spilled out the door of his office.

Shortly before five that afternoon, a high school student who worked as a "runner" for the firm knocked on his door and delivered a FedEx letter. It was just as Layne had told him.

Dear Mr. Jacobson,

We have scheduled a meeting of the List for this Saturday at the Rice Planter's Inn, Georgetown, S.C. The primary purpose of the meeting is to discuss a distribution to the members. The meeting will begin with dinner at 7:00 P.M. Also enclosed is a Power of Attorney, which you need to sign and deliver at that time.

Respectfully,
Desmond LaRochette

Renny slipped the letter into his briefcase. He wanted to go home early, but duty kept him at his desk until he finished the paperwork for a loan closing scheduled the next afternoon. Then, grabbing his briefcase, he headed for the parking garage.

At home there were three messages on his answering machine. The first was from Morris Hogan. "Renny. Hulk here. That was a good-looking woman with you the other night. I haven't been able to get her off my mind and wondered if you could give me her phone number in Michigan. I tried to get you for lunch today, but you were out. Give me a call tonight or in the morning. See ya."

The second was from Gus Eicholtz. "Renny, there have been further developments about the matter we discussed in Georgetown. I am going out of the country for a few days but will try to reach you as soon as I can."

The third was from Jo. "I've been asleep all day and go to work at six this evening. If you get this message in time, please give me a call. If not, I'll call you sometime tomorrow. I had nice dreams about you. Bye."

It was almost six, too late to call. Renny logged on to his computer and sent Jo an e-mail.

Got your phone message. Hope you are rested. Met with Layne today and will be going to Georgetown on Saturday. Can't give details, but it looks promising. Am very interested in nice dreams! Please forward details.

LOL,
Renny

P.S. From now on, LOL means "lots of love."

After eating a sandwich, Renny picked up a book to read, but too agitated by the day's events to concentrate, he decided to rent a movie. At the video store he rejected Arnold Schwarzenegger and chose Tom Hanks and Meg Ryan in *Sleepless in Seattle*. Sitting in his living room, he watched as love's attraction pulled Hanks and Ryan inexorably across the broad expanse of the North American continent toward their rendezvous on top of the Empire State Building. He could relate to the dynamic attraction of love—only in real life it began at a barbecue restaurant in Moncks Corner, South Carolina.

22

Renny and Morris met for lunch at Yogi's the next day. It was a sad occasion; the eatery was closing its doors at the end of the week. No more prison atmosphere, no more peanut shells on the floor, no more two o'clock indigestion from too many chili cheese fries covered in chopped onions.

"What are we going to do?" Morris moaned as they slid into their booth.

"We could always go to the Café Royale," Renny said, referring to a lunch spot with delicate wrought-iron tables, skinny chairs designed with a fashion model's derrière in mind, and a menu of French-sounding entrées with no cholesterol.

"I don't understand how you can joke at a time like this." Morris refused to be comforted. "I've heard there's a good place to eat in Rockingham."

"That's an hour away."

"So what. If we don't eat, we'll die."

"If you die, I'll have your funeral catered by the aforementioned café," Renny said.

"Over my dead body," Morris responded.

"Exactly."

They ordered all their favorite foods, knowing they couldn't eat everything but wanting one last sample. It was an all-American smorgasbord.

As soon as he had eaten enough to blunt his initial appetite, Morris asked, "What's the deal with Jo from Michigan?"

"She's special."

Morris waited. "And? Come on. Out with it."

"You remember the Duke cap you gave me?"

"Yeah. What's that got to do with Jo from Michigan?"

"She wore it when we drove to the mountains on Saturday."

"I knew it!" Morris exclaimed. "She has a lot of class. You've got to give me her address so I can send her a Duke sweatshirt. You know, the one with the big Blue Devil on the front."

"No, I don't think so," Renny said. "She doesn't like the devil."

"Huh?"

"Trust me. Save your money."

Morris chewed another mouthful of hamburger. "Are you going to see her again?"

"Yes. Are you sitting down?"

"Of course, I'm sitting down. You can see me; we're not on the telephone."

"Oh, yeah. Well, she's the one, Morris. I want to marry her."

Morris almost lost his grip on his hamburger. "Whoa, as in diamond ring and white dress?"

"That's right. She hasn't said yes yet, but I asked her at the Clairmont the other night."

Morris took a drink of Coke. "I hear you, but I need more data."

"What kind of data?"

"Everything. How? When? Explain."

"Well, it's different."

"OK," Morris said. "But what does 'different' mean? I know what 'not different' is with all the girls I date. I don't want to marry 'not different.'"

"It's beyond physical attraction, although that's at a level I've never felt. It's a lot about communication."

Morris shook his head in dismay. "Just like the women's magazines say?"

Renny laughed. "Yeah, maybe it is, but when it happens, you don't think about magazines. You want to talk about anything and everything. It's like you and me—only better."

Morris choked and spit a tiny piece of onion onto the table. "Come on. I want the straight answer on this."

Renny chuckled. "OK, let's work through this one level at a time. There's the physical attraction. You know about that."

"Sure. Every day."

"There's the desire to talk and experience things together. You know about that."

"Yeah, I've had that some. Remember Kathy Sue London? We talked about everything and rode horses on the weekends."

"But then there's the spiritual side."

"You've lost me. Is she a New Ager?"

"No, Jo is a born-again Christian. A month ago I would have considered her a good-looking religious fanatic and steered clear of her. Now, one of the main reasons I want to be with her is because of her faith."

"You're serious?"

"Yes. No kidding. I have had the most incredible month of my life. She has helped me see that Christianity is not an activity; it's an encounter with God. It's real."

Morris swallowed, then said, "You've gone to church off and on since you were a kid."

"So what. It was just a social thing. This is real. And"—he paused—"it's real to me. I can already see that the spiritual side of my relationship with Jo is the hinge that opens everything else. It affects the physical, emotional, communication—everything. I know this sounds like junior high, but the first time I held her hand I thought I would come out of my skin. When I kissed her the other night, I went to galaxies I never knew existed. And, Morris, it was right—it was clean—it was the way things are supposed to be."

"Go ahead. I'm listening."

"Even in the dating game, I'm seeing that God's way is *the way*. I don't know much, but there are depths of love, emotion, and relationship that are untouchable apart from the involvement of God in our lives. Knowing Jesus is not cold and sterile. Something very intense has been going on inside me—more intense and alive than anything else I've ever experienced."

"I feel the intensity in what you're saying now. But will this last?"

"That's a good question. It's lasted with Jo for years, and I know people like my landlady and the woman who helped raise me who have been believing this stuff longer than you or I have been alive."

They ate in silence for a few minutes.

"You've rocked my boat today," Morris said finally. "I'm not opposed to what you say, but I've never heard it explained like this in the churches I went to as a kid."

Renny nodded. "Same here. You're my best friend. I want you to know what's going on. You can watch and see what you think."

"OK. It all sounds different coming from you."

After eating more than the legal limit, they left a big tip and said goodbye to their definition of lunchtime culinary excellence. At the front door, Morris said, "I meant to ask you about the Swiss bank account situation. Did you call the guy I mentioned in Switzerland?"

"No, but I think I have the problem worked out. I should know in a week or so."

"Good. Thanks for lunch, Renny."

Jo called midafternoon. "Got your e-mail. Sorry I can't remember a lot of details from my dreams, but I know they were good."

"Try to remember next time. I could use some encouragement."

"I don't want to give you too much encouragement. Or at least too much too soon."

"Every crumb is appreciated, the sooner the better."

"How was the meeting with Thomas Layne?"

"Much better than expected."

"Did he ask about me?"

"Not really. I told him I hoped we would marry and that you had no interest in causing problems for the List. He didn't seem interested or worried. Apparently they are less paranoid about you than we thought."

"Then what was his reason for contacting you?"

"There is going to be a meeting of the List this Saturday in Georgetown to approve a distribution to the members. He wanted my support in approving as large an amount as possible." Renny hoped his truthful, if incomplete, version would satisfy her.

Jo said nothing for a few seconds, then asked, "Did you tell him yes?"

"Sure. I've thought everything through. All I want to do is get enough money in our hands to give us financial security. Then we can both do what we want to do with our lives. The amount Layne was throwing around would do that in spades. Then we can tell the List good-bye."

Jo was silent for a longer period. "I don't like it, Renny. You sound like the men who started this whole thing. It sounds good, but something isn't right about it. The money is not clean."

"Look. Money is not clean or dirty in itself. It's your attitude toward it and what you do with it that matters. That's what I've learned from reading about riches in Matthew. Both our families have a right to our respective shares. In one way, we're only getting half of the amount we should because they refused to recognize your legitimate rights. And once I'm out, they'll have the balance of the Jacobson money, too."

"It's not them I'm thinking about, it's us. Please don't make a final decision on this until we both have time to pray about it and seek to hear from the Lord."

Renny considered another line of argument but realized it was easier to just say, "OK. We'll talk on Friday."

When Renny arrived home, Mrs. Stokes was taking out her garbage. Renny greeted her and said, "I talked with Jo this afternoon."

"Everything fine?"

"Yes. I'm going to Georgetown this Saturday."

"Any problems?"

"No, just more things to take care of about my father's estate. Would you take care of Brandy for me until I get back Sunday evening?"

"I'll be glad to."

"Thanks."

Renny paused at the bottom stairs, wondering if he should ask her to pray for him. No, he didn't want to have to explain the situation and answer well-meaning questions.

Later, Renny picked up his Bible and turned to Matthew. He had continued reading the past couple of days, but since all the problems he had at the church on Sunday it had not been the same. He knew God was out there, but he wasn't sure God had his phone number. Talking with Morris at Yogi's had been the closest he'd felt to God since he resisted the call to publicly acknowledge his new faith. He suspected the presence of the Spirit at lunch was for Morris's benefit; he just enjoyed the overflow. After staring at the words for a few minutes, he closed the book and watched the last three innings of a baseball game on TV.

———

The following morning was Wednesday. No sooner had Renny set his coffee cup on his desk than the phone rang. It was Thomas Layne.

"Talked with Flournoy. He's in. No problem. Wants to put a bullet in Desmond anywhere he can."

"Not literally, I hope."

"Of course not. We'll still be in this together after the changes are made."

"OK. With Eicholtz's proxy, that's five votes to three."

"Correct. Actually, I wouldn't be surprised if Smithfield jumped on board ship once he sees the way the wind is blowing. He is LaRochette's toady, but he has no loyalty to him."

"What about Roget?"

"Doubtful. Roget hangs around Desmond's beach place all the time. He and Desmond are both oily and rub each other the right way, so to speak. Robert has ambitions, but he wants to ride Desmond's coattails. At any rate, we don't need him. Once the vote is in and I explain about the distribution, he won't complain. And don't worry about Desmond. He's a master manipulator, but he'll capitulate when overwhelmed. See you Saturday," Layne said abruptly ending the conversation.

Renny said good-bye to a dead receiver.

He took a sip of hot coffee and tried to remember something he was supposed to do that wasn't on his calendar when the phone rang again.

"Desmond LaRochette on line two."

Renny choked as he swallowed. Picking up the phone, he said "Hello."

"Renny, Desmond LaRochette here."

"Yes sir. Good morning."

"How is everything in Charlotte?"

"Fine, everything's fine." Renny's mind was racing in fourteen directions, none of which had an identifiable destination.

"Good, good. I was calling to make sure you received my letter."

"Yes sir. It came yesterday. Thank you. I'll be there."

"And the power of attorney?"

"Yes, I'll sign it in front of a notary here in the office and bring it to the meeting."

"Excellent. As a courtesy I also wanted to mention something else that's come up in the past couple of days."

Renny swallowed harder than before. "Yes sir?"

"It has to do with our primary account in Switzerland. I'm concerned about the security of the Swiss banking system. You have read, of course, about the gold taken from Jews executed in concentration camps. A lot of it ended up in Swiss bank vaults."

"Yes," Renny said, relieved at the direction of the conversation.

264

"Well, the Swiss have a horrible public relations problem on their hands. I understand they've promised foreign governments, including the U.S., increased access to previously confidential records. Do you follow my concerns?"

"You think the secrecy of the List account is in jeopardy. Why? There's no Nazi link, is there?"

"Of course not, but any threat to secrecy, no matter how remote, is a threat to the continuation of the List and preservation of our assets."

"I see."

"If you were going to open a confidential bank account today, where would you do it?"

Renny thought a second. "Probably the Cayman Islands or one of the other offshore havens."

"My thoughts exactly. Here's where you can help. You work in the banking section of your firm, don't you?"

"Yes, I'm an associate."

"I need some information about our options—the location of suitable banks, types of restrictions, rules on confidentiality, financial stability of potential depositories, rates of return, methods of accessing money. As an expert, you can help us."

Renny looked at the walls of his office. He could almost reach across it in every direction. Oh yes, he was a banking expert. "I'm not really an expert in these matters. Don't you have someone more experienced you can contact?"

"Perhaps, but I'd prefer keeping this in the family. That way we can have a frank discussion about all issues. Do you have some time to work on this before the weekend?"

If Renny could avoid Heywood, he could squeeze some time in the evenings. "Yes. I can work on it today."

"Very good. I would prefer a briefing before we gather with the other members on Saturday. You and I could get together to discuss your findings and recommendations Friday night. I'm staying at my beach house just north of Georgetown on Highway 17. Do you know where the Franklin D. Roosevelt Wildlife Preserve is, near Debordeau Colony Club?"

"Yes. I've been past it many times."

"There's a sand driveway just past the edge of the preserve on the north side. My property is between the preserve and Debordeau. There is an arched iron entranceway on the right. After turning onto the drive you will come to a gate across the road. Punch in 369 and drive up to the house. I'll be waiting for you."

Renny wrote the number on a slip of paper. "OK."

"How soon can you get here?"

Renny turned his calendar to Friday. "I have a full day of work, but I'll leave as soon as I can. Is ten too late?"

"No, that's fine. We should be able to go over everything in a reasonable amount of time. I'll see you then."

"Yes, sir."

"Have a good day."

Renny hit the speed dial for Morris Hogan. "Hey. Are you busy?"

"What do you mean? The folks on the top floor don't pay me to sit around and look pretty."

"OK, OK. I need some information ASAP about offshore banking."

"Have you found another account in your father's estate?"

"No. It's for a client." Renny figured the List qualified as a client. "I need to know the ins and outs. Where's the best place and why. That sort of stuff."

"OK. I should tell you to contact someone at one of the banks you represent so they could bill you $125 an hour for a change."

"Come on, Morris."

"Let me finish. However, because you're my best friend, give me an hour to copy a folder I just happen to have in my office. It has no privileged info and should have everything you need."

"Thanks a million—make that ten million. I'll be over to pick it up."

———

After returning to his office with the file, Renny spent the rest of the morning hiding in the firm library poring over the information. Morris was right. It had everything LaRochette could want: names of bank contacts, safe procedures for transferring funds, security against any breach of confidentiality, balance sheets of specific banks, and recommendations from field representatives who knew the system from A to Z. Before he realized it, he looked up and it was 12:15. Then he remembered: He was supposed to call Paul Bushnell. He went back to his office, grabbed the phone book from his desk, and dialed the number. The church secretary answered.

"Paul Bushnell please."

"I'm sorry, he's out for the afternoon. Can I take a message?"

"No, that's OK. It's not important. I'll give him a call next week."

23

We have made a covenant with death,
and with hell are we at agreement.
ISAIAH 28:15, KJV

Thursday passed in a blur. Renny worked late into the evening on the documents Heywood needed for a loan closing scheduled for Friday afternoon.

While Heywood took care of the closing, Renny was working in his office. His secretary buzzed him. "Call on line three. A Mr. Eicholtz."

Before Renny could pick up the phone, Heywood burst into his office, swearing. "Get it in gear, Renny. I need a secondary note unsecured by collateral directly from the buyer to the seller because of some unrevealed security interests. Why didn't I know there was previously secured collateral involved? Did you double-check the UCC search on the seller?"

"Uh, I'll get right on it." Renny had not double-checked outstanding security interests because he was working on the Cayman Island bank questions. "How much is the side note?"

"Eighty-four thousand at prime plus one. I needed this five minutes ago."

"Yes, sir." Renny was punching keys on his computer before Heywood slammed the door.

His secretary buzzed him again. "Are you going to take the call?"

Renny grabbed the receiver and almost shouted, "Hello!"

No answer. He buzzed his secretary. "Did Mr. Eicholtz leave a number?"

"No. He must have hung up."

Renny had the documents to the parties in less than twenty minutes. When he took the paperwork into the conference room, Heywood introduced him, "This is Renny Jacobson, one of our junior associates. I apologize that he didn't have everything ready on time." He turned to Renny. "You may go now."

After absorbing the collective glares of everyone in the room, Renny slunk out of the conference room. He spent the last hour at work worrying that Barnette Heywood was going to storm back into his office. Leaving a few minutes early, he made sure he didn't walk past Heywood's door.

———

Mrs. Stokes was watching television in her bedroom when Renny stopped in to tell her about his change in plans.

"I have to go to the coast earlier than I thought but I'll still be back Sunday evening."

"That's fine. I'll look out for Brandy."

"Thanks." Renny turned to go, then said, "Pray for me, Mrs. Stokes."

"Oh, I will, I will. God bless you, Renny."

Mrs. Stokes closed the door after a frazzled-looking Renny walked away. Going to the prayer closet, she sat down and asked for help. Slipping to her knees, she started praying.

———

Renny called Jo on his car phone. "How are you?" he asked.

"A little tired, but I'm glad you called. My schedule has been different every day, and I have to leave in a few minutes. Are you on the car phone?"

"Yes."

"You sounded a little fuzzy. Well, I've prayed every chance I could about the List, and I am convinced you should just let it go. You're smart and can work for a living without entangling yourself further in something neither of us fully understands."

For the first time ever, Renny regretted talking to Jo. He decided to face her head-on. "I don't agree. Since we've talked, I've positioned everything to guarantee the distribution. The situation at the law firm is the pits, and I can't see myself staying with it long term. It should all be over in a few days, then I'll back away."

Renny listened to loud static as he passed under a high-voltage power line. "Did you say something?" he asked when he had a clear signal.

"No. I guess I'm too surprised. Don't you think we need to agree about this?"

"I wanted us to agree, too, but ultimately it has to be my decision."

"Then why ask my opinion?"

"I respect your opinion. We just have different ideas about the best way to go."

Again silence.

"Are you on your way to Georgetown now?"

"Yes. I'm seeing LaRochette tonight to discuss opening a new account outside Switzerland. He asked me to do some research about it before the meeting tomorrow."

"Renny, can you hear me?" Even on the car phone Renny could sense desperation in her voice.

"Yes."

"Don't go to Georgetown. Please don't go."

"Jo, I appreciate what you feel, but there are things I have worked out. You don't need to worry."

"Don't be condescending," she said sharply.

"I'm not, or I don't mean to be. We have a simple difference of opinion. I think it's best to do this my way."

"You're not going to listen to me, are you?"

"Yes. I heard you. Just because I'm not going to do what you suggest doesn't mean I'm not listening."

"Well, I can see this conversation has nowhere to go, and I have patients to see who will let me help them."

"Jo—"

"Call me Sunday. Bye."

"Bye."

Renny put the phone in its cradle. *Boy, she's hot. But she'll cool down and be glad once this is over.*

All the way to Georgetown, Renny imagined life as a multimillionaire. His thoughts were different than immediately after his father's death—a nobler thread ran through his dreams and plans. He would become a discreet philanthropist. Maybe build Mama A's church a new sanctuary or gymnasium. He would contribute to worthy charitable causes from art museums to zoo acquisitions, all anonymously so as not to attract attention to himself. He would identify himself as an investor on his tax return, pay all taxes owed, and not worry about an IRS subpoena. He would not invest solely on the amount of anticipated return but would also consider the integrity and societal benevolence of the company or project.

Of course, there would be plenty of money left to enjoy a comfortable life—with Jo. A beach house, mountain house, city house, and vacations all over the world in between. The expenses that made life stressful for others would not be a factor for them. Their children would not have to struggle and scrape; each would be the beneficiary of a well-funded trust that supplied all their needs from infancy through postgraduate education and would leave no doubt of their father's love and care for them.

He would no longer work as most people understood it. Rather, like the aristocracy of times past, he would devote himself to creative pursuits. He could write. And if no publisher recognized his talent and genius, he would publish his works himself.

It took many miles and a lot of imagination to spend $100 million, and when he came back to earth he was only a few miles from Georgetown. It was dark and raining, and he decided to go directly to LaRochette's house. Driving north on Highway 17, he soon recognized the tract of land given many years before to the U.S. government by Bernard Baruch, a wealthy adviser to Franklin D. Roosevelt. The U.S. government owned the property but had never developed it for public use. Turning his wipers on high to clear the rain from the windshield,

Renny slowed. He turned between two small red reflectors that marked the driveway to LaRochette's place.

An electric gate wedged between two ancient live oaks blocked the driveway about two hundred feet from the highway. Renny punched in the access number, and the barrier swung smoothly open. Once past it, the driveway wound over a mile through low-growing trees and dune grass before it opened into a clearing.

LaRochette's beach retreat was worthy of the long entranceway. A French provincial surrounded by massive live oaks, it spread out before the lights of Renny's car in a sprawl of pale gray stucco, steep roofs, and narrow windows. A guesthouse to the right was as large as a typical beach house on the Isle of Palms. The driveway curved in a large arc around a fountain surrounded by low shrubs. Renny parked behind a silver Mercedes coupe. He'd forgotten an umbrella, so he grabbed his briefcase and made a quick dash up a walk of crushed seashells to a covered area in front of the main entrance. His heart was pounding as he rang the bell.

LaRochette, dressed in a blue yachting blazer, white shirt, and gray slacks, answered the door. Every gray hair was neatly in its place.

"Good evening, Renny. Come in out of the storm. Did you have any problem finding the house?"

"No problem at all."

"It's turned into a nasty night, hasn't it?"

Renny came into a two-story foyer dimly lit by recessed lighting that reflected upward from fixtures hidden by dark wooden molding halfway up the wall. A huge grandfather clock started striking the hour as he entered.

"What timing. Just on the strike of ten." LaRochette pointed to the clock. "It's 175 years old, the case was made by slave craftsmen on one of the family plantations, the works imported from Switzerland."

"It's a nice piece," Renny said.

"Come into the library and have a drink. We can talk in there."

LaRochette opened a set of pocket doors that slid noiselessly into the wall and led Renny into one of the most incredible rooms he'd ever seen. The library was the realization of every ideal for a sanctuary dedicated to books. A thick oriental rug covered the wooden floor, and bookcases ten feet in height covered three walls with a rolling ladder that allowed access to the top shelves. Opposite the door was a fireplace framed by burgundy leather chairs. Two matching couches faced each other in the center of the room. An antique secretary and writing desk occupied two corners of the room, and a bar filled another. LaRochette turned up the lights so Renny could take it all in.

"You like it?"

"Amazing. It's what a library should be."

A figure rose from one of the chairs facing the fireplace. It was Robert Roget, dressed casually in a green golf shirt and tan slacks.

"Good evening, Renny."

"Oh, hello, Mr. Roget."

"Call me Robert."

They shook hands. Roget's hand was cool and limp.

LaRochette spoke up. "Robert, pour three glasses of the Maison Prunier."

Roget obviously knew his way around LaRochette's liquor cabinet.

Renny took a sip of the premium brandy. He would make the drink last as long as possible.

LaRochette and Roget sat on one couch and Renny faced them with his briefcase beside him. LaRochette began, "Before we get to business, I wanted to ask if you have had further contact with Miss Johnston?"

"Yes, I have," Renny said nervously. "She recently visited me in Charlotte."

"How is she doing?"

"Fine. I've asked her to marry me."

"Fast work, my boy," LaRochette said, smiling.

"And I believe she will say yes," Renny continued. "Once married, we will, for all practical purposes, be joint members of the List."

"Which means your interest in privacy will be shared by her?" LaRochette said.

"Yes sir, that's what I thought. I don't think she has any desire to cause trouble anyway, but our relationship removes any doubt."

"Sounds good to me," said LaRochette. "How about you, Robert?"

"Ride on and catch the fox, my boy. Every man needs a good woman—or two," he said.

"Now to the business at hand," LaRochette said. "I thought it would be helpful if Robert joined us. Tell us what you learned from your research."

Renny opened the briefcase and organized his notes and papers on a low table between them. "I told Mr. LaRochette that I am not an expert in offshore banking, but I have been able to pull together a lot of relevant information." Renny spent the next hour outlining the pros and cons of different options. LaRochette asked a few questions, Roget none.

"Impressive," LaRochette said when Renny turned over his last sheet. "Our obvious choice is one of two banks—in the Caymans or in the Lesser Antilles. Do you have a preference, Robert?"

"The Caymans are better established, but the Lesser Antilles, more protective. I would lean toward the Caymans because the banks are larger and our money less likely to create a tidal wave."

"I agree," LaRochette said with finality. "Renny, please be prepared to make a presentation on the Cayman banks at the meeting tomorrow night."

"Yes, sir."

LaRochette rose and stretched his legs. "Can I get you another drink?"

"No thanks, I've not finished my first one."

"All right. Before you go, I have a couple of matters to discuss with you. Robert, please get the List."

Roget walked over to the secretary, opened the front, and retrieved the familiar black ledger. He handed it to LaRochette, who set it down on the table.

"Renny, your father, as custodian of the List, held a position of honor and respect. My hope is that his son will follow in his footsteps."

"I'm honored that you think so." Renny took a drink of his brandy and waited.

LaRochette continued, "Over the years there have been petty intrigues and squabbles among the members of the List, but through every situation we have maintained the integrity of the covenant we signed and sealed by our blood. Division on the List is unthinkable and would not be tolerated."

Renny hoped the two men could not hear the pounding of his heart.

LaRochette opened the ledger to the last page and pointed at Renny's signature and the now brownish-red stain beside it. "You have taken your place in the book, and it is my hope that you have taken your place as one of us in your heart and soul, as well. Because you are young and inexperienced, I wanted to caution you against involvement in any controversies that may arise from time to time. They serve no good purpose."

Renny drained his drink. "Yes, sir," he said hoarsely.

"Please accept this as fatherly advice," LaRochette finished with a paternal smile.

"Thank you, sir." Renny picked up his paperwork and put it back in his briefcase. "I guess I need to be leaving. It's been a long day."

LaRochette leaned forward. "Don't rush out. There was something else I wanted to mention to you."

Renny sat back down.

"What I'm about to tell you may sound unusual, but hear me out, if you will." LaRochette lightly touched the cover of the List. "There is a mystical power associated with this book."

"What do you mean?" Renny asked, remembering Jo's vague concern about the List.

"I know that sounds strange, but trust me that the power of agreement by a group of people over a 140-year period has an effect beyond what we see and hear."

"I'm not sure I understand."

"Do you read the Bible?" LaRochette asked.

Startled, Renny said, "On occasion."

"There is a story in the book of Genesis about a group of people who decided to build a tower that would reach the heavens."

"Sure, the Tower of Babel."

"Right. God saw the latent power of their agreement and confounded their plans by confusing their language. As a result, they abandoned their project and were scattered across the earth." LaRochette paused, then continued, "We, too, have a power of agreement, formulated for a good purpose. The latent power of that agreement is attached to this book."

"Why are you telling me this?" Renny's curiosity was greater than any apprehension.

"Let me explain it this way. Your father was aware of this power."

Remembering the message on the tape about the other benefits of the List, Renny said, "Yes, he mentioned that in the instructions he left for me."

"Well, I want to teach you about the power associated with this book and how to use it for your good."

LaRochette's words had a soothing quality that gently carried Renny along a wide, smooth path.

"How does this power work for good?"

"It works for your good, then you share that goodness with others."

That made sense. "Like the use of money," Renny said. "Those who have money can help those who have needs."

"Perfect analogy. Would you like to see what I mean?"

"Why not?" Renny decided he could evaluate the whole matter best by putting it to the test.

"Fine. Put your hand on the List where you signed it. Your left index finger should rest on the spot where you made the mark with your blood."

Feeling slightly silly, Renny did as he was told. "OK. I don't feel anything."

"You shouldn't. In fact you may not feel anything at all. It's similar to faith, believing even when you can't see." LaRochette waited. Roget looked like he was about to fall asleep. "Visualize someone you care about, someone you love."

Renny thought a moment. Jo, Mama A, Aunt Margaret, Morris. He settled on Jo. Closing his eyes, he let her image come before his mind's eye.

"Do you have someone in mind?" LaRochette said.

"Yes."

"Release the power of the List into your life and from you to them. See it flow like a river."

Renny strained to see. "I can't do it. All I see is the person's face framed in gold."

"Good. Imagine light illuminating the picture."

Renny did so, and a tingle ran up his arm. He opened his eyes. "The face disappeared in a blaze of light."

"That's good. The person you saw has been touched by the power of the List."

Roget yawned. "Time for bed."

"Do you have a room at the inn?" LaRochette asked Renny.

"No. I was in a hurry to get here on time and thought I would check in after we finished."

"It's late and the inn may be full tonight. You're welcome to stay here."

Renny looked at his watch. It was almost midnight. Time had passed more quickly than he had realized. "If it's not any trouble."

"Of course not. You're more than welcome."

"Thanks. I'll get my things from the car."

"Your room is upstairs."

Renny didn't realize how tired he was until his head hit the pillow in the massive, canopied bed fifteen minutes later. He wondered if he should reconsider his promise to Layne. LaRochette seemed the better horse in the race. Just before sleep darkened his mind, he devised a plan to help him decide where to place his bet. *If LaRochette is willing to release enough money, then maybe . . .*

The two men met at the bottom of the stairs.

"Was it the girl?"

"Yes, it was the girl."

"How long?"

"I'm not sure. What he lacks in experience is helped by the strength of their attachment. He has great potential."

"And tomorrow?"

"We will have to wait and see."

"Bon soir."

"Bon soir."

24

The easiest person to deceive is one's own self.
BARON LYTTON

R enny awoke to a gray morning sky. He had slept but didn't feel rested. In the daylight he examined his sleeping quarters, a corner bedroom on the seaward side of the house. A plate-glass window facing the ocean, a large skylight, and two tall windows on the north side of the room provided light for a sitting area with a wicker love seat and side chair. A large bathroom with gold fixtures and marble vanity was opposite the foot of the bed. He felt better after he showered and put on a pair of tennis shorts. He positioned one of the chairs so that it faced the picture window and the ocean beyond. Taking his Bible out of his suitcase, he opened it at random and saw his name, Josiah, in the middle of the page. He began in verse 1 of 1 Kings 13:

> By the word of the LORD a man of God came from Judah to Bethel, as Jeroboam was standing by the altar to make an offering. He cried out against the altar by the word of the LORD: "Oh altar, altar! This is what the LORD says: 'A son named Josiah will be born to the house of David. On you he will sacrifice the priests of the high places who now make offerings here, and human bones will be burned on you.'"

It was a gruesome scene. Slaughter of pagan priests and burning human bones. Both his mother and grandfather said he was named after

Josiah in the Bible. Maybe there was another Josiah. He read the commentary at the bottom of the page and noted a reference to 2 Kings 23. As he was turning the pages to find a happier story, LaRochette's voice echoed in the room.

"Good morning, Renny? Can you hear me?"

Renny looked toward the sound and saw an intercom next to the bedroom door. Closing the Bible, he walked over and pressed the talk button. "Yes sir. Good morning."

"Are you ready for breakfast?"

"Yes."

"We have coffee ready, and my cook will have the meal on the table in a couple of minutes. The kitchen is at the bottom of the stairs to the left. We'll be waiting for you."

"Thanks. I'll be right down."

As he descended the long stairway that swept in a semicircle to the foyer, he wondered if his father had ever visited the house. To reach the kitchen, he passed through a long, formal dining room. LaRochette and Roget were drinking coffee and reading newspapers at a circular table surrounded on three sides by a bay window. Outside, the ocean glittered in the morning sun. A platter of bacon and a bowl of steaming scrambled eggs were on the table, and a middle-aged cook set a plate of fresh biscuits beside them.

From behind the paper, Roget mumbled, "Good morning."

"Good morning."

"How would you like your coffee, sir?" the cook asked.

"Cream and sugar, please."

"I asked Marlene to cook a big breakfast this morning," LaRochette said as Renny sat down.

Renny had not eaten anything since a bagel at his desk the previous afternoon, and at the sight of the food, his appetite returned with a vengeance.

Once everything was on the table, the cook disappeared. Three biscuits, two servings of eggs, and several pieces of bacon later, Renny slowed down and sipped his coffee. LaRochette followed at a more leisurely pace; Roget nibbled a few pieces of dry toast as he read the financial section.

"Wonderful breakfast. Can I thank the cook?"

"She has other duties, but I'll be sure to tell her," LaRochette said.

"I was wondering this morning if my father ever stayed here."

"A few times over the years. Living in Charleston, he drove up and back for our meetings in the same day. He was here a week or so before his heart attack. We played a round of golf, didn't we, Robert?"

Roget lowered the paper a couple of inches. "Over at Sea Isle, I believe."

"Yes. I'm glad we had the time together. Who would have thought it would be our last?"

Renny finished the last piece of egg and looked around the kitchen. "Can I ask a question about our business?"

LaRochette smiled. "Of course. The servants are not in this part of the house."

Renny began, "Your letter mentioned a distribution."

"Yes."

"Is that definite?"

"Probably."

"Uh, do you have an amount in mind?"

Roget folded his paper and put it on the table.

"Your first distribution is an exciting time," LaRochette said. "I'll never forget the first time I saw my Swiss account grow by all those zeros."

"My first was the largest distribution ever," Roget added, warming to the change in topic.

LaRochette continued, "Renny, I can't answer your question specifically. The List is a cooperative venture. I don't set the amount. It's determined by a vote of the members."

"Do you have a recommended figure? Your opinion obviously carries a lot of weight."

"Well, it will be substantial."

Renny pressed his lips together in frustration.

"Oh, enough cat and mouse, Desmond. Go ahead and give him an idea."

LaRochette gave Roget a peeved look and stirred his coffee with a silver spoon. "Very well, Renny. One key to the success of the List has been maintaining a long-term perspective. Currently, the world economy is without question entering a downward cycle. In times like these, the better policy is conservative distribution, and I would recommend something in the $1 million range."

Unable to hide his disappointment, Renny said, "But why so little if the principal is so large? The total amount distributed would not equal the amount of interest earned in a month."

"I've had the benefit of many years' experience, and in past distributions during similar economic climates this has been the pattern. Don't let immediate gratification dominate your thinking."

Renny couldn't believe the hypocrisy in what he was hearing. "That's easy for you to say, Mr. LaRochette. Look at the lifestyle you enjoy here in this house. For all I know, you have eleven others like it, one for each month of the year. I have virtually nothing, except a car, my clothes, and a few dollars in a checking account."

LaRochette's face flushed, but the man maintained firm control of his voice. "I understand your feelings. However, what you see here was not built with money distributed from the List. I earned it myself through hard work and fortunate business activities. I don't mean to boast, but the LaRochette family has not relied upon the money from the List for personal use since the 1880s—over one hundred years. We direct all distributions into worthy causes for those less fortunate."

The wind out of his sails, Renny said, "I apologize. I had no idea."

"Apology accepted. Just remember that $1 million is a lot of money."

Renny glanced at Roget for support, but only received a shrug and negative shake of the head. "Is there anything I could say to change your mind?"

"I always try to keep an open mind, but I've given this a lot of thought."

LaRochette drained his coffee cup, and Renny knew the discussion was over.

"Robert and I are going into Georgetown to meet with a business group that owns a couple of restaurants in the area. Have you eaten at the Portside in Charleston?"

Renny remembered the place: large, upscale, good location, popular with tourists. "Yes, a time or two."

"We're negotiating a contract to buy it together with the Inlet Waterway, a local restaurant where I eat every Tuesday when I'm in town. I've spent so much money there, I decided it made sense to buy it and pay myself." LaRochette chuckled. "Would you like to come along for the ride?"

"No, thanks." Renny had no interest in LaRochette's personal business ventures. "I have an errand to run before tonight's meeting."

"You're welcome to stay here as long as you like," LaRochette replied. "Is there anything you need?"

"No. Thanks for your hospitality."

LaRochette and Roget left the kitchen. Renny poured another glass of orange juice and watched sand swirling in the stiff early morning breeze along the beach. He didn't have any errands to run, but he knew LaRochette's invitation was only a courtesy. Now, he had the rest of the day to occupy. He stared, unthinking, out the window for several minutes, then went upstairs and packed his bags.

Downstairs, he stopped at the library entrance. One of the pocket doors was slightly open. Peering through the crack, he scanned the room. It was empty. Walking quickly to the front door, he opened it and looked outside. The silver Mercedes he'd seen the night before was gone.

Treading softly back to the library, he took his bag inside and closed the door. He wanted to see the List. Glancing from side to side to make sure he was alone, he tried to open the front of the secretary. It was locked. Frustrated, he pulled harder, but nothing moved. He started to pick up his suitcase and leave, but the urge to see the List held him. Where was the key? There was a bookcase next to the secretary. Scanning the topics of the volumes, his eye fell on *War and Peace*. The thick book was turned upside down, and when he pulled it out to flip it over, a key fell out on the floor. Voilà! Picking it up, he compared it with the keyhole in the secretary, and in a second he opened the lid.

It was there. He sat on a small brocade-covered chair and examined it with new respect. He read again the words of the original signers and placed his hand on the faded ink. The first meeting would have been a momentous event. The Rice Planter's Inn. Horses and carriages drawn up in front. Daguerreotype images flashed through his mind of men with stern faces, made more solemn by difficulties modern Americans would find unthinkable. What was the discussion that first night? Impassioned speeches by men in peril of financial ruin and death. Men determined to protect their families.

Renny sat bolt upright in the chair. What if Jo's suspicions and his own uneasiness about the List were totally wrong? What if the List's power for good was the same as the touches he'd had from God?

As he flipped through the pages, Renny realized that he wanted the book. It wasn't enough to see it at LaRochette's whim or become custodian "after a proper period of preparation." He wanted it now—to read and handle it whenever he desired. LaRochette's insistence that he bring it to Georgetown made sense. The old man appreciated the book. Renny's father knew its significance. Renny wanted it. He closed the leather cover. Why not take it now? After all, his father had been custodian, and Renny had as much or more right to than anyone else. Alone, he could experiment and develop the power that flowed from it, a power LaRochette said could be used for good.

What good had come to Jo as a result of the previous night? He had a sudden urge to call her and find out. If she had received a blessing, would she reconsider her opinion about his continued involvement with the group?

LaRochette had failed the test. A million dollars. Ridiculous. The old man's parsimony negated his self-serving statements about unity. Layne was the man of the hour. If he agreed to let Renny become custodian, the die was cast. Renny put the List back in the secretary and returned the key to its place under Tolstoy's monumental work. The List would be his soon enough, without the need to sneak it out like a thief.

Slipping out of the library, he quietly shut the doors and left.

The driveway gate opened automatically as his car approached. He turned north toward Pawley's Island and dialed Jo's number from the car phone. There was no answer, and he decided not to leave a message. Finding a deserted spot on the south end of Pawley's, he put on his running shoes and ran on the beach, his face to the wind.

Reaching the place where he and Jo had sat against the log and talked, he stopped, took off his shoes and socks, and waded in the surf. He missed her terribly. Today the waves contained no laughter, and the sandpipers were pitiful companions. Without her presence, the beach was sand, sea, and sun, inanimate objects without the spark of life she ignited wherever she went. Feeling melancholy, he reminded himself that he would see her soon. Then he would have the resources to give her everything she wanted and to surprise her with things she had yet to imagine.

Renting a beach chair and an umbrella, he set them up along a wide section of the strand and lay down in the shade for a nap. Fanned by the breeze, he soon drifted off and descended into a dream. He was in an art gallery, but the pictures were unidentifiable blurs. Frustrated, he began searching for a place to buy a guide to the paintings on display. He came around a corner and saw an exquisite painting of Jo's face framed in gold. While he was staring at the picture and wondering who had painted such a close likeness, a wisp of smoke came up from a corner of the picture, and in a few seconds, to his horror, the image was destroyed in flames. Worried that the gallery would blame him, he ran out as fast as he could. He woke up sweating more from the dream than the heat of the sun. The picture of Jo's face in the frame looked similar to the mental image he'd seen the night before. Unable to go back to sleep, he went for a swim in the surf.

After rinsing off the sand and salt water with a hose next to a beach walkway, he spent the rest of the afternoon walking and wandering through the business section of the island. He went into some shops but bought nothing. Time crawled by, and he decided to drive to Georgetown and register at the inn. He hoped to see Layne privately before the meeting.

On his way into Georgetown, Renny passed a sign on Front Street for the Inlet Waterway Restaurant. Turning around, he drove a couple hundred yards to a dead end. The restaurant faced the street with its back to the river. Painted white with ornate ironwork on the windows, it had a decidedly French look. Just the type of place that would strike LaRochette's fancy.

It was only a few blocks to the Rice Planter's Inn. The familiar desk clerk was on duty. He greeted Renny somberly, "Good afternoon, sir."

"Good afternoon. I'm J. F. Jacobson. There should be a room reserved in my name for the night."

The clerk went down his list, came to the bottom, and started over. "Ah yes, here it is. Room 6. It's upstairs—"

"Yes, I've stayed there before," Renny interrupted, wanting to get upstairs.

"Here is your key." The clerk cleared his throat. "Is Mrs. Jacobson with you this trip?"

Renny couldn't help smiling. "No, but she'll certainly be with me the next time I come. By the way, has Mr. Layne arrived?"

The clerk looked puzzled, consulted his paperwork, and shook his head. "No, not yet, but he'll be in room 8, next door to you."

"Thanks."

Renny settled into his room and lay down on the bed in an attempt to relax. He dozed slightly, but he came awake with a start when he heard a door open and close. He looked out in the hall, but no one was there. He hesitated, then decided to see if Layne had checked in. Knocking softly on Layne's door, he waited and knocked again.

Layne opened the door a crack, and when he saw it was Renny, quickly motioned for him to come inside. "What do you want?" he said sharply.

"I just wanted to make sure everything was set for tonight."

"Of course, of course. Sorry I spoke to you abruptly. I'm nervous about the meeting."

"I talked to LaRochette last night—" Renny began.

"You did what? You idiot!" Layne interrupted.

"No, no. He had asked me to do some research about offshore banking. I didn't mention talking to you or even seeing you."

"All right. Sorry again. Did he say anything I should know?"

"He talked to me about unity, etcetera, but it sounded like a stock speech he gives to all the freshmen. Roget was there, too."

"See, I told you they were comrades."

"You were right—the French connection, so to speak. Anyway, this morning at breakfast I asked LaRochette his opinion about the amount of the distribution. Guess what he said?"

Layne looked at Renny coldly. "Don't play games, just tell me."

Embarrassed by Layne's rebuke, Renny said, "One million."

Renny thought Layne was going to have a fit. "See," he sputtered, "it's always like that. Well, tonight should take care of his stingy ways. I'll try to let the others know before the meeting. That should fortify their resolve for change."

"How will I know when to make the motion?"

"Keep your eye on me. At the appropriate time I'll look at you and tap my glass three times. Make the motion, and we'll go from there."

Layne opened the door and almost pushed Renny into the hall.

"One other thing," Renny whispered hurriedly.

"What?"

"I want to be custodian of the List, like my father."

"Sure, sure. Just do as you're told."

"Without waiting."

"Yes," Layne hissed. "We can't be seen talking like this."

He shut the door in Renny's face.

Renny went back to his room. He didn't like the man, but an alliance with Thomas Layne V was the only logical solution. LaRochette was nobler, but his views were ridiculously conservative, and he was unwilling to release the money. Renny knew what he would do. He had to go for the money and the List.

25

All the world's a stage, and all the
men and women merely players.
AS YOU LIKE IT, ACT 2, SCENE 7

As he straightened his red-and-gold silk tie, Renny practiced making the motion nominating Thomas Layne as president of the List. He wanted a calm and confident tone of voice—not belligerent but firm and sure. When he had achieved the desired effect, he programmed it into his memory and put on his jacket.

Downstairs, the doorman outside the dining room greeted him by name, "Good evening, Mr. Jacobson."

The drinks were already flowing for Roget and Smithfield. LaRochette, a glass of wine in his hand, waved Renny over.

"Good evening, my boy. I hope you had a pleasant day."

"A little slow. I drove up to Pawley's Island."

"Yes, what do they call it? Shabbily elegant."

"Yes, that's it. On my way into town this afternoon I drove by the Inlet Waterway. Nice-looking place."

"I'm glad you approve. Robert and I made great progress today in our negotiations with the sellers. Excuse me. Harry!" LaRochette called to Smithfield, who dutifully responded, and the two men began a private conversation. Renny slid back to a spot near the door.

He missed Jo, wished she were with him, then quickly decided this was not the place for her. He also missed Gus Eicholtz. The big-voiced man would have lightened the atmosphere with his boisterous laugh and spontaneous outbursts.

Layne, Weiss, and Flournoy had not yet arrived. Roget and Smithfield were drinking martinis as fast as they could refill their glasses. At this rate, they would spend the evening under the table. Renny poured a mineral water. He wanted all his wits about him this evening. He was nibbling from the hors d'oeuvre table when Layne, Weiss, and Flournoy made a grand entrance. Layne waved to LaRochette, grabbed the older man's hand, and gave him a hearty hello. Renny was mystified. In a few minutes, LaRochette would have ample reason to say, "Et tu, Brute," but for now Caesar remained unsuspecting of the conspirator's plot.

Weiss pounded Renny on the back. "How have you been?"

"Fine. And you?"

"Couldn't be better." The morose Weiss of the previous meeting had apparently not come to this one.

"What's the reason?" Renny asked.

"My wife is pregnant, and we just found out it is a boy!"

"Congratulations."

"Thanks. I have four daughters, and I never thought we would get it right."

"You have four daughters?"

"Right, but for obvious reasons I've been hanging on for a son. My wife has given me fits about enduring another pregnancy, but it looks like my persistence has paid off."

"Reminds me of rural China," Renny said.

"What in the devil are you talking about?" Weiss asked.

"You know. In some areas unwanted baby girls are taken outside the city and tossed into empty silos to die. Only boys are considered worth keeping."

Weiss glared. "What are you trying to say, Jacobson?"

"Your attitude toward your daughters, Weiss. It stinks."

Before Weiss could respond, Flournoy yelled across the room, "Jerrod! I understand you have good news. Come over here and fill us in."

Renny let him go and poured another glass of water. He ate a few more hors d'oeuvre and cooled off by the time Smithfield joined him at the end of the table. "Desmond tells me you and Ms. Johnston may walk the aisle."

"Yes, I hope so."

"As historian, I can tell you such a step would be a first," the old man said studiously. "There has been very little intermarriage among the member families, never in which both parties knew about the List. It's somewhat surprising considering the relatively small number of aristocratic Southern families."

"Any reason?"

Smithfield furrowed his brow. "None that I can guess except to protect confidentiality. Most members have limited contact with one another outside these meetings. You know how it is; people get together, and before you can blink, the upstairs maid is talking to the butler and the butler is talking to the cook."

Smithfield was unquestionably a nineteenth-century anachronism.

The headwaiter rang a little silver bell, and everyone took his assigned seat at the table. A few glanced awkwardly at the empty seats reserved for the Eicholtz, Maxwell, and Johnston families. Weiss didn't look in Renny's direction. Including the seat reserved for the Hammond family, there were four vacant places.

LaRochette broke the silence. "I know we all feel regret at the additional empty spaces at our table this evening. Of course, Gus Eicholtz is out of the country and could not attend. However"—he looked at Renny and raised his left eyebrow—"can I share your good news about Ms. Johnston?"

Caught off guard, Renny couldn't think of a reason to say no. "Sure."

"Renny and Jo Johnston are engaged to be married. So, in a sense, the Johnston seat will still have a voice at the table."

Before Renny could sputter a correction, Flournoy lifted his glass in the air. "A toast, a toast. To Mr. and Mrs. Renny, er—what is your given name, young Jacobson?"

LaRochette stepped in, "Mr. and Mrs. Josiah Fletchall Jacobson. Long life, prosperity, and many sons."

"Hear, hear." Everyone but Weiss joined in with exuberance.

Soup and salad were followed by roasted leg of lamb rubbed in mustard, seasoned with garlic and accompanied by crisp green beans with almonds and fresh mint jelly. The dinner wine perfectly matched the meal, and dessert was a lemon crepe so light it dissolved as soon as it touched the tongue.

While he ate, Renny tried to maintain occasional eye contact with Layne but had the uneasy impression the older man was avoiding his gaze. As soon as the staff of the inn cleared the table and disappeared into the kitchen, LaRochette stood, tapped his glass, and conversation around the table died down.

"Gentlemen, I am pleased to call to order the 248th meeting of The Covenant List of South Carolina, Limited. I would ask Mr. Smithfield to review the minutes of the last meeting."

Smithfield rose and coughed. "As all of you know, the last meeting was abruptly adjourned following the tragic death of Bart Maxwell. The only business conducted involved our rejection of the claims of Miss Johnston based upon the requirements of our founding documents. Our offer of compensation to her in the amount of $1 million was refused. Is that still her position, Renny?"

"Yes, I'd say so. She was only interested in learning about her father and has no further interest in this group."

"Except for yourself, of course," Smithfield added with unintentional humor that caused a ripple of laughs around the table. "You know what I mean," he sputtered. "At any rate, we never reached a decision about a distribution from the corpus. It has been several years since the last distribution, and under the terms of items four and five of the Covenant we can decide an appropriate amount."

Renny was not watching Smithfield. His eyes were glued to Layne's hand. At that moment Layne picked up a spoon and almost imperceptibly tapped his glass three times. Swallowing his nerves, Renny cleared his throat. "Excuse me. I would like to make a motion."

Everyone turned and stared.

Smithfield looked at LaRochette and said, "I was about to turn the meeting back over to Desmond, but if you have something to bring up, go ahead."

Renny set his expression as he'd practiced in the mirror upstairs. Looking solemnly around the table, he said, "I move for the election of Thomas Layne as president of the List."

Smithfield sat down as if he had been shot. Renny avoided LaRochette's gaze and focused on Jerrod Weiss, who calmly said, "I second the motion."

"Why, it's treason," Roget blurted out.

"Hold on," LaRochette responded. "A motion has been made and seconded. Does anyone want to speak to the issue?"

Renny waited anxiously for Layne to give a speech outlining the progressive changes he envisioned for the List, the most important being a massive, immediate distribution of wealth to them all. All he said was, "I'm honored and will serve if elected."

LaRochette said, "You all know, except for Mr. Jacobson, the leadership my family and I have provided since the founding of this group. I stand on our record."

"I call for the vote," Weiss said.

Regaining his feet and his composure, Smithfield said, "All in favor of the election of Mr. Thomas Layne please signify by raising your right hand."

Renny raised his hand and looked around the table.

No one else moved a muscle.

Renny put his hand down and shook his head. "Maybe I didn't understand. Didn't you ask who supported the election of Mr. Layne?"

"Yes, I did," Smithfield responded. "Apparently you're the only one."

"What!" Renny looked at Layne who stared at him impassively. Then at Weiss who was unsuccessfully trying not to smirk. "You!" he shouted, pointing to Weiss. "You seconded the motion."

"Just because I seconded the motion does not mean that I supported it. All it did was bring the matter to a vote. Parliamentary procedure, you know. I'm satisfied with Desmond's leadership."

His voice now trembling, Renny turned toward Layne. "But you told me—"

"I told you what you wanted to hear."

"Eicholtz's proxy?"

"Did you ever see a proxy?"

"Why, you son of a—"

"Hold on, Renny," LaRochette cut him off.

Renny scanned the impassive faces around the table. "What are you trying to do to me?" he asked, slumping down in his chair.

LaRochette answered, "This was a test, Renny. A loyalty test. A fidelity test. A necessary test."

"Test?" Renny asked numbly.

"That's right. You see, the foundation of this group is unity, an unshakable commitment to one another and our common vision and purpose. Remember that I spoke to you about these matters the other night. It was my way of trying to warn you against divisiveness, but you weren't listening."

Layne continued, "We knew you and Gus Eicholtz talked after the last meeting about your mutual dissatisfaction with our structure. Gus should have known better. You are young and impressionable. We decided it best to make an impression that will last."

"So, you lied to me," Renny said, regaining some heat.

"Don't get self-righteous," Layne said. "You wanted a plan to disrupt this group. We gave you the rope; you hung yourself."

"But not beyond recovery," LaRochette said with a conciliatory smile. "There will be consequences, but you will have opportunity to achieve full reinstatement."

"What consequences?"

"Let me explain in the form of a motion." LaRochette addressed the table as a whole, "I move that we authorize a distribution from the corpus of the List to our individual accounts in the amount of $50 million."

"I second," Roget said quickly.

"All in favor, please raise your hand."

Everyone, including a much meeker Renny, signaled agreement.

LaRochette, his eyes fixed on Renny, continued, "As to consequences. I move that the distribution to the Eicholtz and Jacobson families be delayed until such time as they demonstrate conduct consistent with the founding principles of the List."

Renny clenched his napkin. "No, that's not fair. I'll—"

"I second," Weiss said, interrupting.

"Don't go any farther, Renny," a surprisingly sober Flournoy interjected. Turning to LaRochette, he said, "I suggest we amend the motion to delay distribution only one or two years."

LaRochette waited for anyone else to comment. "I would agree to modify the motion so long as Mr. Jacobson signs the customary power of attorney and understands there will be no distribution of any kind during a two-year probationary period."

"What about Gus?" Flournoy asked.

"We'll need to address that directly with him," LaRochette said.

"You mean you will block withdrawal of monies already in my father's account?" Renny asked, oblivious to the comment about Eicholtz.

"Correct, for the probationary period," LaRochette answered. "Two years is not a long time."

"How much is in my personal account? I don't even know."

LaRochette deferred to Roget who opened a small, leather-bound notebook. "All of our individual accounts have a balance slightly over $16 million."

Renny felt all the energy draining from his body. He was beaten, whipped. Not only had he lost the right to a current distribution but also the ability to access the millions already in his father's account.

"This isn't right," he said.

"Do you agree with the probationary period or not?" Weiss asked in a surly voice.

For the third time he wanted to punch Weiss. But Renny was the one unconscious on the canvas with the referee counting to ten. "OK," he mumbled.

"Pardon?" LaRochette asked.

"I agree."

"Good boy," Flournoy said. "You won't regret it. A little humble pie is good for all of us."

Renny had eaten all the humble pie he could stomach. "May I be excused?" he asked like a small boy who couldn't sit still at the table.

"Does anyone have anything of importance to bring before us?" LaRochette asked.

No one spoke.

"We need to discuss the offshore banking issue, Renny. You know more about that than anyone else, and you're welcome to stay."

"You have the information, and my recommendation is the same as yours," Renny responded. "I have nothing to add to our discussion of last night. If you need me, I'll be in room 6."

"As you wish," LaRochette said in his best fatherly tone. "Don't be too hard on yourself."

"Sure."

Renny slipped out of the room. Closing the door, he heard someone say something he couldn't hear distinctly, but he easily identified Weiss's raucous laugh in response. Renny didn't care; he was past the point of embarrassment and shame.

As he passed the desk, the old clerk stopped him. "Sir, here's an envelope for you mistakenly delivered to another room." Renny took it and trudged up the stairs.

He unlocked the door of his room but didn't turn on the lights. If life was a grand stage, Renny had just finished a scene in which Josiah Fletchall Jacobson was cast as the unknowing fool. Sitting in a chair at the small writing desk, he put his head in his hands and tried to will himself to cry, but no tears came. He couldn't even succeed in getting upset. He was empty. In a state of shock, his body numb and his mind incapable of emotion, he sat unmoving for several minutes. *This must be what the bottom of the barrel looks like.* Then, slipping to his knees, he put his face in the seat of the chair.

"God, I'm sorry for what I've thought and done. Show me the way, because I need help."

For the first time in days, he looked to heaven, stilling his thoughts, plans, and dreams. He waited, and in the darkness, in the emptiness, a tiny flame flickered to life deep in Renny's spirit. It was not strong; he was barely aware of it. But it caused him to lift his face and say, "Thank you." He didn't know what he was thankful for. He just said thank you, and a measure of the heaviness of his heart rolled away. He stayed on his knees, not counting the minutes. Then, getting up and changing clothes, he went outside to the boardwalk along the harbor. Like a captain on a ship's deck, he paced the half-mile length of the boardwalk several times until the stress and tension of the day gave way to fatigue. Thankfully, no one from the List was in sight when he slipped up the stairs to his room.

The envelope was on the bed where he'd dropped it. The outside was blank. Opening it, he took out a single sheet of paper. It was a memo from Roget to LaRochette, an informal asset summary for the List. At the top was the balance on deposit in the corpus accounts in Switzerland. Eicholtz had been wrong. The balance was not $2.5 billion; it was over $3 billion. But there was more. The sheet also contained the Swiss account numbers and balances of all the individual members. Roget and LaRochette each had $32,000,000 beside their names. There was a $0 and an asterisk beside Johnston and Maxwell with a notation at the bottom of the page—"Transferred to R&L via power of attorney, August 28." Everyone else's balance was $16,000,000. At the bottom of the sheet were three additional names with phone numbers: Gerhardt Hesselman, Banc Suisse 011-246-4576; François Meron, Banc Geneve 012-873-0967; Carlos Parmero, Medellín 198-87-926.

Renny folded the sheet, put it back in the envelope, and went downstairs to the front desk. A young boy, not more than seventeen, had taken over for the old desk clerk. The young man was reading a sports magazine.

"Do you have a copy machine? I need to make one copy," Renny asked.

"There's one in the office. I can do it for you."

"I'd rather handle it myself if it's OK," Renny said as casually as he could.

"Sure." The clerk opened a door to a small room behind the counter. It contained a couple of filing cabinets, a small wooden desk, a fax machine, and a desktop copier. He flipped on the copier, and they waited for it to warm up.

"Where are you from?" he asked Renny.

"Charleston originally. Now Charlotte." Renny glanced toward the door.

"Charlotte's a booming town. I'd like to move there once I get out of high school."

"There's plenty of work. That's for sure." Renny heard footsteps and voices on the stairs and positioned himself behind the door.

Someone rang the bell on the desk, and the clerk left Renny in the office. As the boy went past, Renny pushed the door two-thirds shut.

"Good evening. We were looking for Mr. Jacobson. He's in room 6. Have you seen him?" It was Roget and someone else.

"No sir. I don't know any of the guests. This is only my third day on the job. I'm sorry."

"We checked his room and he wasn't in. We're going out for a few minutes. Mr. Jacobson is about five-foot-eight, middle twenties with brown hair. If he comes in, don't say anything. Just make a note of it and let me know when I get back. I'm in room 14. Here's a hundred for your trouble."

"Wow, thanks. I'll be right here."

The copier blinked ready, and Renny made a copy of the sheet as soon as the footsteps faded from the front desk.

The clerk rejoined him. Renny tried to look taller and hoped the clerk wouldn't connect him with Roget's description.

"Thanks for the copy." Renny put the original back in the envelope and the copy in his back pocket. "A Mr. LaRochette is staying here. This envelope needs to be delivered to his room before morning. I don't want you to disturb him, so just slide it under his door around 3:00 A.M. Can you handle that?"

"Sure."

"Here's a fifty for the copy and your delivery service."

"Thanks. I'll check his room number and take it up at three."

"Good. Call me if you come to Charlotte. I'll see if I can help you get a job." Before the clerk could say anything else, Renny was up the stairs and out of sight.

The young man slipped the fifty next to the hundred already in his pocket. On second thought, maybe he should stay in Georgetown. The tips were great.

26

In those days was Hezekiah sick unto death.
2 KINGS 20:1, KJV

As soon as he was in his room, Renny packed his bag. He was not going to talk to Roget; he was leaving. He didn't want to make any decisions; he didn't want to see or talk to the members of the List. He had no plan. He couldn't have given a rational explanation for his sense of urgency—he just wanted to get away. He agreed with Flournoy: Two years was not a long time to wait for millions of dollars, but he wanted to leave Georgetown, and he wanted to leave now. Suitcase in hand, he went quietly down the hall, opened the window to the fire escape, climbed out, and shut the window behind him. In less than a minute he was in his car, backing out of the parking lot, and heading home.

It was almost four in the morning when he cut off his lights and pulled into Mrs. Stokes's driveway. He heard Brandy bark once at the sound of the car.

He didn't wake up until noon the next day. It took him a couple of seconds to remember the previous day's events; then, as the details returned, he rolled over in bed and moaned. After he made a cup of coffee, he picked up the cordless phone and called Jo. Her mother answered.

"Mrs. Edwards. It's Renny. May I speak to Jo?"

"She's in the hospital, Renny."

"What time will she be home?"

"She's not working; she's a patient. They are running tests this morning." Renny could hear the strain in Mrs. Edwards's voice.

Renny sat down on the couch. "What's wrong?"

"They don't know for sure. She started feeling ill Friday night, and by yesterday morning she was so weak she couldn't get out of bed. We took her to the ER, and her blood studies were abnormal. It could be serious."

"How serious?"

"Cancer, leukemia, possibly some other type of blood disorder. We just don't know yet."

Renny stood up. "Can I come and see her?"

"Of course. She wants to see you. I was going to call you later today, but she told me you wouldn't be home until this evening."

"I came back early. I'll get a ticket and be there as soon as I can. What's the name of the hospital?"

"Sparrow in Lansing. The same one where she works. She's in room 3426, but that could change. Just check at the patient information desk."

"OK."

"I'm leaving for the hospital in a few minutes. I'll let her know you're coming."

"Thanks."

Renny called the airline directly. He could catch a flight to Detroit in an hour and a half with a connection to Lansing that would arrive just after 8:00 P.M. He took the dirty clothes out of his suitcase and, not knowing how long he would stay, packed several clean shirts and a couple of pairs of pants. Mrs. Stokes was driving in from church when he walked down the stairs. Renny set his bag beside his car and opened her door when she came to a stop.

"You're early," she said. "How was your time at the coast?"

"Not good, so I came back early. I'm glad I did because I just found out that Jo is in the hospital. Her mother said they are running tests this morning. It could be serious, and I'm flying up to Michigan to be with her."

"Oh no."

"I don't know when I'll be back. Can you take care of things here?"

"Of course."

"I'll call you when I know something."

"Please do. Day or night. Do you want me to check the messages on your answering machine upstairs?"

"Yes. I'll call the office in the morning."

Mrs. Stokes grabbed Renny's hand and held it tight for a moment. "I'll be praying."

Renny put his bag in the car and pulled out of the driveway.

In the kitchen, Mrs. Stokes felt a crushing weight against her chest. Quickly sitting down at the kitchen table, she asked, "Father, what is this?" There was no answer, but she sensed it was the burden of the Lord in response to the pressure that was on Jo, a burden as heavy as any she'd felt in her life. Not bothering to change from her Sunday clothes or fix anything to eat, she went into her prayer closet and closed the door.

———

Several hours later in Lansing the leasing representative at the rental car agency gave Renny directions to the hospital. When he got there, he discovered that they had moved Jo to another room, number 5864. Renny got off the elevator on the fifth floor; he faced double doors emblazoned with a sign that read:

STOP—THIS AREA IS OFF-LIMITS TO VISITORS.
NO ONE BEYOND THIS POINT WITHOUT
PROPER AUTHORIZATION.
FOR ASSISTANCE PLEASE PRESS BUZZER.

Renny pushed the button and waited. A moment later a heavyset nurse wearing blue surgical scrubs, mask, and gloves opened the door a few inches. "Can I help you?"

"I'm trying to locate a patient—Jo Johnston."

"She's on this floor but she cannot see visitors other than immediate family."

"I came all the way from Charlotte—"

"I'm sorry, but my orders provide no exceptions. Only the doctor could approve a visitor. He's with the patient and her mother right now."

"Can you tell them I'm here?"

"Yes. As soon as Dr. Levy is finished, I'll let them know. Your name?"

"Renny Jacobson."

The door clicked shut and Renny slumped down in a chair located in a small waiting area in front of the elevators. A television mounted overhead was playing a mindless sitcom. Renny tried to cut it off, but the controls had been disabled.

Thirty minutes passed. Renny fidgeted impatiently. When the doors opened, a woman with Jo's dark hair and blue eyes came out wearing a mask and gloves. Renny could see she had been crying. "Mrs. Edwards?" he asked, getting up.

"Renny?"

"Yes."

"Hello, Renny. I'm glad you're here, but you can't see Jo. Not yet. We just had a long session with her doctor, and she's exhausted."

"What's wrong? Why the mask and gloves?"

Mrs. Edwards took off the mask and sat down. "It's protection against infection—not to protect us, but to protect Jo. She has a condition known as aplastic anemia. The doctors suspected it after the initial blood tests, and a bone marrow biopsy late this afternoon confirmed it."

"I've never heard of it."

"Dr. Levy, a hematologist, told us it's a rare but extremely serious blood disorder that results from the failure of the bone marrow to produce blood cells. Healthy bone marrow produces platelets, red cells, and white cells, and the part of Jo's bone marrow that does this isn't working."

"So she has no white cells to fight infection?"

"Or red cells or platelets. They can give her transfusions of red cells and platelets but not white cells. That's the reason for all the precautions. It's a reverse quarantine, protecting her from us."

"What caused this? She felt fine when she was with me a few days ago."

"They suspect certain chemicals can trigger a reaction in the bone marrow, but Dr. Levy said in half the cases there is no known cause."

"Can they cure it?"

"There is no medication. She is receiving intravenous antibiotics to ward off infection, but the only hope for a cure is a bone marrow transplant—or a miracle. The best donors are brothers or sisters, and as you know, Jo has neither."

"I'm sorry, Mrs. Edwards."

"Call me Carol, Renny. I know you are, but Jo is not giving up and neither should the rest of us."

"When can I see her?"

"I asked the doctor, and he said no one except hospital staff can come in her room until tomorrow morning. They want to make sure she doesn't have a latent infection. If she doesn't have a fever in the morning, I think you will be able to see her for a few minutes."

Renny put his face in his hands. Looking up, he asked, "What time should I be here?"

"I'm coming at seven, so I would say about seven-thirty."

"Is there anything I can do to help you?"

Jo's mother looked at Renny, and two fresh tears streaked down her cheeks. "Pray," she said, her voice trembling, "pray that my daughter won't die."

———

Renny checked into a hotel near the hospital. As soon as he was in his room he called Mrs. Stokes. "It's bad. She has a blood disorder that could kill her, something called aplastic anemia. She needs a bone marrow transplant."

"Or a miracle," Mrs. Stokes replied.

"That's what her mother said, too."

"Have you seen her yet?"

"No, she's in isolation, but I may get to visit her in the morning."

"Give her my love, and tell her the Lord is helping me fight for her. I'm also going to call two friends and ask them to begin praying."

Renny hung up the phone and began pacing back and forth in the room. He had never prayed for more than a few minutes and had no idea what to say. Talking out loud, he said, "God, what am I supposed to do? I'm not Mrs. Stokes. I've not been a missionary for forty years." He walked from the air conditioner, past the TV, to the bathroom door, and back again. What could he do?

Several minutes passed. Then he remembered what he told Jo on the mountain: "Yea, though I walk through the valley of the shadow of death…" That was it! That was his direction in prayer. He hadn't brought a Bible with him, but finding a Gideon's Bible in the nightstand by the bed, he turned to Psalm 23 and started reading it out loud from beginning to end as he walked. Once, twice, three times. He kept reading it until he had it memorized. Then he quoted it over and over. Different phrases rang through his spirit. He said it softly; he said it as loudly as he dared. It was all for Jo, every word, syllable, and promise. As it grew late and stress and fatigue set in, he took a sheet of hotel stationery and wrote it out:

To Jo:

The Lord is my shepherd; I shall not want. He maketh me to lie down in green pastures: he leadeth me beside the still waters. He restoreth my soul: he leadeth me in the paths of righteousness for his name's sake. Yea, though I walk through the valley of the shadow of death, I will fear no evil: for thou art with me; thy rod and thy staff they comfort me. Thou preparest a table before me in the presence of mine enemies: thou anointest my head with oil; my cup runneth over. Surely goodness and mercy shall follow me all the days of my life: and I will dwell in the house of the Lord for ever.

When his head touched the pillow, he finally said, "Amen."

He arrived at the hospital early the next morning. Carol Edwards was waiting for him outside the quarantine area.

"The blood transfusions are helping, and she's feeling better this morning. She's anxious to see you, so I asked one of the nurses to prep you as soon as she has a minute."

The door opened, and a nurse in her thirties with brown wavy hair, angular features, large brown eyes, and a determined set to her square jaw motioned for Renny and Carol to come inside.

"Renny, this is Anne Bailey, a nurse in this unit. She and Jo are friends here at the hospital. They also attend the same church."

Anne nodded in greeting. "It's good to meet you. I spent last night with Jo and heard her mention your name in her sleep."

"What did she say?"

"Nothing I could decipher. She was somewhat delirious until the fever broke."

"And now?" Renny asked.

"Better, but before you see her I need to tell you the guidelines. Do you have a cold or any other sickness?"

"No."

"You will need to wash up and wear a gown, gloves, mask, and hat. I have a set ready for you by the sink in this bathroom."

Renny suited up.

As they walked down the hall to Jo's room, Anne said, "Don't touch her or take off the mask, please. It's critically important that she not be exposed to anything infectious."

"I understand."

"Carol and I will wait outside while you go in. Here's her room."

Renny knocked lightly and pushed open the door. "Good morning," he said.

"Good morning. Thanks for coming." Jo was propped up in the bed with the tray of breakfast food in front of her. Her skin was so pale and white that it made her blue eyes shine even brighter. "Can I offer you some barbecue?"

"I can't eat it this early in the morning." Renny smiled. "How are you feeling?"

"Better."

Renny approached the bed. "Is this too close?"

"It's not close enough. Take one more giant step."

"I'd better not. Your guardian angel Anne warned me against close contact."

"We'd better obey her; she's been great," Jo said. "She spent all last night with me."

"I've got something for you." Renny took the sheet of motel stationery out of his pocket. "I prayed this for you and wrote it out last night at the hotel." He handed it to Jo.

"From the mountain." Jo nodded. "I'd forgotten."

"Me, too, until I asked the Lord what to pray for you."

"This is good, Renny. This gives me more hope." She sighed. "Thank you."

Renny wanted to take her in his arms and hold her until every atom of illness was driven from her body by the power of his love. But all he could do was say, "You're welcome."

"Tell me about Georgetown. Did things go as you'd hoped?"

Renny shook his head. "No. You were right. It was a waste of time. I shouldn't have gone."

"Are you OK?"

Before Renny could answer, Anne poked her head in the room. "Time's up."

"But he just got here," Jo said.

"And he's about to leave. You have more platelets coming. He can come back this evening."

"And stay longer," Jo said.

"Yes, I think that can be arranged." Anne's features softened when she smiled.

"See you later," Renny said. "Mrs. Stokes sends her love. She's praying."

"Good." Jo's eyes flickered. "I guess I'm more tired than I realized."

Renny went out into the hall, where Anne was talking to Carol.

"You can see the difference the transfusions make. She is totally different from yesterday."

"Do they have a permanent effect?" Carol asked.

"No. The patients usually experience peaks and valleys as the levels of red cells and platelets fluctuate. We need to do a platelet transfusion this morning because they only live in the body for a few days. The red cells can survive a month or more once she's stable. But what we need"—Anne's jaw grew more determined—"is for her body to begin producing cells on its own in the bone marrow."

"We need a miracle," Renny and Carol both said at the same time.

Anne nodded grimly. "You're right."

———

Empty breakfast trays on the glass table in front of them, the three men were enjoying the ocean breeze on the veranda. The youngest spoke. "So, Jacobson flew the coop?"

"Yes. It's tough being the only chicken in a house full of foxes."

"Will he be back?"

"He'll be back."

"Why are you so sure?"

"You know better than to question me. He's drawn to the power, and it will call him back after his emotions cool and wounded feelings heal. He needs to be crushed so that we can rebuild him. He will be a strong one. You'll see."

"I hope you're right."

"Have I ever been wrong?"

27

Curses, not loud but deep ... which the
poor heart fain deny, and dare not.
MACBETH, ACT 5, SCENE 3

W here did you spend the night?" Carol asked Renny as they took off their scrubs. "I should have asked you to stay at our house, but with all that's happened, I wasn't thinking."

"That's OK. I stayed at the Ramada since it's close to the hospital."

"Can you check out and come over now?"

"Yes, but I need to call my office around nine."

"Let's go by the hotel, and you can follow me from there to the house. We'll be home before nine."

After stopping by the hotel, Renny followed Carol's blue Buick along several streets that skirted the campus of Michigan State. East Lansing was a true college town; everything revolved around the university. With the recent return of students for the fall semester, the campus was a bee-hive of activity. Bike riders, joggers, and students carrying books crowded the corners at every traffic light. Dry cleaners, restaurants, and clothing stores all catered to Spartan green.

Leaving the area adjacent to the campus, they passed through neighborhoods where the houses were older and smaller than in newer cities like Charlotte. Renny liked the cozy academic feel of the narrow residential streets that spread out on the north side of the university. The houses exuded what Renny's mother had called personality, an individual style that occasionally matched the character of the occupants. He guessed that one house was the home of a botany professor and another the dwelling of an English literature teacher.

Jo and her mother lived in a small, two-story, brick Cape Cod with a manicured front yard and an expanse of natural woods surrounding it on three sides.

"It's designed for birds, not gardeners," Carol said as she unlocked the door. "You can use the phone in the kitchen."

He called his office. Fortunately, he didn't have any appointments scheduled and his office work could simply pile up on his desk. Mr. Heywood was in a partners' meeting, and Renny left word that he was in Michigan because of a medical emergency involving a close friend.

By the time he hung up, Carol had a fresh pot of coffee ready.

"How would you like it?" she asked.

"Milk and sugar, please."

She led him into the living room and offered him a seat on a mauve-and-cream-colored sofa that faced a picture window overlooking the backyard. Renny immediately noticed two pictures of Jo on the wall. One was an oil portrait painted when she was about six and the other a formal photograph from her high school graduation. He could see the sparkle in her eyes at age six; she really hadn't changed very much.

Carol noticed Renny's interest in the pictures. "Would you like to see some photos of Jo's growing-up years?"

"Would that be OK with you?"

"I need to focus on happier times myself. Let me get a couple of albums."

They sat next to each other on the couch. She began with the naked baby pictures and walked him through diapers, swing sets, bike rides, birthday parties, and early school days. There were even a few pictures of Jo's father. Renny could see the depression that sat on his features. He started to comment but stopped.

"Tell me a story from her life during this time."

Carol thought a moment. "Well, when she was three, I used to rock her every night before putting her to bed. She would curl up in my lap with her favorite blanket, her 'B' she called it, and suck her thumb. Children love repetition, and I would sing the same song to her several times each night. Then I'd ask her, 'Do you know Mommy loves you?' and wait for her to say yes. One night I took the question a step further. When she said yes, I asked her, 'Why does Mommy love you?' She was quiet for a moment, took her thumb out and said, "Cause,' and popped her thumb back in its place. It was the most profound statement of the why of love I'd ever heard. She knew I loved her not for what she did or didn't do or for what she could give me or do for me, but for the simple fact that she was my daughter. It made me understand the love of God for us."

"Like John 3:16?"

"Yes, but at a personal, intimate level. And that's Jo. Since she was a little girl, she has always had the ability to show others the nature of real love." Carol started crying quietly and took a tissue from a box on the coffee table. "It's OK for me to cry like this. I'm not sad; I'm glad for her life and her influence on me and others. I know she's touched you, and you'll never be the same."

Renny didn't trust himself to speak, so they sat in silence until Carol regained her composure. "Come with me. I'll let you see Jo's room."

She led Renny down a short hallway to a corner bedroom. It was decorated in white with a border of bright, cheerful flowers and matching trim around the windows. To allow the most light possible, Jo had chosen shutters instead of curtains. When Renny and her mother entered the room, the shutters were open and the room was almost startling in its brightness. The Star of David Mrs. Stokes had given her hung by a string in front of a windowpane. There were two closets. The larger was filled with clothes and shoes, the smaller with boxes, books, and albums.

"These will give you a more complete glimpse into her life. I know she wouldn't mind you looking through them. If you'll excuse me, I need to be alone for a while."

"Jo won't care?"

"No. I know how she feels about you, Renny."

Renny sat on the floor and pulled out the nearest box. It contained papers from a high school English class. One assignment required the students to describe an embarrassing incident in their life. Jo wrote about the first time she drove alone in her mother's car. She turned the wrong way down a one-way street and ended up stopping in the middle of the road when she came face to face with a local policeman's vehicle.

There were awards, projects, poems, letters to her mother, and more pictures, including two framed photos of Jo with her dates to the junior and senior proms. Both of the guys looked taller than Renny. Too tall for Jo.

Renny read almost every word and examined every piece of memorabilia. In a way, he enjoyed himself, but he also felt moments of sadness because she was not with him to enrich his discoveries. By the time he stretched and stood up, it was lunchtime.

Going out to the kitchen, he found Carol looking in the refrigerator.

"Not much to pick from," she said.

"May I take you out for something?" Renny offered. "We could eat on our way to the hospital."

"That sounds like a good idea. I called a little while ago, and the nurse on duty said we could see Jo earlier than we thought."

"How was she?"

"'Stable' was the word she used."

"Let's go somewhere you and Jo like," Renny said.

"That's easy. There's a small Japanese place not far from the hospital."

The restaurant was not ornate, but Renny quickly discovered why they enjoyed it. The two cooks prepared fried rice, vegetables, fresh meats, and seafood on large griddles in front of the customers. While they were working, the cooks juggled the cooking utensils and carried on a light banter with the patrons.

"Jo loves anything with a teriyaki flavor," Carol said between mouthfuls of steaming fried rice.

"I bet she uses chopsticks."

"Yep, down to the last grain of rice."

"I wish we could take a meal to her."

"I'll check the hospital guidelines for bringing her food from outside. I know she would love to have some."

At the hospital, Carol went first while Renny sat in the waiting room near the elevator. After about fifteen minutes, she came out, and Renny washed his hands and put on the protective gear.

There was a little more color in Jo's cheeks than the night before.

"Mom said you two have been at the house since this morning," she said.

"Yes, she showed me some naked baby pictures and told me an interesting incident or two from your childhood."

"Uh-oh."

"I want to buy you a new blanket."

Jo laughed weakly. "I still have my B. Did you see it? It's in a plastic bag in the closet."

"No, but I enjoyed going through your keepsakes. I hope it was OK for me to learn all your secrets."

"Now that you've found out about my thumbsucking, I have nothing else to hide."

"Everyone should be so pure." Renny resisted the urge to reach out and hold her hand. "How are you feeling?"

"Tired and weak. My hip hurts where they did the bone marrow biopsy."

Renny noticed some red dots on Jo's arms. "What are those spots?"

"They're called petechiae, caused by bleeding under the skin due to my low platelet count. They developed before I received the transfusion last night."

"Do they hurt?"

"No. It's like a little bruise, but there's no pain. Now, tell me about Georgetown. What happened?"

"OK." Renny sighed. "If I know about your thumb, you have a right to know about my foibles. I'll begin at the end." Renny told her about the sting operation orchestrated by the members of the List and the consequences of his failure to pass the loyalty test. "From our lunch in Charlotte to the meeting in Georgetown, Layne played his role like a Shakespearean actor. I never suspected anything."

"What about the probation idea? Are you going to stay with it?"

"I've probably broken probation already since I'm AWOL from the inn. After leaving the meeting with my tail between my legs, the old desk clerk gave me an envelope by mistake. It contained a memo from Roget to LaRochette with a general summary of everyone's financial information. They have already transferred the money from your family's account and Bart Maxwell's account. It looks like it landed with LaRochette and Roget."

"That's not surprising."

"I made a copy of the sheet and arranged for the original to reach LaRochette. Then, all I wanted to do was leave the inn. I went out the window, down the fire escape, and drove most of the night back to Charlotte. When I woke up, I talked with your mother, found out what had happened, and flew up as soon as I could."

"What would the others think if they knew LaRochette took the money from the two accounts?"

"Frankly, I don't know that they would care."

Jo closed her eyes for a few seconds. "Oh yes. You didn't tell me what happened at LaRochette's house the other night. Was it Friday night? It seems a lot longer ago."

"OK. He has a huge place on a large tract of land near Debordeau. Roget was also there. We talked about offshore banking, and LaRochette lectured me about the importance of unity and devotion to the cause. After my neck was in the noose at the meeting, he told me it had been an attempt to warn me, but it would have taken a bigger sign to get my attention. Let's see. . . ." He paused. "There was one other thing that happened." Suddenly, Renny's hands grew clammy, and he felt sick to his stomach.

Jo, who had been listening through half-closed eyelids, pushed herself up in the bed and opened her eyes all the way. "What's wrong? You look as pale as I do."

Renny continued slowly, "LaRochette keeps the List in his library. After we discussed bank issues, he talked to me about becoming custodian like my father and told me the book itself can be a source of power to help people."

"That's not right, Renny."

"I'm afraid that's not all. At his suggestion, I put my hand on the place where I signed and released the power of the List toward someone special to me. You came to mind."

"When was this?" Jo asked sharply.

"About eleven, I guess."

"What happened when you did this?"

"I saw your face in a frame, and it disappeared in a flash of light. I didn't tell LaRochette who I'd thought about, but he said they had been touched by the power of the List."

Jo closed her eyes. "Renny, that's when I first felt sick."

Renny clenched his fists. "But how, but what—I didn't want you to get sick. That wasn't in my mind."

Jo looked at the ceiling. "You didn't know what was going on, but there could be a connection, a curse."

Renny stood. "If I thought I'd done something to hurt you, if I did something to cause this"—he waved his hand toward the stark room— "I'd ask God to let it fall on me!"

"No," Jo said quickly. "That's not the answer. Slow down a second." She closed her eyes again for a moment. "OK. Please come here."

"I am here," Renny said, his eyes downcast.

"No, come right beside the bed."

"But—"

"Just come here and take my hand."

Renny cradled her left hand gently in his right one. Her pale hand was almost as white as the sterile glove that covered his.

With eyes closed, Jo said, "Father, I ask you to release Renny and me from every evil thing connected with the List. I forgive Renny for anything he did without understanding the consequences."

Renny leaned over and buried his face in the sheets.

Jo continued, "Please heal me and do not let evil triumph over me or Renny. In Jesus' name, amen."

Renny was able to choke out an amen.

Jo withdrew her hand from his and stroked his head. "I love you, Renny. No matter what's happened or will happen, I love you."

There was a knock at the door. Renny jumped up and took a step back, wiping his eyes with his sleeve.

Jo said, "Come in."

It was Anne. "Sorry to interrupt, but you need a rest."

Jo nodded. Renny gave her a long look and left the room.

At the sight of Renny's face, Carol asked, "Are you OK?"

"Better than I deserve," he said grimly.

Anne opened the door to the isolation unit. "Carol, we need to let Jo rest for a couple of hours. Come back later. I'll promise you a longer visit then."

"I'm sorry," Renny said as they went down in the elevator, "I took almost all the time."

"Don't apologize. I think your presence will help get her well as much as anything else."

Renny looked away. If she only knew.

He was silent on the trip back to the house. As they pulled into the driveway, he said, "I'll stay here when you go back to the hospital. I want you to have as much time with Jo as you can, and I'd rather be here than in the waiting area."

"OK. Make yourself at home."

Inside, she showed him a guest bedroom on the second floor. It was directly over Jo's room.

"You can stay here. If you need anything, let me know."

"Thanks." Renny shut the door and put his suitcase on the bed. Taking off his shoes to avoid making noise, he started pacing back and forth across the room. He quoted Psalm 23, but it didn't have the power of the previous night. He worried, fretted, analyzed. Nothing happened. He felt he was under a huge brass bowl and nothing could go up or come down. He stared at the ceiling, longing to break through the plaster into the heavens, but his prayers and thoughts didn't go any higher than the top of his head.

Opening the door, he heard Carol leaving for the hospital. He went downstairs to Jo's room. Leaning against the doorframe, he said, "God, please let her come back here." A Bible sat on her nightstand. He picked it up and went into the living room. Sitting on the sofa, he prayed, "What do I need to do to make this right?"

Then, in time-honored—if theologically questionable—fashion, he let the Bible fall open on his lap and read the first words his eyes brought into focus. It was a passage about Paul's ministry in Ephesus:

> Many of those who believed now came and openly confessed their evil deeds. A number who had practiced sorcery brought their scrolls together and burned them publicly. When they calculated the value of the scrolls, the total came to fifty thousand drachmas.

He closed the book. Good theology or not, he had his answer. Like the evil scrolls of Ephesus, the List must be destroyed. Then and only then would Jo be set free from the curse and healed.

Finding a sheet of paper in the kitchen, he wrote:

Dear Jo and Carol,

There is some unfinished business of repentance for me in Georgetown. I would rather be here with you, but I must obey what God has told me to do.

Please pray for me, and I will be praying for you.

Love,
Renny

He put the note on the kitchen table. Calling USAirways, he booked a flight to Detroit that left in two hours. There was no connecting flight to Charlotte until late the next afternoon.

"What about Charleston?" he asked the ticketing agent.

"South Carolina?"

Renny had forgotten there was any other. "Yes."

"There is a late-night flight into Charleston that arrives at midnight."

"I'll take it."

28

*The devil took him to a very high mountain and showed him
all the kingdoms of the world and their splendor. "All this I will
give you," he said, "if you will bow down and worship me."*
MATTHEW 4:8-9, NIV

Renny knew what he had to do, but he wasn't sure how to do it. He
couldn't exactly give Desmond LaRochette a call. "Desmond, old boy.
It's Renny. No hard feelings about the other night. Listen, I need to borrow
the List so I can burn it. When would be a convenient time to pick it up?"

He was in the air from Detroit to Charleston when he hit on a plan.
Desperate problems required desperate solutions, and though desperate,
at least his plan was simple.

Upon landing in Charleston, he checked into a hotel. Exhausted
from emotional strain, he fell asleep and didn't wake up until almost
nine. He quickly called his office. Mr. Heywood was unavailable, so he
left a message that the medical emergency requiring his attention had
not yet been resolved. His work calendar was unraveling, and he told his
secretary to schedule everything she could for the following week. Two
matters could not be postponed, and he dictated a memo over the
phone requesting help from one of the other associates in the banking
law section of the firm.

That taken care of, he tried to call Mama A. She didn't answer, so he
copied her number onto a slip of paper and put it in his pocket. He
would try to reach her later. He also dialed Carol's number, but again
there was no answer. Finally, he phoned Mrs. Stokes. "Good morning.
It's Renny."

"Good morning. How's Jo?"

"They're giving her transfusions, and she seems a little better."

"I know she's in a fight for her life."

"I'm going to help take care of that," Renny said.

"I know you're praying, too."

"Not just that. There is something practical I can do to help."

"Are you giving blood?"

Renny regretted the call. Mrs. Stokes could be frustratingly persistent in a gracious sort of way. He decided to get to the point. "Mrs. Stokes, are curses real? You know, where someone does something and it causes problems for someone else."

Mrs. Stokes didn't answer immediately. "Yes, that sort of thing can happen, but not so much here as in other parts of the world. I've seen the effects myself."

"And you're sure it can be a real thing?"

"Yes. Do you think this is a part of what is happening with Jo?"

"It could be. I've got to go. Bye."

Renny hung up. He'd gotten the information he needed. Mrs. Stokes was not one to exaggerate or fabricate. If she believed in curses, it was enough to validate what he had decided himself.

On her end, the old lady hung up the receiver and gave Brandy a pat on the head.

"Your master may be into something he knows nothing about, girl. I think it's time I took a break from food. These kinds of battles require fasting as well as prayer."

———

After checking out of the hotel, Renny caught a taxi back to the airport and rented a four-wheel-drive Jeep. With all the plane tickets, hotel rooms, and other expenses, he was getting close to the maximum limit on his credit card.

It was noon when he reached Georgetown. He loved the Low Country, but driving down Front Street, he decided Georgetown would not be on his itinerary for a long time. Going north on Highway 17, he passed the entrance to LaRochette's estate and slowed down, looking for any unpaved roads that appeared to head in the direction of the beach. Spotting one, Renny put the vehicle in four-wheel drive and turned off the highway. After three or four hundred yards, the road reached a dead end at the edge of a marsh. He drove back to the highway and resumed his search. Several hundred yards farther along the highway he saw another turnoff. This road skirted the edge of the marsh and after many twists and turns through scrubby pines ended at the base of a huge sand dune.

Renny scrambled up the dune. On the other side was the Atlantic. It was high tide, and the waves were running up to a spot about one hundred feet from the base of the sandy hill. From his vantage point, he looked up and down the deserted beach for a place where he could drive onto the sand, but the row of high, steep dunes stretched unbroken on each side.

He walked south on the hard sand near the water's edge for ten minutes before the top of LaRochette's house came into view. Leaving the open beach, he crept slowly through the dune grass, and as he drew closer to the house, he could hear a lawn mower over the sound of the surf. An older man was cutting a small fringe of grass that encircled the house. Crouching down, he inched forward until he could see the corner of the house and the room where he had spent the night. There was a sturdy-looking trellis covered with purple morning glories extending from the sand up the side of the house.

The silver Mercedes was parked in front, but LaRochette was not in sight. Renny made a mental picture of the location of every bush and tree, then backed slowly away until only the roofline was visible.

Returning to town, he went to a hardware store and bought everything he might need: small flashlight, screwdriver, hammer, razor-blade cutter, and thin, strong rope. Stopping at a medical supply store, he purchased some surgical gloves like the ones he'd worn in Michigan. At a gas station, he added a cheap cigarette lighter with a Confederate flag printed on its side to his equipment—an appropriate implement to burn a Civil War document. Now there was nothing to do but wait until dark.

He tried to reach Carol, but there was still no answer. To pass the time, he went to the small public library near the center of town and found a secluded corner. There was a section on local history, and he found a book about early settlers to the area. Both of his great-great-grandfathers were briefly mentioned. Although he lived in Charleston, J. F. Jacobson had bought a plantation south of Georgetown, and Amos Candler owned a huge tract of land ten miles to the north. He wondered if they had ever met.

He read until the library closed at 5:00. After eating a fast-food supper, he made his first surveillance drive past the Inlet Waterway Restaurant. There was no sign of the silver Mercedes. Good. He hoped LaRochette would not arrive before dark. He checked at 7:00, 7:30, and 8:00. Still no sign of his quarry. At 9:00 he was coming out of the dead-end street when the silver car turned in and flashed past him. In the interior he saw two figures.

It was a go.

Turning off the main highway onto the sandy road, he was sweating in spite of the best efforts of the Jeep's air conditioner. By the time he parked at the base of the sand dune, packed all his gear in a plastic bag, and climbed up the hill, it was completely dark. The moon cast a narrow sliver of light. Walking up the beach, he realized how everything had fallen into place. He knew where the List was kept in the house, the location of the key for the secretary, the skylight in the bedroom, the route from the bedroom to the library, the trelliswork up the side of the house.

Moving from bush to bush, he slowly approached the house. Near the edge of the yard he heard a twig snap and froze. Straining every nerve he peered into the darkness. Another snap was followed by the sound of someone or something passing through the grass. Renny turned, preparing to run toward the beach when a medium-sized doe looked cautiously around a live oak tree to his right. There were hundreds of deer along the coast, and one of their trails apparently skirted LaRochette's property.

Renny watched the deer walk casually across the yard and vanish into the darkness. There was no other sign of activity in or around the darkened house. Renny was not going to need his flashlight; there was an outside light shining brightly at the corner above the trellis. Another blessing.

He moved along the edge of the yard just outside the range of the light until he was perpendicular to the corner of the house, then ran to the trellis. The crisscrossed woodwork was well built, which didn't surprise Renny; nothing but the best for Desmond LaRochette. Putting on the gloves, he slipped his belt through the drawstring of the plastic bag and put his weight on the trellis. It held, and he climbed carefully up.

At close range the glare from the outside light was almost blinding. There was a gap between the top of the trellis and the edge of the roof. Renny grabbed the roof and inched his feet up to the top of the woodwork. He would have to swing his leg up and hope his body followed. Holding his breath, he pushed off. As his foot came up toward the roof, it hit the side of the light, which gave a loud pop and went out.

Hoisting himself onto the eaves, Renny lay still, panting, and counted to ten. Nothing. Taking his flashlight from the bag, he shined it in the direction of the skylight. It was ten feet up and to his left. He carefully slid across the shingles until he could hold on to the casing that surrounded it. He had hoped to unscrew the cover, but it was fastened to its frame with metal rivets. He knew LaRochette would have an alarm system but hoped the bedroom skylight, as a permanent fixture, was not wired. Shining his light around the edge, he saw no sign of a wire or cable connecting to an alarm system.

Rolling over onto his back, he took the cutter, a razor blade set in a metal handle, and set it to cut a half-inch deep. Pressing down he began a cut at the top right corner of the Plexiglas skylight. It took more force than he anticipated, but after several attempts, the blade penetrated the hard plastic, and he laboriously opened a two-foot-long seam down the side of the window.

Sweat was pouring down his face and, after completing one side of the window, he paused for a moment's rest. He was wiping his forehead when suddenly he was caught in the glare of two blinding lights. He covered his eyes with his forearm.

"Don't move!" a deep voice yelled. "I am pointing a gun at your head, and if you make a sudden move I will shoot."

Renny froze. "I don't have a gun. I'm unarmed."

"I don't know that. The bag by your side. Push it away from your body."

Renny pushed the bag away. When he did, a screwdriver rolled out and fell off the edge of the roof.

"Watch it! Another move like that could get you killed!"

A second voice said, "Move slowly down the roof until you reach the edge. Stay on your back."

Renny did as he was told.

"Now roll over slowly and come down the trellis. I assume that's how you climbed up, so you should know what to do."

Renny's foot almost slipped off the top of the wooden structure, but he caught himself and in less than a minute was on the ground facing two very large men who continued to shine their flashlights directly in his face.

"Put your hands on your head, step back, and turn and face the wall."

One of the men expertly frisked him. "He's clean."

"Lie down in the sand."

Renny lay on his back, but one of the men nudged him with his foot. "No, on your face. You need some true grit between your teeth."

One of the men spoke into a microphone clipped to his shirt. "It wasn't a seagull, Mr. LaRochette. We have a young man in his twenties, brown hair, about 150 pounds. He was trying to come through the skylight in the corner bedroom on the north side of the house. . . . Yes, sir." He addressed Renny, "Do you want to tell us your name?"

"Renny Jacobson. Mr. LaRochette knows who I am."

"Oh, really." The man seemed surprised. "His name is Renny Jacobson, sir. He says you know him."

"Yes sir. We'll bring him around."

"Mr. LaRochette wants to talk with him before we call the police."

Renny got shakily to his feet. He was covered in sand and sweat.

"Don't even think about running," one of the men said, grabbing Renny roughly by the arm and jerking him forward.

"If you want to be a cat burglar," the other said as they led Renny around to the front of the house, "you need to be a little lighter on your feet."

Renny didn't answer.

"He's too dirty to take inside. Let's put him in the spare room in the garage."

Coming to a detached three-car garage on the south side of the house, they put him in a small, windowless room with a chair and a couple of tires.

"I'll be right outside, so just sit quietly."

In a few minutes, the door opened. One of the men was explaining to LaRochette, "He triggered a check-status light when he kicked out the security light at the corner of the house. Jack and I saw him on the roof when we came around the north side of the house."

LaRochette shook his head. "Hello, Renny. I'm sorry you're such a mess." Turning, he said, "You can leave us, Rankin. Mr. Jacobson is not a threat to me."

"Yes sir. We'll be outside the door if you need us. Do you want a chair?"

"No, I'll stand," LaRochette replied.

Once they were alone, LaRochette began, "I knew you would come back."

Renny didn't respond.

"Of course, you were attracted to the power of the List. But you are going about everything the wrong way. The List can be yours, but only after you are prepared to handle it. Listen, I know you were embarrassed at the meeting, but if you will let me lead you through the necessary process, you will look back in years ahead and thank me for the discipline and instruction of this time."

Renny maintained his silence.

"Actually, I'm not even upset at tonight's escapade; it just shows me the intensity of your desire to be close to the power. But you don't seize power; you are groomed to assume it."

Renny sighed. "You're totally wrong."

LaRochette raised his eyebrows. "Really. How?"

"I didn't come here to take the List for myself. I came here to destroy it."

"No, I don't believe you. I saw you the other night. You were drawn to it."

"I don't dispute your assessment of the other night. But that was then; this is now."

"What's changed?" LaRochette asked sharply.

"I've changed, or at least I'm trying to change," Renny answered.

"That's my role, to help you change."

Renny looked down at his feet.

LaRochette softened his tone. "Do you realize the danger of your current situation?"

"Yes. I'm in a mess."

"All I have to do is call the police and you will go to jail."

Renny slumped into the chair as the reality of his predicament hit him at a deeper level.

"Let me make it clear to you. I am willing to forget about all this." LaRochette stepped forward and laid his hand on Renny's shoulder. "Unlike your father, I want to help you become all you can be, to reach your full potential. All you have to do is say yes, and I will take you places you've not dreamed existed."

Stung by the accuracy of LaRochette's statement about his father, Renny wavered. LaRochette could have already called the police and had him shipped off to jail. Deep inside, he knew the leader of the List could deliver what he promised. Visions of grandeur danced before his eyes as LaRochette's hand continued to rest lightly on his shoulder. All he had to do was say . . .

"No," he said, pushing away LaRochette's hand. In an instant the visions evaporated. "I don't need a replacement for my earthly father; I already have a heavenly One."

LaRochette abruptly stepped back. "You've sealed your own fate, then." He paused. "And, you're a bigger fool than your father."

"What?" Renny asked, startled.

"I never laid a hand on your father, but your father's heart attack was not due to hardening of the arteries." LaRochette sneered.

"But how?"

"Before the LaRochettes came to Charleston, they owned plantations in Haiti and learned the ways of true power."

"Black magic?"

"A childish term. You wouldn't understand if I told you."

"Do the others know?"

"They know what I tell them. Some more, some less. In fact, I could hasten your own departure if I chose to do so."

Renny felt his chest tighten and his left arm began to tingle.

"But I prefer the unknown time, young Jacobson."

Renny gasped as the tension released.

"Jo has no part in all this," he said when he regained his breath.

"I totally agree." LaRochette chuckled. "She was *your* project. Is she doing well?"

Renny bit his lip.

"She'll be out of her misery soon. Without your help it would have been much more difficult," LaRochette said.

"I didn't mean—"

"Too late for that." LaRochette shook his head. "But my only regret is for you. Someone with your potential doesn't come along every generation. But there will be others, even if I don't get to train them. The List will endure, Renny, but without a Jacobson sharing in the spoils."

LaRochette opened the door. "Rankin, please call the police and have our young burglar deposited in the local jail."

"Yes, sir."

"Good-bye, Mr. Jacobson. There is no *au revoir* for you and me."

29

If any man sin, we have an advocate.

1 JOHN 2:1, KJV

Renny was sitting in the backseat of the police car when the silver Mercedes sped up the drive and parked in its usual place. Roget and Layne, returning from their dinner at the Inlet Waterway, looked curiously in his direction as they walked up to the front door. Renny put his head in his hands.

The officer dropped the plastic bag containing Renny's crude burglary tools in the front seat.

"An investigator will be out in the morning to take pictures of the skylight and interview you and your partner," the officer told Rankin, LaRochette's security chief. "Were there any other signs of attempted entry?"

"Not that we know of. I think he was just getting started when we saw him. He seems like an amateur."

"Amateur or not, he's started with a bang. I'll have multiple warrants issued by a magistrate as soon as we get to the station."

Renny stared out the window as they drove down the long drive.

"Where are you from?" the officer asked.

"Charlotte, no, uh Charleston."

"Pretty confused, huh."

Completely sapped, Renny didn't try to explain. The implications of his predicament and the information LaRochette dumped on him had blown his circuits. He was even more confused about where he was going than where he was from. Reduced to the most basic level of functioning, he was only capable of dealing with simple problems. That's where he started.

"What do I need to do about my rental vehicle?" he asked. "I have a leased Jeep parked on the beach near LaRochette's house."

"That's considerate of you," the officer said, looking curiously at Renny in the rearview mirror. "You know, thinking about the rental car company at a time like this. You can give the information to the booking officer at the jail. They'll make arrangements with the company to pick it up since you won't be needing it for a while."

Oblivious to the officer's mild sarcasm, Renny said, "Thanks."

The radio squawked to life. "We have a domestic D-7 at 675 Trade Street."

"I was over there last night," the officer said to Renny. "One night the husband calls; the next it's the wife." He then spoke into the radio transmitter, "This is Blakely. I'm bringing in a burglary suspect and can't respond."

The Georgetown County Correctional Center was a modern facility built for maximum security—multilevel security doors, cells without windows where day and night were determined by the flick of a light switch, and omnipresent surveillance cameras that removed every vestige of privacy. GCCC had no Barney Fife ready to greet Otis when he stumbled in after a night's binge and make sure that the town drunk had clean sheets, fresh flowers in his cell, and two eggs over easy with buttered toast and hot coffee when he woke up in the morning. Prisoners were processed and incarcerated with sterile, impersonal efficiency.

Renny was taken through two electrically operated steel doors to the booking area. A bored female officer with bleached-blonde hair took his fingerprints and snapped his mug shot: Georgetown County Prisoner 243758. He told her about the rental vehicle, and she gave him a look similar to the one Officer Blakely had given him in the car. She would have someone check into it.

"Take a seat in the hallway. One of the detectives will interview you after the magistrate completes the warrants."

Nobody paid any attention to him as a succession of drunks and kids on drugs were brought in and placed in one of two holding tanks located across the hall from the booking area. Renny's only constant companion was a mild but pervasive smell that could best be described as a mixture of human body odor and hot beer. Every so often someone in one of the two holding tanks would start screaming profanity and banging on the solid metal door. A male officer in the booking area would open a small sliding window in the door and tell the offender to keep quiet or risk transfer to an isolation cell. It seemed to work, and Renny wondered what was so bad about the isolation cells. He didn't want to find out.

After an hour, a slender man in his late thirties with a thin black mustache and a face that appeared incapable of smiling came over to him. "I'm Detective Cook. Come with me."

He led Renny down the hall to a small, windowless room that was bare except for a gray metal table and two folding chairs. It reminded Renny a little of his office at the law firm. As soon as they sat down, the detective took out a sheet of paper and read Renny his Miranda rights.

"Let me get some background information." Detective Cook wrote down Renny's name, address, and birth date. "Now let's get the particulars on your activities this evening."

"I'd like to have a lawyer present before I talk about the charges," Renny said. "I've never been through anything like this before."

Cook's eyes narrowed to slits. "Suit yourself, but you are already crucified, boy. I mean on the c-r-o-s-s. Johnny Cochran couldn't help you."

"Is there a phone I can use?" Renny knew it was pointless to talk.

"At the end of the hall past booking. Long-distance calls are automatically limited to three minutes."

"Thanks."

Cook stood and let Renny pass. "Remember, boy. I said c-r-o-s-s."
Renny didn't turn around.

He had no intention of calling a lawyer first. Jefferson McClintock
didn't make house calls at the Georgetown County Correctional Center
on Tuesday nights, and even if he did, Detective Cook was right in his
blunt description of Renny's situation. He wanted to talk to a lawyer,
but he needed to talk to someone else first. A sleepy voice answered
the phone.

"Mrs. Stokes. It's Renny. I'm sorry to call so late, but I'm in trouble
and only have a few minutes."

"What is it?"

"I'm in the Georgetown County jail. I need you to contact some
people for me. Call Jo's mother, Carol Edwards, early in the morning
and see how Jo is doing. Don't tell her where I am; they've got enough
to worry about. Just tell them I'm still on the coast and unable to reach
them. Then call Agnes Flowers, the lady I told you about." Taking the
slip of paper out of his pocket, he gave her Mama A's number in
Charleston. "Tell her where I am and ask her to pray for me."

"You're not hurt, are you? What in the world has happened?"

"I can't go into it now. I've been arrested for attempted burglary
and only have a few minutes to talk. I'm OK physically, but I've made
a serious mistake in trying to solve some problems."

"My goodness. Let's see, I have Jo's phone number here. Is it the
same as her mother's number?"

"Yes." Renny paused. "Mrs. Stokes, go ahead and call Mama A
tonight. She would be upset if I didn't let her know I needed help. If
nothing else she can pray for me. They're going to take me back to a cell
in a minute."

"All right. Oh, Renny, this is awful."

"It's my fault. Thanks for your help."

The phone clicked off before she could reply.

A young guard took him to a shower where Renny cleaned up and changed into a white cotton jumpsuit with GCCC stenciled on the back in large black letters. He was given a pair of blue flip-flops and told to put his own clothes and personal belongings into a plastic bag. He had over two hundred dollars in his wallet.

"That should keep you in cigarettes and candy bars for a while," the blonde said as she counted the bills on the table. "We'll note the amount on your account for personal purchases."

The guard opened a thick metal door to the main cellblock. Renny had heard enough jailhouse horror stories to cause him to panic, but for some reason, perhaps the immediate result of Mrs. Stokes's intercession, he was surprisingly calm.

"In you go," the guard said, sliding open a cell door.

There were six bunks in the cell. Only two were occupied by sleeping forms; neither acknowledged Renny's entrance. He climbed up on a bunk beside the door where he had a clear view of a camera mounted on the wall and quoted Psalm 23 to himself until he fell asleep.

———

At 7:00 the next morning, bright lights flooded the cellblock. Renny woke up suddenly and for several seconds had no idea where he was. Reality crashed in, and he closed his eyes, hoping everything would change.

"Good morning, up there," a voice from one of the other bunks said.

Renny rolled over and saw a small, balding man in his late forties putting on a pair of steel-rimmed glasses.

"I'm Winston Morgan."

"Renny Jacobson."

"Welcome to the GCCC version of *The Truman Show*," Morgan said with a flourish of his right hand. "Where day is day when they turn on the lights and your every move is viewed by at least two people via countless visible and concealed cameras."

Renny couldn't help but smile.

"Our other companion here, the one pretending to be asleep, is my former codefendant, Ralph Abercrombie. Say good morning to Renny."

A muffled voice said, "Good morning."

"Welcome to the white-collar crime cell," Morgan continued speaking rapidly. "Our breakfast will be served by meticulously groomed attendants in about eight minutes."

"Who are you?" Renny asked.

"I told you who I am. My immediate purpose is to set your mind at ease regarding your cellmates so that your stay on the set of the show will be as pleasant as possible."

Renny hopped down from the bunk and stretched. "Thank you. I woke up feeling lower than I've ever felt before."

"A common condition for the first night in the pokey."

"Why are you and Ralph in here?" Renny asked.

Morgan held up his right index finger. "Lesson number one: Never ask a fellow inmate why he is in jail. If he volunteers the information, fine. But don't ask. You'll find that no one is here because they committed a crime. The most common explanation is that they were framed and double-crossed by their best friend or ex-wife. A close second is they were repre-sented by an idiot lawyer."

"Sorry. I'm afraid I'm guilty with no excuse." Renny decided it was best not to mention his profession.

"Not a good position. But to answer your question, Ralph and I wrote a few too many bad checks—a few hundred too many."

"Oh."

"A few is usually not a serious problem, but a few hundred has a way of attracting major negative attention."

"I guess so."

"But don't worry about us. As codefendants, the authorities initially placed us in separate cells and appointed different lawyers to represent us. Our lawyers convinced us to testify against each other, which we did as persuasively as we could. I said it was all Ralph's fault, and he said it was all my fault. The jury said it was all both our faults."

Renny thought for a moment. "So, you're in both categories—you were double-crossed by your best friend and represented by an idiot lawyer."

"Bingo! You catch on fast, young man. You'll do well here."

A guard with a cart of food trays rumbled down the hall.

"Breakfast in bed again, Ralph. Rise and shine."

———

After breakfast, Renny lay in his bunk praying for Jo. A guard rapped on the bars. "Jacobson, you have a visitor."

Renny ran his fingers through his hair and wished he'd had an opportunity to brush his teeth. "Let us know if it's snowing outside," Morgan joked as Renny, his flip-flops slapping the concrete floor, followed the guard down the hall.

"Will do."

They passed through the main door of the cellblock and went down the hallway past the booking area to the same interview room where Detective Cook had compared Renny's status to Jesus' on the cross. The guard opened the door and let Renny go in.

The door slammed, and one of the largest men Renny had ever seen turned around and faced him. Dressed in a white shirt and khaki slacks, the man extended his hand and smiled. "I'm A. L. Jenkins, your lawyer."

Renny let his hand be swallowed in the lawyer's massive paw. "Hello."

"Sit down," Jenkins said, and they sat across from each other at the small metal table.

"Are you an idiot—I mean, appointed lawyer?" Renny asked.

"No." Jenkins laughed. "I know Agnes Flowers. I've practiced law in Georgetown for ten years, and she called early this morning asking me to see you."

"Did she tell you I was a lawyer, too?"

"Yes, she said you recently started working for a big firm in Charlotte. Could someone from your firm help you?"

Renny couldn't imagine Barnette Heywood's reaction to a request for legal help in his current circumstances. "There aren't any criminal defense lawyers in our firm. I'm sorry about what I said."

"No problem. I know I look more like a right guard for the Packers than an attorney. Actually, I was an offensive lineman in high school and college."

"I was a linebacker," Renny responded. "A small linebacker who would have hated to see you on the other side of the ball. Where did you grow up?"

"Orangeburg. After high school I received a football scholarship to South Carolina State and later went to law school at USC in Columbia."

Renny liked the big man's demeanor.

"If I can, I'd like to help you," the lawyer continued. "I've checked the warrant docket, and you have four charges: criminal trespass, possession of burglary tools, criminal damage to property, and attempted burglary. The first three are misdemeanors; the attempted burglary is a felony."

"How can you help? I was caught on the roof of the house, trying to cut open a skylight."

"Well, it may be possible to get some of the charges dismissed and work out a sentencing agreement as part of a plea bargain on what is left. But first I need to ask you some questions."

"May I ask one first?"

"Sure."

"How much are you going to charge? I'll need to make arrangements to pay."

"No problem. Mrs. Flowers said she would take care of my fee."

Renny's mouth dropped open. "I can't let her do that."

Jenkins shook his head. "Actually, I think you should, or at least let her think she is. She tells me you are a special young man."

Renny felt a rush of emotion at Mama A's expression of love. "How do we let her think she's paying?"

"I'll bill her a small amount, and you can pay the rest without mentioning it to her. Without a trial, my fee should be around twenty-five hundred."

"That's fine. I'm not rich, but I can come up with that much money even if I have to sell something."

"OK. Now, let me ask a few questions. Did you give a statement to the police after you were arrested last night?"

"No. A detective named Cook started to question me and when I told him I would prefer to talk to a lawyer first, he said I was nailed to the—"

"C-r-o-s-s. He needs to get a new line," Jenkins said. "It's good you didn't talk to him. It will be better if we can deal straight with the district attorney's office."

"It's not that I deny what I've done, I just didn't see the point in rehashing everything with him."

"Don't worry. He knows they have what they need without a statement, but you'd be surprised how many people confess even when there is insufficient evidence to convict them otherwise. It just shows that God has put in all of us the desire to be free from a guilty conscience."

"Are you a Christian lawyer?" Renny asked.

"Actually, I'm a Christian who practices law." Jenkins smiled. "That's how I know Agnes Flowers. I've spoken at her church several times, and she invited my family over for dinner one Sunday after the meeting."

"And you live in Georgetown?"

"Yes. I had a hearing scheduled this morning, but it was postponed, and I was available to come see you first thing."

"But, if you're a Christian like Mama A, I mean Mrs. Flowers, how—"

"How can a lawyer who is a Christian represent guilty people?" Jenkins finished Renny's thought.

"Right."

"Remind me to show you the Wall of Faith at my office sometime. Then you'll understand. Now, let's get down to business."

———

Carol met a sleepy-eyed Anne and Dr. Levy inside the quarantine area. "How is she this morning?"

Anne yawned. "Her fever climbed in the night until spiking at 103. It's down some now, but she's still somewhat delirious."

"What's causing the fever?"

Dr. Levy glanced at Jo's chart in his hand. "It's not clear, but minor infections that would be unnoticeable to a healthy person are extremely dangerous for Jo. We're giving her the maximum amount of antibiotics in an effort to knock it out of her system, but without any white blood cells to fight infection, we don't have any allies in her body."

"Are the antibiotics working?"

"We hope so."

"And if they don't work?"

The doctor closed the folder. "We may lose her."

30

And they loved not their lives unto the death.
REVELATION 12:11, KJV

Jenkins put his legal pad down on the table. "OK. You've told me everything that happened last night except the most important thing."

"Which is?" Renny looked puzzled.

"Why? Why did you want to break into LaRochette's house? Mrs. Flowers told me you're from a well-to-do Charleston family, and I know you work for a big law firm in Charlotte. That is not the typical profile for a twenty-five-year-old who tries to burglarize a rich man's beach mansion."

Renny shrugged his shoulders. "Why does it matter? Motive is only important to TV lawyers. The reason I wanted to get inside LaRochette's house is not going to get me off the hook, is it?"

Jenkins nodded. "You're right. But you have told me as much about this disaster as the crew of the *Titanic* knew about the iceberg that sank the ship. If you really want me to help you, I need to know everything."

Renny had faithfully carried the secret of the List so long it had become automatic to exclude any hint of it in conversation with everyone except Jo. But there was a strength in this huge man that made him feel safe. Renny's attempts at solving the problems created by his involvement with the List had failed miserably. Like many other men who had confessed their hidden secrets within the walls of the jailhouse interview room, Renny decided this was the time for him to come clean. Maybe confession would be good for his soul as well.

"How much time do you have?" he asked.

"Enough. My office knows where I am. They can call the jail, and one of the deputies will let me know if I have an emergency. Go ahead, I'm listening."

Renny began with an odd question. "Do you know how many levels of hell there were in Dante's *Inferno*?"

"Uh, nine."

"Well, right now I am at Level Seven, and I don't want to go any lower."

Renny started at the beginning and took the lawyer down the path that led to the interview room at the GCCC. After a few minutes, Jenkins stopped taking notes and just listened. When Renny told him about Jo's illness, tears filled both their eyes.

He finished his tale of woe and said with relief, "And that's the truth, the whole truth, and nothing but the truth. I feel better just getting everything out in the open after wrestling with this by myself for so long."

"Thank you for trusting me," Jenkins said soberly. "We have three things to do. First, I am going to cancel everything on my calendar for the rest of the day and seek guidance from the Lord on your behalf. The next time I see you, I want to have a strategy that has the counsel of Jesus Christ for your situation. He is our Advocate, and unlike earthly lawyers, has never lost a case for a cooperative client. Second, I want you to give me permission to call Agnes Flowers and enlist her prayers on your behalf. I won't tell her everything, but she needs to know enough to appreciate the level of spiritual warfare involved in this situation. Third, I want you to call your landlady in Charlotte and have her fax me the financial information sheet you obtained after the last meeting at the Rice Planter's Inn."

"Will they let me make another call from here?"

"Yes. I'll make sure of it. Here's my card. It has all my phone numbers on it."

"OK."

"Before I leave, I want us to pray together."

"Sure."

The lawyers bowed their heads, and Jenkins began pouring out his soul in prayer. Renny was stunned. For passion and persistence, he had never heard anything like it. It reminded him of the finals of a high school wrestling tournament in which two evenly matched grapplers refuse to yield an inch of territory to the opponent. Jenkins approached God with a determined intensity and an unwillingness to accept no for an answer. At one point, chills ran down Renny's spine, and he opened his eyes to see if angels or some other form of heavenly creatures had come into the room. A. L. quoted passages from the Scriptures with fire and conviction. He beat his fist against the table in opposition to the works of Satan. He beseeched heaven for the manifestation of the will of God for Renny. He invoked the authority of the One who conquered the grave for Jo's deliverance from death. He bound, he loosed, he cried, he sweat, and when he finished by declaring, "In the name of Jesus of Nazareth, the strong Son of God, amen," Renny, for the first time since he started his downward spiral, knew there was a reality to the word *hope*.

In Charlotte, Daisy Stokes had not eaten, slept, or taken a sip of water since Renny's call the night before. Although in good health for a woman of her age, she feared her body could not endure the strain caused by the intensity of the prayer burden for the two young people. Hour after hour passed in the prayer closet. Dawn arrived, but the burden did not lift. Then, suddenly, peace came.

"What is this, Lord? Is it victory?"

"No," came the steady reply to her heart. *"It is the eye of the storm."*

"What do I need to do? My strength is almost gone."

"You can choose to be poured out."

Opening her Bible, she read the words of Paul to Timothy:

For I am already being poured out like a drink offering, and the time has come for my departure. I have fought the good fight, I have finished the race, I have kept the faith. Now there is in store for me the crown of righteousness, which the Lord, the righteous Judge, will award to me on that day—and not only to me, but also to all who have longed for his appearing.

She waited, then lifted her head, and spoke, "If I choose to be poured out, will it bring victory for Renny and Jo?"

"If you choose rightly, you will fulfill my will and have the same epitaph as my servant Paul."

Her understanding expanded by the intensity of the Holy Spirit's presence, Daisy appreciated in a heightened way the excellency and surpassing glory of fulfilling the Lord's will, regardless of the consequences to her own life. Her decision was easy; she'd already made the hard choices along the path of a long life lived in obedience to Jesus.

"Yes," she whispered and immediately the whirlwind of opposition to her prayers again swept over her. But now, energized by a new strength, she beat back the darkness with one of the most powerful weapons in a Christian's arsenal: the increasing brilliance of the Lord's manifest presence upon her life.

———

After Agnes Flowers learned from Mrs. Stokes about Renny's trouble, she went into the kitchen for a drink of water. She was troubled on the surface but she felt a settled resolve deep in her soul, like a soldier going into battle who knew there was no turning back, no chance of a transfer to a safe assignment in the rear, no other option but to go forward and face the enemy. Sitting at the table, she thought about Renny's mother.

"Katharine, your boy's in trouble, but somehow I still don't think the Lord's frettin' and wringin' his hands."

Stretching and lifting her own hands in the air, she said, "What do you want me to do, Lord? Please show me."

Nothing came, so she went to bed and soon fell asleep. She dreamed. She saw herself standing on top of a hill covered with green grass. The terrain was rolling and rocky, not flat and sandy like the Low Country. The landscape reminded her of pictures of Scotland. In the distance, she saw men coming toward her. She could not see who they were, but they were walking resolutely in her direction and would soon ascend the hill where she waited. The closer they came, the more impressed she was by the determination in their bearing. When their faces came into focus, she saw a strength and fortitude that caused her knees to tremble. Although they carried no visible weapons, these were warriors trained for battle, and she knew no foe could stand against them. Up they came to where she stood and stopped. One of the warriors stepped forward. Opening his cloak, he pulled out a double-edged sword that was taller than Agnes and laid it at her feet.

"Pick it up," he commanded.

Agnes looked at the sword and showed the man her hands. "I can't do anythin' with that. It's way too big. I don't even think I belong here."

"Pick it up."

Deciding to show him instead of arguing, she leaned over and grasped the handle, easily lifting the sword over her head; it had no weight at all. Swinging it in front of her, the sword disappeared from view, yet somehow she knew it was still in her hand.

"Where did it go?" she asked.

"It is still there. Its purpose is not to fight what is seen, but what is unseen."

"How could it be so light?"

"You've trained yourself to wield it. The strength to use this sword is not in your flesh; it's in your spirit. You are one of the few on earth who can bend a bow of bronze."

Agnes fell on her knees before the Captain of the Host.

"No." The angel took her hand and lifted her up. "We, too, are here to serve our Lord, and he has assigned us to fight this battle alongside you."

Agnes woke up. She put on her robe and went out to the back porch. The sky was clear and the night air cool on her face. As she rocked, she prayed, and as she prayed, she cut the heavens with a double-edged sword.

———

Renny called Mrs. Stokes as soon as A. L. Jenkins left. "Are you OK?" he asked, disturbed by the obvious weakness of her voice.

"I'm going to be better," she answered cryptically. "I'm glad you called, because I'm going to lie down and rest in a few minutes."

"OK, I'll talk fast. First, did you talk with Jo's mother?"

"No one was home when I called. Do you think I should try to reach her at the hospital?"

"There isn't a phone in Jo's room. Please leave a message on Carol's machine that I've been unable to reach them. I know they're wondering why I haven't called."

"When are you going to tell them what's happened, Renny? You know they would want to help you."

"You're right, but I need to wait. Thanks for calling Mama A. She contacted a lawyer who is a Christian here in Georgetown, and he came by to see me. He is going to pray the rest of the day and let me know what he thinks I should do."

"Sounds like a good lawyer to me."

"He is. One other thing. Upstairs on the coffee table in my living room is a sheet of paper with a list of names, bank account numbers, and dollar amounts on it. Could you fax it to my lawyer sometime today?"

"Yes. I'll do anything to help. There is a fax machine I can use at the church."

Renny gave her Jenkins's fax number. "Thanks, Mrs. Stokes."

With trepidation, Renny phoned the law firm. Surprisingly, Mr. Heywood was in and immediately took his call.

Without any pleasantries, Heywood started right in, "Renny, is it true that you're in jail on a burglary charge in Georgetown, South Carolina?"

"Uh, yes, sir. Well, no, sir, it's attempted burglary."

"That distinction doesn't make a lot of difference to me."

"Well, yeah. I understand. How did you find out I was here?"

"Obviously you didn't call me, did you?"

"No, sir, not until now."

"Let's cut to the heart of the matter, Renny. I have one question. I'm a lawyer, not judge or jury, but I need to know the truth. Are you guilty?"

Unable to think of any other answer, Renny said, "Yes, sir."

"All right. You understand the position this puts us in. We can't have someone associated with the firm who has a criminal record. Anyway, you'll probably lose your license."

"Yes, but—"

"I'm sorry. You're finished at the firm. I'll do everything I can to get you a small severance, at least two weeks' pay. Janice will box up your personal belongings and deliver them to security downstairs. You can have someone pick up your things if you don't, uh, get out for a while."

"Yes sir."

Renny hung up the phone. *Mr. Heywood may not be judge or jury, but he makes quite a swift and efficient executioner.*

Before Renny was taken to the cellblock, he asked one of the guards if there were Bibles available.

"Sure. A local church supplies them for every prisoner. I'll get you one."

"Thanks."

No one was in the cell when the guard slid back the door.

"Where are the two guys who were here this morning?"

"They work outside cleaning patrol cars in the afternoon. They won't be back until supper time."

"How much are they paid?"

"Jailhouse wages, fifty cents an hour. Enough for cigarettes, candy, and stamps."

"Oh."

From fifty million to fifty cents.

Renny sat on an empty bunk and turned to 1 Kings 13, reading again the prophecy predicting the destruction of the altar built by Jeroboam at Bethel. What did Josiah of old do? How could there be a connection between the righteous king of Judah and Renny Jacobson? He read the prophecy of judgment and doom. It was obvious one of Josiah's purposes was to be an instrument of God's wrath against idolatry. But what would that mean today? How could it apply to him?

Flipping the pages to 2 Kings 23, Renny learned that three hundred years had passed from the time of the prophecy in 1 Kings 13 until the birth of the future king Josiah. Upon reaching manhood and assuming the throne, King Josiah renewed the covenant between the people of Judah and the Lord. Renny stopped. Covenant. Covenant List. Still unsure of the connection, he continued. Josiah then embarked on a campaign of religious cleansing that ended at Bethel:

> Even the altar at Bethel, the high place made by Jeroboam son of Nebat, who had caused Israel to sin—even that altar and high place he demolished. He burned the high place and ground it to powder, and burned the Asherah pole also. Then Josiah looked around, and when he saw the tombs that were there on the hillside, he had the bones removed from them and burned on the altar to defile it, in accordance with the word of the LORD proclaimed by the man of God who foretold these things.
>
> The king asked, "What is that tombstone I see?"
>
> The men of the city said, "It marks the tomb of the man of God who came from Judah and pronounced against the altar of Bethel the very things you have done to it."

What Renny read stirred him, but he had no framework for understanding how to bring it forward. He knew the List had become an evil thing in the hands of LaRochette, but his only attempt to receive guidance from Scripture to destroy the List was destroying him instead. His mistake hadn't just burned his fingers; Renny felt as if he had third-degree burns over half his body. The account of King Josiah was harder to apply to his current problems than his idea of burning the List to destroy its influence. He prayed but didn't get any direction. Perhaps he should ask A. L. Jenkins. Already he missed the big man and looked forward to his return.

———

Jo's condition stabilized, but she continued to run a low-grade fever. Dr. Levy placed her in a "bubble," a completely sterile environment created inside a plastic tent.

"She is going to need a bone marrow transplant to have a realistic chance of survival," he told Carol.

"There is no possibility I could be the donor?"

"Unfortunately not. As you know, the best donors are siblings, but since Jo doesn't have any brothers or sisters, I'm searching a database for individuals who have expressed willingness to provide bone marrow for patients like Jo."

"Like organ donors?"

"Not exactly. We need bone marrow from someone who is healthy; a transplant won't work from someone killed in an accident or a suicide. The donor must be willing to undergo the pain of a transplant to help save someone else's life. Not many people are willing to make that type of sacrifice. From those who are, we need a donor who is a match for Jo."

Her voice trembling, Carol asked, "When will you know if there is someone suitable?"

"My staff is working on it now. I'm moving as fast as I can."

Weakened by the fever and low blood count, Jo was not completely coherent, and to an outside observer her mutterings about beings of light and darkness in her room would be classified as delusions. Anne knew otherwise. Working a double shift to care for her friend, she sat by her bed through the night.

"There are more," Jo said, turning her head back and forth.

"More what?" Anne asked.

"Of everything."

Anne held Jo's hand and waited.

"Is it light or dark in here?" Jo asked, staring at the ceiling.

"Do you want me to turn on the light?"

"No, that's Renny's job. He has to do it."

"He's not here now."

"Renny!" Jo cried out suddenly. "No! No!"

Anne wiped the perspiration from Jo's forehead. The fever was rising again. Jo moaned. In spite of the best efforts of medical science and the sacrificial faithfulness of her friend, Jo still needed one thing above anything else—she needed a miracle.

———

The lights dimmed in the library. The three men sat across from one another in leather armchairs. The List lay open on a low table between them.

"I had someone call the hospital in Michigan," LaRochette said. "She's slipping but needs a push over the edge."

"I'm surprised she's not dead," Roget responded. "There is much more resistance than with the others."

LaRochette shrugged. "Her father, H. L. Jacobson, and Bart Maxwell were submitted to the authority of the List. The doorway was open. They were powerless against us."

"But the result will be the same," Roget said.

"Yes, she will not escape. I've seen the end from the beginning."

"And Eicholtz?"

"We're not in a rush. First the girl, then Eicholtz."

"And whenever we choose, young Jacobson," Thomas Layne added, with a cruel smile on his face.

"Later. He needs to suffer at the hands of men before he learns the nature of true torment."

"May I take the lead?" Layne asked.

LaRochette looked at Roget, who nodded.

"Very well. Find your place on the List, and we'll begin."

31

R enny and his cellmates finished supper—slices of bologna and
processed cheese between two pieces of white bread, four bites of
green beans, a square of orange-and-yellow Jell-O, and a red-colored punch
of a vintage Renny hadn't considered fit for drinking since kindergarten.

"Where was the chef tonight?" Renny asked Winston Morgan.

"If you think this is bad, wait until steak night. At least you know
bologna has been ground up by a machine in a meat-packing plant
somewhere. The steak is shipped straight from the shoe recycling center
and covered in gray liquid."

The guard who collected their food trays opened the cell. "Come on,
Jacobson, your lawyer is here to see you."

"My lawyer talked to me twice the whole time he represented me,"
Winston said. "Yours comes twice in one day. How much is he charg-
ing you?"

"Probably not enough," Renny responded as the bars slammed shut.

"You'll need to explain that to me later. I thought I'd heard everything."

The guard took Renny to a different, slightly larger interview room.
Jenkins was waiting with a Bible and legal pad on the table before
him. "Have a seat," he said. "We've got a lot of ground to cover."

"Thanks for coming back so soon," Renny said.

"As of this moment, you're my number one client."

"What do you mean?"

"That's the sense I had when praying for you this afternoon. I'm moving you to the top of the list."

Renny winced.

Drawing a line down the middle of the legal pad, Jenkins continued. "Your bond has been set at $110,000."

"I can't come close to that amount," Renny said.

"It's too high for the nature of the crime, and in the typical case, I'd file a motion to reduce the bond so you could get out of jail pending arraignment and ultimate disposition of your case."

"When are you going to file the motion?"

Jenkins hesitated. "How much do you know about criminal procedure?" he asked.

"Only law school stuff, mostly theory, not much about the nuts and bolts. I've been doing a lot of Regulation Z work at the firm."

"Regulation what?"

"Bank and finance regulations."

"Well, I know nothing about banking regulations."

"And I don't trust my memory of criminal procedure."

"OK. I don't want to file a motion to reduce your bond."

"Why not?" Renny asked sharply. "I want to get out of here as soon as possible."

"I know that, but my sense is that we need to handle your case in an entirely different way."

"How?"

"I believe we need to reach final disposition as soon as possible. I want to move you through the system as quickly as we can. If things go as planned, you'll be out on probation within two or three days."

"That sounds fine with me, but there's no guarantee, is there?"

"No, but to find out where we stand, I need your permission to meet with someone at the D.A.'s office and offer to expedite your case without all the usual formalities and legal maneuvering. You would agree to plead guilty to attempted burglary, and the D.A.'s office would dismiss the misdemeanor charges. Also, the D.A. would not oppose approval by the judge of a first offender petition on your behalf. The petition would provide that once you complete a term of probation, your burglary conviction would be purged from the records and you could truthfully say you had no criminal record on job applications, credit reports, and other background checks."

"No jail time after sentencing?"

"Correct. This procedure is only available for people with no prior problems with the law. You would also have to pay some money to LaRochette to fix his skylight and perform community service time."

"What sort of community service?"

"It can be anything from picking up trash along the roads to providing counseling for troubled youths. Your probation officer would work that out with you."

"OK."

"One of the assistant district attorneys is a lawyer named Virginia Adams. She is tough but fair. My plan is to talk to her in the morning and tell her what I want to do."

"Go ahead. Give it a try."

" Good. Are your cellmates leaving you alone?"

"They're fine. Two guys who wrote a bunch of bad checks."

"Is one of them a short guy who looks like a bookkeeper?" Jenkins asked.

"That's the one."

"I heard him make a plea for mercy that made the judge smile. It was the old 'guilty with an explanation, Your Honor' approach. It didn't work, but it was entertaining."

"After talking with Winston Morgan in the cell, I'm sure it was. Does the judge have to grant the petition you described?"

Jenkins shook his head. "No, but I will talk to him beforehand and get a sense of his opinion."

"That seems risky."

"To some degree, but you don't have a lot of options."

"True," Renny admitted.

"Any other questions?"

"Not right now."

Picking up his Bible, Jenkins said, "All right, let's move from the law to the prophets. I told you I would pray about a spiritual strategy suitable for your situation. I have two passages to start with. The first is in Paul's letter to the Ephesians, chapter 6." Opening his Bible, he read:

> Finally, my brethren, be strong in the Lord, and in the power of his might. Put on the whole armour of God, that ye may be able to stand against the wiles of the devil. For we wrestle not against flesh and blood, but against principalities, against powers, against the rulers of the darkness of this world, against spiritual wickedness in high places.

"Unfortunately, many people reading these verses stop after Paul writes 'we wrestle not.' And that's exactly what they do—nothing. They ignore the practical reality of spiritual evil, and there is no way you can successfully fight an enemy you don't believe exists."

"That's not my situation," Renny said. "I know there is an evil force in all this. It's trying to kill Jo and destroy me. That's why I wanted to burn the List, to break its power or spell over our lives."

"Correct. But even though you knew there was spiritual evil at work, you made a serious mistake in focusing your fight against flesh and blood."

"I'm not sure I follow."

"Let me conduct a friendly cross-examination."

"OK."

"You realized the book, the List as you call it, was a focus of evil power."

"Yes."

"You read in Acts about the books of sorcery burned at Ephesus and concluded the key to destroying the power of the List was to burn the book."

"That's right."

"Why didn't you decide to kill Desmond LaRochette?"

"He deserves killing more than anyone else I can think of at the moment, but to kill him would be murder."

"Isn't he the key person who understands and exercises the evil power of the List?"

"Yes."

"Then, why not kill him?"

Renny thought a moment. "That would be struggling with flesh and blood."

"Correct. And it's the same with the List. The List is only a book, an inanimate object. You didn't think about killing LaRochette because you had enough sense of right and wrong to realize killing him was not the answer to the root problem. Neither is a book the root problem. The List has evil power only because there are evil forces associated with it. I would not want my eight-year-old reading it before he goes to bed, but the key to breaking the List's power is not in destroying the physical pages. The key is combating and defeating the spiritual forces behind it, the principalities, powers, rulers of darkness, and spiritual forces of wickedness in high places."

"How in the world do I do that?"

"It's not a fight fought in this physical world. And that brings me to the next passage of Scripture. It's in the fourth chapter of James: 'Submit yourselves therefore to God. Resist the devil, and he will flee from you. Draw nigh to God, and he will draw nigh to you.'

"The first step in fighting spiritual evil is not running out to do battle; the first step is submitting yourself to God and surrendering to his authority as the Commander in Chief of your own heart. You have to win the battle within, the one inside your own soul, before you can have a chance to win the battle without, the one against external spiritual forces of wickedness and evil."

"I think I see. It's like I've had a fifth column sabotaging everything I've tried to do."

"Exactly. Once you defeat the enemy within, you can receive your battle plan for offensive action against the plans of the devil."

"They didn't teach me this in law school."

"Me either, but in the type of work I do, I've been involved in spiritual warfare for over ten years. A lot of on-the-job training."

"What do I need to do?" Renny asked.

"Let me ask you a few questions first. Where have you made mistakes in dealing with the List?"

"Are you going to stay till midnight? I don't know where to begin."

"OK. This morning you correctly told me that motive is generally irrelevant in a court of law. But unlike most earthly judges, God is very interested in motive. What was your motivation in pursuing involvement in the List?"

"That's easy. Money. I needed money."

"Did you really need money? You had a job, car, place to live, food, clothes . . ."

"Sure, but I wanted a lot of money."

"Which is called?"

Renny thought. "Greed."

"Right. The Bible says, 'The love of money is the root of all evil.' I think your present situation could be marked Exhibit A as proof of that statement."

"Does God want me poor?" Renny asked with frustration.

"Not necessarily. God wants you to be in right relationship with him, whether he blesses you with a little money or a lot. But the List is obviously not a source of money that God is blessing. The whole thing is on the wrong side of God and probably criminal in the eyes of the government as well."

"So what do I do?"

"You need to repent of your greed and place yourself in the hands of God in the area of money and financial security."

A deep part of Renny did not like what Jenkins was telling him.

Letting go of control was not one of his top ten favorite things to do, but the new man within him knew that the lawyer was right. After a few moments, Renny nodded. "OK."

"All right, you tell God."

Eyes closed, Renny said, "Father, I have been greedy. I've made decisions based on greed that have hurt myself and others. I no longer want to live my life controlled in any way by the love of money. I commit myself to you and trust you to bless me and meet my needs. Amen."

"Good. For a new Christian, you know how to pray."

Renny exhaled. "Actually, I'm glad to get that over with. I guess I had to go back to where I stepped out of bounds and begin again. Now, how do we go on the offensive?"

"Not so fast. Can you think of another place you stepped out of bounds?"

"Trying to burglarize LaRochette's house?"

"No, more basic than that. Ask the Lord to show you."

Renny closed his eyes. Many things came to mind. A minute passed. He opened his eyes and met Jenkins's gaze. "I should never have taken the oath or signed the List."

"Yes. That's the bedrock issue. Everything else is built on that foundation."

A sharp pain shot through Renny's right temple. He winced.

"What is it?"

"I'm afraid I'm getting a headache. I've had them off and on since my father's death."

"They're connected to what we're dealing with. We can't stop."

"OK, but sometimes I can reach a point of nausea."

"Not this time. Go ahead and pray, then I have some things to add."

This was much tougher than the issue of greed. Suddenly, Renny was disoriented and unable to formulate a coherent thought or express a complete sentence. The pounding in his head increased, and he wondered if he was about to pass out. Putting his head in his hands, all he could cry out was, "Help, Lord!" But as with blind Bartimaeus, a simple cry for help was all the Lord required.

The anointing of the Holy Spirit came upon A. L. Jenkins, and he took up Renny's cause. Less demonstrative but more intense and focused than in the morning, the lawyer prayed with a specific authority that crystallized the conflict within the small room. Hellish oppression and overcoming faith met in supernatural conflict over Renny's head. Jenkins commanded, bound, and loosed; each word was a forward thrust before which the enemy of Renny's soul grudgingly retreated. At one point, Renny visibly trembled for a few seconds while a specific corner of his inner house was swept clean and Jenkins moved on to another room. Finally, the light of the Word and the power of the Spirit drove the darkness from the farthest corners of Renny's soul. Jenkins paused, caught his breath, and concluded as he had before, "In the name of Jesus of Nazareth, the strong Son of God, amen." Renny put his head on the table. Jenkins waited.

In a few moments, Renny opened his eyes and raised his head. Jenkins smiled. "He is my glory and the lifter of my head."

Renny nodded. "It's gone. Not just my headache. Something I didn't even know was there is gone."

"It is. Now ask the Holy Spirit to fill every room in your house."

Renny didn't need convincing. "Lord Jesus, send the Holy Spirit into every part of who I am. I give myself totally up to you."

Peace came. Then, quiet joy was followed by a confidence in God's goodness. Over it all, an assurance of hope for the future flowed into the newly cleansed and yielded vessel.

"Thank you."

"Thank you, Lord," Jenkins responded.

"Can we wait a minute before doing anything else?" Renny asked. "I need to process what's happening to me."

The two men sat back, both enjoying the presence of the only One who could satisfy the deepest place of need within the human soul. For several minutes, they had silent church.

Jenkins spoke first, "I appreciate you thanking me, Renny, but there are other people who deserve more credit than I do. When I was with the Lord this afternoon, he reminded me of an incident in the life of Moses. As the Israelites were on their journey to the Promised Land, a group of raiders known as the Amalekites began to harass them. Moses sent a military force commanded by his aide Joshua to fight them. Meanwhile, Moses, together with his brother Aaron and a man named Hur, stood on a mountain to watch the battle. At first the Israelites were losing, but when Moses lifted his hands in prayer to heaven, the Israelites began to win. But there was a problem. Moses' arms grew tired, and when he lowered his hands, the Amalekites began to defeat Joshua and his men. To solve the dilemma, Moses sat on a rock while Aaron and Hur held up his hands until Israel won the battle."

"How does that apply to me?"

"You have an Aaron and a Hur, two people who are willing to do what it takes to ensure your victory."

"Agnes Flowers and Daisy Stokes?"

"Yes. They deserve your thanks. They've sustained the fight in the heat of the day when you didn't even know there was a battle being fought."

"You're right." Renny stood. "Now, what do we need to do?"

Jenkins shook his head. "I don't know. The Lord only showed me the strategy for winning the battle in you. What do you think needs to happen?"

Renny thought, then remembered. "Do you know anything about King Josiah?"

Jenkins listened carefully to Renny's story about the prophesied connection between himself and the ancient king of Judah. "There is something to it," he said when Renny finished. "Your next step is to ask the Lord to bring it forward to apply it to today. I'll pray, too."

"When will I see you again?"

"I'll be by in the morning. One other thing. Did Mrs. Stokes fax the financial information sheet to my secretary?"

"I asked her to. You didn't receive it?"

"I haven't gone by the office, but I'll check on the way home."

Renny bit his lip. "There's one other thing I'd like to do before you leave."

"What is it?"

"I want us to pray for Jo."

"Of course. Go ahead."

Renny prayed, "Father, please forgive me for my role in Jo's illness. I repent of my involvement with the power connected to the List and cancel every curse against her, especially those I initiated through my involvement with evil last Friday night. I pray again the promises you gave me for her deliverance from death in Psalm 23. In the name of Jesus, amen."

"Amen. Like I said, you're a fast learner."

———

LaRochette awoke in a cold sweat. He was no stranger to evil, but the raw power and thinly veiled ferocity of the dark forms in the room scared even him.

"What do you want?" he said, his voice trembling.

"You."

"What?" his voice cracked.

"You need us; we need you."

"But why?"

"Just say yes," the voice said with a force that LaRochette could not resist.

"Yes!" he cried out, and the black forms poured in through his open mouth.

32

For we shall all stand before the judgment seat of Christ.
ROMANS 14:10, KJV

Do you think your lawyer would talk to me?" Morgan said from his bunk when Renny finally returned to his cell. Abercrombie was already asleep.

"Why?"

"Listen. I've had as many lawyers as you have fingers and toes, but I've never heard of one spending as much time with a godforsaken accused as yours has with you."

"It's easy. I'm not godforsaken."

"What do you mean?"

"I'm not godforsaken."

"Oh, are you religious?"

"Not the way you think. I used to have enough religion to make me occasionally uncomfortable. Now I have enough to make me regret my years without it."

"Ha! Your years of regret. Think about mine."

Morgan grew quiet. After a few minutes, he said, "Are you asleep?"

"Almost."

"Wake up for a minute and tell me what happened to you."

An hour later, Renny went to sleep with a smile on his face.

———

In the morning, Renny was eating the last bite of powdered eggs when a guard rapped on the bars. "Jacobson. Your lawyer's here to see you."

"I can't believe it. I can't believe it," Morgan said.

"Believe, Winston, believe."

Jenkins was wearing a gray suit, white shirt, and burgundy tie. "Going to court?" Renny asked.

"Yes, I have a motion at 9:00 A.M. in another case, and I'll talk to the assistant D.A. about you as soon as she has a minute."

"OK. What brings you here so early?"

"The sheet your landlady faxed me. It may help us."

"It's amazing, isn't it? But I don't see how it can help me with an attempted burglary charge."

"It can't. I was thinking more about the Josiah prophecy. What if I took it to the IRS?"

"Jo thought about the IRS early on. I guess they could audit everyone on the List and start asking questions. But with all the overseas accounts, I doubt there is a paper trail in the U.S. clear enough to follow."

"Well, I'd like to contact an IRS agent I know in Charleston about it."

"Fine. I think I gave up $16 million plus my percentage of the corpus of the List when we prayed yesterday."

"Any regrets?"

"None."

"OK. I'll get back with you later today."

"If things go well, will I get out tomorrow?"

"Yes, if the judge accepts a plea with probation."

"Thanks."

A. L. caught up with Assistant D.A. Adams around eleven. He gave her a bare-bones account of Renny's situation and obtained her agreement not to oppose a first offender petition. They decided to meet in Judge Kincaid's chambers in the morning and review the case with the judge before court began.

Back in his office, A. L. called the IRS regional office in Charleston. "Greg Barnwell, please."

A voice with a molasses-thick Southern drawl answered. "Barnwell, heah."

"Greg, it's A. L. Jenkins."

"How are you doing, my friend?"

"Can't complain. Listen—I have a client with a situation you may be interested in."

A. L. gave a thumbnail summary of the information on the financial sheet and Renny's version of the functioning of the List.

"Amazing. Are there any Barnwells on the sheet?"

"No. Why?"

"I didn't think so. It would be nice to have some of that money, but my great-great-grandpappy lived in a shack on stilts and caught crayfish for supper."

"How about my ancestors?" Jenkins responded. "They probably called the original members of the group 'massah.'"

"True. Well, if we could get some of that money, it would fund a whole heap of pork-barrel projects for our friends in Washington."

"And give me credit on next year's tax bill."

"Now, A. L. You know we don't give anything to anybody for any reason at any time. However, if this works out, I'm sure an 'attaboy' would be in order for both of us."

"Just do your best." A. L. chuckled. "Mr. Jacobson says the information on the sheet may be stale in a few days. Apparently they are considering a transfer to an account in the Cayman Islands."

"That's a black hole we can't shine a light into right now. Why don't you fax me the sheet and let me talk with the big boss right away."

"I'll send it as soon as we hang up."

In thirty minutes, A. L.'s secretary buzzed his office. "Mr. Barnwell on the phone."

"A. L. Are you sitting down on your big rear end?"

"Yes. What's up?"

"I got the information and talked with Mr. Blankenship. Do you remember the names listed on the bottom, you know, the two Swiss bankers and a man named Carlos Parmero?"

"Yes."

"Where would you guess someone named Parmero lives?"

"Switzerland? Italy?"

"No. Colombia. Not the capital of our fair state, but Colombia the country in South America. The phone number on the sheet is for an office in Medellín, Colombia, the drug center of the Western Hemisphere."

"All right."

"That's not all. Mr. Blankenship received an arrest notice issued by the FBI in Miami a couple of days ago. We get a copy to see if there are assets of high-profile defendants subject to seizure in our region."

"And . . . ?"

"A man named Carlos Parmero with a Colombian passport was on a yacht that caught fire and issued a distress call near Key West. The Coast Guard responded and took the people on board into Miami. Parmero's name surfaced, and a routine check triggered FBI involvement. Bingo. Parmero turned out to be one of the key guys involved in handling funds for the South American drug czars."

"Wow. What are you going to do?"

"I want to send the information you provided to Miami. Also, could you get an affidavit from your client outlining what he knows about the group?"

"I'm on my way."

———

A. L. had a laptop computer and portable printer on the table when Renny came in and sat down.

"How did it go with the D.A.?"

"She's fine. They will drop all the misdemeanor charges and not oppose a first offender petition on the felony. We're going to talk with the judge before court in the morning. You will be brought over at 9:00 A.M., and I'll see you in the courtroom."

"OK, but I'm getting nervous."

"We'll pray Proverbs 21:1; the judge's heart is in the hand of the Lord, and he will direct it. I've seen it happen many times."

"Thanks. Why did you bring the computer and printer?"

"I need an affidavit from you. Let me tell you what happened with the IRS…"

Renny shook his head when A. L. finished. "So, they weren't satisfied with a Swiss bank's rate of return and decided to go out on the open market and double their money in the drug trade."

"Apparently. If this guy Parmero talks, the whole thing could come down."

"When will you find out?"

"I don't know, but I told my contact they needed to act fast. Ready?"

"Yes."

For a man with ham hocks for hands, the lawyer typed with amazing speed.

"Here we go. 'Before the undersigned officer, duly authorized to administer oaths, appeared Josiah Jacobson, who, being duly sworn, states the following on personal knowledge, information, and belief. . . .'"

Fourteen paragraphs later, the big man typed "Further affiant saith not" and sent it to the printer.

"If possible, I would like to soften the blow for Gus Eicholtz. I know there is some retribution planned against him because of our discussions."

"I'll mention that in a cover letter to Barnwell with the affidavit."

While the document was inching out of the printer, A. L. asked, "What are you thinking?"

"I was wondering if this affidavit is connected to the Josiah verses. It could possibly bring down judgment on the List. Can you think of anything else I need to do?"

"Hmm, I'm not sure. Let's get through tomorrow morning first."

As Renny's flip-flops hit the concrete corridor, Daisy Stokes was walking in her bedroom slippers to the kitchen to get a sip of water. Over the last three days she had slept less than ten hours and had lost a noticeable amount of weight from her already spare frame. She had experienced two instances of crushing pain in her chest, and thoughts of a heart attack and sudden death assailed her in an effort to distract her from her mission and purpose. Though she wavered, she repelled the attacks and, like Aaron and Hur, stayed at her post. She called Agnes Flowers, and the two of them spent an hour strategizing, praying, interceding, and encouraging each other. Daisy started to mention the Lord's word about being poured out to her new friend, but she stopped, realizing it was a privilege not to be shared with anyone else.

As she grew weaker, Mrs. Stokes began experiencing the reality of 2 Corinthians 4:16–18: "Therefore we do not lose heart. Though outwardly we are wasting away, yet inwardly we are being renewed day by day. For our light and momentary troubles are achieving for us an eternal glory that far outweighs them all. So we fix our eyes not on what is seen, but on what is unseen. For what is seen is temporary, but what is unseen is eternal."

Knowing that her physical strength was coming to an end, she asked the Lord, "How long?"

He responded: "*Through Shabbat.*" Two more days, through sundown Saturday.

Renny was alone in the cell. Unable to sit still, he paced back and forth with tigerlike restlessness. Something was building inside him, but it had not yet assumed a form he could express. He quoted Psalm 23 and prayed for Jo, but it failed to satisfy the burden within his spirit. He looked up Proverbs 21:1 and spent time asking for favor when he appeared before the judge the next morning. Next, he thanked the Lord for his help in the midst of incredible difficulty and pressure. Yet, the deep-seated unsettledness remained. What was wrong? What had he forgotten to do? What had he failed to consider? Without resolving any of his questions, he lay down on his bunk and tried to sleep, but spent the rest of the night tossing and turning on the thin mattress.

After the sleepless night, Renny better fit the popular concept of a convict. Dark lines under his eyes, it took several splashes of cold water to bring his surroundings into clear focus.

Still wearing his white jumpsuit, he was handcuffed and linked together with leg chains to four other prisoners for transport in a windowless van to the courthouse. A guard with a shotgun sat beside the driver in the front seat of the vehicle. The van parked behind the courthouse, and the prisoners were taken to a special elevator complete with bars across the door. On the third floor, the shotgun-toting guard followed them down a short hall to a special holding cell. Another guard removed the handcuffs and leg irons from all of the prisoners except one, a surly, brooding man who had "love" crudely tattooed across one set of knuckles, "hate" across the other, and a large black spider etched on his neck so that four of its legs and part of its body appeared to be creeping up from beneath his shirt collar.

———

"His Honor will see you now," the judge's secretary told the two lawyers.

A. L. and Virginia Adams entered the private lair of Judge Wray Kincaid, a balding, slender man in his late fifties who rarely smiled and maintained an inscrutable demeanor to all who appeared before him. Surrounded by hundreds of books containing the wisdom of judicial sages long since departed to the place of their own final judgment, Judge Kincaid waved them to two seats before his polished wooden desk.

"Who's so important that you need to see me?" he asked brusquely.

"Josiah Jacobson, Your Honor. He's on today's docket for sentencing on an attempted burglary charge."

Judge Kincaid found Renny's name on the morning's order of business. "Yes?"

"We would like to enter a guilty plea on a first offender petition."

"Do you have the incident file, Ms. Adams?"

"Yes, Your Honor." She handed him the folder.

They waited while the judge scanned the few pages in the file.

"You're sure the defendant has no prior criminal convictions?"

"We found none on the computer," she said.

"He's a lawyer from Charlotte," A. L. said. "He just passed the bar exam, so he would have undergone an extensive background check in North Carolina."

Judge Kincaid's eyes narrowed. "A lawyer. Did he think it appropriate for an officer of the court to come to Georgetown County and attempt to break into a beach house?"

"No, sir, and he wants to enter a guilty plea without any delay."

The judge opened the incident file and squinted at the investigator's handwriting.

"There were no weapons involved?"

"No sir."

"Any indication of threats against the victim, Mr. LaRochette?"

"No sir."

"Ms. Adams, what is your position on the first offender petition?"

"We do not oppose it, Your Honor, and defer to your discretion."

"I imagine you would," the judge said dryly.

"Mr. Jenkins, your client may enter his plea, but I will not commit at this time to accepting the petition. You may so inform your client."

A. L. felt sweat running down inside his shirt. "Yes, Your Honor. Your consideration is appreciated."

"What do you think, Virginia?" A. L. asked as they walked down the hall toward the courtroom.

"The investigative report was routine. I think the judge wants to make young Jacobson twist in the wind for a while."

"He's been doing that longer than the judge realizes. It's time to cut him down."

"I'll try to pick a good time to call the case, A. L. That's all I can do."

A. L. went to the holding cell and Renny came to the bars. "We talked with the judge."

"And?"

"He wouldn't commit beforehand. The D.A. says the investigative report is routine—no weapons, threats of violence. Judge Kincaid may want to dress you down in public. I just don't know."

Renny's shoulders slumped over. "What should I do?"

A. L. thought a moment. "Stand up straight, answer his questions respectfully, and believe in Proverbs 21:1. Remember, the king's heart is in the hand of the Lord. I will be with you to add anything extra."

———

The guards brought the prisoners into the courtroom through a back door and had them sit along the wall to the left of an open area in front of the judge's bench. Also used for public meetings, the courtroom had twenty-five rows of benches. This morning there was a short calendar, and less than seventy-five people were scattered throughout the large room. A. L. and the other lawyers occupied several chairs in front of the "bar," a railing that separated the space in front of the judge from the public seating area. A few police officers lounged in the jury box.

As Judge Kincaid strode into the room, the clerk of court said in a loud voice, "All rise."

Judge Kincaid took his seat, and Ms. Adams began another day's business. After disposing of several bond reduction motions and D.U.I. guilty pleas, she called out, "State versus Jacobson."

A. L. and Renny stepped into the open space before the judge's elevated seat.

"Your Honor, this is Mr. Josiah Jacobson. Ms. Adams and I spoke to you about this case in chambers this morning. Mr. Jacobson would like to enter a plea under the first offender act, and I have prepared a petition for your review." A. L. handed him the papers.

The judge glanced at the documents and peered over half-frame glasses at Renny. "Are you Josiah Jacobson?"

"Yes, sir."

"Do you want to plead guilty to the charge of attempted burglary?"

"Yes, sir."

"Has anyone promised you anything or threatened you in order to persuade you to enter this plea?"

"No, sir."

"Are you entering this plea voluntarily and of your own free will?"

"Yes, sir."

"Have you had opportunity to discuss this charge with your lawyer, Mr. Jenkins?"

"Yes, sir."

The judge paused. "I understand that you yourself are an attorney licensed in North Carolina."

The other lawyers in the courtroom stopped shuffling their papers and stared.

"Yes, Your Honor." Renny's mouth was as dry as stale toast.

"Do you realize that a guilty plea on this charge may be considered a crime of sufficient severity to warrant disciplinary action against you by the State Bar of North Carolina, and that you may be disbarred?"

"Yes, sir."

"Are you in fact guilty of this charge?"

"Yes, sir."

"Tell me what you did."

"I was on the roof of the house trying to cut open a skylight so I could get inside."

"Do you have any prior arrests or convictions?"

"No, sir."

The judge glared over his glasses for several seconds. "Mr. Jenkins has presented me with a request that you be sentenced under the first offender act. Do you understand that I do not have to accept this petition and could sentence you to up to ten years in prison and assess a $10,000 fine?"

Renny swallowed hard. "Yes, Your Honor."

"Do you still want to plead guilty?"

Renny felt the noose tightening around his neck. Maybe the judge was a friend of LaRochette's. "Yes, sir."

"Do you have any questions before I enter sentence?"

"No, sir."

"All right. The court is prepared to enter sentence. I hereby sentence you to three years in the South Carolina State Penitentiary—" He paused. All eyes in the courtroom focused on Renny, who felt his knees begin to buckle. "Said sentence to be served on probation under the terms and conditions of the first offender act. You are also required to perform two hundred hours of community service, pay restitution to the victim for damage to his property, and pay a probation fee of twenty dollars per month during the term of your probation. I am also ordering you not to enter Georgetown County during the term of your probation except for scheduled meetings with your probation officer or to perform your community service obligation. You are further ordered not to go on or about the person or property of Desmond LaRochette and are prohibited from any contact with him initiated by yourself. Do you understand the terms and conditions of your sentence?"

His knees barely functioning, Renny said, "Yes, sir."

"Ms. Adams, please notify Mr. LaRochette of the court's disposition of this case."

"Yes, Your Honor."

"Next case."

A. L. led Renny to a seat next to where the other prisoners were sitting.

"He accepted it, didn't he?" Renny asked anxiously.

"Yes," said A. L. with obvious relief. "The only surprise was the requirement that you get out of Dodge and the restriction against any contact with LaRochette."

"When he said three years in the penitentiary I thought I was going down Dante's hatch to level nine."

A. L. managed a weak grin. "That's just the technical way of ordering probation. It lets the defendant know he is only one mistake away from prison."

Renny watched as a man entered a guilty plea on his third D.U.I. in a year.

"Is this what it will be like when God judges us?" he asked.

A. L. glanced at the hapless defendant who was now the recipient of Judge Kincaid's glare. "Not really. It will be a thousand times—a million times more intense."

Renny shook his head. It was beyond comprehension.

"I know. It affects me every time I stand before the judge with a client. Don't ever forget." A. L. continued, "There won't be any probation available on Judgment Day; it will be all or nothing, heaven or hell. But remember, as a Christian, when you stand before the ultimate Judge, you'll have a lot better Lawyer than me. You'll have the Lord Jesus Christ himself. Not only will he represent you, he'll tell the Judge he's already taken your punishment."

———

LaRochette skillfully tacked the sailboat into the marina entrance. "Robert!" he yelled. "Get ready to tie up at the slip."

After they secured the boat, LaRochette said, "Gus Eicholtz should be back in the country. I want to have a meeting Saturday night to address his late-blooming insubordination. Handle notification and the details at the inn."

"What's your plan?"

LaRochette pursed his lips. "Something different would be appropriate. Yes, something different."

33

Thou shalt compass me about with songs of deliverance.
PSALM 32:7, KJV

Renny met briefly with a probation officer who scheduled a meeting the following week. During the ride back to the jail from the courthouse, one of the other prisoners, a young boy who didn't look more than seventeen, whispered to him, "Did the judge say you are a lawyer?"

"Yes."

"I'm in big trouble. Can you give me any advice?"

Renny looked into the boy's pleading eyes and understood why Jenkins did what he did. "No, but I'll talk to my lawyer for you. What's your name?"

"Billy Adams. I need to do one of those first offender things, too."

"OK. I'll talk with Mr. Jenkins."

"Thanks."

Renny did not return to his cell. A guard left him in the booking area, where the blonde guard gave him his regular clothes and returned his money. Glad to shed his GCCC jumpsuit, he put on his sand-covered shirt and pants.

When Renny returned from changing clothes, the blonde asked, "Do you have any personal belongings in your cell?"

"No, but I didn't get a chance to say good-bye to my cellmates."

The blonde put down her pen. "Are you serious?"

Realizing how silly his comment sounded, Renny said, "Uh, we got to be friends."

"You can send them a letter. Every prisoner needs a pen pal. I'll push the buzzer that unlocks the door down the hall. It leads to the front entrance."

"I need to make a phone call."

"Use the one in the lobby."

He called A. L.'s office. "I'm ready to check out of my free accommodations as soon as you have a chance to pick me up."

"Be there in a minute."

The sun was brighter and the air clearer as he walked across the parking lot to A. L.'s car.

"Let's go by my office for a few minutes, then I want to take you home for a victory lunch."

"Sounds great. I need to locate my rental vehicle. My suitcase was in it."

"You can call from the office."

They parked in front of a restored house a couple of blocks from the courthouse. A. L. shared the building with a workers' compensation lawyer and an insurance broker.

He took Renny into his office, a former bedroom with files stacked in the corners, a large wooden desk, and family pictures on a low credenza. A. L. leafed through his phone messages. "No word from Barnwell," he said. "Oh, here's a phone book. The car rental agency is between here and my house."

Renny dialed the number and found out the Jeep was at the lot.

"Before we go, do you want to see the Wall of Faith?" A. L. asked.

"Sure. Where is it?"

"In the library."

One wall of A. L.'s library had no bookshelves. Instead, he had rows of plain black picture frames, each one containing a couple of pictures and a sheet of handwritten or typed paper.

The big lawyer explained, "In Hebrews 11 there is a list of people:

Abraham, Jacob, Joseph, Moses, and many others who overcame adversity in following the Lord. It's commonly called the 'Hall of Faith' or 'Heroes of Faith' chapter. People sometimes challenge me when they find out I practice criminal law. 'How can you, as a Christian, represent these horrible people?' Part of me wants to grab them by the collar and ask how many down-and-out kids they've led to the Lord in the last year. But I don't argue. Instead, I invite them to visit my office so I can show them this room. My primary job as a Christian is not to curse the darkness in the world but to bring in the light. Each of these frames represents a client in whose life God's light has shone.

"Because I represent so many people, I sometimes can't remember a face. So when I take a case, I usually snap a Polaroid picture of my client and staple it to the file. The picture helps me make contact when we are scheduled to meet in court."

A. L. pointed to one of the frames. "This is Raymond Phillips. He was in jail after his fourth arrest for shoplifting at a local convenience store. When I took this picture nine years ago, he was eighteen years old."

A sullen-looking young man with eyes devoid of hope stared out of the picture.

"Was that picture taken at the jail in one of the interview rooms?" Renny asked, looking closer.

"Yes. The second picture was taken two years ago."

An older, neatly dressed Raymond stood in front of a convenience store with a woman and little girl.

"At the time of the second picture, Raymond was managing the convenience store where he had committed his crimes. Today, he is assistant to the regional manager for this area and directly supervises three stores in the Georgetown area. He serves as a deacon at our church." Also in the frame was a copy of a letter of commendation to Raymond from the vice president of his company.

Renny said, "This is like one of the memorial walls they have in Washington."

"In a way, only it doesn't honor the dead; it honors those who have been brought from death to life by the power of God."

"Do you have a favorite?" he asked.

"Well, my latest addition is always my favorite." He moved to the end of the third row. "This was an unusual situation. Norman Rasbury."

Renny looked at the photograph of an elderly white man with scruffy beard, soiled clothes, and bleary eyes.

"Even though he doesn't drink, Norman was frequently arrested for public drunkenness. He would shuffle along to jail without complaint and sit in the drunk tank until someone familiar with his situation ordered that he be released. Two years ago he was charged with vagrancy, and Judge Kincaid appointed me to represent him. After several sessions of prayer, his mind cleared and he is now a custodian at a local bank." In the second picture, Norman was standing in a hallway with a broom in his hand and a smile on his face.

"What was wrong with him?"

"I never understood the specifics of his problem, but after he committed his life to the Lord, God set him free and gave him a sound mind. The practical effect on his quality of life has been huge. It made me wonder what he could have been in life if he had received help earlier."

A man no one saw as valuable enough to reach out to. Renny nodded. He silently examined several other frames, reading the testimonies of changed lives, seeing the difference of a transformed countenance.

Stepping back from the wall, he asked, "A. L.?"

"What?"

"Could you put my picture on this wall?"

A. L. smiled. "I think you qualify. Let me get my camera while you're still wearing your burglary clothes."

The Jeep was at the lot. The employee on duty didn't know why the vehicle had been towed in and let Renny renew the rental.

Renny had forgotten how hungry he was. Sarah Jenkins had fixed a lunch of seafood quiche, salad, and baked apples with cinnamon for dessert. Everything was on the table when Renny came out of the shower wearing clean clothes.

"I thought you cut a good figure in those jailhouse whites," A. L. said. "They made you look taller."

"You'd look like a huge cloud on a summer day, A. L.," Sarah said.

"Thank you, Sarah," Renny said. "I can see how desperately he needs you to keep him humble."

While they ate, Renny told Sarah about Jo.

"I'll be praying for her," Sarah said.

After Renny finished his last bite of baked apple, Sarah asked, "Where are you going from here?"

"I'm driving to Charleston to see Agnes Flowers and catch a flight to Michigan as soon as possible. With no job, I don't have to be in Charlotte anytime soon."

"If you need a place to stay when you come to Georgetown, you're welcome here," she said.

"That's true," A. L. echoed.

A. L. and Renny walked out together.

"Call me late this afternoon," A. L. said. "Hopefully, I'll know what the Feds are going to do with the information we provided."

"OK." Renny paused. "You know I don't have the words."

The big man put his hand on Renny's shoulder. "You're welcome. It was my privilege."

Renny stopped at a pay phone and called Mrs. Stokes with the news. She had finally contacted Carol Edwards.

"Jo has been fighting an infection so they put her in more restrictive isolation. Even her mother can't go near her."

"What did you tell them about me?"

"Just that you were delayed at the coast and would be in touch as soon as possible."

"OK. I'm on my way to Charleston to see Mama A and then fly to Michigan."

"I want to pay for your ticket, Renny."

Mama A wanted to pay for his lawyer; Mrs. Stokes wanted to buy his plane ticket. Did these women know anything other than giving? He started to say no, but said, "I'll let you know how much it is. Thanks for everything you've been doing. The lawyer told me you and Mama A were like Aaron and Hur in the Bible."

"He did? Remember everything about these days, Renny. Not just the struggles, but also the lessons and victories."

"I'm so worried about Jo. Is she going to be OK?"

"The Lord hasn't shown me, but I believe we'll make it to the next step in the fight."

———

A different Renny walked up Mama A's sidewalk.

"Come in, come in." She shooed him in with her usual greeting. "A. L. told me the Lord is advancing on all fronts. Have a seat, and I'll get you something cool to drink."

She left to get his drink and Renny could hear her singing in the kitchen. She had a new air conditioner that was humming the bass notes.

When she returned, she handed him a glass of lemonade. "The Lord's had me singin' a song of victory most of the afternoon."

"The victory's not won yet. Jo's still sick, I don't have a job, and I have a felony conviction on my record for three years."

"That doesn't keep the Lord's army from singin' the victory. It was when Jehoshaphat praised the Lord before the battle that the enemy was defeated. Praise is a mighty weapon."

Renny smiled wryly. "I think I need some praising lessons. I have to come to Georgetown during my probation. Maybe I can come down and go to church with you."

"I'd love that," she said, patting him on the arm. "You know, my people were praising in the slave cabins long before their circumstances changed. They praised by faith and so must you."

Renny pointed to his white face. "I'm not sure I have what it takes to praise the Lord."

"Nonsense. It's not the color of your skin—it's the attitude of your heart. Let's give it a try right here and now." She gave out a melodic, singsong hum and waited for Renny to follow. Renny didn't budge. "You're right, you need lessons," she said. "Close your eyes and let me take you where it started."

Renny relaxed in his chair and closed his eyes.

"Here's how they used to do it. Everyone would be in the cabins after a day's work, and the stars would begin peekin' out overhead. The bosses were in the big houses, and there was no one to tell them to be quiet. No roar of cars or trucks, no blare of TVs or radios disturbed the sounds of the night. A cricket or two might be a-chirpin' and then someone would let out a hum—umuh. The sound would be picked up and passed around the little cluster of cabins—umuh, umuh, umuh. Then a black poet who never held a pencil or wrote a word would say, 'Jesus.' And the sound of his name would be on everyone's lips. 'Jesus, Jesus, Jesus.'

"On they would go, adding words until they were singin' stories of the great deeds of the God who delivers his people. The pitch rising and falling, the tempo speedin' up and slowin' down, the sounds around the circle from young and old. And you know what? They were free in their spirits long before they were free in their flesh."

Renny smiled and said, "Umuh."

"OK. Umuh," Mama A hummed in a singsong melody.

"Umuh," Renny responded.

"Praise you."

"Praise you."

"Praise you, Lord."

"Praise you, Lord."

"Praise your mighty name."

"Praise your mighty name."

On she led him in antiphonal response until Renny's head was nodding in rhythm, his voice following hers across the hills of spiritual Zion. Barnacles that Renny didn't know existed fell off his spirit, and by the time she said, "Amen and amen," he shouted, "Amen!"

Mama A raised her hands and slapped her knees. "End of lesson one. You did great."

"It was easy opening up with you. I'm not too sure about a group of people."

"Give it time. Drink your lemonade."

Renny took a long swallow. "Thanks for all you've done. I couldn't have made it without you, Mrs. Stokes, and A. L. I know you've been praying."

"It's been a privilege."

"That's what A. L. said."

"It's the truth. What're you goin' to do now?"

"I need to get a ticket to Michigan. I'd like to stay with you until it's time to go to the airport."

"Sure."

———

Renny made a reservation on a red-eye to Detroit with an early morning connection to Lansing.

"Why don't you try to get some rest in the spare bedroom before you leave?"

"Good idea. Let me call A. L.'s office first."

When A. L. picked up, Renny said, "Any word from Barnwell?"

"Not a peep. It's almost quitting time. Maybe they didn't pull it together yet."

"OK. Mama A's been giving me praising lessons."

"Umuh," A. L. responded.

"Don't get me started. I'm going to Michigan late tonight."

"Good. We'll talk soon."

"Bye."

———

Mama A went out on the back porch, and Renny lay down on the bed in the spare bedroom and quickly fell into a deep sleep. In a dream, he saw Mama A's husband, Clarence, standing at the airport ticket counter. He had Renny's plane ticket in his hand, and when Renny asked for it, Clarence smiled and tore it in two. Renny started to get mad, but the gentle smile on the old man's face stopped his anger in its tracks. Renny started to walk past him toward the departure gate, but his feet wouldn't move. Clarence smiled again, stuck his hand in his pocket, and pulled out another ticket. He handed it to Renny, who read the word *Georgetown* on it. Puzzled, he started to say, "You can't fly to Georgetown from Charleston" when the dream ended.

Renny woke up, each detail of the dream clearly etched in his waking memory. It was getting dark, and Mama A was still rocking on the back porch when he came out.

"I had a disturbing dream," he said.

"Sit down and tell me about it."

When he finished, he asked, "Am I supposed to go back to Georgetown? Why?"

Mama A stopped rocking. "I believe the dream is from the Lord. He knew you were determined to go to Michigan and needed something strong to change your mind. Something is not yet finished in Georgetown, and I believe you know it in your spirit."

When she spoke it, Renny knew she was right. He stood up and looked out into the darkening sky. "I've been making my own plans again," he admitted. "You're right."

"Cancel your ticket and spend the night here. I'll seek the Lord for you, and you can go back to Georgetown tomorrow."

"OK. Why was Clarence in the dream?"

"To let me know it was from the Lord."

They spent the rest of the evening in separate parts of the little house, Renny searching his Bible for clues and Mama A waiting before the Lord. Around ten o'clock she called Mrs. Stokes and told her what had happened.

Daisy Stokes listened, then said, "The Lord told me the battle would continue until Saturday evening. Even though Renny is out of jail, I've felt the burden increasing all afternoon."

"I'm to keep a night watch," Mama A said. "Can you get some rest?"

"I don't think so."

"Let me pray for you, then."

"Thanks."

Mama A called forth the refreshing of the Lord for her intercessory comrade.

"Amen," Mrs. Stokes said gratefully when Mama A finished. "The same for you."

"Daisy?"

"Yes."

"Can we meet after this is over? Renny could work it out."

"We'll meet. I'm sure of it. Thanks for calling. Good night."

"Good night."

As Agnes rocked through the night, she watched an incredible display of heat lightning that lasted almost two hours. It all happened so high up in the atmosphere that the resulting thunder was only a distant rumbling.

A verse from Scripture echoed in her mind: "Out of the brightness of his presence bolts of lightning blazed forth. The Lord thundered from heaven; the voice of the Most High resounded. He shot arrows and scattered the enemies, bolts of lightning and routed them."

"Amen," she hummed. "Amen and amen."

34

The next morning Mama A sent Renny off with a blessing instead of breakfast.

In his short Christian experience, Renny had never abstained from food for a spiritual purpose, but in his reading the previous night he had seen the words of Jesus about fasting and had asked Mama A about it the morning.

"Do you fast?"

"Sometimes. Jesus said 'When you fast,' not 'If you fast.'"

"I read about it last night and thought it might be something I need to do today. And, although the specifics are not clear, I'm more confident this morning than I was last night that I need to go back to Georgetown."

"I agree on both counts."

"I was looking forward to some hash browns with onions," Renny said wistfully, his resolve weakening.

"You'll get a double portion the next time, but you've got to obey what the Lord is tellin' you, and your spirit man doesn't need to be distracted by your stomach workin' on a five-course breakfast."

"OK. I'll get my things together and be on my way."

In a few minutes they stood together near the front door.

"Let me pray for you."

"Thanks."

"Here he is, Lord. It's Renny. Release him into the fullness of your purpose this day. Send your holy angels before and behind him. Keep him safe and"—she paused—"pour out on him the fire of the Holy Spirit. In Jesus' name, amen."

Renny felt a breeze on his face and glanced to see if the door was cracked open. It wasn't.

———

It was a clear, sunny morning, and Renny took a slight detour through old Charleston. He drove by his ancestral home place on St. Michael's Alley, but the old house was just an eye-pleasing combination of boards and paint. Nothing that belonged to him was there, and he had no reason to stop. He drove by Jefferson McClintock's office and saw the lawyer's car parked out front. However, there was nothing to discuss with the lawyer, so he didn't stop. He turned left toward the waterfront and passed by the old Planters and Merchants Bank. The safe deposit box was empty now. No need to wake up the sleeping custodian of the vault. Then he drove to the cemetery at St. Alban's. He parked along the street and got out of the car.

It had been less than a month since his visit, but the well-watered grass had closed most of the gaps on his father's grave. The church placed flowers throughout the cemetery on special occasions, but there was nothing on the tombstone this morning except his parents' names.

Standing in front of the tombstone, Renny waited for the familiar feelings of anger and resentment about his father to come out of hiding like soldiers who had been crouching behind rocks and trees during the heat of battle. Some sorrow at missed opportunities and regret at what could have been came to the surface of his thoughts, but surprisingly, rage and anger did not appear. Where were they? He looked at his father's name and resurrected a few of the innumerable hurts and wounds of his upbringing: the pressure of constant criticism, the inability to satisfy expectations, the lonely nights when he needed a father's reassuring word. Nothing. He brought the scene forward to his hardships and sufferings since his father's death: the will, the List, the jail. Nothing. He searched again. Nothing. It was gone! Renny was aware of the hurts and disappointments of his life, but the sharp pain caused by the thorn his father had thrust into his heart was no longer there. He was healed! He was free! He didn't know whether to laugh or cry. As much as anything else he had experienced, this was proof of the power of the gospel. He was a new man. The old had gone; the new had come.

As his emotions calmed, he shifted his thoughts to his mother. Reading her name chiseled in the marble, he waited again. But this time he didn't dread the appearance of enemy forces seeking to destroy his peace of mind. Instead, he inwardly beckoned a sentimental memory or sense of communion with the one whose faith, as well as face, he now shared. But nothing came. Startled by the silence, he tried again to revisit scenes designed to trigger an internal response. Nothing. Why not? Her presence should have been closer now than ever before.

"She is not here," came the quiet response.

"But why? This is the place to visit my memories."

"The grave is not the resting place of those who rest in me."

Not fully comprehending the reply, he nudged the green grass with his shoe for a few moments. Then, as the blades gave way to the pressure, understanding came. He could never focus on this place, these few yards of earth as the basis for communion with his mother. She was as alive to him in Charlotte, Georgetown, or East Lansing as she was in a cemetery in Charleston. In fact, more so. She had sown seeds in his life that would continue to sprout and grow although she was not physically present. Though dead in the flesh, the influence of her life still spoke by the Spirit. Death had no dominion over her. No matter where he was, she was eternally alive.

Walking to his car, Renny knew two things: he had witnessed the final burial of something horribly bad, and he was beginning to understand the resurrection of something tremendously good. Thoughts of the good occupied his mind on the road north toward Georgetown.

———

As he turned down Front Street in Georgetown, a familiar silver Mercedes flashed by. Renny remembered Judge Kincaid's order that he not go near the person or property of Desmond LaRochette. That should have been the easiest part of his probation.

A. L.'s car was parked in front of his office, and Renny pulled in beside it.

"Knock, knock," he said as he let himself in the unlocked front door.

"Who's there?" A. L. boomed out a second before his broad smile graced Renny with its warmth. "What's Brer Rabbit doing back in the brier patch? I thought you were going to Michigan. Don't you remember what happened with the tar baby here a few days ago?"

"I remember," Renny said, grinning. "I need to talk with you."

"Come in. I was just opening my mail before going back home for the rest of the afternoon."

Renny told A. L. about the dream and his decision to come back to Georgetown.

"That's high-level stuff. Do you have any other insight?"

"I'm supposed to fast and pray."

"Would you like to come to the house?"

"No, I don't want to disrupt your Saturday with your family. Could I stay here at the office for a few hours? I could lock up later and bring the key by to you."

"Sure. We're not going anywhere."

After A. L. left, Renny paced the floor for a while, took time to read every frame on the Wall of Faith, and leafed through some of the books in A. L.'s library. As the afternoon marched toward evening, he became increasingly agitated.

"What is it, Lord? What do you want me to do?"

Picking up a Bible A. L. kept on the corner of his desk, Renny began reading in Isaiah. When he came to Chapter 6, his heart began to pound at Isaiah's encounter with the holiness and glory of God. It was as if the words were written specifically for him. Identifying with the prophet of old, he prayed that the Lord would take away his sins, touch his mouth with a coal from the altar, and remove his guilt. Then, he read verse 8: "Then I heard the voice of the Lord saying, 'Whom shall I send? And who will go for us?' And I said, 'Here am I. Send me!'"

The Lord's invitation and the prophet's response hit Renny with intense impact. He felt as if he had been punched in the stomach. It was a message for Isaiah; it was a message for Renny. He knelt on the floor and yielded himself to the will of God. Like Moses at the burning bush every option except abandonment to the will of the Lord lost persuasive appeal. Renny echoed the prophet's words, "Here I am. Send me!"

The Bible on the floor before him, he continued reading:

He said, "Go and tell this people: 'Be ever hearing, but never under-standing; be ever seeing, but never perceiving.' Make the heart of this people calloused; make their ears dull and close their eyes. Otherwise they might see with their eyes, hear with their ears, understand with their hearts, and turn and be healed."

Then I said, "For how long, O Lord?"

And he answered: "Until the cities lie ruined and without inhabi-tant, until the houses are left deserted and the fields ruined and rav-aged, until the Lord has sent everyone far away and the land is utterly forsaken."

Renny put his forehead to the pages. Time passed. How long he didn't know. He waited until a sense of completion entered his spirit.

Getting up from the floor, he left the building and locked the door. As he drove toward A. L.'s house he passed the Rice Planter's Inn. He saw them on the front porch. Roget was holding the door open for Layne and Weiss. Turning down a side street, Renny came up behind the old building. The familiar cars were in the parking lot. LaRochette, Roget, Smithfield, Weiss, Layne, Flournoy, Eicholtz—all were present. There was going to be a meeting tonight. Renny knew what he had to do.

———

Sarah Jenkins opened the door. "Come in."

"Thanks. I'm just here for a few minutes. Is A. L. around?"

"He's upstairs supervising bath time. I'll let him know you're here."

The big man came into the dining room, drying his hands on a towel. "Well?" he asked.

"There is a meeting of the List tonight. I drove past the inn, and all of them are there, even Eicholtz. I'm supposed to go."

"Whew. Are you sure?"

"This time I'm sure."

"What are you going to do?"

"I'll know when I get there."

"As your attorney, I have to remind you that if LaRochette is there, your presence will violate the terms of probation, and Judge Kincaid can send you to prison."

"I thought of that, but I have no option."

"You've got a lot of courage, Renny."

"I'm at peace whatever happens."

A. L. came closer and put his big hand on Renny's shoulder. "As your friend, my spirit says do whatever the Lord has put in your heart. He will take care of the consequences."

"Thanks. I need to go."

"Go with God."

35

All these things shall come upon this generation.
MATTHEW 23:36, KJV

Renny parked next to the silver Mercedes, a definite violation of Judge Kincaid's order to stay away from Desmond LaRochette. Soon, there would be no doubt. A. L. was right. A face-to-face encounter with LaRochette would trigger revocation of his probation, and within a week he would be sleeping in a hot prison cell somewhere in rural South Carolina. He forced himself to concentrate on the present. Turning off the engine, he waited. He wanted to make sure everyone would be in his place.

It was dusk when he got out of his vehicle and walked to the front of the inn. A storm was churning the ocean, and a stiff breeze from the east opposed him as he faced the ancient structure. Suddenly, he heard someone call his name.

"Renny!" a wailing voice separated itself from the wind and demanded his attention.

He jerked his head around to see who had cried out. A car passed by on the street, but there was no one but himself in front of the inn or on the sidewalk. A second, stronger gust of wind rushed past him.

"Renny!" the voice came again, and with it an involuntary shudder ran down his spine. "You fool," it added with a sneer. The voice was not without, but within.

He wavered. And when he did, a seed of fear quickly sprouted in his heart and enveloped him in darkness. What did he think he was going to do? He was blindly walking to his own execution. *Here I am, Mr. LaRochette. Finish the job you started the other night. A heart attack at age twenty-six would be a novel way to die. Good evening, Mr. Layne. Do you need someone to mock tonight? I'm your man, the one with the bull's-eye on his chest.*

Yes, he was a fool. If he had a sensible bone in his body, he would leave, drive to the nearest airport, and fly to Michigan as soon as possible. He had been deceived once into thinking he could destroy the power of the List. Where had it landed him? In jail with a felony conviction. Now he was about to make an even greater blunder. After all, he was only one man. How could he be so deceived about his capabilities?

In a softer, less strident tone, the voice urged, "Your place is beside Jo. She needs you." Of course. What could be more important than being with the woman he loved? He started to turn around.

But his legs didn't move. Trying to clear the fog that surrounded him, he shook his head and took a deep breath. He needed to sort this out.

What about the verses he'd read hours before in A. L.'s office? The call? His response? The strength and confidence that had entered his spirit? The power of the Scriptures? The affirmation from A. L.? What was real? This or that? Where did his destiny lie? What would happen if he cut and ran?

"Be safe," the dark voice responded.

Renny closed his eyes and through clenched teeth, whispered, "Jesus." It was all he could think to say.

At the mention of the Name, a tiny spark of light flickered to life in his heart. He watched, wishing he could cup his hands around it to protect it. Surely it would be snuffed out by the swirling darkness. But as he watched, it grew. And with each passing moment, the expanding light relentlessly drove back the fearful blackness that moments before had threatened to engulf him and cause him to flee. As the light increased, his confidence rekindled, too.

Then he felt the power of the Word push in past the barrier of his consciousness. It was different from the experience at A. L.'s office. More immediate. More present. At his core he felt a stirring, an awareness, a pressure. It built; it grew. Another shudder ran through his body. But instead of opening the door to fear, this time the involuntary movement shook off the remaining barnacles of fear. Instead of fear, faith rose in his heart. The light swelled. Resolve returned. The darkness fled.

Strength to face the future entered him, and when he commanded his legs to move forward, they obeyed. An unseen confirming hand gently rested on his shoulder, and he didn't look back. There was no turning back. He climbed the steps to the porch and opened the front door.

———

LaRochette called the 249th meeting of the List to order in the cozy dining room. The waiters served the meal and retired to the kitchen. Two fresh bottles of dinner wine made the rounds of empty glasses. Between mouthfuls, Weiss made a poor attempt at telling a joke, which resulted in a few forced chuckles from one end of the table. Gus Eicholtz asked Layne whether Renny was coming to the meeting. Before Layne could answer, the door opened.

When a famous or powerful person entered a room, ordinary conversation ceases once those present become aware of who is in their midst. Renny Jacobson was not famous in the eyes of men, nor did he possess power according to earthly perceptions. But he did not walk into the dining room of the Rice Planter's Inn as an inexperienced twenty-six-year-old who had been cruelly deceived by evil men, wiser and more devious than he. He stood before them robed with the delegated authority of the Judge of the universe, the One before whom every knee in heaven and on earth would bow.

Smithfield saw him first and dropped his spoon into his soup. Layne stopped in midsentence and turned pale. Weiss grunted and looked away. Eicholtz started to voice a greeting but couldn't force his lips to form the words. Total silence descended on the room.

Only LaRochette had the strength to fight through the resistance. He rose to his feet. "Renny, what a sur—"

Renny cut him off with a wave of his hand. LaRochette opened and closed his mouth like a fish out of water. Nothing came out, and after a moment he sat down in his chair with a thud.

Renny, his face set like flint with a strength and determination beyond voluntary control, met the eyes of everyone in the room. One by one he commanded their attention and looked into their souls. Few could bear his gaze for more than a few seconds before looking down or glancing away. Smithfield quickly found the napkin in his lap the most interesting thing within reach. Layne tried to adopt his patented smirk, but his face refused to cooperate and he nervously broke eye contact. Weiss attempted to generate a belligerent bluster but ended up flushing red in unexplainable embarrassment. Flournoy cleared his throat but didn't speak.

The evil within LaRochette cried out in rage for release when Renny's eyes met his, and the legion of reinforced dark hosts in the older man's soul revealed their presence. But all they could do was glare. Held fast in chains of darkness, they were rendered impotent in the presence of the One who lived in Renny's spirit. Only Eicholtz did not seek to challenge Renny. He nodded and bowed his head.

With the old portrait of John C. Calhoun behind him, Renny stood on the same spot where Amos Candler, his mother's great-grandfather, had pleaded with J. F. Jacobson and the other men assembled that dark Confederate night not to bind themselves in a deceptive covenant of greed. Almost 140 years later, the competing influences in his family line— Jacobson on one side, Candler on the other—reached their climax with Renny at the center of the battle. In the end, the power of God's goodness promised to a thousand generations of those who loved him reigned supreme upon the field of conflict. Renny chose the way of the Lord.

Clothed in the spiritual mantle of his Candler ancestor, Renny's authority was unquestionably established in the moments of unspoken confrontation. No longer the disenfranchised youngster, he now held the keys of dominion in time and space over the assembled group.

Then, in rapid progression, words without origin in conscious memory began forming in his understanding. He let the burden build until the full fruition of the word sown in the spiritual atmosphere over a century before by his godly ancestor came forth with the multiplied power of a whirlwind. The conflict of generations played its final card, and when Renny spoke, it was not the volume of his voice, but the irresistible intensity of the Spirit that caused heaven and earth to give way before his declaration of judgment.

Renny declared:

Upon this generation will come the triumph of Almighty God against every source of spiritual evil in heavenly places connected with this covenant. Upon this generation will come the vengeance of the Lord Jesus Christ for everything you have measured out to others in greed, violence, and murder. Upon this generation will come the full measure of retribution for the sins of all who have united with you in wickedness. The cup of God's wrath is full, and he now breaks every tentacle of your evil power and brings you to confusion and utter destruction.

Renny stopped, and the building shuddered as a strong blast of wind swept in from the sea. Once again he stared at each man to see if any wanted to dispute his proclamation. Unable to move, they sat frozen in their seats. None responded. LaRochette couldn't breathe, and his face turned bright red. The full effect of the word released, Renny turned on his heels and left the room.

Outside, it was calm. Low in the eastern sky Renny saw the first glimmer of the evening star.

———

As the sound of the closing door died away, LaRochette gasped for air. "It's not that easy . . . uh, to break the power of our unity." Drawing from his internal reservoir of evil, he found renewed strength to continue. "Jacobson will go to prison for his little escapade. And he cannot revoke by a few words the covenant he made in our presence and sealed with his own blood." Taking the List, he opened it. "See, the proof of his unity and submission to us. Right here it reads—" LaRochette stopped and paled.

"What is it, Desmond?" Roget asked.

LaRochette stepped back as Roget reached across the table, grabbed the book, and ran his finger down the page Renny had signed.

"It's gone! His name is not here!"

Gus Eicholtz jumped to his feet and jerked the book out of Roget's hands to see for himself. "What fools we've been!"

Turning back a page, he found where his name appeared and marked through it with a bold stroke of his pen. "Strike my name as well," he said and bolted out of the room, slamming the door behind him.

———

For the past three days Jo had been sleeping twenty hours a day due to fatigue and fever. During the brief spells of wakefulness, she continued to be disoriented and delirious. Dr. Levy had been unable to locate a suitable bone marrow donor and was fighting desperately to keep Jo alive until a possible match could be found. Exhausted and emotionally spent, Carol had gone home for a few hours' rest.

When Renny uttered his proclamation breaking the power of the List over the lives of those it had touched, Jo rolled over in bed and opened her eyes. She was hungry. Moving her arms, she felt stronger than she had at any time since entering the hospital. Her legs felt better, too. She wanted to get out of bed. Fully awake, she sat up. She pushed the call button and a very tired Anne responded in a few seconds.

"What's wrong?"

"It's not what's wrong. Something is right. My arms and legs feel much better, and I don't have a trace of fever. Take my temperature, and let's do a blood test."

Anne felt Jo's cool forehead. "Praise the Lord. I'll get someone from the lab to draw blood."

Jo's temperature was 98.6, but she stayed under the isolation tent until the lab completed the blood work. Her red cell, white cell, and platelet counts were all within normal limits.

Anne came running in with tears streaming down her face and told Jo the results. "I called your mom. She's on her way over. Dr. Levy is assisting with a surgery, but I left word for him to come as soon as he can."

"It's a miracle," Jo said.

"Yes." Anne smiled through her tears. "That's what you needed. A miracle."

36

And I will restore to you ... And ye shall eat in plenty,
and be satisfied, and praise the name of the LORD your God,
that hath dealt wondrously with you.
JOEL 2:25-26, KJV

L aRochette returned to the dining room and faced the still-shaken
remnant of the Covenant List of South Carolina, Limited.

"I talked with the police department. A magistrate is going to issue
a warrant for Jacobson's arrest for violating the terms of his probation
in coming here tonight. They are also going to charge him with ter-
rorist threats based on my summary of what he told us. Once he's in
jail, he will have plenty of time to rue the error of his ways."

"I may send him a postcard from the Virgin Islands. 'Wish you
were here,'" Weiss said in an effort to sound gleeful.

There was a loud knock at the door, and it flew open. "Nobody move!"

Five men, two in dark business suits and three wearing black shirts
emblazoned with DEA, burst into the room. The DEA officers quickly
blocked the two exits from the room. One of the men dressed in a suit
spoke, "I'm Special Agent Max Logan with the Federal Bureau of
Investigation. This is Agent Jackson, and these other officers are with
the Drug Enforcement Agency. We have warrants for the arrest of the
following persons . . ."

LaRochette tried to register a protest, but Agent Jackson interrupted
him and ordered him to face the wall and put his hands on top of his
head. In ten minutes, LaRochette aged ten years. True to Renny's
words, a group of confused and defeated men was frisked, handcuffed,

and led out single file to waiting government sedans. They were separated from one another and transported to an FBI detention center in Charleston.

———

Renny was driving back to Charleston when the Georgetown police called A. L.'s house and informed him of the warrant for Renny's arrest.

"I don't know where he is, but I will advise him to turn himself in as soon as I can contact him."

A. L. hung up the receiver with a heavy heart. The phone rang again. It was Greg Barnwell. "Did you hear the big news yet?"

"Unfortunately. The police just called and said there was a warrant for Jacobson's arrest."

"What? They oughta give the boy a medal, not throw him back in the lockup."

"What are you talking about?"

"The big news is the bust the FBI and DEA made an hour ago on those rich guys your client put us onto. This is not for public dissemination, but you have a right to know. The old fellows were congregating at an old inn in Georgetown like fat cats around a dinner dish. The agents scooped 'em up without a meow or a scratch. They were all there except the one named Eicholtz."

"Tell me more."

"You're not going to represent them, are you?"

"You're kidding. I think I have a conflict of interest."

"No doubt you do. Well, the DEA took the information you supplied and used it to squeeze that Parmero character in Miami. He saw the handwriting on the wall and agreed to turn state's evidence. He gave us more than enough information to get multicount indictments this morning in Miami from a special grand jury investigating the Colombian drug trade. The federal district judge also issued seizure orders on all the accounts in Switzerland. It may take a while, but I think the national debt could be substantially reduced."

"Wow."

"The details will probably never come out, but in terms of money subject to seizure, it may be the biggest drug bust in history."

"Incredible. Thanks for letting me know."

"The thanks go to you and your client."

"Hey, since we're such heroes, can you get someone to help with Jacobson's situation here in Georgetown? Apparently he confronted the group before your men arrived, violating his parole agreement not to have contact with LaRochette, the leader of the organization."

"Sure. I'll pass it on and ask someone to call the local authorities as soon as possible."

"Great. You should get a promotion, Greg."

"Who knows? At the least I'll get an afternoon off to go fishin'."

Oblivious to the furor foaming in his wake, Renny was as lighthearted and free as he had been since—well, forever.

Mama A was still awake when he knocked on her door.

"A. L. called an hour ago and said he had some bad news and some better news. He wanted you to call him if you came by here."

Renny went into the kitchen and dialed A. L.'s number. "Do I want to know the bad news?" he asked.

"Don't worry," the big lawyer said. "LaRochette orchestrated a warrant for your arrest. However, I can guarantee that as we speak he is not thinking about pressing charges against you. Within the hour he should be arriving in Charleston, courtesy of the FBI and DEA. The federal authorities are going to contact the law enforcement officials here about the warrant for your arrest, and I will try to see Judge Kincaid about the matter on Monday morning."

"What happened?"

"The Feds were on your heels. They must have arrived at the inn within minutes after you left."

"Was everybody arrested?"

"All except Eicholtz were picked up on multicount indictments. The Colombian contact is cooperating with the government."

"It happened," Renny said deliberately.

"What do you mean?"

"The message I had for the group. They could not resist the presence of God's power within me. I can't describe what happened; it was the Lord's judgment against evil, just like King Josiah in the Bible."

"You broke the power of evil in the spiritual realm. Now the Lord is using the sword of the government to execute judgment on the earth."

"Yeah."

"Well done, Renny."

Renny paused. "So, did I make it to the Wall of Faith?"

A. L. laughed. "Without a doubt. You're my new favorite case."

———

Both Renny and Mama A went to bed and slept like rocks. Renny caught an early flight to Detroit and arrived in Lansing before noon. He drove straight to the hospital and took the elevator to the fifth floor. The middle-aged nurse responded to the buzzer.

"I want to see Jo Johnston, please."

"She's been moved to another room. You need to check at the patient information desk downstairs in the lobby."

Renny retraced his steps and saw Carol Edwards walking across the lobby. Waving, he ran over to her. "How's Jo?"

"She's fine."

"No more fever or infection?"

"More than that. No more anything. She's completely healed."

Renny's mouth dropped open. "When? How?"

"Last night. I'd gone home to rest for a few hours, not sure if she'd still be with us when I returned to the hospital. But she woke up and felt better. They performed blood tests, and everything was completely normal. They repeated the tests this morning and got the same results. So Dr. Levy moved her to a regular room."

"Did you say seven-thirty?"

"Yes."

Renny shook his head. "Incredible."

"Yes, it is," Carol responded, not realizing what Renny was referring to. "She may be released tomorrow."

"Can I see her?"

"I'm on my way up to her room now."

Carol knocked on the door. "You have a visitor. I'll be back in a minute."

Renny wasn't prepared for his reaction when he saw Jo sitting up in bed with the full bloom of health on her cheeks and a bright smile on her face. That would have been enough. But when their eyes met, her joy at seeing him and the pure love that flowed out of her heart and into his overcame him. He sat down by the bed, put his face into the sheet beside her, and wept. Her own eyes moist, Jo didn't speak. She simply stroked his head with her hand. The tension generated by the overwhelming pressures of the previous few days flowed out of Renny. His internal spring had been wound to the breaking point, and in her presence he was finally able to let everything go.

"Feel better?" she asked when he raised his tear-streaked face.

He nodded.

"Me, too."

He held her hand to his cheek and kissed it.

"That's nice. Tell me, what have you been doing while I was in never-never land?"

Renny wiped his eyes and sat up in the chair. "I have a story only you can fully appreciate."

"I'm all ears."

"I don't know how to begin."

Jo put her index finger to her cheek. "Either 'Once upon a time' or 'It was a dark and stormy night.'"

"That's an easy choice," Renny responded. "It was a dark and stormy night . . ." Renny talked until they brought Jo's lunch and finished his summary of the past days' events as she ate the last bite of dessert.

"All right," Jo said after asking a few questions. "Would it be accurate for me to tell my mother that I'm in love with an unemployed, convicted felon with an outstanding warrant for his arrest?"

"As long as you keep the I'm-in-love part, you can tell her whatever you want."

"So, when do we get married?"

Renny jumped up from the chair. "Do they have a chaplain on call here at the hospital?"

"Let's allow a few days for planning. Get Mom, and we'll tell her."

Renny was unable to reach Mrs. Stokes with the news, but he called Mama A to let her know.

"Congratulations. Have you set a date?"

"Not yet."

"Have you talked to Mrs. Stokes?"

"No, she didn't answer."

"She called me a couple hours ago. She wasn't feeling well and asked me to pray. I'm concerned about her."

"I'll phone a friend in Charlotte and have him check on her."

When Morris Hogan arrived at the house, he had to break a pane in the kitchen door to get inside. Daisy Stokes was unconscious on the floor with Brandy lying beside her, resting her head on the old woman's arm. Morris called 911, followed the ambulance to the hospital, and dialed the number for Jo's hospital room. Renny answered.

"She had a heart attack," Morris said. "She was alive but unconscious at the time they admitted her to cardiac ICU."

"Oh no."

"What are you going to do?"

"I don't know yet. I need to be in two places at once. Can you take care of Brandy until I get back?"

"Sure."

"Thanks, Morris. I'll explain things to you as soon as I come home."

Renny put down the receiver and told Jo the news.

"You need to go to her, Renny," Jo said without hesitation.

"But I just got here."

"And I'm fine. We're going to spend the rest of our lives together."

Renny started to protest but knew she was right. "OK."

"As soon as I get out of here I'm coming to join you."

"Are you up to doing that?"

"Yes. I'll be able to do anything I need to do."

———

It was midnight when Renny's plane touched down in Charlotte. He made it home, greeted a wildly excited Brandy, and fell exhausted into bed. The next morning he was not able to see Mrs. Stokes, whose status was critical but stable. He drove back home and called Mama A.

"She's in God's hands, Renny. Whatever happens."

"There's nothing I need to do?" he asked.

"I'm sure she would like to see you. That's all I can say."

Renny called Jo's hospital room, and no one answered. He tried Carol at their house, and a familiar voice answered.

"You're home?"

"Been here a couple of hours."

"How do you feel?"

"A little weak, but I get stronger with every meal. I've already booked a ticket and will be in Charlotte at 5:05 this afternoon."

Renny wrote down the flight number. "I'll meet you at the gate."

Just before lunch, Renny called A. L. "Any news?"

"The whole town's buzzing about the arrests. You wouldn't believe some of the wild rumors. The funny thing to me is that the wildest rumor is nowhere near as bizarre as the actual truth."

"Did you talk to the judge?"

"Yes. He'd already received a call from the U.S. Attorney's office.

Whoever talked to him must have told him you were some kind of national hero. He dismissed the warrants and told me he would entertain a motion suspending the balance of your probation and clearing your record under the first offender act immediately. I made an oral motion, which he granted. I expect to have an order by this afternoon."

"Great!" Renny felt another boulder roll off his shoulders.

"That's not all," A. L. said. "Are you sitting down?"

"Go for it."

"There is the possibility of a reward."

"Reward?"

"Yes, something through the DEA. A bureaucrat from Washington phoned and asked me some questions about the information that led to the arrests. Your name was the only one worth mentioning."

"How much?"

"If they obtain a conviction or guilty plea, it would be $150,000."

Renny laughed. "Is that per defendant?"

"I asked that myself," A. L. responded with a chuckle. "It's per transaction, and the government considers this whole matter a single transaction."

"Of course they do. Well, at least I can pay my lawyer and my credit card bill."

"And have a little left over, I'd imagine," A. L. said.

———

Renny and Jo drove directly to the hospital from the airport. On the way he told her about the possibility of the reward. "It's better than nothing," he said nonchalantly.

"Nothing! That's a lot more than nothing, and, unlike the millions you didn't get, it's clean."

"You're getting your spunkiness back, I see."

One of the nurses in ICU asked them to wait while she checked Mrs. Stokes's status. In a minute she returned. "She's very, very weak. You can both go back for a couple of minutes."

Daisy Stokes's small figure looked even smaller wrapped in intravenous tubing and surrounded by banks of monitors. But she was conscious and managed a weak smile when Renny walked into view. Jo followed, and when Mrs. Stokes saw her, a tear glistened in the corner of her eye. She motioned them to come closer.

In a hoarse voice she said to Renny, "Let me have your hand." She held it and looked at Jo, who extended her hand as well. Mrs. Stokes put Renny's on top of Jo's and then rested her own hand on top of them both.

"Blessing," she said. "Blessing," she repeated, a little stronger.

Renny and Jo waited as she closed her eyes and breathed heavily a few times.

"On the nightstand in my bedroom—" She paused, attempted to speak further, but slipped into unconsciousness.

Jo gently picked up Mrs. Stokes's hand from its place on top of theirs and laid it beside her. A nurse came in and indicated that time was up.

Renny and Jo rode in silence to the house. Jo sat in the kitchen while Renny went to Mrs. Stokes's bedroom. He returned with a single sheet of paper. Written in Mrs. Stokes's handwriting, he read the following:

Last Will and Testament

I, Daisy Kenilworth Stokes, make this Will to dispose of all my earthly possessions.

1) I give all money in my bank accounts to the Chinese Evangelization Society for use in the work that is dear to my heart at Kaohsiung. I also direct that my automobile be sold and the money given to CES for the same purpose.

2) I give all the rest of my estate, including my house and land located in Mecklenburg County, North Carolina, to Josiah Fletchall Jacobson. It is my hope that this house will serve as a home for him and Jo Johnston upon their marriage.

3) I ask that Sharon Watson serve as legal representative of my estate.

Renny shook his head and handed the piece of paper to Jo. "It's a holographic will, signed and dated by Mrs. Stokes just a few days ago."

"What?"

"A will in her own handwriting. Completely legal. I should know."

Jo read the document silently. "Who is Sharon Watson?"

"A lady Mrs. Stokes prays with at her church."

"What do you think, Renny?" Jo asked, handing the paper back to Renny.

"I don't know what to think about this. Mrs. Stokes has no family that I'm aware of, and she's known me less than six months."

"She loves us," Jo said simply. "She wants to bless us."

"My lawyer said Mrs. Stokes and Mama A carried us through this situation by their prayers."

Jo thought a moment. "It was more than that. In a way, I think Mrs. Stokes gave her life for us."

Renny went upstairs to check his answering machine while Jo put her things in the blue bedroom. She looked in the prayer closet and whispered, "Thank you, Mrs. Stokes, for giving this room to me."

She and Renny sat down in the quiet of the living room.

"Guess who left a message on my answering machine?"

"Who?"

"Gus Eicholtz. He said he wanted to talk with me. He's turning himself in to the authorities and said he was going to cooperate with them. What do you think?"

"I think he is seeking God, and you should help him find him."

"You're right."

They sat in silence, letting the peace that followed victory wash over them.

"Renny?"

"Yes."

"I can probably get a job at one of the hospitals in town."

"Do you want to do that?"

"I think so."

"I could see if one of the other law firms would take me in."

"No, I don't think so."

"Why not?"

"I want you to write your book."

"About the best barbecue restaurants?"

"No, that would be your second book."

"What about?"

Jo sat up straight and looked Renny in the eye. "I think we just lived it."

Renny nodded. "I'll start tomorrow."

EPILOGUE

Blessing, and honour, and glory, and power, be unto him that sitteth upon the throne, and unto the Lamb for ever and ever.
REVELATION 5:13, KJV

The hall was so vast that its dimensions could not be calculated in units of measure understood on earth. Millions were present—a host on the right and a host on the left—yet the room remained mostly unfilled, waiting for the great final harvest at the end of the age to sweep the full measure of the redeemed into the place prepared for them before the foundation of the world. Then, the wedding feast could begin.

The focus of all in the room never strayed far from the One who sat on the throne. From his Presence came a light and glory that never faded in brilliance nor lost its captivating beauty. To earthly eyes, the light was blinding, but to those qualified to behold with heavenly vision, even a fleeting glimpse of the glorified Messiah was reward enough for lives lived in sacrifice for others.

Three figures, two male and one female, stepped from the throng on the left and came together in an open space. Though still recognizable to those who knew them on earth, they now possessed a pure beauty that caused worldly perceptions of attractiveness to appear cheap and tawdry. No longer bound by the earth, they reflected the light of heaven. They were overcomers. They were part of the great cloud of witnesses.

"It is finished," the eldest said.

"Yes," the others answered.

"Did you know the manner in which the Master would fulfill the word he gave you?" the woman asked.

"I was not shown the exact nature of the conflict the young one would face. I knew he would come forth from my lineage, but I did not know he would also be descended from one who signed the Covenant."

"The battle was intense," the other man said.

"He was in the crucible of good and evil. Warfare from competing generations reached its climax in his struggle."

"Yes, but there was prayer," the woman said.

The two men nodded in agreement. The elder spoke, "Yes, the enemy's allies and our Lord's children often make the same mistake—they both underestimate the power of prevailing prayer."

A fourth figure, a dark-skinned man, joined them.

"She persevered, Clarence," Katharine said.

"Yes, together with the other one, she won the victory."

"Ah yes, the other one will join us soon," Amos Candler said. "I saw her soul laid on the altar. She, too, has overcome."

"And she will receive a crown on the final day," Nathaniel Candler added.

The four figures faced the throne where they had spent uncountable seasons in worship and intercession. Of course, petitions presented in the great hall were different from those that originated on earth. Intercession by the overcomers did not focus so much on the situation or circumstance that needed divine intervention as upon the majesty of him who sits upon the throne. They knew that in him alone rested the ultimate authority and power to effect change on the earth.

Prompted by a common awareness, the four turned and watched as another figure walked gracefully toward them from the grand entrance to the hall.

Katharine stepped forward to greet her. "Welcome home, Daisy."

Lifting their hands, the group of five faced the throne and released themselves in unhindered adoration and praise.

SPECIAL PREVIEW OF

ROBERT WHITLOW'S

The Sacrifice

WESTBOW
PRESS
A Division of Thomas Nelson Publishers
Since 1798

visit us at www.westbowpress.com

1

Roll, Jordan, roll. Come down to the river and be baptized.
Roll, Jordan, roll. Pass through the waters to the other side.
Roll, Jordan, roll. In dying you'll become alive.
Roll, Jordan, roll.

The members of Hall's Chapel weren't in a hurry. In some cases, friends and relatives had prayed and waited decades for this moment. Prodigals had come home; those wandering in the wilderness of sin had come to the edge of the promised land. The celebration of salvation was a time to be savored. The voices of the congregation gathered along Montgomery Creek flowed over the water in triumph. Refrain followed refrain in affirmation of a faith as unrelenting as the force of the current rushing past the white frame church. Tambourines joined the voices. Hands clapped in syncopated rhythm.

Dressed in white robes, the five candidates for baptism walked forward to the edge of the stream and faced the rest of the congregation. The small crowd grew quiet.

A heavyset woman in a baptismal garment lifted her hands in the air and cried out at the top of her voice, "Thank you, Jesus!"

Her declaration was greeted with a chorus of "Yes, Lord!" and "Amen!"

Bishop Moore joined the converts and introduced each one using their new first name—"brother" or "sister." From this day forward they would be part of the larger family of God's children who had met on the banks of the creek for almost 150 years. The former slaves who founded the church took seriously the command to love one another and passed on a strong sense of community that had not been lost by subsequent generations.

Each new believer stepped into the edge of the water and gave a brief testimony of the journey that had brought him or her to the river of God's forgiveness. The stories were similar, yet each one unique.

When it was her turn, the woman who had cried out shed a few tears that fell warm from her dark cheeks into the cool water at her bare feet. Some who knew her had doubted she would ever let go of the bitterness and unforgivingness that had dominated her life for more than twenty-five years, but the chains had been broken, the captive set free. Other testimonies followed until all five confirmed their faith in the presence of the gathered witnesses.

Bishop Moore waded into the water. Much of the stream bottom in the valley was covered with smooth rocks that made footing treacherous for the trout fishermen who crowded the stream each April, but the church deacons had cleared away the rocks and made a safe path to the small pool where Bishop Moore waited for the first candidate. A teenage boy walked gingerly forward into the cold water that inched up his legs to his waist. His family looked on with joy.

Bishop Moore held up his right hand and said in a loud voice, "Michael Lindale Wallace, I baptize you in the name of the Father, the Son, and the Holy Ghost."

Then, putting his hand over Mike's face, the bishop laid the young man back into the water. Bishop Moore didn't do a quick baptism. He wanted people to remember their moment under the water, so he went deep and stayed long. The five had been cautioned by the lady who gave them their robes to take a deep breath.

After several seconds, the bishop lifted Mike out of the water and proclaimed, "Buried in likeness to his death in baptism; raised to walk in newness of resurrection life."

The sputtering boy managed a big smile. His father shouted, "Hallelujah!"

Mike splashed through the water toward the shore. The next in line was the woman who had shed the tears. She stepped deeper into the water.

The first shot didn't cause a stir. One of the elders later told the police detective, "I thought it was a firecracker."

The second shot knifed through the water about three feet from the woman wading toward the bishop. The bullet left a line of bubbles before disappearing into the sandy bottom.

The third shot shattered the windshield of a car parked next to the sanctuary. At the sound of the splintering glass, pandemonium broke out. The air was filled with screams. People began running away from the water. Some ran toward the sanctuary. Others hid behind cars and trucks. Several children who were not standing near their parents froze, unsure what to do.

The fourth shot passed through the bottom of the new dress Alisha Mason was wearing. At that moment, the teenager didn't know how close she'd come to serious injury. (It was several days before she took out the dress and saw the place where the bullet almost nicked her left calf.) She hid behind a tree.

The fifth shot hit the church above the front door. It was the only bullet recovered by the sheriff's department.

Hurriedly glancing over his shoulder, Bishop Moore scrambled toward the bank as quickly as his aging legs could carry him. Out of the corner of his eye, he saw a figure running downstream through the dense underbrush on the other side of the stream.

———

Papers from a real-estate development contract were neatly stacked in rows across the wooden surface of Scott Ellis's desk. He ran his fingers through his short brown hair as he searched for a paragraph that he wanted to move from one section of the document to another. Stocky and muscular, the young lawyer had taken off his coat and hung it on a wooden hanger on the inside of his office door. The phone on a small, antique table beside his desk buzzed.

"Harold Garrison on line four," the receptionist said.

Scott didn't recognize the name. "Did he say what it was about?"

"No. Mr. Humphrey talked to him and told me to forward the call to you."

"Okay, I'll take it."

Scott knew from the receptionist's response that Mr. Garrison was a potential client referred down the line from the firm's senior partner. He couldn't dodge the call. Leland Humphrey would ask him about it later. He punched the flashing button.

"Scott Ellis, here."

"Yeah, this here is Harold Garrison. My son is in trouble with the law, and I have to talk to someone today."

Scott looked at his calendar. "What kind of trouble?"

"He's locked up at the jail for teenagers."

"The youth detention center?"

"Yeah. The police picked him up this past weekend. I'm leaving town tonight and need to see a lawyer before I get on the road."

"What are the charges?" Scott asked.

"Uh, the summons from the juvenile court said he's unruly and delinquent."

"That could mean a lot of things. Did anyone at the detention center tell you anything more specific?"

"Yeah, a guy wrote it down on a piece of paper." The phone was quiet for a few seconds. "It says 'assault with a deadly weapon with intent to inflict serious injury, assaulting by pointing a gun, and criminal damage to property.'"

"Those are serious charges."

"Lester says it's a big mistake. He ain't never been in any kind of trouble before."

"Lester is your son?"

"Yeah."

"How old is he?"

"Sixteen. He'll be seventeen in less than a month."

Scott's calendar was clear at three o'clock. "Can you come in at three this afternoon?"

"Yeah, but I need to know you're a fighter. I want someone who can win."

"I've had some success," Scott responded.

Actually, he'd appeared in juvenile court two times since graduating from law school. In his first case, he represented a student who was suspended from school for fighting. The other matter involved a young man charged with illegal possession of a few pills. Scott worked out deals for both clients that involved supervised probation. He wasn't sure that met Mr. Garrison's definition for success, but the juvenile court process was informal and the results predictable. He was confident that he could do as well as any other attorney in town.

"How much is this going to cost me?" Mr. Garrison asked.

Scott thought quickly. "Did Mr. Humphrey mention a fee?"

"He said it might be $2,500 if it has to go to a hearing."

"That sounds right."

"Do I have to bring all of it this afternoon?"

Scott hesitated. The cardinal rule of criminal cases was to get the entire fee up front, but he didn't want to lose the chance for courtroom experience.

"Can you do that?" he asked.

"Only if y'all take cash. I don't have no checking account."

"Yes, sir. Cash will be fine."

Scott Wesley Ellis, the newest associate of Humphrey, Balcomb and Jackson, checked the time on the small digital clock that divided his working day into the six-minute intervals billable by the law firm at rates of $115 to $160 per hour. He quickly completed a billing slip: "Initial phone call—Garrison case."

Scott's cream-colored office was at the end of the hall on the second floor of the firm's two-story, brick building. Everything in the office was there for a reason. Scott's diplomas and his law license were framed and hung in a razor-straight row behind his desk. A picture of his father at the main entrance to Fort Bragg stood at attention next to a similar photo of Scott taken at the same location twenty-five years later. Inside the top drawer of his desk every pen and paper clip was in its place. The young lawyer didn't have to look twice when he needed something.

The dark-colored wooden surface of his desk and the small antique table where his phone rested were always shiny. Scott tried to keep clutter in the office to a minimum. There weren't any pleadings or documents on the floor, and stray letters or memos found a home in the proper file or ended up in the trash can without lingering in paperwork limbo. As much as possible in the midst of a developing law practice, Scott tried to manage the flow of work from his in-box across his desk and into his out-box. For him, outward organization was a key to efficiency.

As a child, Scott had ridden his bicycle past Humphrey, Balcomb and Jackson on his way to the barbershop. He never imagined that one day he would enter the building as an attorney himself. The same shiny brass nameplate was still there, but the firm had expanded over the years from three to seven attorneys. Lawyers, secretaries, and paralegals occupied every available inch of both floors.

From his office window, Scott could see the steeple of the First Baptist Church and the southwest corner of the Blanchard County Courthouse. One of the advantages of practicing law in a small town was convenient access to the halls of justice, and all the law firms in Catawba clustered around the courthouse like baby chicks around a hen.

Scott's salary was smaller than his counterparts an hour down the road in the office towers of Charlotte, but at the smaller firm he had the opportunity to sit at the feet of Mr. Humphrey, a true Southern orator whose courtroom demeanor was so compelling that other attorneys would listen and take notes in the gallery when he gave a closing argument. Scott wanted to be a trial lawyer, and if there was courtroom potential in his future, he believed Leland Humphrey could call it forth.